DEFINITELY DEAD

ALSO BY THE AUTHOR IN LARGE PRINT

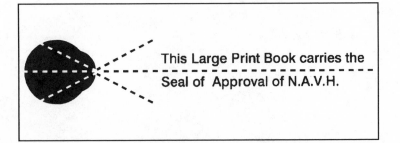

DEFINITELY DEAD

CHARLAINE HARRIS

WHEELER PUBLISHING
An imprint of Thomson Gale, a part of The Thomson Corporation

THOMSON
————✶————™
GALE

Detroit • New York • San Francisco • New Haven, Conn. • Waterville, Maine • London • Munich

LIBRARY OF CONGRESS CATALOGING-IN-PUBLICATION DATA

Harris, Charlaine.
  Definitely dead / by Charlaine Harris.
    p. cm.
  "A Southern vampire novel" — T.p. verso.
  ISBN 1-59722-291-7 (alk. paper)
    1. Waitresses — Fiction. 2. Telepathy — Fiction. 3. Vampires — Fiction. 4.
Louisiana — Fiction. 5. Large type books. I. Title.
  PS3558.A6427D47 2006b
  813'.54—dc22   2006012233

Published in 2006 by arrangement with Ace Books, an imprint of The Berkley Publishing Group, a division of Penguin Group (USA) Inc.

Printed in the United States of America on permanent paper
10 9 8 7 6 5 4 3 2 1

Obviously, this book was finished months before Hurricane Katrina struck the Gulf Coast. Since much of the plot is set in New Orleans, I struggled with whether I would leave *Definitely Dead* as it was, or include the catastrophe of August and September. After much thought, since Sookie's visit takes place in the early spring of the year, I decided to let the book remain as it was originally written.

My heart goes out to the people of the beautiful city of New Orleans and to all the people of the coastal areas of Mississippi, my home state. My thoughts and prayers will be with you as you rebuild your homes and your lives.

ACKNOWLEDGMENTS

My thanks to so many people: Jerrilyn Farmer's son's Latin teacher; Toni L. P. Kelner and Steve Kelner, friends and sounding boards; Ivan Van Laningham, who has both knowledge and opinions about many, many subjects; Dr. Stacy Clanton, about whom I can say the same; Alexandre Dumas, author of the fabulous *The Three Musketeers,* which everyone ought to read; Anne Rice, for vampirizing New Orleans; and to the reader at Uncle Hugo's who guessed the plot of this book in advance . . . hats off to you all!

1

I was draped over the arm of one of the most beautiful men I'd ever seen, and he was staring into my eyes. "Think . . . Brad Pitt," I whispered. The dark brown eyes still regarded me with remote interest.

Okay, I was on the wrong track.

I pictured Claude's last lover, a bouncer at a strip joint.

"Think about Charles Bronson," I suggested. "Or, um, Edward James Olmos." I was rewarded by the beginnings of a hot glow in those long-lashed eyes.

In a jiffy, you would've thought Claude was going to hike up my long rustling skirt and yank down my low-cut push-up bodice and ravish me until I begged for mercy. Unfortunately for me — and all the other women of Louisiana — Claude batted for another team. Bosomy and blond was not Claude's ideal; tough, rough, and brooding, with maybe a little whisker stubble, was what lit his fire.

"Maria-Star, reach in there and pull that lock of hair back," Alfred Cumberland directed from behind the camera. The photographer was a heavyset black man with graying hair and mustache. Maria-Star Cooper took a quick step in front of the camera to rearrange a stray strand of my long blond hair. I was bent backward over Claude's right arm, my invisible (to the camera, anyway) left hand desperately clutching the back of his black frock coat, my right arm raised to rest gently on his left shoulder. His left hand was at my waist. I think the pose was meant to suggest that he was lowering me to the ground to have his way with me.

Claude was wearing the black frock coat with black knee pants, white hose, and a white frothy shirt. I was wearing a long blue dress with a billowing skirt and a score of petticoats. As I've mentioned, the dress was scanty on the topside, with the little sleeves pushed down off my shoulders. I was glad the temperature in the studio was moderately warm. The big light (it looked to my eyes like a satellite dish) was not as hot as I'd expected.

Al Cumberland was snapping away as Claude smoldered down at me. I did my best to smolder right back. My personal life had been, shall we say, *barren* for the past few weeks, so I was all too ready to smolder. In fact, I was ready to burst into flames.

Maria-Star, who had beautiful light-toast skin and curly dark hair, was standing ready with a big makeup case and brushes and combs to perform last-minute repairs. When Claude and I had arrived at the studio, I'd been surprised to find that I recognized the photographer's young assistant. I hadn't seen Maria-Star since the Shreveport pack-leader had been chosen a few weeks before. I hadn't had much of a chance to observe her then, since the packmaster contest had been frightening and bloody. Today, I had the leisure to see that Maria-Star had completely recovered from being hit by a car this past January. Werewolves healed quickly.

Maria-Star had recognized me, too, and I'd been relieved when she smiled back at me. My standing with the Shreveport pack was, to say the least, uncertain. Without exactly volunteering to do so, I'd unwittingly thrown in my lot with the unsuccessful contestant for the packleader's job. That contestant's son, Alcide Herveaux, whom I'd counted as maybe more than a friend, felt I'd let him down during the contest; the

11

new packleader, Patrick Furnan, knew I had ties to the Herveaux family. I'd been surprised when Maria-Star chatted away while she was zipping the costume and brushing my hair. She applied more makeup than I'd ever worn in my life, but when I stared into the mirror I had to thank her. I looked great, though I didn't look like Sookie Stackhouse.

If Claude hadn't been gay, he might have been impressed, too. He's the brother of my friend Claudine, and he makes his living stripping on ladies' night at Hooligans, a club he now owns. Claude is simply mouthwatering; six feet tall, with rippling black hair and large brown eyes, a perfect nose, and lips just full enough. He keeps his hair long to cover up his ears: they've been surgically altered to look rounded like human ears, not pointed as they originally were. If you're in the know supernaturally, you'll spot the ear surgery, and you'll know Claude is a fairy. I'm not using the pejorative term for his sexual orientation. I mean it literally; Claude's a fairy.

"Now the wind machine," Al instructed Maria-Star, and after a little repositioning, she switched on a large fan. Now we appeared to be standing in a gale. My hair billowed out in a blond sheet, though Claude's tied-back ponytail stayed in place. After a few shots to capture that look, Maria-Star unbound Claude's hair and directed it over one shoulder, so it would blow forward to form a backdrop for his perfect profile.

"Wonderful," Al said, and snapped some more. Maria-Star moved the machine a couple of times, causing the windstorm to strike from different directions. Eventually Al told me I could stand up. I straightened gratefully.

"I hope that wasn't too hard on your arm," I told Claude, who was looking cool and calm again.

"Nah, no problem. You have any fruit juice around?" he asked Maria-Star. Claude was not Mr. Social Skills.

The pretty Were pointed to a little refrigerator in the corner of the studio. "Cups are on the top," she told Claude. She followed him with her eyes and sighed. Women frequently did that after they'd actually talked to Claude. The sigh was a "what a pity" sigh.

After checking to make sure her boss was still fiddling intently with his gear, Maria-Star gave me a bright smile. Even though she was a Were, which made her thoughts hard to read, I was picking up on the fact that she had something she wanted to tell me . . . and she wasn't sure how I was going to take it.

Telepathy is no fun. Your opinion of yourself suffers when you know what others think of you. And telepathy makes it almost impossible to date regular guys. Just think about it. (And remember, I'll know — if you are, or if you aren't.)

"Alcide's had a hard time of it since his dad was defeated," Maria-Star said, keeping her voice low. Claude was occupied with studying himself in a mirror while he drank his juice. Al Cumberland had gotten a call on his cell phone and retreated to his office to hold his conversation.

"I'm sure he has," I said. Since Jackson Herveaux's opponent had killed him, it was only to be expected that Jackson's son was having his ups and his downs. "I sent a memorial to the ASPCA, and I know they'll notify Alcide and Janice," I said. (Janice was Alcide's younger sister, which made her a non-Were. I wondered how Alcide had explained their father's death to his sister.) In acknowledgment, I'd received a printed thank-you note, the kind the funeral home gives you, without one personal word written on it.

"Well . . ." She seemed to be unable to spit it out, whatever was stuck in her throat.

I was getting a glimpse of the shape of it. Pain flickered through me like a knife, and then I locked it down and pulled my pride around me. I'd learned to do that all too early in life.

I picked an album of samples of Alfred's work and began to flip through them, hardly looking at the photographs of brides and grooms, bar mitzvahs, first communions, twenty-fifth wedding anniversaries. I closed that album and laid it down. I was trying to look casual, but I don't think it worked.

With a bright smile that echoed Maria-Star's own expression, I said, "Alcide and I weren't ever truly a couple, you know." I might have had longings and hopes, but they'd never had a chance to ripen. The timing had always been wrong.

Maria-Star's eyes, a much lighter brown than Claude's, widened in awe. Or was it fear? "I heard you could do that," she said. "But it's hard to believe."

"Yeah," I said wearily. "Well, I'm glad you and Alcide are dating, and I have no right to mind, even if I did. Which I don't." That came out kind of garbled (and it wasn't entirely true), but I think Maria-Star got my intention: to save my face.

When I hadn't heard from Alcide in the weeks following his father's death, I'd known that whatever feelings he'd had for me were quenched. That had been a blow, but not a fatal one. Realistically, I hadn't expected anything more from Alcide. But gosh darn it, I liked him, and it always smarts when you find out you've been replaced with apparent ease. After all, before his dad's death Alcide had suggested we live together. Now he was shacking up with this young Were, maybe planning to have puppies with her.

I stopped that line of thought in its tracks. Shame on me! No point in being a bitch. (Which, come to think of it, Maria-Star actually was, at least three nights a month.)

Double shame on me.

"I hope you're very happy," I said.

She wordlessly handed me another album, this one stamped EYES ONLY. When I opened it, I realized that the Eyes were supernatural. Here were pictures of ceremonies humans never got to see . . . a vampire couple dressed in elaborate costume, posed before a giant ankh; a young man in the middle of changing into a bear, presumably for the first time; a shot of a Were pack with all its members in wolf form. Al Cumberland, photographer of the weird. No wonder he had been Claude's first choice for his pictures, which Claude hoped would launch

16

him on a cover-model career.

"Next shot," called Al, as he bustled out of his office, snapping his phone shut. "Maria-Star, we just got booked for a double wedding in Miss Stackhouse's neck of the woods." I wondered if he'd been engaged for regular human work or for a supernatural event, but it would be rude to ask.

Claude and I got up close and personal again. Following Al's instructions, I pulled up the skirt to display my legs. In the era my dress represented, I didn't think women tanned or shaved their legs, and I was brown and smooth as a baby's bottom. But what the hey. Probably guys hadn't walked around with their shirts unbuttoned, either.

"Raise your leg like you're going to wrap it around him," Alfred directed. "Now Claude, this is your chance to shine. Look like you're going to pull your pants off at any second. We want the readers to pant when they look at you!"

Claude's portfolio of shots would be used when he entered the Mr. Romance competition, orchestrated each year by *Romantic Times Bookclub* magazine.

When he'd shared his ambition with Al (I gathered they'd met at a party), Al had advised Claude to have some pictures made

17

with the sort of woman that often appeared on the cover of romance novels; he'd told the fairy that Claude's dark looks would be set off by a blue-eyed blonde. I happened to be the only bosomy blonde of Claude's acquaintance who was willing to help him for free. Of course, Claude knew some strippers who would have done it, but they expected to be paid. With his usual tact, Claude had told me this on our way to the photographer's studio. Claude could have kept these details to himself, which would have left me feeling good about helping out my friend's brother — but in typical Claude fashion, he shared.

"Okay, Claude, now off with the shirt," Alfred called.

Claude was used to being asked to take off his clothes. He had a broad, hairless chest with impressive musculature, so he looked very nice indeed without his shirt. I was unmoved. Maybe I was becoming immune.

"Skirt, leg," Alfred reminded me, and I told myself that this was a job. Al and Maria-Star were certainly professional and impersonal, and you couldn't get cooler than Claude. But I wasn't used to pulling my skirt up in front of people, and it felt pretty personal to me. Though I showed this much leg when I wore shorts and never raised a blush, somehow the pulling up of the long skirt was a little more loaded with sexuality. I clenched my teeth and hiked up the material, tucking it at intervals so it would stay in position.

"Miss Stackhouse, you have to look like you're enjoying this," Al said. He peered at me from around his camera, his forehead creased in a definitely unhappy way.

I tried not to sulk. I'd told Claude I'd do him a favor, and favors should be done willingly. I raised my leg so my thigh was parallel with the floor, and pointed my bare toes to the floor in what I hoped was a graceful position. I put both hands on Claude's naked shoulders and looked up at him. His skin felt warm and smooth to the touch — not erotic or arousing.

"You look *bored*, Miss Stackhouse," Alfred said. "You're supposed to look like you want to jump his bones. Maria-Star, make her look more . . . more." Maria darted over to push the little puff sleeves farther down my arms. She got a little too enthusiastic, and I was glad the bodice was tight.

The fact of the matter was, Claude could look beautiful and bare all day long, and I still wouldn't want him. He was grumpy and he had bad manners. Even if he'd been hetero, he wouldn't have been my cup of tea — after I'd had ten minutes' conversation with him.

Like Claude earlier, I'd have to resort to fantasy.

I thought of Bill the vampire, my first love in every way. But instead of lust, I felt anger. Bill was dating another woman, had been for a few weeks.

Okay, what about Eric, Bill's boss, the former Viking? Eric the vampire had shared my house and my bed for a few days in January. Nope, that way lay danger. Eric knew a secret I wanted to keep hidden for the rest of my days; though, since he'd had amnesia when he'd stayed at my place, he wasn't aware it was in his memory somewhere.

A few other faces popped into my mind — my boss, Sam Merlotte, the owner of Merlotte's Bar. No, don't go there, thinking about your boss naked is *bad.* Okay, Alcide Herveaux? Nope, that was a no-go, especially since I was in the company of his current girlfriend. . . . Okay, I was clean out of fantasy material and would have to fall back on one of my old fictional favorites.

But movie stars seemed bland after the supernatural world I'd inhabited since Bill came into Merlotte's. The last remotely erotic experience I'd had, oddly enough, had involved my bleeding leg getting licked. That had been . . . unsettling. But even under the circumstances, it had made things deep inside me twitch. I remembered how Quinn's bald head had moved while he cleaned my scrape in a very personal way, the firm grip his big warm fingers had had on my leg. . . .

"That'll do," Alfred said, and began snapping away. Claude put his hand on my bare thigh when he could feel my muscles begin to tremble from the effort of holding the position. Once again, a man had a hold of my leg. Claude gripped my thigh enough to give it some support. That helped considerably, but it wasn't a bit erotic.

"Now some bed shots," Al said, just when I'd decided I couldn't stand it any more.

"No," Claude and I said in chorus.

"But that's part of the package," Al said. "You don't need to undress, you know. I don't do that kind of picture. My wife would kill me. You just lie down on the bed like you are. Claude hikes up on one elbow and looks down at you, Miss Stackhouse."

"No," I said firmly. "Take some pictures of him standing by himself in the water. That would be better." There was a fake pond over in the corner, and shots of

21

Claude, apparently naked, dripping water over his bare chest, would be extremely appealing (to any woman who hadn't actually met him).

"How does that grab you, Claude?" Al asked.

Claude's narcissism chimed in. "I think that would be great, Al," he said, trying not to sound too excited.

I started for the changing room, eager to shed the costume and get back into my regular jeans. I glanced around for a clock. I was due at work at five-thirty, and I had to drive back to Bon Temps and grab my work uniform before I went to Merlotte's.

Claude called, "Thanks, Sookie."

"Sure, Claude. Good luck with the modeling contracts." But he was already admiring himself in a mirror.

Maria-Star saw me out. "Goodbye, Sookie. It was good to see you again."

"You, too," I lied. Even through the reddish twisted passages of a Were mind, I could see that Maria-Star couldn't understand why I would pass up Alcide. After all, the Were was handsome in a rugged way, an entertaining companion, and a hot-blooded male of the heterosexual persuasion. Also, he now owned his own surveying company and was a wealthy man in his own right.

The answer popped into my head and I spoke before I thought. "Is anyone still looking for Debbie Pelt?" I asked, much the same way you poke a sore tooth. Debbie had been Alcide's longtime on-again, off-again lover. She'd been a piece of work.

"Not the same people," Maria-Star said. Her expression darkened. Maria-Star didn't like thinking about Debbie any more than I did, though doubtless for different reasons. "The detectives the Pelt family hired gave up, said they'd be fleecing the family if they'd kept on. That's what I heard. The police didn't exactly say it, but they'd reached a dead end, too. I've only met the Pelts once, when they came over to Shreveport right after Debbie disappeared. They're a pretty savage couple." I blinked. This was a fairly drastic statement, coming from a Were.

"Sandra, their daughter, is the worst. She was nuts about Debbie, and for her sake they're still consulting people, some way-out people. Myself, I think Debbie got abducted. Or maybe she killed herself. When Alcide abjured her, maybe she lost it big-time."

"Maybe," I murmured, but without conviction.

"He's better off. I hope she stays missing," Maria-Star said.

My opinion had been the same, but unlike Maria-Star, I knew exactly what had happened to Debbie; that was the wedge that had pushed Alcide and me apart.

"I hope he never sees her again," Maria-Star said, her pretty face dark and showing a little bit of her own savage side.

Alcide might be dating Maria-Star, but he hadn't confided in her fully. Alcide knew for a fact that he would never see Debbie again. And that was my fault, okay?

I'd shot her dead.

I'd more or less made my peace with my act, but the stark fact of it kept popping back up. There's no way you can kill someone and get to the other side of the experience unchanged. The consequences alter your life.

Two priests walked into the bar.

This sounds like the opening of a million jokes. But these priests didn't have a kangaroo with them, and there was not a rabbi sitting at the bar, or a blonde, either. I'd seen plenty of blondes, one kangaroo in a zoo, no rabbis. However, I'd seen these two priests plenty of times before. They had a standing appointment to have dinner together every other week.

Father Dan Riordan, clean shaven and ruddy, was the Catholic priest who came to the little Bon Temps church once a week on Saturday to celebrate mass, and Father Kempton Littrell, pale and bearded, was the Episcopal priest who held Holy Eucharist in the tiny Episcopal church in Clarice once every two weeks.

"Hello, Sookie," Father Riordan said. He was Irish; really Irish, not just of Irish extraction. I loved to hear him talk. He wore thick glasses with black frames, and he was in his forties.

"Evening, Father. And hi to you, Father Littrell. What can I get you all?"

"I'd like Scotch on the rocks, Miss Sookie. And you, Kempton?"

"Oh, I'll just have a beer. And a basket of chicken strips, please." The Episcopal priest wore gold-rimmed glasses, and he was younger than Father Riordan. He had a conscientious heart.

"Sure." I smiled at the two of them. Since I could read their thoughts, I knew them both to be genuinely good men, and that made me happy. It's always disconcerting to hear the contents of a minister's head and find out they're no better than you, and not only that, they're not trying to be.

Since it was full dark outside, I wasn't

25

surprised when Bill Compton walked in. I couldn't say the same for the priests. The churches of America hadn't come to grips with the reality of vampires. To call their policies confused was putting it mildly. The Catholic Church was at this moment holding a convocation to decide whether the church would declare all vampires damned and anathema to Catholics, or accept them into the fold as potential converts. The Episcopal Church had voted against accepting vampires as priests, though they were allowed to take communion — but a substantial slice of the laity said that would be over their dead bodies. Unfortunately, most of them didn't comprehend how possible that was.

Both the priests watched unhappily as Bill gave me a quick kiss on the cheek and settled at his favorite table. Bill barely gave them a glance, but unfolded his newspaper and began to read. He always looked serious, as if he were studying the financial pages or the news from Iraq; but I knew he read the advice columns first, and then the comics, though he often didn't get the jokes.

Bill was by himself, which was a nice change. Usually, he brought the lovely Selah Pumphrey. I loathed her. Since Bill had been my first love and my first lover, maybe

I would never be completely over him. Maybe he didn't want me to be. He did seem to drag Selah into Merlotte's every single date they had. I figured he was waving her in my face. Not exactly what you did if you didn't care any more, huh?

Without his having to ask, I took him his favorite beverage, TrueBlood type O. I set it neatly in front of him on a napkin, and I'd turned to go when a cool hand touched my arm. His touch always jolted me; maybe it always would. Bill had always made it clear I aroused him, and after a lifetime of no relationships and no sex, I began walking tall when Bill made it clear he found me attractive. Other men had looked at me as if I'd become more interesting, too. Now I knew why people thought about sex so much; Bill had given me a thorough education.

"Sookie, stay for a moment." I looked down into brown eyes, which looked all the darker in Bill's white face. His hair was brown, too, smooth and sleek. He was slim and broad-shouldered, his arms hard with muscles, like the farmer he had been. "How have you been?"

"I'm fine," I said, trying not to sound surprised. It wasn't often Bill passed the time of day; small talk wasn't his strong point. Even when we'd been a couple, he had not been what you'd call chatty. And even a vampire can be a workaholic; Bill had become a computer geek. "Have things been well with you?"

"Yes. When will you go to New Orleans to claim your inheritance?"

Now I was truly startled. (This is possible because I can't read vampire minds. That's why I like vampires so much. It's wonderful to be with someone who's a mystery to me.) My cousin had been murdered almost six weeks ago in New Orleans, and Bill had been with me when the Queen of Louisiana's emissary had come to tell me about it . . . and to deliver the murderer to me for my judgment. "I guess I'll go through Hadley's apartment sometime in the next month or so. I haven't talked to Sam about taking the time off."

"I'm sorry you lost your cousin. Have you been grieving?"

I hadn't seen Hadley in years, and it would have been stranger than I can say to see her after she'd become a vampire. But as a person with very few living relations, I hated to lose even one. "A bit," I said.

"You don't know when you might go?"

"I haven't decided. You remember her lawyer, Mr. Cataliades? He said he'd tell me when the will had gone through probate. He promised to keep the place intact for me, and when the queen's counselor tells you the place'll be intact, you have to believe it'll be untouched. I haven't really been too interested, to tell you the truth."

"I might go with you when you head to New Orleans, if you don't mind having a traveling companion."

"Gee," I said, with just a dash of sarcasm, "Won't Selah mind? Or were you going to bring her, too?" That would make for a merry trip.

"No." And he closed down. You just couldn't get anything out of Bill when he was holding his mouth like that, I knew from experience. Okay, color me confused.

"I'll let you know," I said, trying to figure him out. Though it was painful to be in Bill's company, I trusted him. Bill would never harm me. He wouldn't let anyone else harm me, either. But there's more than one kind of harm.

"Sookie," Father Littrell called, and I hurried away.

I glanced back to catch Bill smiling, a small smile with a lot of satisfaction packed into it. I wasn't sure what it meant, but I liked to see Bill smile. Maybe he was hoping to revive our relationship?

Father Littrell said, "We weren't sure if you wanted to be interrupted or not." I looked down at him, confused.

"We were a tad concerned to see you consorting with the vampire for so long, and so intently," Father Riordan said. "Was the imp of hell trying to bring you under his spell?"

Suddenly his Irish accent wasn't charming at all. I looked at Father Riordan quizzically. "You're joking, right? You know Bill and I dated for a good while. Obviously, you don't know much about imps from hell if you believe Bill's anything like one." I'd seen things *much* darker than Bill in and about our fair town of Bon Temps. Some of those things had been human. "Father Riordan, I understand my own life. I understand the nature of vampires better than you ever will. Father Littrell," I said, "you want honey mustard or ketchup with your chicken strips?"

Father Littrell chose honey mustard, in a kind of dazed way. I walked away, working to shrug the little incident off, wondering what the two priests would do if they knew what had happened in this bar a couple of months before when the bar's clientele had ganged up to rid me of someone who was trying to kill me.

Since that someone had been a vampire, they'd probably have approved.

Before he left, Father Riordan came over to "have a word" with me. "Sookie, I know you're not real happy with me at the moment, but I need to ask you something on behalf of someone else. If I've made you less inclined to listen by my behavior, please ignore that and give these people the same consideration you would have."

I sighed. At least Father Riordan tried to be a good man. I nodded reluctantly.

"Good girl. A family in Jackson has contacted me . . ."

All my alarms started going off. Debbie Pelt was from Jackson.

"The Pelt family, I know you've heard of them. They're still searching for news of their daughter, who vanished in January. Debbie, her name was. They called me because their priest knows me, knows I serve the Bon Temps congregation. The Pelts would like to come to see you, Sookie. They want to talk to everyone who saw their daughter the night she vanished, and they feared if they just showed up on your doorstep, you might not see them. They're afraid you're angry because their private detectives have interviewed you, and the police have talked to you, and maybe you might be indignant about all that."

"I don't want to see them," I said. "Father Riordan, I've told everything I know." That was true. I just hadn't told it to the police or the Pelts. "I don't want to talk about Debbie any more." That was also true, very true. "Tell them, with all due respect, there's nothing left to talk about."

"I'll tell them," he said. "But I've got to say, Sookie, I'm disappointed."

"Well, I guess it's been a bad night for me all around," I said. "Losing your good opinion, and all."

He left without another word, which was exactly what I'd wanted.

2

It was close to closing time the next night when another odd thing happened. Just as Sam gave us the signal to start telling our customers this would be their last drink, someone I thought I'd never see again came into Merlotte's.

He moved quietly for such a large man. He stood just inside the door, looking around for a free table, and I noticed him because of the quick gleam of the dim bar light on his shaven head. He was very tall, and very wide, with a proud nose and big white teeth. He had full lips and an olive complexion, and he was wearing a sort of bronze sports jacket over a black shirt and slacks. Though he would have looked more natural in motorcycle boots, he was wearing polished loafers.

"Quinn," Sam said quietly. His hands became still, though he'd been in the middle of mixing a Tom Collins. "What is he doing here?"

"I didn't know you knew him," I said, feeling my face flush as I realized I'd been thinking about the bald man only the day before. He'd been the one who'd cleaned the blood from my leg with his tongue — an interesting experience.

"Everyone in my world knows Quinn," Sam said, his face neutral. "But I'm surprised you've met him, since you're not a shifter." Unlike Quinn, Sam's not a big man; but he's very strong, as shifters tend to be, and his curly red-gold hair haloes his head in an angelic way.

"I met Quinn at the contest for packmaster," I said. "He was the, ah, emcee." Naturally, Sam and I had talked about the change of leadership in the Shreveport pack. Shreveport isn't too far from Bon Temps, and what the Weres do is pretty important if you're any kind of a shifter.

A true shape-shifter, like Sam, can change into anything, though each shape-shifter has a favorite animal. And to confuse the issue, all those who can change from human form to animal form call themselves shape-shifters, though very few possess Sam's versatility. Shifters who can change to only one animal are were-animals: weretigers (like Quinn), werebears, werewolves. The wolves are the only ones who call themselves simply Weres, and they consider themselves superior in toughness and culture to any of the other shape-shifters.

Weres are also the most numerous subset of shifters, though compared to the total vampire population, there are mighty few of them. There are several reasons for this. The Were birthrate is low, infant mortality is higher than in the general population of humans, and only the first child born of a pure Were couple becomes a full Were. That happens during puberty — as if puberty weren't bad enough already.

Shape-shifters are very secretive. It's a hard habit to break, even around a sympathetic and strange human like me. The shifters have not come into the public view yet, and I'm learning about their world in little increments.

Even Sam has many secrets that I don't know, and I count him as a friend. Sam turns into a collie, and he often visits me in that form. (Sometimes he sleeps on the rug by my bed.)

I'd only seen Quinn in his human form.

I hadn't mentioned Quinn when I told Sam about the fight between Jackson Herveaux and Patrick Furnan for the

Shreveport pack leadership. Sam was frowning at me now, displeased that I'd kept it from him, but I hadn't done it purposely. I glanced back at Quinn. He'd lifted his nose a little. He was sampling the air, following a scent. Who was he trailing?

When Quinn went unerringly to a table in my section, despite the many empty ones in the closer section that Arlene was working, I knew he was trailing me.

Okay, mixed feelings on that.

I glanced sideways at Sam to get his reaction. I had trusted him for five years now, and he had never failed me.

Now Sam nodded at me. He didn't look happy, though. "Go see what he wants," he said, his voice so low it was almost a growl.

I got more and more nervous the closer I came to the new customer. I could feel my cheeks redden. Why was I getting so flustered?

"Hello, Mr. Quinn," I said. It would be stupid to pretend I didn't recognize him. "What can I get you? I'm afraid we're about to close, but I have time to serve you a beer or a drink."

He closed his eyes and took a deep breath, as if he were inhaling me. "I'd recognize you in a pitch-black room," he said, and he smiled at me. It was a broad and beautiful smile.

I looked off in another direction, pinching back the involuntary grin that rose to my lips. I was acting sort of . . . shy. I never acted shy. Or maybe *coy* would be a better term, and one I disliked. "I guess I should say thank you," I ventured cautiously. "That's a compliment?"

"Intended as one. Who's the dog behind the bar who's giving me the stay-away look?"

He meant *dog* as a statement of fact, not as a derogatory term.

"That's my boss, Sam Merlotte."

"He has an interest in you."

"I should hope so. I've worked for him for round about five years."

"Hmmm. How about a beer?"

"Sure. What kind?"

"Bud."

"Coming right up," I said, and turned to go. I knew he watched me all the way to the bar because I could feel his gaze. And I knew from his mind, though his was a closely guarded shifter mind, that he was watching me with admiration.

"What does he want?" Sam looked almost . . . bristly. If he'd been in dog form, the

37

hair on his back would have been standing up.

"A Bud," I said.

Sam scowled at me. "That's not what I meant, and you know it."

I shrugged. I had no idea what Quinn wanted.

Sam slammed the full glass down on the bar right by my fingers, making me jump. I gave him a steady look to make sure he noted that I'd been displeased, and then I took the beer to Quinn.

Quinn gave me the cost of the beer and a good tip — not a ridiculously high one, which would have made me feel bought — which I slipped into my pocket. I began making the rounds of my other tables. "You visiting someone in this area?" I asked Quinn as I passed him on my way back from clearing another table. Most of the patrons were paying up and drifting out of Merlotte's. There was an afterhours place that Sam pretended he didn't know about, way out in the country, but most of the Merlotte's regulars would be going home to bed. If a bar could be family-oriented, Merlotte's was.

"Yes," he said. "You."

That left me with nowhere to go, conversationally.

I kept on going and unloaded the glasses from my tray so absently that I almost dropped one. I couldn't think of when I'd been so flustered.

"Business or personal?" I asked, the next time I was close.

"Both," he said.

A little of the pleasure drained away when I heard about the business part, but I was left with a sharpened attention . . . and that was a good thing. You needed all your wits honed when you dealt with the supes. Supernatural beings had goals and desires that regular people didn't fathom. I knew that, since for my entire life I have been the unwilling repository for human, "normal," goals and desires.

When Quinn was one of the few people left in the bar — besides the other barmaids and Sam — he stood and looked at me expectantly. I went over, smiling brightly, as I do when I'm tense. I was interested to find that Quinn was almost equally tense. I could feel the tightness in his brain pattern.

"I'll see you at your house, if that's agreeable to you." He looked down at me seriously. "If that makes you nervous, we can meet somewhere else. But I want to talk to you tonight, unless you're exhausted."

That had been put politely enough. Arlene and Danielle were trying hard not to stare — well, they were trying hard to stare when Quinn wouldn't catch them — but Sam had turned his back to fiddle around with something behind the bar, ignoring the other shifter. He was behaving very badly.

Quickly I processed Quinn's request. If he came out to my house, I'd be at his mercy. I live in a remote place. My nearest neighbor is my ex, Bill, and he lives clear across the cemetery. On the other hand, if Quinn had been a regular date of mine, I'd let him take me home without a second thought. From what I could catch from his thoughts, he meant me no harm.

"All right," I said, finally. He relaxed, and smiled his big smile at me again.

I whisked his empty glass away and became aware that three pairs of eyes were watching me disapprovingly. Sam was disgruntled, and Danielle and Arlene couldn't understand why anyone would prefer me to them, though Quinn gave even those two experienced barmaids pause. Quinn gave off a whiff of otherness that must be perceptible to even the most prosaic human. "I'll be through in just a minute," I said.

"Take your time."

I finished filling the little china rectangle on each table with packages of sugar and sweetener. I made sure the napkin holders were full and checked the salt and pepper shakers. I was soon through. I gathered my purse from Sam's office and called good-bye to him.

Quinn pulled out to follow me in a dark green pickup truck. Under the parking lot lights, the truck looked brand spanking new, with gleaming tires and hubcaps, an extended cab, and a covered bed. I'd bet good money it was loaded with options. Quinn's truck was the fanciest vehicle I'd seen in a long time. My brother, Jason, would have drooled, and he's got pink and aqua swirls painted on the side of *his* truck.

I drove south on Hummingbird Road and turned left into my driveway. After following the drive through two acres of woods, I reached the clearing where our old family home stood. I'd turned the outside lights on before I left, and there was a security light on the electric pole that was automatic, so the clearing was well lit. I pulled around back to park behind the house, and Quinn parked right beside me.

He got out of his truck and looked around him. The security light showed him a tidy yard. The driveway was in excellent repair, and I'd recently repainted the tool shed in the back. There was a propane tank, which no amount of landscaping could disguise, but my grandmother had planted plenty of flower beds to add to the ones my family had established over the hundred-and-fifty-odd years the family had lived here. I'd lived on this land, in this house, from age seven, and I loved it.

There's nothing grand about my home. It started out as a family farmhouse and it's been enlarged and remodeled over the years. I keep it clean, and I try to keep the yard in good trim. Big repairs are beyond my skills, but Jason sometimes helps me out. He hadn't been happy when Gran left me the house and land, but he'd moved to our parents' house when he'd turned twenty-one, and I'd never made him pay me for my half of that property. Gran's will had seemed fair to me. It had taken Jason a while to admit that had been the right thing for her to do.

We'd become closer in the past few months.

I unlocked the back door and led Quinn into the kitchen. He looked around him curiously as I hung my jacket on one of the chairs pushed under the table in the middle of the kitchen where I ate all my meals.

"This isn't finished," Quinn said.

The cabinets were resting on the floor,

ready to be mounted. After that, the whole room would have to be painted and the countertops installed. Then I'd be able to rest easy.

"My old kitchen got burned down a few weeks ago," I said. "The builder had a cancellation and got this done in record time, but then when the cabinets didn't arrive on time, he put his crew on another job. By the time the cabinets got here, they were almost through there. I guess they'll come back eventually." In the meantime, at least I could enjoy being back in my own home. Sam had been tremendously kind in letting me live in one of his rent houses (and gosh, I'd enjoyed the level floors and the new plumbing and the neighbors), but there was nothing like being home.

The new stove was in, so I could cook, and I'd laid a sheet of plywood over the top of the cabinets so I could use it as a work station while I was cooking. The new refrigerator gleamed and hummed quietly, quite unlike the one Gran had had for thirty years. The newness of the kitchen struck me every time I crossed the back porch — now larger and enclosed — to unlock the new, heavier back door, with its peephole and deadbolt.

"This is where the old house begins," I

said, going from the kitchen into the hall. Only a few boards had had to be replaced in the floor in the rest of the house, and everything was freshly cleaned and painted. Not only had the walls and ceilings been smoke-stained, but I'd had to eradicate the burned smell. I'd replaced some curtains, tossed out a throw rug or two, and cleaned, cleaned, cleaned. This project had occupied every extra waking moment I'd had for quite a while.

"A good job," Quinn commented, studying how the two parts had been united.

"Come into the living room," I said, pleased. I enjoyed showing someone the house now that I knew the upholstery was clean, there were no dust bunnies, and the glass over the pictures was simply gleaming. The living room curtains had been replaced, something I'd wanted to do for at least a year.

God bless insurance, and God bless the money I'd earned hiding Eric from an enemy. I'd gouged a hole in my savings account, but I'd had it when I needed it, and that was something for which I could be grateful.

The fireplace was laid ready for a fire, but it was just too warm to justify lighting one. Quinn sat in an armchair, and I sat across from him. "Can I get you a drink — a beer, or some coffee or iced tea?" I asked, conscious of my role as hostess.

"No, thanks," he said. He smiled at me. "I've wanted to see you again since I met you in Shreveport."

I tried to keep my eyes on him. The impulse to look down at my feet or my hands was almost overwhelming. His eyes really were the deep, deep purple I remembered. "That was a tough day for the Herveauxes," I said.

"You dated Alcide for a while," he observed, in a neutral kind of voice.

I thought of a couple of possible answers. I settled for, "I haven't seen him since the packmaster contest."

He smiled widely. "So he's not your steady?"

I shook my head.

"Then you're unattached?"

"Yes."

"No toes I'd be stepping on?"

I tried to smile, but my effort was not a happy one. "I didn't say that." There were toes. Those toes wouldn't be happy piggies. But they didn't have any right to be in the way.

"I guess I can handle some disgruntled exes. So will you go out with me?"

45

I looked at him for a second or two, scouring my mind for considerations. From his brain I was getting nothing but hopefulness: I saw no deceit or self-serving. When I examined the reservations I had, they dissolved into nothing.

"Yes," I said. "I will." His beautiful white smile sparked me to smile in return, and this time my smile was genuine.

"There," he said. "We've negotiated the pleasure part. Now for the business part, which is unrelated."

"Okay," I said, and put my smile away. I hoped I'd have occasion to haul it out later, but any business he would have with me would be supe-related, and therefore cause for anxiety.

"You've heard about the regional summit?"

The vampire summit: the kings and queens from a group of states would gather to confer about . . . vampire stuff. "Eric said something about it."

"Has he hired you to work there yet?"

"He mentioned he might need me."

"Because the Queen of Louisiana found out I was in the area, and she asked me to request your services. I think her bid would have to cancel out Eric's."

"You'd have to ask Eric about that."

"I think you would have to *tell* him. The queen's wishes are Eric's orders."

I could feel my face fall. I didn't want to tell Eric, the sheriff of Louisiana's Area Five, anything. Eric's feelings for me were confused. I can assure you, vamps don't like feeling confused. The sheriff had lost his memory of the short time he'd spent hiding in my house. That memory gap had driven Eric nuts; he liked being in control, and that meant being cognizant of his own actions every second of the night. So he'd waited until he could perform an action on my behalf, and as payment for that action he'd demanded my account of what had passed while he stayed with me.

Maybe I'd carried the frankness thing a little too far. Eric wasn't exactly surprised that we'd had sex; but he was stunned when I told him he'd offered to give up his hard-won position in the vampire hierarchy and to come live with me.

If you knew Eric, you'd know that was pretty much intolerable to him.

He didn't talk to me any more. He stared at me when we met, as if he were trying to resurrect his own memories of that time, to prove me wrong. It made me sad to see that the relationship we'd had — not the secret happiness of the few days he'd spent with

me, but the entertaining relationship between a man and a woman who had little in
common but a sense of humor — didn't
seem to exist any more.

I knew it was up to me to tell him that his
queen had superseded him, but I sure didn't
want to.

"Smile's all gone," Quinn observed. He
looked serious himself.

"Well, Eric is a . . ." I didn't know how to
finish the sentence. "He's a complicated
guy," I said lamely.

"What shall we do on our first date?"
Quinn asked. So he was a good subject
changer.

"We could go to the movies," I said, to
start the ball rolling.

"We could. Afterward, we could have dinner in Shreveport. Maybe Ralph and Ka-
coo's," he suggested.

"I hear their crawfish etouffee is good," I
said, keeping the conversational ball rolling.

"And who doesn't like crawfish etouffee?
Or we could go bowling."

My great-uncle had been an avid bowler.
I could see his feet, in their bowling shoes,
right in front of me. I shuddered. "Don't
know how."

"We could go to a hockey game."

"That might be fun."

"We could cook together in your kitchen, and then watch a movie on your DVD."

"Better put that one on a back burner." That sounded a little too personal for a first date, not that I've had that much experience with first dates. But I know that proximity to a bedroom is never a good idea unless you're sure you wouldn't mind if the flow of the evening took you in that direction.

"We could go see *The Producers.* That's coming to the Strand."

"Really?" Okay, I was excited now. Shreveport's restored Strand Theater hosted traveling stage productions ranging from plays to ballet. I'd never seen a real play before. Wouldn't that be awfully expensive? Surely he wouldn't have suggested it if he couldn't afford it. "Could we?"

He nodded, pleased at my reaction. "I can make the reservations for this weekend. What about your work schedule?"

"I'm off Friday night," I said happily. "And, um, I'll be glad to chip in for my ticket."

"I invited you. My treat," Quinn said firmly. I could read from his thoughts that he thought it was surprising that I had offered. And touching. Hmmm. I didn't like that. "Okay then. It's settled. When I get back to my laptop, I'll order the tickets on-line. I know there are some good ones left, because I was checking out our options before I drove over."

Naturally, I began to wonder about appropriate clothes. But I stowed that away for later. "Quinn, where do you actually live?"

"I have a house outside Memphis."

"Oh," I said, thinking that seemed a long way away for a dating relationship.

"I'm partner in a company called Special Events. We're a sort of secret offshoot of Extreme(ly Elegant) Events. You've seen the logo, I know. E(E)E?" He made the parentheses with his fingers. I nodded. E(E)E did a lot of very fancy event designing nationally. "There are four partners who work full-time for Special Events, and we each employ a few people full-or part-time. Since we travel a lot, we have places we use all over the country; some of them are just rooms in houses of friends or associates, and some of them are real apartments. The place I stay in this area is in Shreveport, a guesthouse in back of the mansion of a shifter."

I'd learned a lot about him in two minutes flat. "So you put on events in the supernatural world, like the contest for packmaster." That had been a dangerous job and one requiring a lot of specialized paraphernalia. "But what else is there to do? A packmaster's contest can only come up every so now and then. How much do you have to travel? What other special events can you stage?"

"I generally handle the Southeast, Georgia across to Texas." He sat forward in his chair, his big hands resting on his knees. "Tennessee south through Florida. In those states, if you want to stage a fight for packmaster, or a rite of ascension for a shaman or witch, or a vampire hierarchal wedding — and you want to do it right, with all the trimmings — you come to me."

I remembered the extraordinary pictures in Alfred Cumberland's photo gallery. "So there's enough of that to keep you busy?"

"Oh, yes," he said. "Of course, some of it is seasonal. Vamps get married in the winter, since the nights are so much longer. I did a hierarchal wedding in New Orleans in January, this past year. And then, some of the occasions are tied to the Wiccan calendar. Or to puberty."

I couldn't begin to imagine the ceremonies he arranged, but a description would have to wait for another occasion. "And you have three partners who do this full-time, too? I'm sorry. I'm just grilling you, seems like.

But this is such an interesting way to make a living."

"I'm glad you think so. You gotta have a lot of people skills, and you gotta have a mind for details and organization."

"You have to be really, really, tough," I murmured, adding my own thought.

He smiled, a slow smile. "No problem there."

Yep, didn't seem as though toughness was a problem for Quinn.

"And you have to be good at sizing up people, so you can steer clients in the right direction, leave them happy with the job you've done," he said.

"Can you tell me some stories? Or is there a client confidentiality clause with your jobs?"

"Customers sign a contract, but none of them have ever requested a confidentiality clause," he said. "Special Events, you don't get much chance to talk about what you do, obviously, since the clients are mostly still traveling beneath the surface of the regular world. It's actually kind of a relief to talk about it. I usually have to tell a girl I'm a consultant, or something bogus like that."

"It's a relief to me, too, to be able to talk without worrying I'm spilling secrets."

"Then it's lucky we found each other,

huh?" Again, the white grin. "I'd better let you get some rest, since you just got off work." Quinn got up and stretched after he'd reached his full height. It was an impressive gesture on someone as muscular as he was. It was just possible Quinn knew how excellent he looked when he stretched. I glanced down to hide my smile. I didn't mind one bit that he wanted to impress me.

He reached for my hand and pulled me to my feet in one easy motion. I could feel his focus centered on me. His own hand was warm and hard. He could crack my bones with it.

The average woman would not be pondering how fast her date could kill her, but I'll never be an average woman. I'd realized that by the time I became old enough to understand that not every child could understand what her family members were thinking about her. Not every little girl knew when her teachers liked her, or felt contempt for her, or compared her to her brother (Jason had an easy charm even then). Not every little girl had a funny uncle who tried to get her alone at every family gathering.

So I let Quinn hold my hand, and I looked up into his pansy-purple eyes, and for a minute I indulged myself by letting his admiration wash over me like a bath of approval.

Yes, I knew he was a tiger. And I don't mean in bed, though I was willing to believe he was ferocious and powerful there, too.

When he kissed me good night, his lips brushed my cheek, and I smiled.

I like a man who knows when to rush things . . . and when not to.

3

I got a phone call the next night at Merlotte's. Of course, it's not a good thing to get phone calls at work; Sam doesn't like it, unless there's some kind of home emergency. Since I get the least of any of the barmaids — in fact, I could count the calls I'd gotten at work on one hand — I tried not to feel guilty when I gestured to Sam that I'd take the call back at the phone on his desk.

"Hello," I said cautiously.

"Sookie," said a familiar voice.

"Oh, Pam. Hi." I was relieved, but only for a second. Pam was Eric's second in command, and she was his child, in the vampire sense.

"The boss wants to see you," she said. "I'm calling from his office."

Eric's office, in the back of his club, Fangtasia, was well soundproofed. I could barely hear KDED, the all-vampire radio station, playing in the background: Clapton's version of "After Midnight."

"Well, lah-de-dah. He's too lofty to make his own phone calls?"

"Yes," Pam said. That Pam — *literal-minded* was the phrase for her.

"What's this about?"

"I am following his instructions," she said. "He tells me to call the telepath, I call you. You are summoned."

"Pam, I need a little more explanation than that. I don't especially want to see Eric."

"You are being recalcitrant?"

Uh-oh. I hadn't had that on my Word of the Day calendar yet. "I'm not sure I understand." It's better to just go on and confess ignorance than try to fake my way through.

Pam sighed, a long-suffering gust of sound. "You're digging in your heels," she clarified, her English accent making itself known. "And you shouldn't be. Eric treats you very well." She sounded faintly incredulous.

"I'm not giving up work *or* free time to drive over to Shreveport because Mr. High and Mighty wants me to jump to do his bidding," I protested — reasonably, I thought. "He can haul his ass over here if he wants to tell me something. Or he can pick up the telephone his ownself." So there.

"If he had wanted to pick up the phone 'his ownself,' as you put it, he would have done so. Be here Friday night by eight, he bids me tell you."

"Sorry, no can do."

A significant silence.

"You won't come?"

"I can't. I have a date," I said, trying to keep any trace of smugness out of my voice.

There was another silence. Then Pam snickered. "Oh, that's rich," she said, abruptly switching to American vernacular. "Oh, I'm going to love telling him that."

Her reaction made me begin to feel uneasy. "Um, Pam," I began, wondering if I should backpedal, "listen . . ."

"Oh, no," she said, almost laughing out loud, which was very un-Pam-like.

"You tell him I did say thanks for the calendar proofs," I said. Eric, always thinking of ways to make Fangtasia more lucrative, had come up with a vampire calendar to sell in the little gift shop. Eric himself was Mr. January. He'd posed with a bed and a long white fur robe. Eric and the bed were set against a pale gray background hung with giant glittering snowflakes. He wasn't wearing the robe: oh, no. He wasn't wearing anything. He had one bent knee on the rumpled bed, and the other foot was on the floor, and he was looking directly at the camera, smoldering. (He could have taught Claude a few lessons.) Eric's blond hair fell in a tousled mane around his shoulders, and his right hand gripped the robe tossed on the bed, so the white fur rose just high enough to cover his kit 'n' kaboodle. His body was turned just slightly to flaunt the curve of his world-class butt. A light trail of dark blond hair pointed south of his navel. It practically screamed, "Carrying concealed!"

I happened to know that Eric's pistol was more of a .357 Magnum than a snub-nose.

Somehow I'd never gotten past looking at January.

"Oh, I'll let him know," Pam said. "Eric said many people wouldn't like it if I were in the calendar made for women . . . so I'm in the one for men. Would you like me to send you a copy of my picture, as well?"

"That surprises me," I told her. "It really does. I mean, that you wouldn't mind posing." I had a hard time imagining her participation in a project that would pander to human tastes.

"Eric tells me to pose, I pose," she said matter-of-factly. Though Eric had considerable power over Pam since he was her maker, I have to say that I'd never known Eric to ask Pam to do anything she wasn't ready to do. Either he knew her well (which, of course, he did) or Pam was willing to do just about anything.

"I have a whip in my picture," Pam said. "The photographer says it'll sell a million." Pam had wide-ranging tastes in the area of sex.

After a long moment while I contemplated the mental image that raised, I said, "I'm sure it will, Pam. But I'll give it a pass."

"We'll all get a percentage, all of us who agreed to pose."

"But Eric will get a bigger percentage than the rest."

"Well, he's the sheriff," Pam said reasonably.

"Right. Well, bye." I started to hang up.

"Wait, what am I to tell Eric?"

"Just tell him the truth."

"You know he'll be angry." Pam didn't sound at all scared. In fact, she sounded gleeful.

"Well, that's his problem," I said, maybe a bit childishly, and this time I did hang up. An angry Eric would surely be my problem, too.

I had a nasty feeling I'd taken a serious

step in denying Eric. I had no idea what would happen now. When I'd first gotten to know the sheriff of Area Five, I'd been dating Bill. Eric had wanted to use my unusual talent. He'd simply held hurting Bill over my head to get me to comply. When I'd broken up with Bill, Eric had lacked any means of coercion until I'd needed a favor from him, and then I'd supplied Eric with the most potent ammunition of all — the knowledge that I'd shot Debbie Pelt. It didn't matter that he'd hidden her body and her car and he couldn't himself remember where; the accusation would be enough to ruin the rest of my life, even if it was never proved. Even if I could bring myself to deny it.

As I carried out my duties in the bar the rest of that night, I found myself wondering if Eric really would reveal my secret. If Eric told the police what I'd done, he'd have to admit he'd had a part in it, wouldn't he?

I was waylaid by Detective Andy Bellefleur when I was on my way to the bar. I've known Andy and his sister Portia all my life. They're a few years older than me, but we'd been through the same schools, grown up in the same town. Like me, they'd been largely raised by their grandmother. The detective and I have had our ups and downs.

Andy had been dating a young school-teacher, Halleigh Robinson, for a few months now.

Tonight, he had a secret to share with me and a favor to ask.

"Listen, she's going to order the chicken basket," he said, without preamble. I glanced over to their table, to make sure Halleigh was sitting with her back to me. She did. "When you bring the food to the table, make sure this is in it, covered up." He stuffed a little velvet-covered box into my hand. There was a ten-dollar bill under it.

"Sure, Andy, no problem," I said, smiling.

"Thanks, Sookie," he said, and for once he smiled back, a simple and uncomplicated and terrified smile.

Andy had been right on the money. Halleigh ordered the chicken basket when I went to their table.

"Make that extra fries," I said to our new cook when I turned in the order. I wanted plenty of camouflage. The cook turned from the grill to glare at me. We've had an assortment of cooks, of every age, color, gender, and sexual preference. We even had a vampire, once. Our current cook was a middle-aged black woman named Callie Collins. Callie was heavy, so heavy I didn't know how she could get through the hours she spent standing on her feet in the hot kitchen. "Extra fries?" Callie said, as if she'd never heard of such a thing. "Uh-huh. People get extra fries when they pay for them, not because they friends of yours."

It could be that Callie was so sharp-edged because she was old enough to remember the bad old days when blacks and whites had different schools, different waiting rooms, different water fountains. I didn't remember any of those things, and I was not willing to take into account Callie's bundle of baggage every time I talked to her.

"They paid extra," I lied, not wanting to call an explanation through the service pass-through that anyone close enough could overhear. I'd put a dollar of my tip into the till, instead, to make up the money. Despite our differences, I wished Andy and his schoolteacher well. Anyone who was going to be Caroline Bellefleur's granddaughter-in-law deserved a romantic moment.

When Callie called up the basket, I trotted over to get it. Slipping the little box under the fries was harder than I imagined, and it required a bit of surreptitious rearrangement. I wondered if Andy had realized that the velvet would get greasy and salty.

Oh well, this wasn't my romantic gesture, but his.

I carried the tray to the table with happy anticipation. In fact, Andy had to warn me (with a severe glance) to pull my face into more neutral lines as I served their food. Andy already had a beer in front of him, and she had a glass of white wine. Halleigh wasn't a big drinker, as befitted an elementary school teacher. I turned away as soon as the food was on the table, even forgetting to ask them if they needed anything else, like a good waitress should.

It was beyond me to try to stay detached after that. Though I tried not to be obvious, I watched the couple as closely as I could. Andy was on pins and needles, and I could hear his brain, which was simply agitated. He really wasn't sure whether he'd be accepted, and his mind was running through the list of things she might object to: the fact that Andy was almost ten years older, his hazardous profession . . .

I knew the moment when she spied the box. Maybe it wasn't nice of me to eavesdrop mentally on a very special moment, but to tell you the truth, I didn't even think of that at the time. Though ordinarily I keep myself well guarded, I'm used to dropping into people's heads if I spy something interesting. I'm also used to believing that my ability is a minus, not a plus, so I guess I feel entitled to whatever fun I can have with it.

I had my back to them, clearing off a table, which I should have left for the busboy to do. So I was close enough to hear.

She was frozen for a long moment. "There's a box in my food," she said, finally, keeping her voice very low because she thought she'd upset Sam if she made a fuss.

"I know," he said. "It's from me."

She knew then; everything in her brain began to accelerate, and the thoughts practically tripped over themselves in their eagerness.

"Oh, Andy," she whispered. She must have opened the box. It was all I could do not to turn around and look right along with her.

"Do you like it?"

"Yes, it's beautiful."

"Will you wear it?"

There was a silence. Her head was so confused. Half of it was going "Yippee!" and half of it was troubled.

"Yes, with one stipulation," she said slowly.

I could feel his shock. Whatever Andy had expected, it wasn't this.

"And that would be?" he asked, suddenly sounding much more like a cop than a lover.

"We have to live in our own place."

"What?" Again, she'd surprised Andy.

"I've always gotten the idea that you assumed you'd stay in the family home, with your grandmother and your sister, even after you got married. It's a wonderful old house, and your grandmother and Portia are great women."

That was tactful. Good for Halleigh.

"But I'd like to have a home of my own," she said gently, earning my admiration.

And then I really had to haul ass; I had tables to tend to. But as I refilled beer mugs, cleared empty plates, and took more money to Sam at the cash register, I was filled with awe at Halleigh's stand, since the Bellefleur mansion was Bon Temps's premier residence. Most young women would give a finger or two to live there, especially since the big old house had been extensively remodeled and freshened with the influx of money from a mysterious stranger. That stranger was actually Bill, who'd discovered that the Bellefleurs were descendants of his. He'd known they wouldn't accept money from a vampire, so he'd arranged the whole "mysterious legacy" ruse, and Caroline Bellefleur had jumped into spending it on the mansion with as much relish as Andy ate a cheeseburger.

Andy caught up with me a few minutes later. He snagged me on the way to Sid Matt Lancaster's table, so the aged lawyer had to wait a bit extra for his hamburger and fries.

"Sookie, I have to know," he said urgently, but in a very low tone.

"What, Andy?" I was alarmed at his intensity.

"Does she love me?" There were edges of humiliation in his head, that he'd actually asked me. Andy was proud, and he wanted some kind of assurance that Halleigh didn't want his family name or his family home as he'd found other women had. Well, he'd found out about the home. Halleigh didn't want it, and he would move into some humble, small house with her, if she really loved him.

No one had ever demanded this of me before. After all the years of wanting people to believe in me, understand my freakish talent, I found I didn't enjoy being taken seriously, after all. But Andy was waiting for an answer, and I couldn't refuse. He was one of the most dogged men I'd ever met.

"She loves you as much as you love her," I said, and he let go of my arm. I continued on my way to Sid Matt's table. When I glanced back at him, he was staring at me.

Chew on that, Andy Bellefleur, I thought. Then I felt a little ashamed of myself. But he shouldn't have asked, if he didn't want to know the answer.

There was something in the woods around my house.

I'd gotten ready for bed as soon as I'd come home, because one of my favorite moments in every twenty-four hours is when I get to put on my nightgown. It was warm enough that I didn't need a bathrobe, so I was roaming around in my old blue knee-length sleep tee. I was just thinking of shutting the kitchen window, since the March night was getting a little chilly. I'd been listening to the sounds of the night while I washed dishes; the frogs and the bugs had been filling the air with their chorus.

Suddenly, the noises that had made the night seem as friendly and busy as the day had come to a stop, cut off in midcry.

I paused, my hands immersed in the hot soapy water. Peering out into the darkness didn't help a bit, and I realized how visible I must be, standing at an open window with its curtains flung wide apart. The yard was lit up with the security light, but beyond the trees that ringed the clearing, the woods lay dark and still.

Something was out there. I closed my eyes and tried to reach out with my brain, and I found some kind of activity. But it wasn't clear enough to define.

I thought about phoning Bill, but I'd called him before when I'd been worried about my safety. I couldn't let it become a habit. Hey, maybe the watcher in the woods was Bill himself? He sometimes roamed around at night, and he came to check on me from time to time. I looked longingly over at the telephone on the wall at the end of the counter. (Well, where the counter would be when it was all put together.) My new telephone was portable. I could grab it, retreat to my bedroom, and call Bill in a snap of the fingers, since he was on my speed dial. If he answered the phone, I'd know whatever was out in the woods was something I needed to worry about.

But if he was home, he'd come racing over here. He'd hear my call like this: "Oh, Bill, please come save me! I can't think of anything to do but call a big, strong vampire to come to my rescue!"

I made myself admit that I really knew that whatever was in the woods, it wasn't Bill. I'd gotten a brain signal of some kind. If the lurker had been a vampire, I would have sensed nothing. Only twice had I gotten a flicker of a signal from a vampire brain, and it had been like a flash of electricity in an outage.

And right by that telephone was the back door — which wasn't locked.

Nothing on earth could keep me at the sink after the fact of the open door had occurred to me. I simply ran for it. I stepped out onto the back porch, flipped the latch on the glass door there, and jumped back into the kitchen proper and locked the big wooden door, which I'd had outfitted with a thumb latch and a deadbolt.

I leaned against the door after it was safely locked. Better than anyone I could think of, I knew the futility of doors and locks. To a vampire, the physical barrier was nothing — but a vampire had to be invited in. To a Were, doors were of more consequence, but still not much of a problem; with their incredible strength, Weres could go wherever they damn well chose. The same held true of other shifters.

Why didn't I just hold an open house?

However, I felt wonderfully better with two locked doors between me and whatever was in the woods. I knew the front door was locked and bolted, since it hadn't been opened in days. I didn't get that many visitors, and I normally entered and departed through the back.

I crept back to the window, which I closed and locked. I drew the curtains, too. I'd done everything to increase my security I could do. I went back to the dishes. I got a wet circle on the front of my sleep tee because I had to lean against the edge of the sink to steady my shaking legs. But I made myself continue until all the dishes were safely in the drainer and the sink had been wiped clean.

I listened intently after that. The woods were still silent. No matter how I listened with every sense at my disposal, that faint signal did not impinge on my brain again. It was gone.

I sat in the kitchen for a while, brain still in high gear, but then I forced myself to follow my usual routine. My heart rate had returned to normal by the time I brushed my teeth, and as I climbed into bed I had almost persuaded myself that nothing had happened out there in the silent darkness. But I'm careful about being honest inside. I knew some creature had been out in my woods; and that creature had been something bigger and scarier than a raccoon.

Quite soon after I'd turned my bedside light off, I heard the bugs and the frogs

resume their chorus. Finally, when it continued uninterrupted, I slept.

4

I punched in the number of my brother's cell phone when I got up the next morning. I hadn't spent a very good night, but at least I'd gotten a bit of sleep. Jason answered on the second ring. He sounded a little preoccupied when he said, "Hello?"

"Hi, Brother. How's it going?"

"Listen, I need to talk to you. I can't right now. I'll be there, probably in a couple of hours." He hung up without saying goodbye, and he'd sounded pretty worried about something. Good. I needed another complication.

I glanced at the clock. A couple of hours would give me enough time to get cleaned up and run into town to go to the grocery store. Jason would be getting here about noon, and if I knew him he'd expect me to feed him lunch. I yanked my hair into a ponytail and then doubled the elastic band around it, making it into a kind of topknot.

I had a little fan of the ends waving above my head. Though I tried not to admit it to myself, I thought this slapdash hairstyle was fun-looking and kind of cute.

It was one of those crisp, cool March mornings, the kind that promises a warm afternoon. The sky was so bright and sunny that my spirits rose, and I drove to Bon Temps with the window rolled down, singing along with the radio at the top of my voice. I would've sung along with Weird Al Yankovic that morning.

I drove past woods, the occasional house, and a field full of cows (and a couple of buffalo; you never know what people will raise).

The disc jockey played "Blue Hawaii" as a golden oldie, and I wondered where Bubba was — not my own brother, but the vampire now known only as Bubba. I hadn't seen him in three or four weeks. Maybe the vamps of Louisiana had moved him to another hiding place, or maybe he'd wandered off, as he does from time to time. That's when you get your long articles in the papers they keep by the grocery checkout stand.

Though I was having a blissful moment of being happy and content, I had one of those stray ideas you get at odd moments. I thought, *How nice it would be if Eric were here with me in the car. He'd look so good with the wind blowing his hair, and he'd enjoy the moment.* Well, yeah, before he burned to a crisp.

But I realized I'd thought of Eric because it was the kind of day you wanted to share with the person you cared about, the person whose company you enjoyed the most. And that would be Eric as he'd been while he was cursed by a witch: the Eric who hadn't been hardened by centuries of vampire politics, the Eric who had no contempt for humans and their affairs, the Eric who was not in charge of many financial enterprises and responsible for the lives and incomes of quite a few humans and vampires. In other words, Eric as he would never be again.

Ding-dong, the witch was dead, and Eric was restored to his character as it was now. The restored Eric was wary of me, was fond of me, and didn't trust me (or his feelings) an inch.

I sighed heavily, and the song vanished from my lips. It was nearly quenched in my heart until I told myself to stop being a melancholy idiot. I was young, I was healthy. The day was beautiful. And I had an actual date for Friday night. I promised myself a big treat. Instead of going directly to the grocery store, I went by Tara's Togs, owned and operated by my friend Tara Thornton.

I hadn't seen Tara in a while. She'd gone on a vacation to visit an aunt in south Texas, and since she'd returned she'd been working long hours at the store. At least, that's what she'd said when I'd called her to thank her for the car. When my kitchen had burned, my car had burned with it, and Tara had loaned me her old car, a two-year-old Malibu. She'd acquired a brand-new car (never mind how) and hadn't gotten around to selling the Malibu.

To my astonishment, about a month ago, Tara had mailed me the title and the bill of sale, with a letter telling me the car was now mine. I'd called to protest, but she had stonewalled me, and in the end, there didn't seem to be anything to do but accept the gift graciously.

She intended it as payment, since I'd extricated her from a terrible situation. But to help her, I'd had to indebt myself to Eric. I hadn't minded. Tara had been my friend all my life. Now she was safe, if she was smart enough to stay away from the supernatural world.

Though I was grateful and relieved to have the newest vehicle I'd ever owned, I would have been happier to have her uninterrupted friendship. I'd stayed away, since I assumed that I reminded her of too many bad things. But I was in the mood to try to rip down that veil. Maybe Tara had had enough time.

Tara's Togs was in a strip mall on the south side of Bon Temps. There was one other car parked in front of the store. I decided it might be good that a third party would be there; it would depersonalize the meeting.

Tara was serving Andy Bellefleur's sister Portia when I went in, so I began flicking through the size tens, and then the eights. Portia was sitting at the Isabelle table, which was extremely interesting. Tara is the local representative for Isabelle's Bridal, a national company that produces a catalog that's become the bible of all things wedding-related. You can try on samples of the bridesmaid dresses at the local outlet, so you can order the right size, and each dress comes in about twenty colors. The wedding dresses are just as popular. Isabelle's has twenty-five models. The Company also offers wedding shower invitations, decorations, garters, bridesmaids' gifts, and any bit of wedding paraphernalia you can imagine. However, Isabelle's was pretty much a middle-class phenomenon, and Portia was definitely an upper-class woman.

Since she lived with her grandmother and

her brother in the Bellefleur mansion on Magnolia Street, Portia had grown up in a sort of decayed gothic splendor. Now that the mansion was repaired and her grandmother entertained more, Portia had looked noticeably happier when I'd glimpsed her around town. She didn't come into Merlotte's that much, but when she was in the bar she had more time to spare for other people, and she smiled occasionally. A plain woman just past thirty, Portia's best feature was her thick, shining chestnut hair.

Portia was thinking *wedding,* and Tara was thinking *money.*

"I have to talk with Halleigh again, but I think we'll need four hundred invitations," Portia was saying, and I thought my jaw would drop.

"All right, Portia, if you don't mind paying the rush fee, we can have those in ten days."

"Oh, good!" Portia was definitely pleased. "Of course, Halleigh and I will be wearing different dresses, but we thought we might try to pick out the same bridesmaid's dress. Maybe in different colors. What do you think?"

I thought I was going to choke on my own curiosity. Portia was going to be married, too? To that stick of an accountant she'd been dating, the guy from Clarice? Tara caught a glimpse of my face over the top of the standing rack of dresses. Portia was looking at the catalog, so Tara winked at me. She was definitely pleased to have a rich customer, and we were definitely okay with each other. Relief flooded me.

"I think having the same style in different colors — coordinating colors, of course — would be really original," Tara said. "How many bridesmaids are there going to be?"

"Five apiece," Portia said, her attention on the page before her. "Can I take a copy of the catalog home? That way, Halleigh and I can look at it tonight."

"I only have one extra copy; you know, one of the ways Isabelle's makes money is charging an arm and a leg for the darn catalog," Tara said with a charming smile. Tara can lay it on when she needs to. "I'll let you take it home, if you cross your heart you'll bring it back tomorrow!"

Portia made the childish gesture, and tucked the thick catalog under her arm. She was wearing one of her "lawyer suits," a brownish tweedy-looking straight skirt and jacket with a silk blouse underneath. She had on beige hose and low-heeled pumps, and she carried a matching purse. Bo-ring.

Portia was excited, and her brain was cartwheeling with happy images. She knew she would look a little old as a bride, especially compared to Halleigh; but by God, she was finally going to be a bride. Portia would get her share of the fun, the presents, the attention, and the clothes, to say nothing of the validation of having a husband of her own. She looked up from the catalog and spied me lurking by the slacks rack. Her happiness was profound enough to encompass even me.

"Hello, Sookie!" she said, practically beaming. "Andy told me what a help you were to him, fixing up his little surprise for Halleigh. I really appreciate it."

"It was fun," I said, with my own version of a gracious smile. "Is it true that congratulations are in order for you, as well?" I know, you're not supposed to congratulate the bride, only the groom, but I didn't think Portia would mind.

Sure enough, she didn't. "Well, I am getting married," she confessed. "And we decided to have a double ceremony with Andy and Halleigh. The reception will be at the house."

Of course. Why have a mansion, if you couldn't have the reception there?

"That's going to be a lot of work, setting up a wedding by — when?" I said, trying to sound sympathetic and concerned.

"April. Tell me about it," Portia said, laughing. "Grandmother is already half-crazy. She's called every caterer she knows to try to book someone for the second weekend, and finally landed Extreme(ly Elegant) Events because they had a cancellation. Plus, the guy who runs Sculptured Forest in Shreveport is coming to see her this afternoon."

Sculptured Forest was the premier landscape planning center and nursery in the area, at least if you went by their omnipresent ads. Hiring both Sculptured Forest and Extreme(ly Elegant) Events meant that this double wedding would be the primo social occasion of the Bon Temps year.

"We're thinking an outdoor wedding at the house, with tents in the back yard," Portia said. "In case of rain, we'll have to move it to the church, and have the reception at the Renard Parish Community Building. But we'll keep our fingers crossed."

"Sounds wonderful." I really couldn't think of anything else to say. "How are you going to keep working, with all this wedding stuff to do?"

"Somehow I'll manage."

I wondered what the rush was. Why weren't the happy couples waiting until summer, when Halleigh wouldn't be working? Why not wait, so Portia could free her calendar for a proper wedding and honeymoon? And wasn't the man she'd been dating an accountant? Surely a wedding during tax season was the worst possible scheduling.

Oooo . . . maybe Portia was pregnant. But if she was in the family way, she wasn't thinking about it, and I hardly thought she would be doing otherwise. Gosh, if I ever found out I was pregnant, I'd be so happy! If the guy loved me and would marry me, that is — because I wasn't tough enough to raise a kid by myself, and my grandmother would roll over in her grave if I was an unmarried mother. Modern thinking on that subject had completely passed my grandmother by, without even ruffling her hair with its passage.

While all these thoughts were buzzing around in my head, it took me a minute to process Portia's words. "So try to keep the second Saturday in April free," she said with as close to a charming smile as Portia Bellefleur could manage.

I promised I would, trying not to trip over my own tongue with astonishment. She must be high on wedding fever. Why would my presence be desired at the wedding? I was no big buddy of any of the Bellefleurs.

"We're asking Sam to bartend at the reception," she continued, and my world realigned into a more familiar pattern. She wanted me there to assist Sam.

"An afternoon wedding?" I asked. Sam sometimes took outside bartending jobs, but Saturday was usually our heavy day at Merlotte's.

"No, night," she said, "but I already talked to Sam this morning, and he's agreed."

"Okay," I said.

She read more into my tone than I'd put there, and she flushed. "Glen has some clients that he wants to invite," she said, though I'd asked for no explanation. "They can only come after dark." Glen Vicks was the accountant. I was glad I'd retrieved his last name from my memory. Then everything clicked into place, and I understood Portia's embarrassment. Portia meant that Glen's clients were vampires. Well, well, well. I smiled at her.

"I'm sure it'll be a lovely wedding, and I look forward to being there," I said, "since you were kind enough to invite me." I'd deliberately misunderstood her, and as I'd foreseen, she flushed even redder. Then a related idea occurred to me, one so important I bent one of my personal rules.

"Portia," I said slowly, wanting to be sure she got my meaning, "you should invite Bill Compton."

Now Portia loathed Bill — disliked all vampires — but when she'd been forwarding one of her own plots, she'd dated Bill briefly. Which had been odd, because afterward Bill had discovered Portia was actually his great-great-great-great-great-granddaughter, or something like that.

Bill had gone along with her pretense of interest in him. At the time, he'd just wanted to find out what her goal was. He'd realized that it made Portia's skin crawl to be around him. But when he'd discovered the Bellefleurs were his only surviving kin, he'd anonymously given them a whacking great bunch of money.

I could "hear" that Portia thought I was purposely reminding her of the few times she'd dated Bill. She didn't want to be reminded of it, and it angered her that I'd done so.

"Why do you suggest that?" she asked coldly, and I gave her high points for not just stalking out of the shop. Tara was being studiously busy over by the Isabelle table, but I knew she could hear our conversation. Nothing wrong with Tara's hearing.

I had a ferocious internal debate. Finally,

what Bill wanted prevailed over what I wanted for him. "Never mind," I said reluctantly. "Your wedding, your list."

Portia was looking at me as if she really saw me for the first time. "Are you still dating him?" she asked.

"No, he's dating Selah Pumphrey," I said, keeping my voice even and empty.

Portia gave me an unreadable look. Without another word, she went out to her car.

"What was all that about?" Tara asked.

I couldn't explain, so I changed the subject to one closer to Tara's retailing heart. "I'm delighted you're getting the business," I said.

"You and me both. If she didn't have to pull it together in such a short time, you can bet Portia Bellefleur wouldn't ever go Isabelle," Tara said frankly. "She'd drive to Shreveport and back a million times running errands, if she had the lead time. Halleigh is just trailing along in Portia's wake, poor thing. She'll come in this afternoon, and I'll show her the same things I've shown Portia, and she'll have to buckle under. But it's all good for me. They're getting the whole package, because the Isabelle system can deliver it all on time. Invitations, thank-you notes, dresses, garters, bridesmaids' gifts, even the mother-of-the-bride gowns

— Miss Caroline will be buying one, and Halleigh's mother — they're getting it all here, either from my stock or from Isabelle's book." She looked me up and down. "What brought you in, by the way?"

"I need a date outfit to wear to a play in Shreveport," I said, "and I have to go to the grocery and get back at home to cook Jason's lunch. So, you got anything to show me?"

Tara's smile turned predatory. "Oh," she said, "just a few things."

5

I was glad Jason was a little late. I'd finished the bacon and I was putting the hamburgers in the frying pan when he arrived. I had already opened the package of buns and put two on Jason's plate, and put a bag of potato chips on the table. I'd poured him a glass of tea and set it beside his place.

Jason came in without knocking, as he always did. Jason hadn't changed that much, at least to the eyes, since he'd become a werepanther. He was still blond and attractive, and I mean attractive in the old way; he was good to look at, but he was also the kind of man that everyone looks at when he comes into a room. On top of that, he'd always had a mean streak. But since his change, he'd somehow been acting like a better person. I hadn't decided why that was. Maybe being a wild animal once a month satisfied some craving he hadn't known he had.

Since he'd been bitten, not born, he didn't change completely; he became a sort of hybrid. At first, he'd been disappointed about that. But he'd gotten over it. He'd been dating a full werepanther named Crystal for several months now. Crystal lived in a tiny community some miles out in the country — and let me tell you, out in the country from Bon Temps, Louisiana, is really *out in the country.*

We said a brief prayer and began eating. Jason didn't dig in with his usual gusto. Since the hamburger tasted good to me, I figured whatever was on his mind was important. I couldn't read it out of his brain. Since my brother had become a Were, his thoughts had not been as clear to me.

Mostly, that was a relief.

After two bites, Jason put down his hamburger, and his body posture changed. He was ready to talk. "I got something I got to tell you," he said. "Crystal doesn't want me to tell anyone, but I'm really worried about her. Yesterday, Crystal . . . she had a miscarriage."

I shut my eyes for a few seconds. I had about twenty thoughts in that brief time, and I couldn't complete a one of them. "I'm so sorry," I said. "I hope Crystal's all right?"

Jason looked at me over a plate of food

he'd completely forgotten. "She won't go to the doctor."

I stared at him blankly. "But she has to," I said reasonably. "She needs a D & C." I wasn't sure what "D & C" stood for, but I knew after you'd miscarried, you went to a hospital and that's what they did there. My friend and co-worker Arlene had had a D & C after her miscarriage, and she'd told me about it several times. *Several* times. "They go in and . . ." I began, but Jason cut me off in midstream.

"Hey, I don't need to know," he said, looking very uncomfortable. "I just know that since Crystal's a werepanther, she didn't want to go to the hospital. She had to go when she got gored by that razorback, just like Calvin had to go when he got shot, but they both got well so fast that there was some comment in the doctors' lounge, she heard. So she won't go now. She's at my house, but she's . . . she's not doing well. She's getting worse, not better."

"Uh-oh," I said. "So what's happening?"

"She's bleeding too heavy, and her legs don't work right." He swallowed. "She can hardly stand up, much less walk."

"Have you called Calvin?" I asked. Calvin Norris, Crystal's uncle, is the leader of the tiny Hotshot panther community.

"She don't want me to tell Calvin. She's scared Calvin'll kill me for knocking her up. Crystal didn't want me to tell you, either, but I got to have help."

Though her mom wasn't living, Crystal had female relatives galore in Hotshot. I'd never had a baby, I'd never even been pregnant, and I wasn't a shifter. Any one of them would know more about the situation than I did. I told Jason this.

"I don't want her to sit up long enough to go back to Hotshot, specially in my truck." My brother looked as stubborn as a mule.

For an awful minute, I thought that Jason's big concern was Crystal bleeding on his upholstery. I was about to hop down his throat, when he added, "The shocks need replacing, and I'm scared the bouncing of the truck on that bad road would make Crystal worse."

Then her kin could come to Crystal. But I knew before I spoke that Jason would find a reason to veto that, too. He had some kind of plan. "Okay. What can I do?"

"Didn't you tell me that time when you got hurt, there was a special kind of doctor the vamps called to look at your back?"

I didn't like to think about that night. My back still bore the scars of the attack. The poison on the maenad's claws had nearly

89

killed me. "Yes," I said slowly, "Dr. Ludwig." Doctor to all that was weird and strange, Dr. Ludwig was herself an oddity. She was extremely short — very, very short. And her features were not exactly regular, either. It would come as an extreme surprise to me if Dr. Ludwig were at all human. I'd seen her a second time at the contest for packmaster. Both times, I'd been in Shreveport; so the chances were good that Dr. Ludwig actually lived there.

Since I didn't want to overlook the obvious, I fished a Shreveport directory out of the drawer below the wall-mounted telephone. There was a listing for a Doctor Amy Ludwig. Amy? I bit back a burst of laughter.

I was very nervous about approaching Dr. Ludwig on my own, but when I saw how worried Jason was, I couldn't protest over making one lousy phone call.

It rang four times. A machine picked up. A mechanical voice said, "You have reached the telephone of Dr. Amy Ludwig. Dr. Ludwig is not accepting new patients, insured or uninsured. Dr. Ludwig does not want pharmaceutical samples, and she does not need insurance of any kind. She is not interested in investing her money, or giving to charities she hasn't personally selected." There was a long silence, during which time most callers presumably hung up. I didn't. After a moment, I heard another click on the line.

"Hello?" asked a gruff little voice.

"Dr. Ludwig?" I asked cautiously.

"Yes? I don't accept new patients, you know! Too busy!" She sounded both impatient and cautious.

"I'm Sookie Stackhouse. Is this the Dr. Ludwig who treated me in Eric's office at Fangtasia?"

"You are the young woman poisoned by the maenad's claws?"

"Yes. I saw you again a few weeks ago, remember?"

"And where was that?" She remembered quite well, but she wanted another proof of my identity.

"An empty building in an industrial park."

"And who was running the show there?"

"A big bald guy named Quinn."

"Oh, all right." She sighed. "What do you want? I'm rather busy."

"I have a patient for you. Please come to see her."

"Bring her to me."

"She's too sick to travel."

I heard the doctor muttering to herself, but I couldn't make out the words.

"Pooh," the doctor said. "Oh, very well,

Miss Stackhouse. Tell me what the problem is."

I explained as best I could. Jason was moving around the kitchen, because he was too worried to sit still.

"Idiots. Fools," Dr. Ludwig said. "Tell me how to get to your house. Then you can take me where the girl is."

"I may have to leave for work before you can get here," I said, after glancing at the clock and calculating how long it would take the doctor to drive from Shreveport. "My brother will be here waiting."

"Is he the responsible party?"

I didn't know if she was talking about the bill for her services, or the pregnancy. Either way, I told her that Jason definitely was the responsible party.

"She's coming," I told my brother, after I'd given the doctor directions and hung up. "I don't know how much she charges, but I told her you'd pay."

"Sure, sure. How will I know her?"

"You can't mistake her for anyone you know. She said she'd have a driver. She wouldn't be tall enough to see over the steering wheel, so I should have figured on that."

I did the dishes while Jason fidgeted. He called Crystal to check on her, seemed okay with what he'd heard. Finally, I asked him to go outside and knock old dirt-dauber nests off the tool shed. He couldn't seem to settle down, so he might as well be useful.

I thought about the situation while I started a load of laundry and put on my barmaid outfit (black pants, white boat-neck tee with *Merlotte's* embroidered over the left breast, black Adidas). I was not a happy camper. I was worried about Crystal — and I didn't like her. I was sorry she'd lost the baby because I know that's a sad experience, but I was happy because I really didn't want Jason to marry the girl, and I was pretty sure he would have if the pregnancy had continued. I cast around for something to make me feel better. I opened the closet to look at my new outfit, the one I'd bought at Tara's Togs to wear on my date. But I couldn't even get any enjoyment out of it.

Finally, I did what I'd planned on doing before I'd heard Jason's news: I got a book and settled in a chair on the front porch, reading a few sentences every now and then in between admiring the pear tree in the front yard, which was covered in white blossoms and humming with bees.

The sun was beaming, the daffodils were just past their prime, and I had a date for Friday. And I'd already done my good deed for the day, in calling Dr. Ludwig. The coil of worry in my stomach eased up a little.

From time to time, I could hear vague sounds traveling my way from the backyard; Jason had found something to keep him occupied after he'd dealt with the nests. Maybe he was pulling up weeds in the flower beds. I brightened. That would be nice, since I didn't have my grandmother's enthusiasm for gardening. I admired the results, but I didn't enjoy the whole process as she had.

After checking my watch repeatedly, I was relieved to see a rather grand pearl Cadillac pull into the front parking area. There was a tiny shape in the front passenger seat. The driver's door opened, and a Were named Amanda got out. She and I had had our differences, but we'd parted on fair terms. I was relieved to see someone I knew. Amanda, who looked exactly like a middle-class soccer mom, was in her thirties. Her red hair looked natural, quite unlike my friend Arlene's.

"Sookie, hey," she said. "When the doctor told me where we were going, I was relieved, since I knew how to get here already."

"You're not her usual driver? Hey, I like the haircut, by the way."

"Oh, thanks." Amanda's hair was newly

short, cut in a careless, almost boyish style that oddly suited her. I say oddly, because Amanda's body was definitely womanly.

"Haven't got used to it yet," she admitted, running her hand over her neck. "Actually, it's usually my oldest boy that drives Dr. Ludwig, but he's in school today, of course. Is it your sister-in-law that's ailing?"

"My brother's fiancée," I said, trying to put a good face on it. "Crystal. She's a panther."

Amanda looked almost respectful. Weres often have only contempt for other shape-shifters, but something as formidable as a panther would get their attention. "I heard there was a cluster of panthers out here somewhere. Never met one before."

"I have to get to work, but my brother's going to lead you over to his place."

"So, you're not really close to your brother's fiancée?"

I was taken aback at the implication that I was less than concerned about Crystal's welfare. Maybe I should have hurried over to her bedside and left Jason here to guide the doctor? I suddenly saw my enjoyment of my moments of peace as a callous disregard for Crystal. But now was no time to wallow in guilt.

"Truthfully," I said, "no, I'm not that close

to her. But Jason didn't seem to think there was anything I could do for her, and my presence wouldn't exactly be soothing since she's not any fonder of me than I am of her."

Amanda shrugged. "Okay, where is he?"

Jason came around the corner of the house just then, to my relief. "Oh, great," he said. "You're the doctor?"

"No," Amanda said. "The doctor's in the car. I'm the driver today."

"I'll lead you over there. I been on the phone with Crystal, and she's not getting any better."

I felt another wave of remorse. "Call me at work, Jason, and let me know how she's doing, okay? I can come over after work and spend the night, if you need me."

"Thanks, Sis." He gave me a quick hug and then looked awkward. "Uh, I'm glad I didn't keep it a secret like Crystal wanted me to. She didn't think you'd help her."

"I'd like to think I was at least a good enough person to help someone who needed it, no matter if we were close or not." Surely Crystal hadn't imagined that I'd be indifferent, or even pleased, that she was ailing?

Dismayed, I watched the two very different vehicles start down the driveway on their way back to Hummingbird Road. I locked up and got in my own car in no very

96

happy mood.

Continuing the theme of an eventful day, when I walked through the back door of Merlotte's that afternoon, Sam called to me from his office.

I went in to see what he wanted, knowing ahead of time that a few other people were waiting in there. To my dismay, I found that Father Riordan had ambushed me.

There were four people in Sam's office, besides my boss. Sam was unhappy, but trying to keep a good face on. A little to my surprise, Father Riordan wasn't happy about the people that had accompanied him, either. I suspected I knew who they were. Crap. Not only did Father Riordan have the Pelts in tow, but a young woman of about seventeen, who must be Debbie's sister, Sandra.

The three new people looked at me intently. The older Pelts were tall and slim. He wore glasses and was balding, with ears that stuck out of his head like jug handles. She was attractive, if a bit overly made up. She was wearing a Donna Karan pants set and carrying a bag with a famous logo on it. Heels, too. Sandra Pelt was more casual, her jeans and T-shirt fitting her narrow figure very tightly.

I hardly heard Father Riordan formally

introduce the Pelts, I was so overwhelmed with irritation that they were intruding themselves into my life to such an extent. I'd told Father Riordan I didn't want to meet them, yet here they were. The older Pelts ate me up with their avid eyes. *Savage,* Maria-Star had termed them. *Desperate* was the word that came to my mind.

Sandra was a different kettle of fish altogether: since she was the second child, she wasn't — couldn't be — a shifter like her folks, but she wasn't altogether a regular human, either. But something caught at my brain, made me pause. Sandra Pelt *was* a shifter of some kind. I'd heard the Pelts described as much more involved with their second daughter than they'd been with Debbie. Now, getting bits of information from them, I saw why that might be. Sandra Pelt might be underage, but she was formidable. She was a full Were.

But that couldn't be, unless . . .

Okay. Debbie Pelt, werefox, had been adopted. I'd learned that the Weres were prone to fertility problems, and I assumed that the Pelts had given up on having their own little Were, and had adopted a baby that was at least some kind of shape-shifter, if not their own kind. Even a full-blooded fox must have seemed preferable to a plain human. Then the Pelts had adopted another daughter, a Were.

"Sookie," Father Riordan said, his Irish voice charming but unhappy, "Barbara and Gordon showed up on my doorstep today. When I told them you'd said all you wanted to say about Debbie's disappearance, they weren't content with that. They insisted I bring them here with me."

My intense anger at the priest receded a bit. But another emotion filled its place. I was anxious enough about the encounter to feel my nervous smile spread across my face. I beamed at the Pelts, caught the backwash of their disapproval.

"I'm sorry for your situation," I said. "I'm sorry you're left wondering what happened to Debbie. But I don't know what else I can tell you."

A tear ran down Barbara Pelt's face, and I opened my purse to remove a tissue. I handed it to the woman, who patted her face. "She thought you were stealing Alcide from her," Barbara said.

You're not supposed to speak ill of the dead, but in Debbie Pelt's case, that was just plain impossible. "Mrs. Pelt, I'm going to be frank," I told her. Just not too frank. "Debbie was engaged to someone else at the time of her disappearance, a man named

Clausen, if I remember correctly." Barbara Pelt nodded, reluctantly. "That engagement left Alcide at perfect liberty to date anyone he liked, and we did spend time together briefly." No lies there. "We haven't seen each other in weeks, and he's dating someone else now. So Debbie really was mistaken in what she thought."

Sandra Pelt bit her lower lip. She was lean, with clear skin and dark brown hair. She wore little makeup, and her teeth were dazzlingly white and even. Her hoop earrings could provide a perch for a parakeet; they were that big. She had a narrow body and expensive clothes: top of the mall chain.

Her expression was angry. She didn't like what I was saying, not one little bit. She was an adolescent, and there were strong surges of emotion in the girl. I remembered what my life had been like when I'd been Sandra's age, and I pitied her.

"Since you knew both of them," Barbara Pelt said carefully, not acknowledging my words, "you must have known that they had — they have — a strong love-hate relationship, no matter what Debbie did."

"Oh, *that's* true," I said, and maybe I didn't sound respectful enough. If there was anyone I'd done a big favor to in killing Debbie Pelt, that person was Alcide

Herveaux. Otherwise, he and la Pelt would have been tearing each other up for years, if not the rest of their lives.

Sam turned away when the phone rang, but I glimpsed a smile on his face.

"We just feel that there must be something you know, some tiny little thing, that would help us discover what happened to our daughter. If — if she's met her end, we want her killer to come to justice."

I looked at the Pelts for a long moment. I could hear Sam's voice in the background as he reacted with astonishment to something he was hearing over the telephone.

"Mr. and Mrs. Pelt, Sandra," I said. "I talked to the police when Debbie vanished. I cooperated with them fully. I talked to your private investigators when they came here, to my place of work, just like you've done. I let them come into my home. I answered their questions." Just not truthfully.

(I know, the whole edifice was a lie, but I was doing the best I could.)

"I am very sorry for your loss and I sympathize with your anxiety to discover what's happened to Debbie," I continued, speaking slowly so I could pick my words. I took a deep breath. "But this has got to end. Enough's enough. I can't tell you a thing other than what I've already told you."

To my surprise, Sam edged around me and went into the bar, moving fast. He didn't say a word to anyone in the room. Father Riordan glanced after him, startled. I became even more anxious for the Pelts to leave. Something was up.

"I understand what you're saying," Gordon Pelt said stiffly. It was the first time the man had spoken. He didn't sound happy to be where he was, or to be doing what he was doing. "I realize we haven't gone about this in the best way, but I'm sure you'll excuse us when you think about what we've been through."

"Oh, of course," I said, and if that wasn't a complete truth, it wasn't a complete lie, either. I shut my purse and stowed it in the drawer in Sam's desk where all the servers kept their purses, and I hurried out to the bar.

I felt the upheaval wash over me. Something was wrong; almost every brain in the bar was broadcasting a signal combining excitement with anxiety bordering on panic.

"What's up?" I asked Sam, sidling behind the bar.

"I just told Holly that the school called. Holly's little boy is missing."

I felt the chill start at the base of my spine

and work up. "What happened?"

"Danielle's mom usually picks up Cody from school when she picks up Danielle's little girl, Ashley." Danielle Gray and Holly Cleary had been best friends all through high school and their friendship had continued through the failure of both their marriages. They liked to work the same shift. Danielle's mother, Mary Jane Jasper, had been a lifesaver for Danielle, and from time to time her generosity had spilled over to include Holly. Ashley must be about eight, and Danielle's son, Mark Robert, should now be four. Holly's only child, Cody, was six. He was in the first grade.

"The school let someone else pick Cody up?" I'd heard that the teachers were on the alert for unauthorized spouses picking up their kids.

"No one knows what happened to the little guy. The teacher on duty, Halleigh Robinson, was standing outside watching the kids get in their cars. She says Cody suddenly remembered he'd left a picture for his mom on his desk, and he ran back into the school to get it. She doesn't remember seeing him come out, but she couldn't find him when she went in to check."

"So Mrs. Jasper was there waiting for Cody?"

"Yes, she was the only one left, sitting there in her car with her grandchildren."

"This is very scary. I don't suppose David knows anything?" David, Holly's ex, lived in Springhill and had remarried. I registered the departure of the Pelts: one less irritant.

"Apparently not. Holly called him at his job, and he was there and had been all afternoon, no doubt about it. He called his new wife, and she had just gotten back from picking up her own kids at the Springhill school. The local police went by their house and searched, just to be sure. Now David's on his way here."

Holly was sitting at one of the tables, and though her face was dry, her eyes had the look of someone who'd seen inside Hell. Danielle was crouched on the floor beside her, holding her hand and speaking to Holly urgently and quietly. Alcee Beck, one of the local detectives, was sitting at the same table. A pad and pen were in front of him, and he was talking on his cell phone.

"They've searched the school?"

"Yeah, that's where Andy is now. And Kevin and Kenya." Kevin and Kenya were two uniformed patrol officers. "Bud Dearborn is on the phone setting up an Amber Alert."

I spared a thought for how Halleigh must

be feeling right now; she was only twenty-three or so, and this was her first teaching job. She hadn't done anything wrong, at least that I could tell — but when a kid goes missing, no one escapes blame.

I tried to think how I could help. This was a unique opportunity for my little disability to work for the greater good. I'd kept my mouth shut for years about all kinds of things. People didn't want to know what I knew. People didn't want to be around someone who could do what I could do. The way I survived was keeping my mouth shut, because it was easy for the humans around me to forget or disbelieve, when the evidence of my odd talent wasn't shoved in their face.

Would you want to be around a woman who knew you were cheating on your spouse, and with whom? If you were a guy, would you want to be around a woman who knew that you secretly wanted to wear lacy underwear? Would you want to hang with a gal who knew your most secret judgments on other people and all your hidden flaws?

No, I thought not.

But if a child was involved, how could I hold back?

I looked at Sam, and he looked back at me sadly. "It's hard, isn't it, *cher*?" he said.

"What are you going to do?"

"Whatever I have to. But I have to do it now," I said.

He nodded. "Go on down to the school," he said, and I left.

6

I didn't know how I was going to accomplish this. I didn't know who would acknowledge that I could help.

There was a crowd at the elementary school, of course. A group of about thirty adults was standing on the grass on the street side of the sidewalk in front of the school, and Bud Dearborn, the sheriff, was talking to Andy on the front lawn. Betty Ford Elementary was the same school I'd attended. The building had been fairly new then, a straightforward single-level brick building with a main hall containing the offices, the kindergarten, the first-grade classrooms, and the cafeteria. There a wing to the right for the second grade, a wing to the left for the third. A small recreational building was behind the school in the large playground, attainable by a covered walkway. It was used for the children's bad-weather exercise sessions.

Of course there were flagpoles in front of the school, one for the American flag and one for the Louisiana flag. I loved driving by when they were snapping in the breeze on a day like today. I loved thinking of all the little children inside, busy being children. But the flags had been taken down for the day, and only the tied-down ropes moved in the stiff wind. The green lawn of the school was dotted with the occasional candy wrapper or crumpled notebook paper. The school custodian, Madelyn Pepper (always called "Miss Maddy"), was sitting on a plastic chair right outside the main school doors, her rolling cart beside her. Miss Maddy had been the custodian for many years. Miss Maddy was a very slow woman, mentally, but she was a hard worker, and absolutely reliable. She looked much the same as she had when I had gone to school there: tall, husky, and white, with a long fall of dyed platinum hair. She was smoking a cigarette. The principal, Mrs. Garfield, had had a running battle with Miss Maddy for years about her habit, a battle that Miss Maddy had always won. She smoked outside, but she smoked. Today, Mrs. Garfield was completely indifferent to Miss Maddy's bad habit. Mrs. Garfield, the wife of a Methodist-Episcopal minister, was dressed in a mustard-color business suit, plain hose, and black pumps. She was just as strained as Miss Maddy, and a lot less guarded about showing it.

I worked my way through the front of the little crowd, not certain how to go about doing what I had to do.

Andy saw me first, and touched Bud Dearborn on the shoulder. Bud had a cell phone to his ear. Bud turned to look at me. I nodded at them. Sheriff Dearborn was not my friend. He'd been a friend of my father's, but he'd never had the time of day for me. To the sheriff, people fell into two categories: people who broke the law and could be arrested, and people who did not break the law and could not be. And most of those were people who just hadn't been caught breaking the law yet; that was what Bud believed. I fell somewhere in between. He felt sure I was guilty of something, but he couldn't figure out what it was.

Andy didn't like me much, either, but he was a believer. He jerked his head to the left, almost imperceptibly. I couldn't see Bud Dearborn's face clearly, but his shoulders stiffened in anger, and he leaned forward a little, his whole body posture saying that he was furious with his detective.

I worked my way out of the knot of anxious and curious citizens and slipped around the third-grade wing to the back of the school. The playground, about the size of half a football field, was fenced in, and the gate was ordinarily locked with a chain secured by a padlock. It had been opened, presumably for the convenience of the searchers. I saw Kevin Pryor, a thin young patrol officer who always won the 4K race at the Azalea Festival, bending over to peer into a culvert right across the street. The grass in the ditch was high, and his dark uniform pants were dusted with yellow. His partner, Kenya, who was as buxom as Kevin was thin, was across the street on the other side of the block, and I watched her head move from side to side as she scanned the surrounding yards.

The school took up a whole block in the middle of a residential area. All the houses around were modest homes on modest lots, the kind of neighborhood where there were basketball goals and bicycles, barking dogs, and driveways brightened with sidewalk chalk.

Today every surface was dusted in a light yellow powder; it was the very beginning of pollen time. If you rinsed off your car in town in your driveway, there would be a ring of yellow around the storm drain. Cats' bellies were tinged yellow, and tall dogs had yellow paws. Every other person you talked to had red eyes and carried a cache of tissues.

I noticed several thrown down around the playground. There were patches of new green grass and patches of hard-packed dirt, in areas where the children congregated the most. A big map of the United States had been painted on the concrete apron right outside the school doors. The name of each state was painted carefully and clearly. Louisiana was the only state colored bright red, and a pelican filled up its outline. The word *Louisiana* was too long to compete with the pelican, and it had been painted on the pavement right where the Gulf of Mexico would be.

Andy emerged from the rear door, his face set and hard. He looked ten years older.

"How's Halleigh?" I asked.

"She's in the school crying her eyes out," he said. "We have to find this boy."

"What did Bud say?" I asked. I stepped inside the gate.

"Don't ask," he said. "If there's anything you can do for us, we need all the help we can get."

"You're going out on a limb."

"So are you."

"Where are the people that were in the school when he ran back in?"

"They're all in here, except for the principal and the custodian."

"I saw them outside."

"I'll bring them in. All the teachers are in the cafeteria. It has that little stage at one end. Sit behind the curtain there. See if you can get anything."

"Okay." I didn't have a better idea.

Andy set off for the front of the school to gather up the principal and the custodian.

I stepped into the end of the third-grade corridor. There were bright pictures decorating the walls outside every classroom. I stared at the drawings of rudimentary people having picnics and fishing, and tears prickled my eyes. For the first time, I wished I were psychic instead of telepathic. Then I could envision what had happened to Cody, instead of having to wait for someone to think about it. I'd never met a real psychic, but I understood that it was a very uncertain talent to have, one that was not specific enough at times, and too specific at others. My little quirk was much more reliable, and I made myself believe I could help this child.

As I made my way to the cafeteria, the smell of the school evoked a rush of memories. Most of them were painful; some were pleasant. When I'd been this small, I'd had no control over my telepathy and no idea what was wrong with me. My parents had put me through the mental health mill to try to find out, which had further set me off from my peers. But most of my teachers had been kind. They'd understood that I was doing my best to learn — that somehow I was constantly distracted, but it wasn't through my own choice. Inhaling the scent of chalk, cleaner, paper, and books brought it all back.

I remembered all the corridors and doorways as if I'd just left. The walls were a peach color now, instead of the off-white I remembered, and the carpet was a sort of speckled gray in place of brown linoleum; but the structure of the school was unchanged. Without hesitation, I slipped through a back door to the little stage, which was at one end of the lunchroom. If I remembered correctly, the space was actually called the "multipurpose room." The serving area could be shut off with folding doors, and the picnic tables that lined the room could be folded and moved aside. Now they were taking up the floor in orderly rows, and the people sitting at them were all adults, with the exception of some teachers' children who'd been in the classrooms

113

with their mothers when the alarm had been raised.

I found a tiny plastic chair and set it back behind the curtains on stage left. I closed my eyes and began to concentrate. I lost the awareness of my body as I shut out all stimuli and began to let my mind roam free.

It's my fault, my fault, my fault! Why didn't I notice he hadn't come back out? Or did he slip by me? Could he have gotten into a car without my noticing?

Poor Halleigh. She was sitting by herself, and the mound of tissues by her showed how she'd been spending her waiting time. She was completely innocent of anything, so I resumed my probing.

Oh my God, thank you God that it's not my son that's missing. . . .

. . . go home and have some cookies . . .

Can't go to the store and pick up some hamburger meat, maybe I can call Ralph and he can go by Sonic . . . but we ate fast food last night, not good . . .

His mom's a barmaid, how many lowlifes does she know? Probably one of them.

It went on and on, a litany of harmless thoughts. The children were thinking about snacks and television, and they were also scared. The adults, for the most part, were very frightened for their own children and

114

worried about the effect of Cody's disappearance on their own families and their own class.

Andy Bellefleur said, "In just a minute Sheriff Dearborn will be in here, and then we'll divide you into two groups."

The teachers relaxed. These were familiar instructions, as they themselves had often given.

"We'll ask questions of each of you in turn, and then you can go. I know you're all worried, and we have patrol officers searching the area, but maybe we can get some information that will help us find Cody."

Mrs. Garfield came in. I could feel her anxiety preceding her like a dark cloud, full of thunder. Miss Maddy was right behind her. I could hear the wheels of her cart, loaded with its lined garbage can and laden with cleaning supplies. All the scents surrounding her were familiar. Of course, she started cleaning right after school. She would have been in one of the classrooms, and she probably hadn't seen anything. Mrs. Garfield might have been in her office. The principal in my day, Mr. Heffernan, had stood outside with the teacher on duty until all the children were gone, so that parents would have a chance to talk to him if they had questions about their child's progress . . . or lack thereof.

I didn't lean out from behind the dusty curtain to look, but I could follow the progress of the two easily. Mrs. Garfield was a ball of tension so dense it charged the air around her, and Miss Maddy was equally surrounded by the smell of all the cleaning products and the sounds of her cart. She was miserable, too, and above all she wanted to get back to her routine. Maddy Pepper might be a woman of limited intelligence, but she loved her job because she was good at it.

I learned a lot while I was sitting there. I learned that one of the teachers was a lesbian, though she was married and had three children. I learned that another teacher was pregnant but hadn't told anyone yet. I learned that most of the women (there were no male teachers at the elementary school) were stressed out by multiple obligations to their families, their jobs, and their churches. Cody's teacher was very unhappy, because she liked the little boy, though she thought his mother was weird. She did believe Holly was trying hard to be a good mother, and that offset her distaste for Holly's goth trappings.

But nothing I learned helped me discover Cody's whereabouts until I ventured into

Maddy Pepper's head.

When Kenya came up behind me, I was doubled over, my hand over my mouth, trying to cry silently. I was not capable of getting up to look for Andy or anyone else. I knew where the boy was.

"He sent me back here to find out what you know," Kenya whispered. She was massively unhappy about her errand, and though she'd always liked me okay, she didn't think I could do anything to help the police. She thought Andy was a fool for stalling his career by asking me to sit back there, concealed.

Then I caught something else, something faint and weak.

I jumped to my feet and grabbed Kenya by the shoulder. "Look in the garbage can, the one loaded on the cart, right now!" I said, my voice low but (I hoped) urgent enough to light a fire under Kenya. "He's in the can, he's still alive!"

Kenya wasn't rash enough to leap out from behind the curtain, jump down from the stage, and dash over to the custodian's cart. She gave me a hard, hard, look. I stepped out from behind the curtain to watch as Kenya made her way down the little stairs at the front of the stage, and went over to where Maddy Pepper was sitting, her fingers tapping against her legs. Miss Maddy wanted a cigarette. Then she realized that Kenya was approaching her, and a dull alarm sounded in her brain. When the custodian saw Kenya actually touch the edge of the large garbage can, she leaped to her feet and yelled, "I didn't mean to! I didn't mean to!"

Everyone in the room turned to the commotion, and everyone's face wore identical expressions of horror. Andy strode over, his face hard. Kenya was bent over the can, rummaging, tossing a snowstorm of used tissues over her shoulder. She froze for a second when she found what she'd been looking for. She bent over, almost in danger of falling into the can.

"He's alive," she called to Andy. "Call 911!"

"She was mopping when he ran back into the school to get the picture," Andy said. We were sitting in the cafeteria all by ourselves. "I don't know if you could hear all that, there was so much noise in the room."

I nodded. I'd been able to hear her thoughts as she'd spoken. All these years on her job, and she'd never had a problem with a student that wasn't easily resolved with a few strong words on her part. Then, today, Cody had come running into the classroom, pollen all over his shoes and pants cuffs, tracking up Maddy's freshly mopped floor. She'd yelled at him, and he'd been so startled that his feet had slipped on the wet floor. The little boy had gone over backward and hit his head on the floor. The corridor had indoor-outdoor carpeting to reduce the noise, but the classrooms did not, and his head had bounced on the linoleum.

Maddy had thought she'd killed him, and she'd hastily concealed his body in the nearest receptacle. She'd realized she'd lose her job if the child was dead, and on an impulse she'd tried to hide him. She had no plan and no idea of what would happen. She hadn't figured out how she'd dispose of his body, and she hadn't counted on how miserable she'd feel about the whole thing, how guilty.

To keep my part of it silent, which the police and I both agreed was absolutely the best idea, Andy suggested to Kenya that she'd suddenly realized the only receptacle in the school she hadn't searched was Maddy Pepper's trash can. "That's exactly what I thought," Kenya said. "I should search it, at least poke around and see if an abductor had tossed something into it."

119

Kenya's round face was unreadable. Kevin looked at her, his brows drawn together, sensing something beneath the surface of the conversation. Kevin was no fool, especially where Kenya was concerned.

Andy's thoughts were clear to me. "Don't ever ask me to do this again," I told him.

He nodded in acquiescence, but he was lying. He was seeing before him a vista of cleared cases, of malefactors locked up, of how clean Bon Temps would be when I'd told him who all the criminals were and he'd found a way to charge them with something.

"I'm not going to do it," I said. "I'm not going to help you all the time. You're a detective. You have to find things out in a legal way, so you can build a court case. If you use me all the time, you'll get sloppy. The cases will fall through. You'll get a bad reputation." I spoke desperately, helplessly. I didn't think my words would have any effect.

"She's not a Magic 8 Ball," Kevin said.

Kenya looked surprised, and Andy was more than surprised; he thought this was almost heresy. Kevin was a patrolman; Andy was a detective. And Kevin was a quiet man, listening to all his co-workers, but not often offering a comment of his own. He was notoriously mother-ridden; maybe he'd learned at his mother's knee not to offer opinions.

"You can't shake her and come up with the right answer," Kevin continued. "You have to find out the answer on your own. It's not right to take over Sookie's life so you can do your job better."

"Right," said Andy, unconvinced. "But I would think any citizen would want her town to be rid of thieves and rapists and murderers."

"What about adulterers and people who take extra papers out of the newspaper dispensers? Should I turn those in, too? What about kids who cheat on their exams?"

"Sookie, you know what I mean," he said, white-faced and furious.

"Yeah, I know what you mean. Forget it. I helped you save that child's life. Don't make me even think about regretting it." I left the same way I'd come, out the back gate and down the side of the school property to where I'd left my car. I drove back to work very carefully, because I was still shaking with the intensity of the emotions that had flowed through the school this afternoon.

At the bar, I found that Holly and Danielle had left — Holly to the hospital to be with her son, and Danielle to drive her there because she was so shaky.

"The police would have taken Holly, gladly," Sam said. "But I knew Holly didn't have anyone but Danielle here, so I thought I might as well let Danielle go, too."

"Of course, that leaves me to serve by myself," I said tartly, thinking I was getting punished doubly for helping Holly out.

He smiled at me, and for a second I couldn't help but smile back. "I've called that Tanya Grissom. She said she'd like to help out, just on a fill-in basis."

Tanya Grissom had just moved to Bon Temps, and she'd come into Merlotte's right away to put in an application. She'd put herself through college waitressing, she'd told Sam. She'd pulled down over two hundred dollars a night in tips. That wasn't going to happen in Bon Temps, and I'd told her so frankly.

"Did you call Arlene and Charlsie first?" I realized I'd overstepped my bounds, because I was only a waitress/barmaid, not the owner. It wasn't for me to remind Sam he should call the women with longer time in before he called the newcomer. The newcomer was definitely a shape-shifter, and I was afraid Sam was prejudiced in her favor.

Sam didn't look irritated, just matter-of-fact. "Yeah, I called them first. Arlene said she had a date, and Charlsie was keeping her grandbaby. She's been hinting pretty heavily that she won't be working much longer. I think she's going to keep the baby full-time when her daughter-in-law goes back to work."

"Oh," I said, disconcerted. I'd have to get used to someone new. Of course, barmaids come and barmaids go, and I'd seen quite a few pass through the employee door of Merlotte's in my — gosh, now five — years of working for Sam. Merlotte's was open until midnight on weeknights and until one on Friday and Saturday. Sam had tried opening on Sunday for a while, but it didn't pay. So now Merlotte's was closed on Sunday, unless it had been rented for a private party.

Sam tried to rotate our times so everyone got a chance to work the more lucrative night shift, so some days I worked eleven to five (or six-thirty, if we became extra busy) and sometimes I worked five to closing. He'd experimented with times and days until we'd all agreed on what worked best. He expected a little flexibility from us, and in return he was good about letting us off for funerals and weddings and other milestones.

I'd had a couple of other jobs before I'd started working for Sam. He was the easiest person to work for, by far. He'd become more than my employer somewhere along the way; he was my friend. When I'd found out he was a shape-shifter, it hadn't bothered me a bit. I'd heard rumors in the shifting community that the Weres were thinking of going public, the way the vampires had. I worried about Sam. I worried about people in Bon Temps accepting him. Would they feel he'd been deceiving them all these years, or would they take it in stride? Since the vampires had made their carefully orchestrated revelation, life as we knew it had changed, all over the world. Some countries, after the initial shock had worn off, had begun working to include vampires in the mainstream of life; others had pronounced vampires nonhuman and urged their citizens to kill vampires on sight (easier said than done).

"I'm sure Tanya will be fine," I said, but I sounded uncertain, even to my own ears. Acting on an impulse — and I can only suppose the tidal wave of emotions I'd experienced that day had something to do with this — I threw my arms around Sam and gave him a hug. I smelled clean skin and hair and the slight sweet smell of a light aftershave, an undertone of wine, a whiff of beer . . . the Sam smell. I drew it into my lungs like oxygen.

Surprised, Sam hugged me back, and for a second the warmth of his embrace made me feel almost light-headed with pleasure. Then we both backed off, because after all, this was our workplace and there were a few customers scattered around. Tanya came in, so it was good we were out of the clinch. I didn't want her to think this was routine.

Tanya was shorter than my five foot six, and she was a pleasant-looking woman in her late twenties. Her hair was short and straight and shiny, a medium brown that almost matched her eyes. She had a small mouth and a button nose and a nice figure. I had absolutely no reason to dislike her, but I wasn't happy to see her. I was ashamed of myself. I should give Tanya a fair chance to show her true character.

After all, I'd discover it sooner or later. You can't hide what you really are, not from me — not if you're a regular human person. I try not to listen in, but I can't block everything out. When I'd dated Bill, he'd helped me learn how to close my mind. Since then, life had been easier — more pleasant, more relaxed.

Tanya was a smiling woman, I'd give her that. She smiled at Sam, and she smiled at me, and she smiled at the customers. It wasn't a nervous smile, like mine, the grin that says "I'm hearing a clamor inside my head and I'm trying to look normal on the outside"; Tanya's smile was more of a "I'm really cute and perky and will endear myself to everyone" kind of smile. Before she picked up a tray and started working, Tanya asked a list of sensible questions, and I could tell she'd had experience.

"What's wrong?" Sam asked.

"Nothing," I said. "I just . . ."

"She seems nice enough," he said. "Do you think there's something wrong with her?"

"Nothing I know of," I said, trying to sound brisk and cheerful. I knew I was smiling that jittery smile. "Look, Jane Bodehouse is signaling for another round. We'll have to call her son again."

Tanya turned around and looked at me just then, as if she felt my eyes on her back. Her own smile was gone, replaced with a look so level that my estimate of her capacity for serious action instantly upgraded. We stood for a moment, regarding each other steadily, and then she beamed at me and continued to the next table, asking the man there if he was ready for another beer.

Suddenly I thought, *I wonder if Tanya is interested in Sam.* I didn't like the way I felt when I thought about that. I decided the day had been exhausting enough without creating a new worry. And no call from Jason.

After work, I went home with a lot on my mind: Father Riordan, the Pelts, Cody, Crystal's miscarriage.

I drove down my graveled driveway through the woods, and when I pulled into the clearing and drove behind the house to park at the back door, its isolation struck me all over again. Living in town for a few weeks had made the house seem even lonelier, and though I loved being back in the old place, it didn't feel the same as it had before the fire.

I'd seldom felt worried living by myself in this isolated spot, but over the past few months my vulnerability had been impressed on me. I'd had a few close calls, and twice there'd been intruders in my house waiting for me when I'd come in. Now I had installed some really good locks on my doors, I had peepholes front and back, and my brother had given me his Benelli shotgun to keep for good.

I had some big lights on the corners of the house, but I didn't like to leave them on all night. I was considering the purchase of one of those motion-detector lights. The drawback was, since I lived in a large clearing in the middle of the woods, critters often crossed my yard at night, and the light would come on when every little possum rambled across the grass.

The second point about a light coming on was . . . *So what?* The kind of thing I was scared of wasn't going to be intimidated by a light. I'd just be able to see it better before it ate me. Furthermore, there were no neighbors that a light might startle or rouse. Strange, I reflected, that I'd seldom had a frightened moment when my grandmother had been alive. She'd been a tough little lady for a woman in her late seventies, but she couldn't have defended me against a flea. Somehow, the simple fact of not being alone had made me feel safer.

After all this thinking about danger, I was in a tense state when I got out of my car. I'd passed a truck parked in front, and I unlocked the back and went through the house to open the front door with the miserable feeling that I was about to have to go through a scene. The quiet interlude on my front porch watching the bees in the pear tree seemed a week ago, instead of hours.

Calvin Norris, leader of the Hotshot werepanthers, got out of his truck and came up the steps. He was a bearded man in his early forties, and he was a serious man whose responsibilities sat squarely on his shoulders. Evidently Calvin had just gotten off work. He was wearing the blue shirt and blue jeans all the Norcross crew leaders wore.

"Sookie," he said, nodding to me.

"Please come in," I answered, though I was reluctant. However, Calvin had never been anything but civil to me, and he had helped me rescue my brother a couple of months ago, when Jason had been held hostage. At the least, I owed him civility.

"My niece called me when the danger had passed," he said heavily, taking a seat on the couch after I'd waved my hand to show he was welcome to stay. "I think you saved her life."

"I'm real glad to hear Crystal's better. All I did was make a phone call." I sat in my favorite old chair, and I noticed I was slumping with weariness. I forced my shoulders back. "Dr. Ludwig was able to stop her bleeding?"

Calvin nodded. He looked at me steadily, his strange eyes solemn. "She's going to be okay. Our women miscarry a lot. That's why we were hoping . . . Well."

I flinched, the weight of Calvin's hopes that I'd mate with him resting heavily on my shoulders. I'm not sure why I felt guilty; because of his disappointment, I guess. After all, it was hardly my fault that the idea had limited appeal for me.

"I guess Jason and Crystal will be getting hitched," Calvin said matter-of-factly. "I have to say, I'm not crazy about your brother, but then I'm not the one marrying him."

I was nonplussed. I didn't know if this wedding was Jason's idea, or Calvin's, or Crystal's. Jason certainly hadn't been thinking marriage this morning, unless it was something he'd neglected to mention in the turmoil of his worry about Crystal. I said, "Well, to be honest, I'm not crazy about Crystal. But I'm not the one marrying her." I took a deep breath. "I'll do my best to help them out, if they decide to . . . do that. Jason's about all I've got, as you know."

"Sookie," he said, and his voice was suddenly far less certain, "I want to talk about something else, too."

Of course he did. No way was I going to dodge this bullet.

"I know that something you got told, when you came out to the house, put you off me. I'd like to know what it was. I can't fix it, if I don't know what's broken."

I took a deep breath, while I considered

my next words very carefully. "Calvin, I know that Terry is your daughter." When I'd gone to see Calvin when he'd gotten out of the hospital after being shot, I'd met Terry and her mother Maryelizabeth at Calvin's house. Though they clearly didn't live there, it was equally clear that they treated the place as an extension of their own home. Then Terry had asked me if I was going to marry her father.

"Yes," Calvin said. "I would've told you if you'd asked me."

"Do you have other children?"

"Yes. I have three other children."

"By different mothers?"

"By three different mothers."

I'd been right. "Why is that?" I asked, to be sure.

"Because I'm pure-blooded," he said, as if it were self-evident. "Since only the first child of a pureblood couple turns out to be a full panther, we have to switch off."

I was profoundly glad I'd never seriously considered marrying Calvin, because if I had, I would have thrown up right then. What I'd suspected, after witnessing the succession-to-packmaster ritual, was true. "So it's not the woman's first child, period, that turns out to be a full-blooded shape-shifter . . . it's her first child with a specific man."

"Right." Calvin looked surprised that I hadn't known that. "The first child of any given pureblood couple is the real thing. So if our population gets too small, a pure-blooded male has to mate with as many pure-blooded women as he can, to increase the pack."

"Okay." I waited for a minute, to collect myself. "Did you think that I would be okay with you impregnating other women, if we got married?"

"No, I wouldn't expect that of an out-sider," he answered, in that same matter-of-fact voice. "I think it's time I settled down with one woman. I've done my duty as leader."

I tried not to roll my eyes. If it had been anyone else I would have sniggered, but Calvin was an honorable man, and he didn't deserve that reaction.

"Now I want to mate for life, and it would be good for the pack if I could bring new blood into the community. You can tell that we've bred with each other for too long. My eyes can hardly pass for human, and Crystal takes forever to change. We have to add something new to our gene pool, as the scientists call it. If you and I had a baby, which was what I was hoping, that baby wouldn't ever be a full Were; but he or she might breed into the community, bring new blood and new skills."

"Why'd you pick me?"

He said, almost shyly, "I like you. And you're real pretty." He smiled at me then, a rare and sweet expression. "I've watched you at the bar for years. You're nice to everyone, and you're a hard worker, and you don't have no one to take care of you like you deserve. And you know about us; it wouldn't be any big shock."

"Do other kinds of shape-shifters do the same thing?" I asked this so quietly, I could hardly hear myself. I stared down at my hands, clenched together in my lap, and I could hardly breathe as I waited to hear his answer. Alcide's green eyes filled my thoughts.

"When the pack begins to grow too small, it's their duty to," he said slowly. "What's on your mind, Sookie?"

"When I went to the contest for the Shreveport packmaster, the one who won — Patrick Furnan — he had sex with a young Were girl, though he was married. I began to wonder."

"Did I ever stand a chance with you?" Calvin asked. He seemed to have drawn his own conclusions.

Calvin could not be blamed for wanting to preserve his way of life. If I found the means distasteful, that was my problem.

"You definitely interested me," I said. "But I'm just too human to think of having my husband's children all around me. I'd just be too . . . it would just throw me off all the time, knowing my husband had had sex with almost every woman I saw day-to-day." Come to think of it, Jason would fit right into the Hotshot community. I paused for a second, but he remained silent. "I hope that my brother will be welcomed into your community, regardless of my answer."

"I don't know if he understands what we do," Calvin said. "But Crystal's already miscarried once before, by a full-blood. Now she's miscarried this baby of your brother's. I'm thinking this means Crystal had better not try any more to have a panther. She may not be able to have a baby of your brother's. Do you feel obliged to talk to him about that?"

"It shouldn't be up to me to discuss that with Jason . . . it should be up to Crystal." I met Calvin's eyes. I opened my mouth to remark that if all Jason wanted was babies, he shouldn't get married; but then I recognized that was a sensitive subject, and I stopped while I was ahead.

Calvin shook my hand in an odd, formal way when he left. I believed that marked the end of his courtship. I had never been deeply attracted to Calvin Norris, and I'd never seriously thought about accepting his offer. But I'd be less than honest if I didn't admit that I'd fantasized about a steady husband with a good job and benefits, a husband who came straight home after his shift and fixed broken things on his days off. There were men who did that, men who didn't change into anything other than their own form, men who were alive twenty-four/seven. I knew that from reading so many minds at the bar.

I'm afraid that what really struck me about Calvin's confession — or explanation — is what it might reveal to me about Alcide.

Alcide had sparked my affection, and my lust. Thinking of him did make me wonder what marriage to him would be like, wonder in a very personal way, as opposed to my impersonal speculation about health insurance that Calvin had inspired. I'd pretty much abandoned the secret hope Alcide had inspired in me, after I'd been forced to shoot his former fiancée; but something in me had clung to the thought, something I'd kept secret even from myself, even after I'd found out he was dating Maria-Star. As recently as this day, I'd been stoutly denying to the Pelts that Alcide had any interest in me. But something lonely inside me had nursed a hope.

I got up slowly, feeling about twice my actual age, and went into the kitchen to get something out of the freezer for my supper. I wasn't hungry, but I'd eat unwisely later if I didn't fix something now, I told myself sternly.

But I never cooked a meal for myself that night.

Instead, I leaned against the refrigerator door and cried.

7

The next day was Friday; not only was it my day off this week, but I had a date, so it was practically a red-letter day. I refused to ruin it by moping. Though it was still cool for such a pastime, I did one of my favorite things: I put on a bikini, greased myself up, and went to lie in the sun on the adjustable chaise lounge I'd gotten at Wal-Mart on sale at the end of the previous summer. I took a book, a radio, and a hat into the front yard, where there were fewer trees and flowering plants to encourage bugs that bit. I read, sang along with the tunes on the radio, and painted my toenails and fingernails. Though I was goose-pimply at first, I warmed up quickly along with the sun, and there was no breeze that day to chill me.

I know sunbathing is bad and evil, and I'll pay for it later, etc., etc., but it's one of the few free pleasures available to me.

No one came to visit, I couldn't hear the

phone, and since the sun was out, the vampires weren't. I had a delightful time, all by myself. Around one o'clock, I decided to run into town for some groceries and a new bra, and I stopped at the mailbox out by Hummingbird Road to see if the mail carrier had run yet. Yes. My cable bill and my electric bill were in the mailbox, which was a downer. But lurking behind a Sears sales brochure was an invitation to a wedding shower for Halleigh. Well . . . gosh. I was surprised, but pleased. Of course, I'd lived next to Halleigh in one of Sam's duplexes for a few weeks while my house was being repaired after the fire, and we'd seen each at least once a day during that time. So it wasn't a complete stretch, her putting me on her list of invitees. Plus, maybe she was relieved that the Cody situation had been cleared up so quickly?

I didn't get many invitations, so receiving it added to my sense of well-being. Three other teachers were giving the shower, and the invitation designated kitchen gifts. How timely, since I was on my way to the Wal-Mart Supercenter in Clarice.

After a lot of thought, I bought a two-quart Corning Ware casserole dish. Those were always handy. (I also got fruit juice, sharp cheddar, bacon, gift paper, and a really pretty blue bra and matching panties, but that's beside the point.)

After I'd gotten home and unloaded my purchases, I wrapped the boxed casserole dish in some silvery paper and stuck a big white bow on it. I wrote the date and time of the shower on my calendar, and I put the invitation on top of the present. I was on top of the shower situation.

Riding high on a crest of virtue, I wiped down the inside and outside of my new refrigerator after I'd eaten lunch. I washed a load of clothes in my new washer, wishing for the hundredth time that my cabinets were in place since I was tired of looking for things in the clutter on the floor.

I walked through the house to make sure it looked nice, since Quinn was picking me up. Not even letting myself think, I changed my sheets and cleaned my bathroom — not that I had any intention of falling into bed with Quinn, but it's better to be prepared than not, right? Besides, it just made me feel good, knowing that everything was clean and nice. Fresh towels in both bathrooms, a light dusting around the living room and bedroom, a quick circuit with the vacuum. Before I got in the shower, I even swept the porches, though I knew they would be covered again in a yellow haze before I got back from my date.

I let the sun dry my hair, probably getting it full of pollen, too. I put on my makeup carefully; I didn't wear a lot, but it was fun to apply it for something more interesting than work. A little eye shadow, a lot of mascara, some powder and lipstick. Then I put on my new date underwear. It made me feel special from the skin on out: midnight blue lace. I looked in the full-length mirror to check out the effect. I gave myself a thumbs-up. You have to cheer for yourself, right?

The outfit I'd bought from Tara's Togs was royal blue and made out of some heavy knit that hung beautifully. I zipped up the pants and put on the top. It was sleeveless and it wrapped across my breasts and tied. I experimented with the depth of cleavage, at last picking a degree of revelation I was sure toed the line between sexy and cheap.

I got my black wrap out of the closet, the one Alcide had given me to replace one Debbie Pelt had vandalized. I'd need it later in the evening. I slipped into my black sandals. I experimented with jewelry, finally settling on a plain gold chain (it had been my grandmother's) and plain ball earrings.

Hah!

There was a knock on the front door, and

I glanced at the clock, a bit surprised that Quinn was fifteen minutes early. I hadn't heard his truck, either. I opened the door to find not Quinn, but Eric, standing there.

I am sure he enjoyed my gasp of surprise.

Never open your door without checking. Never assume you know who's on the other side. That's why I'd gotten the peepholes! Stupid me. Eric must have flown, since I couldn't see a car anywhere.

"May I come in?" Eric asked politely. He had looked me over. After appreciating the view, he realized it hadn't been designed with him in mind. He wasn't happy. "I suppose you're expecting company?"

"As a matter of fact I am, and actually, I'd rather you stayed on that side of the doorsill," I said. I stepped back so he couldn't reach me.

"You told Pam that you didn't want to come to Shreveport," he said. Oh yes, he was angry. "So here I am, to find out why you don't answer my call." Usually, his accent was very slight, but tonight I noticed that it was pronounced.

"I didn't have time," I said. "I'm going out tonight."

"So I see," he said, more quietly. "Who are you going out with?"

"Is that really any of your business?" I met

his eyes, challengingly.

"Of course it is," he said.

I was disconcerted. "And that would be why?" I rallied a little.

"You should be mine. I have slept with you, I have cared for you, I have . . . assisted you financially."

"You paid me money you owed me, for services rendered," I answered. "You may have slept with me, but not recently, and you've shown no signs of wanting to do so again. If you care for me, you're showing it in a mighty strange way. I never heard that 'total avoidance aside from orders coming from flunkies' was a valid way to show caring." This was a jumbled sentence, okay, but I knew he got it.

"You're calling Pam a flunky?" He had a ghost of smile on his lips. Then he got back to being miffed. I could tell because he began dropping his contractions. "I do not have to hang around you to show you. I am sheriff. You . . . you are in my retinue."

I knew my mouth was hanging open, but I couldn't help it. "Catching flies," my grandmother had called that expression, and I felt like I was catching plenty of them. "Your retinue?" I managed to splutter. "Well, *up* you and your retinue. You don't tell me what to do!"

"You are obliged to go with me to the conference," Eric said, his mouth tense and his eyes blazing. "That was why I called you to Shreveport, to talk to you about travel time and arrangements."

"I'm not obliged to go anywhere with you. You got outranked, buddy."

"Buddy? *Buddy?*"

And it would have degenerated from there, if Quinn hadn't pulled up. Instead of arriving in his truck, Quinn was in a Lincoln Continental. I felt a moment of sheer snobbish pleasure at the thought of riding in it. I'd selected the pants outfit at least partly because I thought I'd be scrambling up into a pickup, but I was just as pleased to slither into a luxurious car. Quinn came across the lawn and mounted the porch with an understated speed. He didn't look as though he was hurrying, but suddenly he was there, and I was smiling at him, and he looked wonderful. He was wearing a dark gray suit, a dark purple shirt, and a tie that blended the two colors in a paisley pattern. He was wearing one earring, a simple gold hoop.

Eric had fang showing.

"Hello, Eric," Quinn said calmly. His deep voice rumbled along my spine. "Sookie, you look good enough to eat." He smiled at me, and the tremors along my spine spread into another area entirely. I would never have believed that in Eric's presence I could think another man was attractive. I'd have been wrong to think so.

"You look very nice, too," I said, trying not to beam like an idiot. It was not cool to drool.

Eric said, "What have you been telling Sookie, Quinn?"

The two tall men looked at each other. I didn't believe I was the source of their animosity. I was a symptom, not the disease. Something lay underneath this.

"I've been telling Sookie that the queen requires Sookie's presence at the conference as part of her party, and that the queen's summons supercedes yours," Quinn said flatly.

"Since when has the queen given orders through a shifter?" Eric said, contempt flattening his voice.

"Since this shifter performed a valuable service for her in the line of business," Quinn answered, with no hesitation. "Mr. Cataliades suggested to Her Majesty that I might be helpful in a diplomatic capacity, and my partners were glad to give me extra time to perform any duties she might give me."

I wasn't totally sure I was following this,

but I got the gist of it.

Eric was incensed, to use a good entry from my Word of the Day calendar. In fact, his eyes were almost throwing sparks, he was so angry. "This woman has been mine, and she will be mine," he said, in tones so definite I thought about checking my rear end for a brand.

Quinn shifted his gaze to me. "Babe, are you his, or not?" he asked.

"Not," I said.

"Then let's go enjoy the show," Quinn said. He didn't seem frightened, or even concerned. Was this his true reaction, or was he presenting a façade? Either way, it was pretty impressive.

I had to pass by Eric on my way to Quinn's car. I looked up at him, because I couldn't help it. Being close to him while he was this angry was not a safe thing, and I needed to be on my guard. Eric was seldom crossed in serious matters, and my annexation by the Queen of Louisiana — his queen — was a serious matter. My date with Quinn was sticking in his throat, too. Eric was just going to have to swallow.

Then we were both in the car, belted in, and Quinn did an expert backing maneuver to point the Lincoln back to Hummingbird Road. I breathed out, slowly and carefully.

It took a few quiet moments for me to feel calm again. Gradually my hands relaxed. I realized the silence had been building. I gave myself a mental shake. "Do you go to the theater often, as you're traveling around?" I asked socially.

He laughed, and the deep, rich sound of it filled up the car. "Yes," he said. "I go to the movies and the theater and any sporting event that's going on. I like to see people do things. I don't watch much television. I like to get out of my hotel room or my apartment and watch things happen or make them happen myself."

"So do you dance?"

He gave me a quick glance. "I do."

I smiled. "I like to dance." And I was actually pretty good at dancing, not that I got many chances to practice. "I'm no good at singing," I admitted, "but I really, really enjoy dancing."

"That sounds promising."

I thought we'd have to see how this evening went before we made any dancing dates, but at least we knew there was something we both liked to do. "I like movies," I said. "But I don't think I've ever been to any live sports besides high school games. But those, I do attend. Football, basketball, baseball . . . I go to 'em all, when my job will let me."

"Did you play a sport in school?" Quinn asked. I confessed that I'd played softball, and he told me he'd played basketball, which, considering his height, was no surprise at all.

Quinn was easy to talk to. He listened when I spoke. He drove well; at least he didn't curse at the other drivers, like Jason did. My brother tended to be on the impatient side when he drove.

I was waiting for the other shoe to drop. I was waiting for that moment — you know the one I mean — the moment when your date suddenly confesses to something you just can't stomach: he reveals himself as a racist or homophobe, admits he'd never marry anyone but another Baptist (Southerner, brunette, marathon runner, whatever), tells you about his children by his first three wives, describes his fondness for being paddled, or relates his youthful experiences in blowing up frogs or torturing cats. After that moment, no matter how much fun you have, you know it's not going anywhere. And I didn't even have to wait for a guy to tell me this stuff verbally; I could read it right out of his head before we even dated.

Never popular with the regular guys, me.

Whether they admitted it or not, they couldn't stand the idea of going out with a girl who knew exactly how often they jacked off, had a lusty thought about another woman, or wondered how their teacher looked with her clothes off.

Quinn came around and opened my door when we parked across the street from the Strand, and he took my hand as we crossed the street. I enjoyed the courtesy.

There were lots of people going into the theater, and they all seemed to look at Quinn. Of course, a bald guy as tall as Quinn is going to get some stares. I was trying not to think about his hand; it was very large and very warm and very dry.

"They're all looking at you," he said, as he pulled the tickets from his pocket, and I pressed my lips together to keep from laughing.

"Oh, I don't think so," I said.

"Why else would they be staring?"

"At you," I said, amazed.

He laughed out loud, that deep laugh that made me vibrate inside.

We had very good seats, right in the middle and toward the front of the theater. Quinn filled up his seat, no doubt about it, and I wondered if the people behind him could see. I looked at my program with some curiosity, found I didn't recognize the names of any of the actors in the production, and decided I didn't care at all. I glanced up to find that Quinn was staring at me. I felt my face flood with color. I'd folded my black wrap and placed it in my lap, and I had the abrupt desire to pull my top higher to cover every inch of my cleavage.

"Definitely looking at you," he said, and smiled. I ducked my head, pleased but self-conscious.

Lots of people have seen *The Producers.* I don't need to describe the plot, except to say it's about gullible people and lovable rascals, and it's very funny. I enjoyed every minute. It was marvelous to watch people performing right in front of me on such a professional level. The guest star, the one whom the older people in the audience seemed to recognize, swashed through the lead role with this amazing assurance. Quinn laughed too, and after the intermission he took my hand again. My fingers closed around his quite naturally, and I didn't feel self-conscious about the contact.

Suddenly it was an hour later, and the play was over. We stood up along with everyone else, though we could tell it would take a while for the theater to clear out. Quinn took my wrap and held it for me, and I threw it around me. He was sorry I was covering myself up — I got that directly from his brain.

"Thank you," I said, tugging on his sleeve to make sure he was looking at me. I wanted him to know how much I meant it. "That was just great."

"I enjoyed it, too. You want to go get something to eat?"

"Okay," I said, after a moment.

"You had to think about it?"

I had actually sort of flash-thought about several different items. If I'd enumerated them, it'd have run something like, *He must be having a good time or he wouldn't suggest more of the evening. I have to get up and go to work tomorrow but I don't want to miss this opportunity. If we go to eat I have to be careful not to spill anything on my new clothes. Will it be okay to spend even more of his money, since the tickets cost so much?*

"Oh, I had to consider the calories," I said, patting my rear end.

"There's nothing wrong with you, front or back," Quinn said, and the warmth in his eyes made me feel like basking. I knew I was curvier than the ideal. I'd actually heard Holly tell Danielle that anything over a size eight was simply disgusting. Since a day I got into an eight was a happy day for me, I'd felt pretty forlorn for all of three minutes. I would have related this conversation to Quinn if I hadn't been sure it would sound like I was angling for a compliment.

"Let the restaurant be my treat," I said.

"With all due respect to your pride, no, I won't." Quinn looked me right in the eyes to make sure I knew he meant it.

We'd reached the sidewalk by that time. Surprised at his vehemence, I didn't know how to react. On one level, I was relieved, since I have to be careful with my money. On another level, I knew it was right for me to offer and I would have felt good if he'd said that would be fine.

"You know I'm not trying to insult you, right?" I said.

"I understand that you're being equal."

I looked up at him doubtfully, but he was serious.

Quinn said, "I believe you are absolutely as good as me in every way. But I asked you out, and I am providing the financial backup for our date."

"What if I asked you out?"

He looked grim. "Then I'd have to sit back and let you take care of the evening," he said. He said it reluctantly, but he said it. I looked away and smiled.

Cars were pulling out of the parking lot at a steady pace. Since we'd taken our time leaving the theater, Quinn's car was looking lonely in the second row. Suddenly, my mental alarm went off. Somewhere close, there was a lot of hostility and evil intent. We had left the sidewalk to cross the street to the parking lot. I gripped Quinn's arm and then let it go so we could clear for action.

"Something's wrong," I said.

Without replying, Quinn began scanning the area. He unbuttoned his suit coat with his left hand so he could move without hindrance. His fingers curled into fists. Since he was a man with a powerful protective urge, he stepped ahead of me, in front of me.

So of course, we were attacked from behind.

8

In a blur of movement that couldn't be broken down into increments my eye could clearly recognize, a beast knocked me into Quinn, who stumbled forward a step. I was on the ground underneath the snarling half man, half wolf by the time Quinn wheeled, and as soon as he did, another Were appeared, seemingly out of nowhere, to leap on Quinn's back.

The creature on top of me was a brand-new fresh half Were, so young he could only have been bitten in the past three weeks. He was in such a frenzy that he had attacked before he had finished with the partial change that a bitten Were can achieve. His face was still elongating into a muzzle, even as he tried to choke me. He would never attain the beautiful wolf form of the full-blooded Were. He was "bitten, not blood," as the Weres put it. He still had arms, he still had legs, he had a body covered with hair, and he had a wolf's head. But he was just as savage as a full-blood.

I clawed at his hands, the hands that were gripping my neck with such ferocity. I wasn't wearing my silver chain tonight. I'd decided it would be tacky, since my date was himself a shifter. Being tacky might have saved my life, I thought in a flash, though it was the last coherent thought I had for a few moments.

The Were was straddling my body, and I brought my knees up sharply, trying to give him a big enough jolt that he'd loosen his hold. There were shrieks of alarm from the few remaining pedestrians, and a higher, more piercing shriek from Quinn's attacker, whom I saw flying through the air as if he'd been launched from a cannon. Then a big hand grasped my attacker by his own neck and lifted him. Unfortunately, the half beast who had his hands wrapped around my throat didn't let me go. I began to rise from the pavement, too, my throat becoming more and more pinched by the grip he had on me.

Quinn must have seen my desperate situation, because he struck the Were on top of me with his free hand, a slap that rocked the Were's head back and simply knocked him for a loop so thoroughly that he let go of my neck.

Then Quinn grabbed the young Were by the shoulders and tossed him aside. The boy landed on the pavement and didn't move.

"Sookie," Quinn said, hardly sounding out of breath. Out of breath is what I was, struggling to get my throat to open back up so I could gulp in some oxygen. I could hear a police siren, and I was profoundly thankful. Quinn slipped his arm under my shoulders and held me up. Finally I breathed in, and the air was wonderful, blissful. "You're breathing okay?" he asked. I gathered myself enough to nod. "Any bones broken in your throat?" I tried to raise my hand to my neck, but my hand wasn't cooperating just at the moment.

His face filled my scope of vision, and in the dim light of the corner lamp I could see he was pumped. "I'll kill them if they hurt you," he growled, and just then, that was delightful news.

"Bitten," I wheezed, and he looked horrified, checking me over with hands and eyes for the bite mark. "Not me," I elaborated. "Them. Not born Weres." I sucked in a lot of air. "And maybe on drugs," I said. Awareness dawned in his eyes.

That was the only explanation for such insane behavior.

A heavyset black patrolman hurried up to me. "We need an ambulance at the Strand," he was saying to someone on his shoulder. No, it was a little radio set. I shook my head.

"You need an ambulance, ma'am," he insisted. "Girl over there says the man took you down and tried to choke you."

"I'm okay," I said, my voice raspy and my throat undeniably painful.

"Sir, you with this lady?" the patrolman asked Quinn. When he turned, the light flashed off his name pin; it said *Boling*.

"Yes, I am."

"You . . . ah, you got these punks offa her?"

"Yes."

Boling's partner, a Caucasian version of Boling, came up to us then. He looked at Quinn with some reservation. He'd been examining our assailants, who had fully changed to human form before the police had arrived. Of course, they were naked.

"The one has a broken leg," he told us. "The other is claiming his shoulder's dislocated."

Boling shrugged. "Got what was coming to 'em." It might have been my imagination, but he, too, seemed a bit more cautious when he looked at my date.

"They got more than they expected," his

partner said neutrally. "Sir, do you know either of these kids?" He tilted his head toward the teenagers, who were being examined by a patrolman from another car, a younger man with a more athletic build. The boys were leaning against each other, looking stunned.

"I've never seen them before," Quinn said. "You, babe?" He looked down at me questioningly. I shook my head. I was feeling better enough that I felt at a distinct disadvantage, being on the ground. I wanted to get up, and I said so to my date. Before the police officers could tell me once again to wait for an ambulance, Quinn managed to get me to my feet with as little pain as possible.

I looked down at my beautiful new outfit. It was really dirty. "How does the back look?" I asked Quinn, and even I could hear the fear in my voice. I turned my back to Quinn and looked at him anxiously over my shoulder. Quinn seemed a little startled, but he dutifully scanned my rear view.

"No tearing," he reported. "There may be a spot or two where the material got a little scraped across the pavement."

I burst into tears. I probably would have started crying no matter what, because I was feeling a powerful reaction to the adrenaline that had surged through my body when we'd been attacked, but the timing was perfect. The police got more avuncular the more I cried, and as an extra bonus, Quinn pulled me into his arms and I rested my cheek against his chest. I listened to his heartbeat when I quit sobbing. I'd gotten rid of my nervous reaction to the attack and disarmed the police at the same time, though I knew they'd still wonder about Quinn and his strength.

Another policeman called from his place by one of the assailants, the one Quinn had thrown. Our two patrolmen went to answer the summons, and we were briefly alone.

"Smart," Quinn murmured into my ear.

"Mmmm," I said, snuggling against him.

He tightened his arms around me. "You get any closer, we're going to have to excuse ourselves and get a room," he whispered.

"Sorry." I pulled back slightly and looked up at him. "Who you reckon hired them?"

He may have been surprised I'd figured that out, but you couldn't tell by his brain. The chemical reaction that had fueled my tears had made his mental snarl extra complicated. "I'm definitely going to find out," he said. "How's your throat?"

"Hurts," I admitted, my voice raspy. "But I know there's nothing really wrong with it.

And I don't have health insurance. So I don't want to go to the hospital. It would be a waste of time and money."

"Then we won't go." He bent and kissed my cheek. I turned my face up to him, and his next kiss landed in exactly the right spot. After a gentle second, it flared into something more intense. We were both feeling the aftereffects of the adrenaline rush.

The sound of a throat clearing brought me back into my right mind as effectively as if Officer Boling had thrown a bucket of cold water on us. I disengaged and buried my face against Quinn's chest again. I knew I couldn't move away for a minute or two, since his excitement was pressed right up against me. Though these weren't the best circumstances for evaluation, I was pretty sure Quinn was proportional. I had to resist the urge to rub my body against his. I knew that would make things worse for him, from a public viewpoint — but I was in a much better mood than I had been, and I guess I was feeling mischievous. And frisky. Very frisky. Going through this ordeal together had probably accelerated our relationship the equivalent of four dates.

"Did you have other questions for us, Officer?" Quinn asked, in a voice that was not perfectly calm.

"Yes, sir, if you and the lady will come down to the station, we need to take your statements. Detective Coughlin will do that while we take the prisoners to the hospital."

"All right. Does that have to be tonight? My friend needs to rest. She's exhausted. This has been quite an ordeal for her."

"It won't take long," the officer said mendaciously. "You sure you've never seen these two punks before? Because this seems like a real personal attack, you don't mind me saying so."

"Neither of us knows them."

"And the lady still refuses medical attention?"

I nodded.

"Well, all right then, folks. Hope you don't have no more trouble."

"Thank you for coming so quickly," I said, and turned my head a little to meet Officer Boling's eyes. He looked at me in a troubled way, and I could hear in his head that he was worried about my safety with a violent man like Quinn, a man who could throw two boys several feet in the air. He didn't realize, and I hoped he never would, that the attack had been personal. It had been no random mugging.

We went to the station in a police car. I wasn't sure what their thinking was, but

160

Boling's partner told us that we'd be returned to Quinn's vehicle, so we went along with the program. Maybe they didn't want us to have a chance to talk to each other alone. I don't know why; I think the only thing that could have aroused their suspicion was Quinn's size and expertise in fighting off attackers.

In the brief seconds we had alone before an officer climbed into the driver's seat, I told Quinn, "If you think something at me, I'll be able to hear you — if you need me to know something urgently."

"Handy," he commented. The violence seemed to have relaxed something inside him. He rubbed his thumb across the palm of my hand. He was thinking he'd like to have thirty minutes in a bed with me, right now, or even fifteen; hell, even ten, even in the backseat of a car, would be fantastic. I tried not to laugh, but I couldn't help it, and when he realized that I'd read all that clearly, he shook his head with a rueful smile.

We have somewhere to go after this, he thought deliberately. I hoped he didn't mean he was going to rent a room or take me to his place for sex, because no matter how attractive I found him, I wasn't going to do that tonight. But his brain had mostly cleared of lust, and I perceived his purpose was something different. I nodded.

So don't get too tired, he said. I nodded again. How I was supposed to prevent exhaustion, I wasn't sure, but I'd try to hoard a little energy.

The police station was much like I expected it to be. Though there's a lot to be said for Shreveport, it has more than its fair share of crime. We didn't excite much attention at all, until officers who'd been on the scene put their heads together with police in the building, and then there were a few stolen glances at Quinn, some surreptitious evaluations. He was formidable-looking enough for them to credit ordinary strength as the source of his defeat of the two muggers. But there was just enough strangeness about the incident, enough peculiar touches in the eyewitness reports . . . and then my eye caught a familiar weathered face. Uh-oh.

"Detective Coughlin," I said, remembering now why the name had sounded familiar.

"Miss Stackhouse," he responded, with about as much enthusiasm as I had shown. "What you been up to?"

"We got mugged," I explained.

"Last time I saw you, you were engaged

162

to Alcide Herveaux, and you'd just found one of the most sickening corpses I've ever seen," he said easily. His belly seemed to have gotten even bigger in the few months since I'd met him at a murder scene here in Shreveport. Like many men with a disproportionate belly, he wore his khaki pants buttoned underneath the overhang, so to speak. Since his shirt had broad blue and white stripes, the effect was that of a tent overhanging packed dirt.

I just nodded. There was really nothing to say.

"Mr. Herveaux doing okay after the loss of his father?" Jackson Herveaux's body had been found half-in, half-out of a feed tank filled with water on an old farm belonging to the family. Though the newspaper had tap-danced around some of the injuries, it was clear wild animals had chewed at some of the bones. The theory was that the older Herveaux had fallen into the tank and broken his leg when he hit the bottom. He had managed to get to the edge and haul himself halfway out, but at that point he had passed out. Since no one knew he'd visited the farm, no one came to his rescue, the theory went, and he'd died all by himself.

Actually, a large crowd had witnessed

Jackson's demise, among them the man beside me.

"I haven't talked to Alcide since his dad was found," I said truthfully.

"My goodness, I'm sure sorry that didn't work out," Detective Coughlin said, pretending he didn't see that I was standing with my date for the evening. "You two sure made a nice-looking couple."

"Sookie is pretty no matter who she's with," Quinn said.

I smiled up at him, and he smiled back. He was sure making all the right moves.

"So if you'll come with me for a minute, Miss Stackhouse, we'll get your story down on paper and you can leave."

Quinn's hand tightened on mine. He was warning me. Wait a minute, who was the mind reader around here? I squeezed right back. I was perfectly aware that Detective Coughlin thought I must be guilty of *something,* and he'd do his best to discover what. But in fact, I was not guilty.

We had been the targets, I'd picked that from the attackers' brains. But why?

Detective Coughlin led me to a desk in a roomful of desks, and he fished a form out of a drawer. The business of the room continued; some of the desks were unoccupied and had that "closed for the night"

164

look, but others showed signs of work in progress. There were a few people coming in and out of the room, and two desks away, a younger detective with short white-blond hair was busily typing on his computer. I was being very careful, and I'd opened my mind, so I knew he was looking at me when I was looking in another direction, and I knew he'd been positioned there by Detective Coughlin, or at least prodded to get a good hard look at me while I was in the room.

I met his eyes squarely. The shock of recognition was mutual. I'd seen him at the packmaster contest. He was a Were. He'd acted as Patrick Furnan's second in the duel. I'd caught him cheating. Maria-Star had told me his punishment had been having his head shaved. Though his candidate won, this punishment had been exacted, and his hair was just now growing in. He hated me with the passion of the guilty. He half rose from his chair, his first instinct being to come over to me and beat the crap out of me, but when he absorbed the fact that someone had already tried to do that, he smirked.

"Is that your partner?" I asked Detective Coughlin.

"What?" He'd been peering at the computer through reading glasses, and he glanced over at the younger man, then back at me. "Yeah, that's my new partner. The guy I was with at the last crime scene I saw you at, he retired last month."

"What's his name? Your new partner?"

"Why, you going after him next? You can't seem to settle on one man, can you, Miss Stackhouse?"

If I'd been a vampire, I could have made him answer me, and if I were really skilled, he wouldn't even know he'd done it.

"It's more like they can't settle on me, Detective Coughlin," I said, and he gave me a curious look. He waved a finger toward the blond detective.

"That's Cal. Cal Myers." He seemed to have called up the right form, because he began to take me through the incident once again, and I answered his questions with genuine indifference. For once, I had very little to hide.

"I did wonder," I said, when we'd concluded, "if they'd taken drugs."

"You know much about drugs, Miss Stackhouse?" His little eyes went over me again.

"Not firsthand, but of course, from time to time someone comes into the bar who's taken something they shouldn't. These young men definitely seemed . . . influenced by something."

"Well, the hospital will take their blood, and we'll know."

"Will I have to come back?"

"To testify against them? Sure."

No way out of it. "Okay," I said, as firmly and neutrally as I could. "We through here?"

"I guess we are." He met my eyes, his own little brown eyes full of suspicion. There was no point in my resenting it; he was absolutely right, there was something fishy about me, something he didn't know. Coughlin was doing his best to be a good cop. I felt suddenly sorry for him, floundering through a world he only knew the half of.

"Don't trust your partner," I whispered, and I expected him to blow up and call Cal Myers over and ridicule me to him. But something in my eyes or my voice arrested that impulse. My words spoke to a warning that had been sounding surreptitiously in his brain, maybe from the moment he'd met the Were.

He didn't say anything, not one word. His mind was full of fear, fear and loathing . . . but he believed I was telling him the truth. After a second, I got up and left the squad room. To my utter relief, Quinn was waiting for me in the lobby.

A patrolman — not Boling — took us back to Quinn's car, and we were silent during the drive. Quinn's car was sitting in solitary splendor in the parking lot across from the Strand, which was closed and dark. He pulled out his keys and hit the keypad to open the doors, and we got in slowly and wearily.

"Where are we going?" I asked.

"The Hair of the Dog," he said.

9

The Hair of the Dog was off Kings Highway, not too far from Centenary College. It was an old brick storefront. The large windows facing the street were covered with opaque cream curtains, I noticed, as we turned in to the left side of the building to lurch through an alley that led to a parking area at the back. We parked in the small, weedy lot. Though it was poorly lit, I could see that the ground was littered with empty cans, broken glass, used condoms, and worse. There were several motorcycles, a few of the less expensive compact cars, and a Suburban or two. The back door had a sign on it that read NO ENTRANCE — STAFF ONLY.

Though my feet were definitely beginning to protest the unaccustomed high heels, we had to pick our way through the alley to the front entrance. The cold creeping down my spine intensified as we grew close to the door. Then it was like I'd hit a wall, the spell gripped me that suddenly. I stopped dead. I struggled to go forward, but I couldn't move. I could smell the magic. The Hair of the Dog had been warded. Someone had paid a very good witch a handsome amount of money to surround the door with a go-away spell.

I fought not to give in to a compulsion to turn and walk in another direction, any other direction.

Quinn took a few steps forward, and turned to regard me with some surprise, until he realized what was happening. "I forgot," he said, that same surprise sounding in his voice. "I actually forgot you're human."

"That sounds like a compliment," I said, with some effort. Even in the cool night, my forehead beaded with sweat. My right foot edged forward an inch.

"Here," he said, and scooped me up, until he was holding me just like Rhett carried Scarlett O'Hara. As his aura wrapped around me, the unpleasant go-away compulsion eased. I drew a deep breath of relief. The magic could no longer recognize me as human, at least not decisively. Though the bar still seemed unattractive and mildly repellent, I could enter without wanting to be sick.

Maybe it was the lingering effects of the spell, but after we'd entered it, the bar *still* seemed unattractive and mildly repellent. I wouldn't say all conversation ceased when we walked in, but there was a definite lull in the noise that filled the bar. A jukebox was playing "Bad Moon Rising," which was like the Were national anthem, and the motley collection of Weres and shifters seemed to reorient themselves.

"Humans are not allowed in this place!" A very young woman leaped across the bar in one muscular surge and strode forward. She was wearing fishnet stockings and high-heeled boots, a red leather bustier — well, a bustier that wished it was made of red leather, it was probably more like Naugahyde — and a black band of cloth that I supposed she called a skirt. It was like she'd pulled a tube top on, and then worked it down. It was so tight I thought it might roll up all at once, like a window shade.

She didn't like my smile, correctly reading it as a comment on her ensemble.

"Get your human ass out of here," she said, and growled. Unfortunately, it didn't sound too threatening, since she hadn't had any practice at putting the menace into it, and I could feel my smile widen. The dress-challenged teen had the poor impulse control of the very new Were, and she pulled her hand back to punch me.

Then Quinn snarled.

The sound came from deep in his belly, and it was thunderous, the deep sound of it penetrating every corner of the bar. The bartender, a biker type with beard and hair of considerable length and tattoos that covered his bare arms, reached down below the bar. I knew he was pulling out a shotgun.

Not for the first time, I wondered if I shouldn't start going armed everywhere I went. In my law-abiding life, I had never seen the need until the past few months. The jukebox cut off just then, and the silence of the bar was just as deafening as the noise had been.

"Please don't get the gun out," I said, smiling brightly at the bartender. I could feel it stretching my lips, that too-bright grin that made me look a little nuts. "We come in peace," I added, on a crazy impulse, showing them my empty palms.

A shifter who'd been standing at the bar laughed, a sharp bark of startled amusement. The tension began to ratchet down a notch. The young woman's hand dropped to her side, and she took a step back. Her gaze flickered from Quinn to me and back again. Both the bartender's hands were in sight now.

"Hello, Sookie," said a familiar voice. Amanda, the red-haired Were who'd been chauffeuring Dr. Ludwig the day before, was sitting at a table in a dark corner. (Actually, the room seemed to be full of dark corners.)

With Amanda was a husky man in his late thirties. Both were supplied with drinks and a bowl of snack mix. They had company at the table, a couple sitting with their backs to me. When they turned, I recognized Alcide and Maria-Star. They turned cautiously, as if any sudden movement might trigger violence. Maria-Star's brain was a motley jumble of anxiety, pride, and tension. Alcide's was just conflicted. He didn't know how to feel.

That made two of us.

"Hey, Amanda," I said, my voice as cheerful as my smile. It wouldn't do to let the silence pile up.

"I'm honored to have the legendary Quinn in my bar," Amanda said, and I realized that, whatever other jobs she might have, she owned the Hair of the Dog. "Are you two out for an evening on the town, or is there some special reason for your visit?"

Since I had no idea why we were there, I had to defer to Quinn for an answer, which didn't make me look too good, in my opinion.

"There's a very good reason, though I've long wanted to visit your bar," Quinn said in a courtly, formal style that had come out of nowhere.

Amanda inclined her head, which seemed to be a signal for Quinn to continue.

"This evening, my date and I were attacked in a public place, with civilians all around us."

No one seemed awfully upset or astonished by this. In fact, Miss Fashion-Challenged shrugged her bare skinny shoulders.

"We were attacked by Weres," Quinn said.

Now we got the big reaction. Heads and hands jerked and then became still. Alcide half rose to his feet and then sat down again.

"Weres of the Long Tooth pack?" Amanda asked. Her voice was incredulous.

Quinn shrugged. "The attack was a killing one, so I didn't stop to ask questions. Both were very young bitten Weres, and from their behavior, they were on drugs."

More shocked reaction. We were creating

quite the sensation.

"Are you hurt?" Alcide asked me, as if Quinn weren't standing right there.

I tilted my head back so my neck would be visible. I wasn't smiling anymore. By now the bruises left by the boy's hands would be darkening nicely. And I'd been thinking hard. "As a friend of the pack, I didn't expect anything to happen to me here in Shreveport," I said.

I figured my status as friend of the pack hadn't changed with the new regime, or at least I hoped it hadn't. Anyway, it was my trump card, and I played it.

"Colonel Flood did say Sookie was a friend of the pack," Amanda said unexpectedly. The Weres all looked at each other, and the moment seemed to hang in the balance.

"What happened to the cubs?" asked the biker behind the bar.

"They lived," Quinn said, giving them the important news first. There was a general feeling that the whole bar gave a sigh; whether of relief or regret, I couldn't tell you.

"The police have them," Quinn continued. "Since the cubs attacked us in front of humans, there was no way around police involvement." We'd talked about Cal Myers on our way to the bar. Quinn had caught only a glimpse of the Were cop, but of course he'd known him for what he was. I wondered if my companion would now raise the issue of Cal Myers's presence at the station, but Quinn said nothing. And truthfully, why comment on something the Weres were sure to already know? The Were pack would stand together against outsiders, no matter how divided they were among themselves.

Police involvement in Were affairs was undesirable, obviously. Though Cal Myers's presence on the force would help, every scrutiny raised the possibility that humans would learn of the existence of creatures that preferred anonymity. I didn't know how they'd flown (or crawled, or loped) under the radar this long. I had a conviction that the cost in human lives had been considerable.

Alcide said, "You should take Sookie home. She's tired."

Quinn put his arm around me and pulled me to his side. "When we've received your assurance that the pack will get to the bottom of this unprovoked attack, we'll leave."

Neat speech. Quinn seemed to be a master of expressing himself diplomatically and firmly. He was a little overwhelming, truthfully. The power flowed from him in a steady stream, and his physical presence was undeniable.

"We'll convey all this to the packmaster," Amanda was saying. "He'll investigate, I'm sure. Someone must have hired these pups."

"Someone converted them to start with," Quinn said. "Unless your pack has degraded to biting street punks and sending them out to scavenge?"

Okay, hostile atmosphere now. I looked up at my large companion and discovered that Quinn was nearasthis to losing his temper.

"Thank you all," I said to Amanda, my bright smile again yanking at the corners of my mouth. "Alcide, Maria-Star, good to see you. We're going to go now. Long drive back to Bon Temps." I gave Biker Bartender and Fishnet Girl a little wave. He nodded, and she scowled. Probably she wouldn't be interested in becoming my best friend. I wriggled out from under Quinn's arm and linked his hand with mine.

"Come on, Quinn. Let's hit the road."

For a bad little moment, his eyes didn't recognize me. Then they cleared, and he relaxed. "Sure, babe." He said good-bye to the Weres, and we turned our backs on them to walk out. Even though the little crowd included Alcide, whom I trusted in most ways, it was an uncomfortable moment for me.

I could feel no fear, no anxiety, coming from Quinn. Either he had great focus and control, or he really wasn't scared of a bar full of werewolves, which was admirable and all, but kind of . . . unrealistic.

The correct answer turned out to be "great focus and control." I found out when we got to the dim parking lot. Moving quicker than I could track, I was against the car and his mouth was on mine. After a startled second, I was right in the moment. Shared danger does that, and it was the second time — on our first date — that we'd been in peril. Was that a bad omen? I dismissed that rational thought when Quinn's lips and teeth traveled down to find that vulnerable and sensitive place where the neck curves into the shoulder. I made an incoherent noise, because along with the arousal I always felt when kissed there, I felt undeniable pain from the bruises that circled my neck. It was an uncomfortable combination.

"Sorry, sorry," he muttered into my skin, his lips never stopping their assault. I knew if I lowered my hand, I'd be able to touch him intimately. I'm not saying I wasn't tempted. But I was learning a little caution as I went along . . . probably not enough, I reflected with the sliver of my mind that wasn't getting more and more involved with the heat that surged up from my lowest nerve bundle to meet the heat generated by Quinn's lips. Oh, geez. Oh, oh, oh.

I moved against him. It was a reflex, okay? But a mistake, because his hand slipped under my breast and his thumb began stroking. I shuddered and jerked. He was doing a little gasping, too. It was like jumping onto the running board of a car that was already speeding down the dark road.

"Okay." I breathed, pulled away a little. "Okay, let's stop this now."

"Ummm," he said in my ear, his tongue flicking. I jerked.

"I'm not doing this," I said, trying to sound definite. Then my resolve gathered. "Quinn! I'm not having sex with you in this nasty parking lot!"

"Not even a little bit of sex?"

"No. Definitely not!"

"Your mouth" (here he kissed it) "is saying one thing, but your body" (he kissed my shoulder) "is saying another."

"Listen to the mouth, buster."

"Buster?"

"Okay. Quinn."

He sighed, straightened. "All right," he said. He smiled ruefully. "Sorry. I didn't plan on jumping you like that."

"Going into a place where you're not exactly welcome, and getting out unhurt, that's some excitement," I said.

He expelled a deep breath. "Right," he said.

"I like you a lot," I said. I could read his mind fairly clearly, just at this instant. He liked me, too; right at the moment, he liked me a whole bunch. He wanted to like me right up against the wall.

I battened my hatches. "But I've had a couple of experiences that have been warnings for me to slow down. I haven't been going slow with you tonight. Even with the, ah, special circumstances." I was suddenly ready to sit down in the car. My back was aching and I felt a slight cramp. I worried for a second, then thought of my monthly cycle. That was certainly enough to wear me out, coming on top of an exciting, and bruising, evening.

Quinn was looking down at me. He was wondering about me. I couldn't tell what his exact concern was, but suddenly he asked, "Which of us was the target of that attack outside the theater?"

Okay, his mind was definitely off sex now.

Good. "You think it was just one of us?"

That gave him pause. "I had assumed so," he said.

"We also have to wonder who put them up to it. I guess they were paid, in some form — either drugs or money, or both. You think they'll talk?"

"I don't think they'll survive the night in jail."

10

They didn't even rate the front page. They were in the local section of the Shreveport paper, below the fold. JAILHOUSE HOMICIDES, the headline read. I sighed.

Two juveniles awaiting transport from the holding cells to the Juvenile Facility were killed last night sometime after midnight.

The newspaper was delivered every morning to the special box at the end of my driveway, right beside my mailbox. But it was getting dark by the time I saw the article, while I was sitting in my car, about to pull out onto Hummingbird Road and go to work. I hadn't ventured out today until now. Sleeping, laundry, and a little gardening had taken up my day. No one had called, and no one had visited, just like the ads said. I'd thought Quinn might phone, just to check up on my little injuries . . . but not.

The two juveniles, brought into the police station on charges of assault and battery, were put in one of the holding cells to wait for the morning bus to arrive from the Juvenile Facility. The holding cell for juvenile offenders is out of sight from that for adult offenders, and the two were the only juveniles incarcerated during the night. At some point, the two were strangled by a person or persons unknown. No other prisoners were harmed, and all denied seeing any suspicious activity. Both the youths had extensive juvenile records. "They had had many encounters with the police," a source close to the investigation said.

"We're going to look into this thoroughly," said Detective Dan Coughlin, who had responded to the original complaint and was heading the investigation of the incident for which the youths were apprehended. "They were arrested after allegedly attacking a couple in a bizarre manner, and their deaths are equally bizarre." His partner, Cal Myers, added, "Justice will be done."

I found that especially ominous.

Tossing the paper on the seat beside me, I pulled my sheaf of mail out of the mailbox and added it to the little pile. I'd sort through it after my shift at Merlotte's.

I was in a thoughtful mood when I got to the bar. Preoccupied with the fate of the two assailants of the night before, I hardly flinched when I found that I would be working with Sam's new employee. Tanya was as bright-eyed and efficient as I'd found her previously. Sam was very happy with her; in fact, the second time he told me how pleased he was, I told him a little sharply that I'd already heard about it.

I was glad to see Bill come in and sit at a table in my section. I wanted an excuse to walk away, before I would have to respond to the question forming in Sam's head: *Why don't you like Tanya?*

I don't expect to like everyone I meet, any more than I expect everyone to like me. But I usually have a basis for disliking an individual, and it's more than an unspecified distrust and vague distaste. Though Tanya was some kind of shape-shifter, I should have been able to read her and learn enough to either confirm or disprove my instinctive suspicion. But I couldn't read Tanya. I'd get a word here and there, like a radio station that's fading out. You'd think I'd be glad to find someone my own age and sex who could perhaps become a friend. Instead, I was disturbed when I realized she was a closed book. Oddly, Sam hadn't said a word about her essential nature. He hadn't said, "Oh, she's a weremole," or "She's a true shifter, like me," or anything like that.

I was in a troubled mood when I strode over to take Bill's order. My bad mood compounded when I saw Selah Pumphrey standing in the doorway scanning the crowd, probably trying to locate Bill. I said a few bad words to myself, turned on my heel, and walked away. Very unprofessional.

Selah was staring at me when I glanced at their table after a while. Arlene had gone over to take their order. I simply listened to Selah; I was in a rude mood. She was wondering why Bill always wanted to meet her here, when the natives were obviously hostile. She couldn't believe that a discerning and sophisticated man like Bill could ever have dated a barmaid. And the way she'd heard it, I hadn't even gone to college, and furthermore, my grandmother had gotten *murdered.*

That made me sleazy, I guess.

I try to take things like this with a grain of

salt. After all, I could have shielded myself pretty effectively from these thoughts. People who eavesdrop seldom hear good about themselves, right? An old adage, and a true one. I told myself (about six times in a row) that I had no business listening to her, that it would be too drastic a reaction to go slap her upside the head or snatch her baldheaded. But the anger swelled in me, and I couldn't seem to get it under control. I put three beers down on the table in front of Catfish, Dago, and Hoyt with unnecessary force. They looked up at me simultaneously in astonishment.

"We do something wrong, Sook?" Catfish said. "Or is it just your time of the month?"

"You didn't do anything," I said. And it wasn't my time of the month — oh. Yes, it was. I'd had the warning with the ache in my back, the heaviness in my stomach, and my swollen fingers. My little friend had come to visit, and I felt the sensation even as I realized what was contributing to my general irritation.

I glanced over at Bill and caught him staring at me, his nostrils flaring. He could smell the blood. A wave of acute embarrassment rolled over me, turning my face red. For a second, I glimpsed naked hunger on his face, and then he wiped his features clean of all expression.

If he wasn't weeping with unrequited love on my doorstep, at least he was suffering a little. A tiny pleased smile was on my lips when I glimpsed myself in the mirror behind the bar.

A second vampire came in an hour later. She looked at Bill for a second, nodded to him, and then sat at a table in Arlene's section. Arlene hustled over to take the vamp's order. They spoke for a minute, but I was too busy to check in on them. Besides, I'd just have heard the vamp filtered through Arlene, since vampires are silent as the grave (ho ho) to me. The next thing I knew, Arlene was wending her way through the crowd to me.

"The dead gal wants to talk to you," she said, not moderating her voice in the least, and heads turned in our direction. Arlene is not long on subtlety — or tact, for that matter.

After I made sure all my customers were happy, I went to the vamp's table. "What can I do for you?" I asked, in the lowest voice I could manage. I knew the vamp could hear me; their hearing is phenomenal, and their vision is not far behind in acuity.

"You're Sookie Stackhouse?" asked the vamp. She was very tall, just under six feet, and she was of some racial blend that had turned out awfully well. Her skin was a golden color, and her hair was thick and coarse and dark. She'd had it cornrowed, and her arms were weighed down with jewelry. Her clothes, in contrast, were simple; she wore a severely tailored white blouse with long sleeves, and black leggings with black sandals.

"Yes," I said. "Can I help you?" She was looking at me with an expression I could only identify as doubtful.

"Pam sent me here," she said. "My name is Felicia." Her voice was as lilting and exotic as her appearance. It made you think about rum drinks and beaches.

"How-de-do, Felicia," I said politely. "I hope Pam is well."

Since vampires don't have variable health, this was a stumper for Felicia. "She seems all right," the vamp said uncertainly. "She has sent me here to identify myself to you."

"Okay, I know you now," I said, just as confused as Felicia had been.

"She said you had a habit of killing the bartenders of Fangtasia," Felicia said, her lovely doe eyes wide with amazement. "She said I must come to beg your mercy. But you just seem like a human, to me."

That Pam. "She was just teasing you," I

said as gently as I could. I didn't think Felicia was the sharpest tool in the shed. Super hearing and super strength do not equal super intelligence. "Pam and I are friends, sort of, and she likes to embarrass me. I guess she likes to do the same thing to you, Felicia. I have no intention of harming anyone." Felicia looked skeptical. "It's true, I have a bad history with the bartenders of Fangtasia, but that's just, ah, coincidence," I babbled on. "And I am really, truly just a human."

After chewing that over for a moment, Felicia looked relieved, which made her even prettier. Pam often had multiple reasons for doing something, and I found myself wondering if she'd sent Felicia here so I could observe her attractions — which of course would be obvious to Eric. Pam might be trying to stir up trouble. She hated a dull life.

"You go back to Shreveport and have a good time with your boss," I said, trying to sound kind.

"Eric?" the lovely vampire said. She seemed startled. "He's good to work for, but I'm not a lover of men."

I glanced over at my tables, not only checking to see if anyone urgently needed a drink, but to see who'd picked up on that line of dialogue. Hoyt's tongue was practically hanging out, and Catfish looked as though he'd been caught in the headlights. Dago was happily shocked. "So, Felicia, how'd you end up in Shreveport, if you don't mind me asking?" I turned my attention back to the new vamp.

"Oh, my friend Indira asked me to come. She said servitude with Eric is not so bad." Felicia shrugged, to show how "not so bad" it was. "He doesn't demand sexual services if the woman is not so inclined, and he asks in return only a few hours in the bar and special chores from time to time."

"So he has a reputation as a good boss?"

"Oh, yes." Felicia looked almost surprised. "He's no softie, of course."

Softie was not a word you could use in the same sentence as *Eric.*

"And you can't cross him. He doesn't forgive that," she continued thoughtfully. "But as long as you fulfill your obligations to him, he'll do the same for you."

I nodded. That more or less fit with my impression of Eric, and I knew Eric very well in some respects . . . though not at all in others.

"This will be much better than Arkansas," Felicia said.

"Why'd you leave Arkansas?" I asked,

because I just couldn't help it. Felicia was the simplest vampire I'd ever met.

"Peter Threadgill," she said. "The king. He just married your queen."

Sophie-Anne Leclerq of Louisiana was by no means *my* queen, but out of curiosity, I wanted to continue the conversation.

"What's so wrong with Peter Threadgill?"

That was a poser for Felicia. She mulled it over. "He holds grudges," she said, frowning. "He's never pleased with what he has. It's not enough that he's the oldest, strongest vampire in the state. Once he became king — and he'd schemed for years to work his way up to it — he still wasn't content. There was something wrong with the state, you see?"

"Like, 'Any state that would have me for a king isn't a good state to be king of'?"

"Exactly," Felicia said, as if I were very clever to think of such a phrase. "He negotiated with Louisiana for months and months, and even Jade Flower got tired of hearing about the queen. Then she finally agreed to the alliance. After a week of celebrating, the king grew sullen again. Suddenly, that wasn't good enough. She had to love him. She had to give up everything for him." Felicia shook her head at the vagaries of royalty.

"So it wasn't a love match?"

"That's the last thing vampire kings and queens marry for," Felicia said. "Now he is having his visit with the queen in New Orleans, and I'm glad I'm at the other end of the state."

I didn't grasp the concept of a married couple visiting, but I was sure that sooner or later I'd understand.

I would have been interested in hearing more, but it was time for me to get back to my section and work. "Thanks for visiting, Felicia, and don't worry about a thing. I'm glad you're working for Eric," I said.

Felicia smiled at me, a dazzling and toothy experience. "I'm glad you don't plan on killing me," she said.

I smiled back at her, a bit hesitantly.

"I assure you, now that I know who you are, you won't get a chance to creep up on me," Felicia continued. Suddenly, the true vampire looked out from Felicia's eyes, and I shivered. It could be fatal to underestimate Felicia. Smart, no. Savage, yes.

"I don't plan on creeping up on anyone, much less a vampire," I said.

She gave me a sharp nod, and then she glided out the door as suddenly as she'd come in.

"What was all that about?" Arlene asked

me, when we happened to be at the bar waiting for orders at the same time. I noticed Sam was listening, as well.

I shrugged. "She's working at Fangtasia, in Shreveport, and she just wanted to make my acquaintance."

Arlene stared at me. "They got to check in with you, now? Sookie, you need to shun the dead and involve yourself more with the living."

I stared right back. "Where'd you get an idea like that?"

"You act like I can't think for myself."

Arlene had never worked out a thought like that in her life. Arlene's middle name was *tolerance,* mostly because she was too easygoing to take a moral stance.

"Well, I'm surprised," I said, sharply aware of how harshly I'd just evaluated someone I'd always looked on as a friend.

"Well, I been going to church with Rafe Prudhomme."

I liked Rafe Prudhomme, a very quiet man in his forties who worked for Pelican State Title Company. But I'd never had the chance to get to know him well, never listened in to his thoughts. Maybe that had been a mistake. "What kind of church does he go to?" I said.

"He's been attending that Fellowship of

the Sun, that new church."

My heart sank, almost literally. I didn't bother to point out that the Fellowship was a collection of bigots who were bound together by hatred and fear. "It's not really a church, you know. There's a branch of the Fellowship close to here?"

"Minden." Arlene looked away, the very picture of guilt. "I knew you wouldn't like that. But I saw the Catholic priest, Father Riordan, there. So even the ordained people think it's okay. We've been the past two Sunday evenings."

"And you believe that stuff?"

But one of Arlene's customers yelled for her, and she was definitely glad to walk away.

My eyes met Sam's, and we looked equally troubled. The Fellowship of the Sun was an antivampire, antitolerance organization, and its influence was spreading. Some of the Fellowship enclaves were not militant, but many of them preached hatred and fear in its most extreme form. If the Fellowship had a secret underground hit list, I was surely on it. The Fellowship founders, Steve and Sarah Newlin, had been driven out of their most lucrative church in Dallas because I'd interfered with their plans. I'd survived a couple of assassination attempts since then,

but there was always the chance the Fellowship would track me down and ambush me.
They'd seen me in Dallas, they'd seen me
in Jackson, and sooner or later they'd figure
out who I was and where I lived.

I had plenty to worry about.

The next morning, Tanya showed up at my house. It was Sunday, and I was off work, and I felt pretty cheerful. After all, Crystal was healing, Quinn seemed to like me, and I hadn't heard any more from Eric, so maybe he would leave me alone. I try to be optimistic. My gran's favorite saying from the Bible was, "Sufficient unto the day is the evil thereof." She had explained that that meant that you don't worry about tomorrow, or about things you can't change. I tried to practice that philosophy, though most days it was hard. Today it was easy.

The birds were tweeting and chirping, the bugs were buzzing, and the pollen-heavy air was full of peace as if it were yet another plant emission. I was sitting on the front porch in my pink robe, sipping my coffee, listening to *Car Talk* on Red River Radio, and feeling really good, when a little Dodge Dart chugged up my driveway. I didn't recognize the car, but I did recognize the driver. All my peacefulness vanished in a puff of suspicion. Now that I knew about the proximity of a new Fellowship conclave, Tanya's inquisitive presence seemed even more suspicious. I was not happy to see her at my home. Common courtesy forbade me from warning her off, with no more provocation than I'd had, but I wasn't giving her any welcoming smile when I lowered my feet to the porch and stood.

"Good morning, Sookie!" she called as she got out of her car.

"Tanya," I said, just to acknowledge the greeting.

She paused halfway to the steps. "Um, everything okay?"

I didn't speak.

"I should have called first, huh?" She tried to look winsome and rueful.

"That would have been better. I don't like unannounced visitors."

"Sorry, I promise I'll call next time." She resumed her progress over the stepping stones to the steps. "Got an extra cup of coffee?"

I violated one of the most basic rules of hospitality. "No, not this morning," I said. I went to stand at the top of the steps to block her way onto the porch.

"Well . . . . Sookie," she said, her voice uncertain. "You really are a grump in the morning."

I looked down at her steadily.

"No wonder Bill Compton's dating someone else," Tanya said with a little laugh. She knew immediately she'd made an error. "Sorry," she added hastily, "maybe I haven't had enough coffee myself. I shouldn't have said that. That Selah Pumphrey's a bitch, huh?"

Too late now, Tanya. I said, "At least you know where you stand with Selah." That was clear enough, right? "I'll see you at work."

"Okay. I'll call next time, you hear?" She gave me a bright, empty smile.

"I hear you." I watched her get back into the little car. She gave me a cheerful wave and, with a lot of extra maneuvering, she turned the Dart around and headed back to Hummingbird Road.

I watched her go, waiting until the sound of the engine had completely died away before I resumed my seat. I left my book on the plastic table beside my lawn chair and sipped the rest of my coffee without the pleasure that had accompanied the first few mouthfuls.

Tanya was up to something.

She practically had a neon sign flashing above her head. I wished the sign would be obliging enough to tell me what she was, who she worked for, and what her goal might be, but I guessed I'd just have to find that out myself. I was going to listen to her head every chance I got, and if that didn't work — and sometimes it doesn't, because not only was she a shifter, but you can't make people think about what you need to them to, on demand — I would have to take more drastic action.

Not that I was sure what that would be.

In the past year, somehow I'd assumed the role of guardian of the weird in my little corner of our state. I was the poster girl for interspecies tolerance. I'd learned a lot about the other universe, the one that surrounded the (mostly oblivious) human race. It was kind of neat, knowing stuff that other people didn't. But it complicated my already difficult life, and it led me into dangerous byways among beings who desperately wanted to keep their existence a secret.

The phone rang inside the house, and I stirred myself from my unhappy thoughts to answer it.

"Hey, babe," said a warm voice on the other end.

"Quinn," I said, trying not to sound too

happy. Not that I was emotionally invested in this man, but I sure needed something positive to happen right now, and Quinn was both formidable and attractive.

"What are you doing?"

"Oh, sitting on my front porch drinking coffee in my bathrobe."

"I wish I was there to have a cup with you."

Hmmm. Idle wish, or serious "ask me over"?

"There's plenty in the pot," I said cautiously.

"I'm in Dallas, or I'd be there in a flash," he said.

Deflation. "When did you leave?" I asked, because that seemed the safest, least prying question.

"Yesterday. I got a call from the mother of a guy who works for me from time to time. He quit in the middle of a job we were working on in New Orleans, weeks ago. I was pretty pissed at him, but I wasn't exactly worried. He was kind of a free-floating guy, had a lot of irons in the fire that took him all over the country. But his mom says he still hasn't shown up anywhere, and she thinks something's happened to him. I'm looking around his house and going through his files to help her out, but I'm reaching a dead end. The track seems to have ended in New Orleans. I'll be driving back to Shreveport tomorrow. Are you working?"

"Yes, early shift. I'll be off around five-ish."

"So can I invite myself over for dinner? I'll bring the steaks. You got a grill?"

"As a matter of fact, I do. It's pretty old, but it works."

"Got coals?"

"I'd have to check." I hadn't cooked out since my grandmother had died.

"No problem. I'll bring some."

"Okay," I said. "I'll fix everything else."

"We have a plan."

"See you at six?"

"Six it is."

"Okay, good-bye then."

Actually, I would have liked to talk to him longer, but I wasn't sure what to say, since I'd never had the experience of much idle chitchat with boys. My dating career had begun last year, when I'd met Bill. I had a lot of catching up to do. I was not like, say, Lindsay Popken, who'd been Miss Bon Temps the year I graduated from high school. Lindsay was able to reduce boys to drooling idiots and keep them trailing after her like stunned hyenas. I'd watched her at it often and still could not understand the phenomenon. It never seemed to me she talked about anything in particular. I'd even listened to her brain, but it was mostly full of white noise. Lindsay's technique, I'd concluded, was instinctive, and it was based on never saying anything serious.

Oh well, enough of reminiscence. I went into the house to see what I needed to do to get it ready for Quinn's visit the next evening and to make a list of necessary purchases. It was a happy way to spend a Sunday afternoon. I'd go shopping. I stepped into the shower contemplating a pleasurable day.

A knock at my front door interrupted me about thirty minutes later as I was putting on some lipstick. This time I looked through the peephole. My heart sank. However, I was obliged to open the door.

A familiar long black limo was parked in my drive. My only previous experience with that limo led me to expect unpleasant news and trouble.

The man — the being — standing on my front porch was the personal representative and lawyer for the vampire queen of Louisiana, and his name was Mr. Cataliades, emphasis on the second syllable. I'd first met Mr. Cataliades when he'd come to let me know that my cousin Hadley had died, leaving her estate to me. Not only had Hadley died, she'd been murdered, and the vampire responsible had been punished right before my eyes. The night had been full of multiple shocks: discovering not only that Hadley had left this world, but she'd left it as a vampire, and she'd been the favorite of the queen, in a biblical sense.

Hadley had been one of the few remaining members of my family, and I felt her loss; at the same time, I had to admit that Hadley, in her teenage years, had been the cause of much grief to her mother and much pain to my grandmother. If she'd lived, maybe she'd have tried to make up for that — or maybe she wouldn't. She hadn't had the chance.

I took a deep breath. I opened the door. "Mr. Cataliades," I said, feeling my anxious smile stretch my lips unconvincingly. The queen's lawyer was a man composed of circles, his face round and his belly rounder, his eyes beady and circular and dark. I didn't think he was human — or perhaps not wholly human — but I wasn't sure what he could be. Not a vampire; here he was, in broad daylight. Not Were, or shifter; no red buzz surrounding his brain.

"Miss Stackhouse," he said, beaming at

me. "What a pleasure to see you again."

"And you also," I said, lying through my teeth. I hesitated, suddenly feeling achy and jumpy. I was sure Cataliades, like all the other supes I encountered, would know I was having my time of the month. Just great. "Won't you come in?"

"Thank you, my dear," he said, and I stepped aside, filled with misgivings, to let this creature enter my home.

"Please, have a seat," I said, determined to be polite. "Would you care for a drink?"

"No, thank you. You seem to be on your way somewhere." He was frowning at the purse I'd tossed on my chair on my way to the door.

Okay, something I wasn't understanding, here. "Yes," I said, raising my eyebrows in query. "I had planned on going to the grocery store, but I can put that off for an hour or so."

"You're not packed to return to New Orleans with me?"

"What?"

"You received my message?"

"What message?"

We stared at each other, mutually dismayed.

"I sent a messenger to you with a letter from my law office," Mr. Cataliades said.

"She should have arrived here four nights ago. The letter was sealed with magic. No one but you could open it."

I shook my head, my blank expression telling him what I needed to say.

"You are saying that Gladiola didn't get here? I expected her to arrive here Wednesday night, at the latest. She wouldn't have come in a car. She likes to run." He smiled indulgently for just a second. But then the smile vanished. If I'd blinked, I would have missed it. "Wednesday night," he prompted me.

"That was the night I heard someone outside the house," I said. I shivered, remembering how tense I'd been that night. "No one came to the door. No one tried to break in. No one called to me. There was only the sense of something moving, and all the animals fell silent."

It was impossible for someone as powerful as the supernatural lawyer to look bewildered, but he did look very thoughtful. After a moment he rose ponderously and bowed to me, gesturing toward the door. We went back outside. On the front porch, he turned to the car and beckoned.

A very lean woman slid from behind the wheel. She was younger than me, maybe in her very early twenties. Like Mr. Cataliades, she was only partly human. Her dark red hair was spiked, her makeup laid on with a trowel. Even the striking outfit of the girl in the Hair of the Dog paled in comparison to this young woman's. She wore striped stockings, alternating bands of shocking pink and black, and her ankle boots were black and extremely high-heeled. Her skirt was transparent, black, and ruffled, and her pink tank top was her sole upper garment.

She just about took my breath away.

"Hi, howareya?" she said brightly, her smile revealing very sharp white teeth a dentist would fall in love with, right before he lost a finger.

"Hello," I said. I held out my hand. "I'm Sookie Stackhouse."

She covered the ground between us very speedily, even in the ridiculous heels. Her hand was tiny and bony. "Pleasedtameetya," she said. "Diantha."

"Pretty name," I said, after I figured out it wasn't another run-on sentence.

"Thankya."

"Diantha," Mr. Cataliades said, "I need you to conduct a search for me." '

"To find?"

"I'm very afraid we are looking for Glad's remains."

The smile fell from the girl's face.

"No shit," she said quite clearly.

"No, Diantha," the lawyer said. "No shit."

Diantha sat on the steps and pulled off her shoes and her striped tights. It didn't seem to bother her at all that without the tights, her transparent skirt left nothing to the imagination. Since Mr. Cataliades's expression didn't change in the least, I decided I could be worldly enough to ignore it, too.

As soon as she'd disencumbered herself, the girl was off, moving low to the ground, sniffing in a way that told me she was even less human than I'd estimated. But she didn't move like the Weres I'd observed, or the shape-shifting panthers. Her body seemed to bend and turn in a way that simply wasn't mammalian.

Mr. Cataliades watched her, his hands folded in front of him. He was silent, so I was, too. The girl darted around the yard like a demented hummingbird, vibrating almost visibly with an unearthly energy.

For all that movement, I couldn't hear her make a sound.

It wasn't long before she stopped at a clump of bushes at the very edge of the woods. She was bent over looking at the ground, absolutely still. Then, not looking up, she raised her hand like a schoolchild who'd discovered the correct answer.

"Let us go see," Mr. Cataliades suggested, and in his deliberate way he strode across the driveway, then the grass, to a clump of wax myrtles at the edge of the woods. Diantha didn't look up as we neared, but remained focused on something on the ground behind the bushes. Her face was streaked with tears. I took a deep breath and looked down at what held her attention.

This girl had been a little younger than Diantha, but she too was thin and slight. Her hair had been dyed bright gold, in sharp contrast with her milk chocolate skin. Her lips had drawn back in death, giving her a snarl that revealed teeth as white and sharp as Diantha's. Oddly enough, she didn't seem as worse for wear as I would have expected, given the fact that she might have been out here for several days. There were only a few ants walking over her, not at all the usual insect activity . . . and she didn't look bad at all for a person who'd been cut in two at the waist.

My head buzzed for a minute, and I was a little scared I would go down on one knee. I'd seen some bad stuff, including two massacres, but I'd never seen anyone divided like this girl had been. I could see her insides. They didn't look like human insides. And it appeared the two halves had been separately seared shut. There was very little leakage.

"Cut with a steel sword," Mr. Cataliades said. "A very good sword."

"What shall we do with her remains?" I asked. "I can get an old blanket." I knew without even asking that we would not be calling the police.

"We have to burn her," Mr. Cataliades said. "Over there, on the gravel of your parking area, Miss Stackhouse, would be safest. You're not expecting any company?"

"No," I said, shocked on many levels. "I'm sorry, why must she be . . . burned?"

"No one will eat a demon, or even a half demon like Glad or Diantha," he said, as if explaining that the sun rises in the east. "Not even the bugs, as you see. The ground will not digest her, as it does humans."

"You don't want to take her home? To her people?"

"Diantha and I are her people. It's not our custom to take the dead back to the place where they were living."

"But what killed her?"

Mr. Cataliades raised an eyebrow.

"No, of course she was killed by something cutting through her middle, I'm seeing that! But what wielded the blade?"

"Diantha, what do you think?" Mr. Cataliades said, as if he were conducting a class.

"Something real, real strong and sneaky," Diantha said. "It got close to Gladiola, and she weren't no fool. We're not easy to kill."

"I have seen no sign of the letter she was carrying, either." Mr. Cataliades leaned over and peered at the ground. Then he straightened. "Have you got firewood, Miss Stackhouse?"

"Yessir, there's a good bit of split oak in the back by the toolshed." Jason had cut up some trees the last ice storm had downed.

"Do you need to pack, my dear?"

"Yes," I said, almost too overwhelmed to answer. "What? What for?"

"The trip to New Orleans. You can go now, can't you?"

"I . . . I guess so. I'll have to ask my boss."

"Then Diantha and I will take care of this while you are getting permission and packing," Mr. Cataliades said, and I blinked.

"All right," I said. I didn't seem to be able to think very clearly.

"Then we need to leave for New Orleans," he said. "I'd thought I'd find you ready. I thought that Glad had stayed to help you."

I wrenched my gaze from the body to stare up at the lawyer. "I'm just not understanding this," I said. But I remembered some-thing. "My friend Bill wanted to go to New Orleans when I went to clean out Hadley's apartment," I said. "If he can, if he can ar-range it, would that be all right with you?"

"You want Bill to go," he said, and there was a tinge of surprise in his voice. "Bill is in favor with the queen, so I wouldn't mind if he went."

"Okay, I'll have to get in touch with him when it's full dark," I said. "I hope he's in town."

I could have called Sam, but I wanted to go somewhere away from the strange funeral on my driveway. When I drove off, Mr. Cat-aliades was carrying the limp small body out of the woods. He had the bottom half.

A silent Diantha was filling a wheelbarrow with wood.

12

"Sam," I said, keeping my voice low, "I need a few days off." When I'd knocked on his trailer door, I'd been surprised to find he had guests, though I'd seen the other vehicles parked by Sam's truck. JB du Rone and Andy Bellefleur were perched on Sam's couch, beer and potato chips set handily on the coffee table. Sam was engaging in a male bonding ritual. "Watching sports?" I added, trying not to sound astonished. I waved over Sam's shoulder to JB and Andy, and they waved back: JB enthusiastically, and Andy less happily. If you can be said to wave ambivalently, that was what he did.

"Uh, yeah, basketball. LSU's playing . . . oh, well. You need the time off right now?"

"Yes," I said. "There's kind of an emergency."

"Can you tell me about it?"

"I have to go to New Orleans to clean out my cousin Hadley's apartment," I said.

"And that has to be right now? You know Tanya is still new, and Charlsie just quit, she says for good. Arlene's not as reliable as she used to be, and Holly and Danielle are still pretty shaky since the school incident."

"I'm sorry," I said. "If you want to let me go and get someone else, I'll understand." It broke my heart to say that, but in fairness to Sam, I had to.

Sam shut the trailer door behind him and stepped out on the porch. He looked hurt. "Sookie," he said, after a second, "you've been completely reliable for at least five years. You've only asked for time off maybe two or three times total. I'm not going to fire you because you need a few days."

"Oh. Well, good." I could feel my face redden. I wasn't used to praise. "Liz's daughter might be able to come help."

"I'll call down the list," he said mildly. "How are you getting to New Orleans?"

"I have a ride."

"Who with?" he asked, his voice gentle. He didn't want me to get mad at his minding my business. (I could tell that much.)

"The queen's lawyer," I said, in an even quieter voice. Though tolerant of vampires in general, the citizens of Bon Temps might get a little excitable if they knew that their state had a vampire queen, and that her secret government affected them in many ways. On the other hand, given the disrepute of Louisiana politics, they might just think it was business as usual.

"You're going to clean out Hadley's apartment?"

I'd told Sam about my cousin's second, and final, death.

"Yes. And I need to find out about whatever she left me."

"This seems real sudden." Sam looked troubled. He ran a hand over his curly red-gold hair until it stood out from his head in a wild halo. He needed a haircut.

"Yes, to me, too. Mr. Cataliades tried to tell me earlier, but the messenger was killed."

I heard Andy yelling at the television as some big play roused his excitement. Strange, I'd never thought of Andy as a sports guy, or JB either, for that matter. I'd never added up all the time I'd heard men thinking about assists and three-pointers when the women with them were talking about the need for new kitchen drapes or Rudy's bad grade in algebra. When I did add it up, I wondered if the purpose of sports wasn't to give guys a safe alternative to thornier issues.

"You shouldn't go," Sam said instantly.

"It sounds like it could be dangerous."

I shrugged. "I have to," I said. "Hadley left it to me; I have to do it." I was far from as calm as I was trying to look, but it didn't seem to me like it would do any good to kick and scream about it.

Sam began to speak, then reconsidered. Finally, he said, "Is this about money, Sook? Do you need the money she left you?"

"Sam, I don't know if Hadley had a penny to her name. She was my cousin, and I have to do this for her. Besides . . ." I was on the verge of telling him the trip to New Orleans had to be important in some way, since someone was trying so hard to keep me from going.

But Sam tended to be a worrier, especially if I was involved, and I didn't want to get him all worked up when nothing he could say would dissuade me from going. I don't think of myself as a stubborn person, but I figured this was the last service I could perform for my cousin.

"What about taking Jason?" Sam suggested, taking my hand. "He was Hadley's cousin, too."

"Evidently, he and Hadley were on the outs toward the end," I said. "That's why she left her stuff to me. Besides, Jason's got a lot on his plate right now."

"What, something besides bossing Hoyt around and screwing every woman who'll stand still long enough?"

I stared at Sam. I'd known he was not a big fan of my brother's, but I hadn't known his dislike went this deep.

"Yes, actually," I said, my voice as cold and frosty as a beer mug. I wasn't about to explain my brother's girlfriend's miscarriage while I was standing on a doorstep, especially given Sam's antagonism.

Sam looked away, shaking his head in disgust with himself. "I'm sorry, Sookie, I'm really sorry. I just think Jason should pay more attention to the only sister he's got. You're so loyal to him."

"Well, he wouldn't let anything happen to me," I said, bewildered. "Jason would stand up for me."

Before Sam said, "Of course," I caught the flicker of doubt in his mind.

"I have to go pack," I said. I hated to walk away. No matter his feelings about Jason, Sam was important to me, and leaving him with this unhappiness between us shook me a bit. But I could hear the men roaring at some play inside the trailer, and I knew I had to let him get back to his guests and his Sunday afternoon pleasure. He gave me a kiss on the cheek.

"Call me if you need me," he said, and he looked as if he wanted to say a lot more. I nodded, turned away, and went down the steps to my car.

"Bill, you said you wanted to go to New Orleans with me when I went to close out Hadley's estate?" Finally it was full dark, and I was able to call Bill. Selah Pumphrey had answered the phone and called Bill to talk to me in a very chilly voice.

"Yes."

"Mr. Cataliades is here, and he wants to leave real shortly."

"You could have told me earlier, when you knew he was coming." But Bill didn't sound truly angry, or even surprised.

"He sent a messenger, but she was killed in my woods."

"You found the body?"

"No, a girl who came with him did. Her name's Diantha."

"Then it was Gladiola who died."

"Yes," I said, surprised. "How did you know?"

Bill said, "When you come into a state, it's only polite to check in with the queen or king if you're staying for any length of time. I saw the girls from time to time, since they function as the queen's messengers."

I looked at the telephone in my hands with as much thoughtfulness as if it'd been Bill's face. I couldn't help but think all these thoughts in quick succession. Bill wandered in my woods . . . Gladiola had been killed in my woods. She'd been killed without noise, efficiently and accurately, by someone well versed in the lore of the supernatural, someone who'd known to use a steel sword, someone who'd been strong enough to sweep a sword through Gladiola's entire body.

These were characteristics of a vampire — but any number of supernatural creatures could do the same.

To get close enough to wield the sword, the killer had been super quick or quite innocuous-looking. Gladiola hadn't suspected she was going to be killed.

Maybe she had known the murderer.

And the way Gladiola's little body had been left, tossed in the bushes carelessly . . . the killer hadn't cared if I found her body or not, though of course the demonic lack of putrefaction had played a role there. Her *silence* was all the killer had wanted. Why had she been killed? Her message, if I was getting the whole story from the heavy lawyer, had simply been for me to prepare for my trip to New Orleans. I was going, anyway, though she hadn't had a chance to deliver it. So what had been gained by silencing her? Two or three more days of ignorance on my part? It didn't seem to me that was much motivation.

Bill was waiting for me to end the long pause in our conversation, one of the things I'd always liked about him. He didn't feel the need to fill conversational pauses.

"They burned her in the driveway," I said.

"Of course. It's the only way to dispose of anything with demon blood," Bill said, but absently, as if he'd been thinking deep thoughts about something else.

" 'Of course'? How was I supposed to know that?"

"At least you know now. Bugs won't bite them, their bodies won't corrupt, and sex with them is corrosive."

"Diantha seems so perky and obedient."

"Of course, when she's with her uncle."

"Mr. Cataliades is her uncle," I said. "Glad's uncle, too?"

"Oh, yes. Cataliades is mostly demon, but his half brother Nergal is a full demon. Nergal's had several half-human children. All by different mothers, obviously."

I wasn't sure why this was so obvious, and I wasn't about to ask him.

"You're letting Selah listen to all this?"

"No, she's in the bathroom showering."

Okay, still feeling jealous. And envious: Selah had the luxury of ignorance, while I did not. What a nicer world it was when you didn't know about the supernatural side of life.

Sure. Then you just had to worry about famine, war, serial killers, AIDS, tsunamis, old age, and the Ebola virus.

"*Can* it, Sookie," I said to myself, and Bill said, "Pardon me?"

I shook myself. "Listen, Bill, if you want to go to New Orleans with me and the lawyer, be over here in the next thirty minutes. Otherwise, I'll assume you have other fish to fry." I hung up. I would have a whole drive to the Big Easy to think about all this.

"He'll be here, or not, in the next thirty minutes," I called out the front door to the lawyer.

"Good to hear," Mr. Cataliades called back. He was standing by Diantha while she was hosing the black smudge off my gravel.

I trotted back to my room and packed my toothbrush. I ran down my mental checklist. I'd left a message on Jason's answering machine, I'd asked Tara if she'd mind running out to get my mail and my papers every day, I'd watered my few houseplants (my grandmother believed that plants, like birds and dogs, belonged outside; ironically enough, I'd gotten some houseplants when she died, and I was trying hard to keep them alive).

Quinn!

He wasn't with his cell phone, or wasn't answering it, at any rate. I left a voice mail message. Only our second date, and I had to cancel it.

I found it hard to figure out exactly how much to tell him. "I have to go to New Orleans to clean out my cousin's apartment," I said. "She lived in a place on Chloe Street, and I don't know if there's a phone or not. So I guess I'll just call you when I get back? I'm sorry our plans changed." I hoped he would at least be able to tell I was genuinely regretful that I wouldn't be able to eat dinner with him.

Bill arrived just as I was carrying my bag out to the car. He had a backpack, which struck me as funny. I suppressed my smile when I saw his face. Even for a vampire, Bill looked pale and drawn. He ignored me.

"Cataliades," he said, with a nod. "I'll hitch a ride with you, if that suits you. Sorry about your loss." He nodded to Diantha, who was alternating long, furious monologues in a language I didn't understand with the sort of frozen-faced stare I associated with deep shock.

"My niece died an untimely death," Cataliades said, in his deliberate way. "She will not go unavenged."

"Of course not," Bill said, in his cool voice. While Diantha reached in to pop the trunk, Bill moved to the back of the car to toss his backpack into its depths. I locked my front door behind me and hurried down the steps to put my bag in with his. I caught a glimpse of his face before he registered my approach, and that glimpse shook me.

Bill looked desperate.

13

There were moments on the drive south when I felt like sharing all my thoughts with my companions. Mr. Cataliades drove for a couple of hours, and then Diantha took the wheel. Bill and the lawyer didn't have a lot of small talk, and I had too many things on my mind for social chitchat, so we were a silent bunch.

I was as comfortable as I'd ever been in a vehicle. I had the rear-facing seat all to myself, while Bill and the lawyer sat opposite me. The limo was the last word in automotive luxury, at least in my eyes. Upholstered in leather and padded to the nth degree, the limo boasted lots of leg room, bottles of water and synthetic blood, and a little basket of snacks. Mr. Cataliades was real fond of Cheetos.

I closed my eyes and thought for a while. Bill's brain, naturally, was a null to me, and Mr. Cataliades's brain was very nearly so.

His brain emitted a low-level buzz that was almost soothing, while the same emanation, from Diantha's brain, vibrated at a higher pitch. I'd been on the edge of a thought when I'd been talking with Sam, and I wanted to pursue it while I could still catch hold of its tail. Once I'd worked it through, I decided to share it.

"Mr. Cataliades," I said, and the big man opened his eyes. Bill was already looking at me. Something was going on in Bill's head, something weird. "You know that Wednesday, the night your girl was supposed to appear on my doorstep, I heard something in the woods."

The lawyer nodded. Bill nodded.

"So we assume that was the night she was killed."

Again with the double nods.

"But why? Whoever did it had to know that sooner or later you would contact me, or come to see me, to find out what had happened. Even if the killer didn't know the message Gladiola was bringing, they'd figure that she'd be missed sooner rather than later."

"That's reasonable," Mr. Cataliades said.

"But on Friday night, I was attacked in a parking lot in Shreveport."

I got my money's worth out of that statement, I can tell you. If I'd hooked both the men up to electroshock machines and given them a jolt, the reaction couldn't have been more dynamic.

"Why didn't you tell me?" Bill demanded. His eyes were glowing with anger, and his fangs were out.

"Why should I? We don't date any more. We don't see each other regularly."

"So this is your punishment for my dating someone else, keeping something so serious from me?"

Even in my wildest fantasies (which had included such scenes as Bill breaking up with Selah in Merlotte's, and his subsequent public confession to me that Selah had never measured up to my charms), I'd never envisioned such a reaction. Though it was very dark in the car's interior, I thought I saw Mr. Cataliades roll his eyes. Maybe he thought that was over the top, too.

"Bill, I never set out to punish you," I said. At least I didn't think I had. "We just don't share details of our lives any more. Actually, I was out on a date when the attack occurred. I believe I'm used to us not being part of the scenery."

"Who was your date?"

"Not that it's actually your business, but it is pertinent to the rest of the story. I'm dating Quinn." We'd had one date and planned another. That counted as "dating," right?

"Quinn the tiger," Bill said expressionlessly.

"Hats off to you, young lady!" Mr. Cataliades said. "You are courageous and discerning."

"I'm not really asking for approval," I said as neutrally as I could manage. "Or disapproval, for that matter." I waved my hand to show that topic was off the table. "Here's what I want you to know. The attackers were very young Weres."

"Weres," Mr. Cataliades said. As we sped through the darkness, I couldn't decipher his expression or his voice. "What kind of Weres?"

Good question. The lawyer was on the ball. "Bitten Weres," I said. "And I believe they were on drugs, as well." That gave them pause.

"What happened during the attack and afterward?" Bill said, breaking a long silence.

I described the attack and its aftermath.

"So Quinn took you to the Hair of the Dog," Bill said. "He thought that was an appropriate response?"

I could tell Bill was furious, but as usual, I didn't know why.

"It may have worked," Cataliades said. "Consider. Nothing else has happened to her, so apparently Quinn's threat took root."

I tried not to say "Huh?" but I guess Bill's vampire eyes could see it on my face.

"He challenged them," Bill said, sounding even colder than usual. "He told them you were under his protection, and that they harmed you at their peril. He accused them of being behind the attack, but at the same time reminded them that even if they didn't know of it, they were responsible for bringing the one who planned it to justice."

"I got all that on the spot," I said patiently. "And I think Quinn was warning them, not challenging them. Big difference. What I didn't get was . . . nothing should happen in the pack without Patrick Furnan's knowledge, right? Since he's the grand high poobah now. So why not go straight to Patrick? Why go to the local watering hole?"

"What a very interesting question," Cataliades said. "What would your answer be, Compton?"

"The one that springs to mind . . . Quinn might know there's a rebellion fomenting against Furnan already. He's added fuel to it by letting the rebels know that Furnan is trying to kill a friend of the pack."

We're not talking armies here. There

might be thirty-five members of the pack, maybe a little more with servicemen from Barksdale Air Force Base added in. It would take only five people to make a rebellion.

"Why don't they just take him out?" I asked. I'm not politically minded, as I guess you can tell.

Mr. Cataliades was smiling at me. It was dark in the car, but I just knew it. "So direct, so classic," he said. "So American. Well, Miss Stackhouse, it's like this. The Weres can be savage, oh yes! But they do have rules. The penalty for killing the pack-leader, except by open challenge, is death."

"But who would, ah, enact that penalty, if the pack kept the killing secret?"

"Unless the pack is willing to kill the whole Furnan family, I think the Furnan family would be delighted to inform the Were hierarchy of Patrick's murder. Now maybe you know the Shreveport Weres better than most. Are there ruthless killers among them who wouldn't mind slaughtering Furnan's wife and children?"

I thought about Amanda, Alcide, and Maria-Star. "That's a whole different kettle of fish. I see that."

"Now vampires, you'd find many more who were up for that kind of treachery," the lawyer said. "Don't you think so, Mr. Compton?"

There was a curious silence. "Vampires have to pay a price if they kill another vampire," Bill said stiffly.

"If they're affiliated with a clan," Mr. Cataliades said mildly.

"I didn't know vampires had clans," I said. Learning something new all the time, that was me.

"It's a fairly new concept. It's an attempt to regularize the vampire world so it looks more palatable to humans. If the American model catches on, the vampire world will resemble a huge multinational corporation more than a loosely ruled collection of vicious bloodsuckers."

"Lose some of the color and tradition, gain some of the profits," I murmured. "Like Wal-Mart versus Dad's Downtown Hardware." Mr. Cataliades laughed.

"You're right, Miss Stackhouse. Exactly. There are those in both camps, and the summit we'll attend in a few weeks will have this item high on the agenda."

"To get from what's going to take place weeks from now and get back to something a little more on topic, why would Patrick Furnan try to kill me? He doesn't like me, and he knows I'd stand with Alcide if I had to make a choice between 'em, but so what? I'm not important. Why would he plan all this — find the two boys who would do it, bite them, send them out to get me and Quinn — if there wasn't some big payoff?"

"You have a knack for asking good questions, Miss Stackhouse. I wish my answers were as good."

Well, I might as well keep my thoughts to myself if I wasn't going to get any information out of my companions.

The only reason to kill Gladiola, at least the only reason that this direct human could see, was to delay my getting the message that I needed to be ready to leave for New Orleans. Also, Gladiola would have provided some buffer between me and anything that came after me, or at the least she would have been more alert to the attack.

As it was, she'd been lying dead in the woods when I'd gone on my date with Quinn. Whoa. How had the young wolves known where to find me? Shreveport isn't that big, but you couldn't guard every road into town on the off chance I'd show up. On the other hand, if a Were had spotted Quinn and me going into the theater, they'd have known I'd be there for a couple of hours, and that was time enough to arrange something.

If this mastermind had known even earlier, it would have been even easier . . . if someone, say, had known beforehand that Quinn had asked me to go the theater. Who'd known I had a date with Quinn? Well, Tara: I'd told her when I bought my outfit. And I'd mentioned it to Jason, I thought, when I'd called him to inquire after Crystal. I'd told Pam I had a date, but I didn't remember telling her where I was going.

And then there was Quinn himself.

I was so grieved by this idea that I had to suppress tears. It was not like I knew Quinn that well or could judge his character based on the time I'd spent with him. . . . I'd learned over the past few months that you couldn't really know someone that quickly, that learning a person's true character might take years. It had shaken me profoundly, since I'm used to knowing people very well, very quickly. I know them better than they ever suspect. But making mistakes about the character of a few supernaturals had caught me flatfooted, emotionally. Used to the quick assessment my telepathy made possible, I'd been naïve and careless.

Now I was surrounded by such creatures.

I snuggled into a corner of the broad seat and shut my eyes. I had to be in my own world for a while, with no one else allowed inside. I fell asleep in the dark car, with a semidemon and a vampire sitting across from me and a half demon in the driver's seat.

When I woke up, I had my head in Bill's lap. His hand was gently stroking my hair, and the familiar touch of his fingers brought me peace and a stirring of that sensual feeling that Bill had always been able to rouse in me.

It took a second for me to remember where we were and what we were doing, and then I sat up, blinking and tousled. Mr. Cataliades was quite still on the opposite seat, and I thought he was asleep, but it was impossible to be sure. If he'd been human, I would've known.

"Where are we?" I asked.

"Almost there," Bill said. "Sookie . . ."

"Hmm?" I stretched and yawned and longed for a toothbrush.

"I'll help you go through Hadley's apartment if you want me to."

I had a feeling he'd changed his mind about what he was going to say, at the last minute.

"If I need help, I know where to go," I answered. That should be ambiguous enough. I was beginning to get a mighty bad feeling about Hadley's apartment. Maybe Hadley's legacy to me was more in the nature of a curse than a blessing. And yet she'd pointedly excluded Jason, because he had failed her when she'd needed help, so Hadley presumably had meant her bequest to be a boon. On the other hand, Hadley had been a vampire, no longer human, and that would have changed her. Oh, yeah.

Looking out the window, I could see streetlights and a few other cars moving through the gloom. It was raining, and it was four in the morning. I wondered if there was an IHOP anywhere nearby. I'd been to one, once. It had been wonderful. That had been on my only previous trip to New Orleans, when I'd been in high school. We'd been to the aquarium and the slave museum and the church on Jackson Square, the St. Louis Cathedral. It had been wonderful to see something new, to think about all the people who had passed through the same area, what they must have looked like in the clothes of their time. On the other hand, a telepath with poor shielding is not going to have a great time with a bunch of teenagers.

Now my companions were much less easy to read, and quite a bit more dangerous.

We were on a quiet residential street when the limousine pulled to a curb and stopped.

"Your cousin's apartment," Mr. Cataliades said as Diantha opened the door. I was
out and on the sidewalk while Mr. Cataliades maneuvered himself into the right position to exit, and Bill was stuck behind him.

I was facing a six-foot wall with an opening for the driveway. It was hard to tell, in
the uncertain glow of a streetlight, what lay
within, but it seemed to be a small courtyard
with a very tight circular drive. In the
middle of the drive was an explosion of
greenery, though I couldn't discern the
individual plants. In the right front corner
was a tool shed. There was a two-story
building forming an L. To take advantage of
the depth of the lot, the building was
oriented with the L inverted. Right next
door was a similar building, at least as far
as I could tell. Hadley's was painted white,
with dark green shutters.

"How many apartments are here, and
which one is Hadley's?" I asked Mr. Cataliades, who was steaming along behind me.

"There's the bottom floor, where the
owner lives, and the top floor, which is
yours now for as long as you want it. The
queen has been paying the rent until the
estate was probated. She didn't think it fair
that Hadley's estate should do so." Even for
Mr. Cataliades, this was a formal speech.

My reaction was muted by my exhaustion, and I could only say, "I can't think why she didn't just put Hadley's stuff into storage. I could have gone through it all at one of the rental places."

"You'll get used to way the queen does things," he said.

Not if I had anything to say about it. "For right now, can you just show me how to get into Hadley's apartment, so I can unpack and get some sleep?"

"Of course, of course. And dawn is coming, so Mr. Compton needs to go to the queen's headquarters to gain shelter for the day." Diantha had already started up the stairs, which I could just make out. They curved up the short part of the L, which lay to the back of the lot. "Here is your key, Miss Stackhouse. As soon as Diantha comes down, we'll leave you to it. You can meet the owner tomorrow."

"Sure," I said, and trudged up the stairs, holding to the wrought-iron handrail. This wasn't what I had envisioned at all. I thought Hadley would have a place like one of the apartments at the Kingfisher Arms, the only apartment building in Bon Temps. This was like a little bitty mansion.

Diantha had put my sports bag and my big carryall by one of two doors on the second floor. There was a broad roofed gallery running below the windows and doors of the second floor, which would provide shade for people sitting inside on the ground floor. Magic trembled around all those French windows and the doors. I recognized the smell and feel of it, now. The apartment had been sealed with more than locks.

I hesitated, the key in my hand.

"It will recognize you," called the lawyer from the courtyard. So I unlocked the door with clumsy hands, and pushed the door open. Warm air rushed out to meet me. This apartment had been closed for weeks. I wondered if anyone had come in to air it out. It didn't smell actively bad, just stale, so I knew the climate control system had been left on. I fumbled around for the switch of the nearest light, a lamp on a marble-topped pedestal to the right of the door. It cast a pool of golden light on the gleaming hardwood floors and some faux antique furniture (at least I was assuming it was faux). I took another step inside the apartment, trying to imagine Hadley here, Hadley who'd worn black lipstick to have her senior picture made and bought her shoes at Payless.

"Sookie," Bill said behind me, by way of letting me know that he was standing right outside the doorway. I didn't tell him he could come in.

"I have to get to bed now, Bill. I'll see you tomorrow. Do I have the queen's phone number?"

"Cataliades stuck a card in your purse while you were sleeping."

"Oh, good. Well, night."

And I shut the door in his face. I was rude, but he was hovering, and I just wasn't up for talking to him. It had shaken me, finding my head in his lap when I woke; it was like we were still a couple.

After a minute I heard his footsteps going back down the stairs. I was never more relieved to be alone in my life. Thanks to the night spent in a car and the brief sleep I'd had, I felt disoriented, rumpled, and desperately in need of a toothbrush. Time to scope out the place, with emphasis on bathroom discovery.

I looked around carefully. The shorter segment of the upside-down L was the living room, where I now stood. Its open plan included a kitchen against the far right wall. On my left, forming the long side of the L, was a hall lined with French windows that opened directly onto the gallery. The wall that formed the other side of the hall was punctuated with doors.

Bags in hand, I started down the hall, peering into each open door. I didn't find the light switch that would illumine the hall, though there must be one, since there were fixtures at regular intervals on the ceiling.

But enough moonlight streamed through the windows of the rooms to enable me to see as much as I needed. The first room was a bathroom, thank God, though after a second I realized it wasn't Hadley's. It was very small and very clean, with a narrow shower stall, a toilet and sink; no toiletries, no personal clutter. I passed it by and glanced in the next doorway, discovering that it opened into a small room that had probably been intended as the guest bedroom. Hadley had set up a computer desk loaded with computer gear, not items of great interest to me.

In addition to a narrow daybed, there was a bookshelf crammed full with boxes and books, and I promised myself I'd go through that tomorrow. The next door was shut, but I cracked it open to peer inside for a second. It was the door to a narrow, deep, walk-in closet lined with shelves full of items that I didn't take the time to identify.

To my relief, the next door was that of the main bathroom, the one with the shower and the tub and a large sink with a dressing table built in. The surface of the surround was littered with cosmetics and an electric curler, still plugged in. Five or six bottles of perfume were lined up on a shelf, and there were crumpled towels in the hamper, spotted with dark blotches. I put my face right down to them; at that range, they emitted an alarming reek. I couldn't understand why the smell hadn't pervaded the entire apartment. I picked up the whole hamper, unlocked the French window on the other side of the hall, and set it outside. I left the light on in the bathroom, because I intended to revisit it shortly.

The last door, set at right angles to all the others and forming the end of the hall, led into Hadley's bedroom. It was big enough, though not as big as my bedroom at home. It held another large closet, crammed full with clothes. The bed was made, not a Hadley trademark, and I wondered who'd been in the apartment since Hadley had been killed. Someone had entered before the place had been sealed by magic. The bedroom, of course, was completely darkened. The windows had been covered by beautifully painted wood panels, and there were two doors to the room. There was just enough space between them for a person to stand.

I set my bags on the floor by Hadley's chest of drawers, and I rooted around until I found my cosmetics bag and my tampons. Trudging back into the bathroom, I extricated my toothbrush and toothpaste from the small bag and had the delight of brushing my teeth and washing my face. I felt a little more human after that, but not much. I switched out the bathroom light and pulled back the covers on the bed, which was low and broad. The sheets startled me so much that I stood there with my lips curled. They were disgusting: black satin, for God's sake! And not even real satin, but some synthetic. Give me percale or 100% cotton, any day. However, I wasn't going to hunt down another set of sheets at this hour of the morning. Besides, what if this was all she had?

I climbed into the king-size bed — well, I slithered into the king-size bed — and after an uneasy wiggle or two to get used to the feel of them, I managed to fall asleep between those sheets just fine.

14

Someone was pinching my toe and saying "Wake up! Wake up!" I roared back to consciousness in a terrified rush, my eyes opening on the unfamiliar room streaming with sunshine. A woman I didn't know was standing at the foot of the bed.

"Who the hell are you?" I was irritated, but not scared. She didn't look dangerous. She was about my age, and she was very tan. Her chestnut hair was short, her eyes a bright blue, and she was wearing khaki shorts and a white shirt that hung open over a coral tank top. She was rushing the season a little.

"I'm Amelia Broadway. I own the building."

"Why are you in here waking me up?"

"I heard Cataliades in the courtyard last night, and I figured he'd brought you back to clean out Hadley's apartment. I wanted to talk to you."

241

"And you couldn't wait until I woke up? And you used a key to get in, instead of ringing the doorbell? What's wrong with you?"

She was definitely startled. For the first time, Amelia Broadway looked as if she realized she could have handled the situation better. "Well, see, I've been worried," she said in a subdued way.

"Yeah? Me, too," I said. "Join the club. I'm plenty worried right now. Now get out of here and wait for me in the living room, okay?"

"Sure," she said. "I can do that."

I let my heart rate get back to normal before I slid out of bed. Then I made the bed quickly and pulled some clothes out of my bag. I shuffled into the bathroom, catching a quick glimpse of my uninvited guest as I went from bedroom to bath. She was dusting the living room with a cloth that looked suspiciously like a man's flannel shirt. O-kay.

I showered as quickly as I could, slapped on a little makeup, and came out barefoot but clad in jeans and a blue T-shirt.

Amelia Broadway stopped her housecleaning and stared at me. "You don't look a thing like Hadley," she said, and I couldn't decide by her tone if she thought that was a good thing or a bad thing.

"I'm not at all like Hadley, all the way through," I said flatly.

"Well, that's good. Hadley was pretty awful," Amelia said unexpectedly. "Whoops. Sorry, I'm not tactful."

"Really?" I tried to keep my voice level, but a trace of sarcasm may have leaked through. "So if you know where the coffee is, can you point me in that direction?" I was looking at the kitchen area for the first time in the daylight. It had exposed brick and copper, a stainless steel food preparation area and a matching refrigerator, and a sink with a faucet that cost more than my clothes. Small, but fancy, like the rest of the place.

All this, for a vampire who didn't really need a kitchen in the first place.

"Hadley's coffeepot is right there," Amelia said, and I spotted it. It was black and it kind of blended in. Hadley had always been a coffee freak, so I'd figured that even as a vampire she'd kept a supply of her favorite beverage. I opened the cabinet above the pot, and behold — two cans of Community Coffee and some filters. The silvery seal was intact on the first one I opened, but the second can was open and half full. I inhaled the wonderful coffee smell with quiet pleasure. It seemed amazingly fresh.

After I fixed the pot and punched a button to set it perking, I found two mugs and set them beside it. The sugar bowl was right by the pot, but when I opened it, I found only a hardened residue. I pitched the contents into the trash can, which was lined but empty. It had been cleaned out after Hadley's death. Maybe Hadley had had some powdered creamer in the refrigerator? In the South, people who don't use it constantly often keep it there.

But when I opened the gleaming stainless steel refrigerator, I found nothing but five bottles of TrueBlood.

Nothing had brought home to me so strongly the fact that my cousin Hadley had died a vamp. I'd never known anyone before and after. It was a shock. I had so many memories of Hadley, some of them happy and some of them unpleasant — but in all of those memories, my cousin was breathing and her heart was beating. I stood with my lips compressed, staring at the red bottles, until I'd recovered enough to shut the door very gently.

After a vain search in the cabinets for Cremora, I told Amelia I hoped she took her coffee black.

"Yes, that'll be fine," Amelia said primly.

She was obviously trying to be on her better behavior, and I could only be grateful for that. Hadley's landlady was perched on one of Hadley's spindle-legged armchairs. The upholstery was really pretty, a yellow silky material printed with dark red and blue flowers, but I disliked the fragile style of the furniture. I like chairs that look as though they could hold big people, heavy people, without a creak or a groan. I like furniture that looks as though it won't be ruined if you spill a Coke on it, or if your dog hops up on it to take a nap. I tried to settle myself on the loveseat opposite the landlady's. Pretty, yes. Comfortable, no. Suspicion confirmed.

"So what are you, Amelia?"

"Beg pardon?"

"What are you?"

"Oh, a witch."

"Figured." I hadn't caught the sense of the supernatural that I get from creatures whose very cells have been changed by the nature of their being. Amelia had acquired her "otherness." "Did you do the spells to seal off the apartment?"

"Yes," she said rather proudly. She gave me a look of sheer evaluation. I had known the apartment was warded with spells; I had known she was a member of the other world, the hidden world. I might be a regular human, but I was in the know. I read all these thoughts as easily as if Amelia had spoken them to me. She was an exceptional broadcaster, as clear and clean as her complexion. "The night Hadley died, the queen's lawyer phoned me. Of course, I was asleep. He told me to shut this sucker up, that Hadley wouldn't be coming back, but the queen wanted her place kept intact for her heir. I came up and began cleaning early the next morning." She'd worn rubber gloves, too; I could see that in her mental picture of herself the morning after Hadley had died.

"You emptied the trash and made the bed?"

She looked embarrassed. "Yes, I did. I didn't realize 'intact' meant 'untouched.' Cataliades got here and let me have it. But I'm glad I got the trash out of here, anyway. It's strange, because someone went through the garbage bin that night, before I could put it out for pickup."

"I don't guess you know if they took anything?"

She cast me an incredulous look. "It's not like I inventory the trash," she said. She added, reluctantly, "It had been treated with a spell, but I don't know what the spell was for."

Okay, that wasn't good news. Amelia wasn't even admitting it to herself; she didn't want to think about the house being the target for supernatural assault. Amelia was proud because her wards had held, but she hadn't thought to ward the garbage bin.

"Oh, I got all her potted plants out and moved them down to my place for easier care, too. So if you want to take 'em back to Hole-in-the-Road with you, you're welcome."

"Bon Temps," I corrected. Amelia snorted. She had the born city dweller's contempt for small towns. "So you own this building, and you rented the upstairs to Hadley when?"

"About a year ago. She was a vamp already," Amelia said. "And she was the queen's girlfriend, had been for quite a while. So I figured it was good insurance, you know? No one's going to attack the queen's honeybun, right? And no one's going to break into her place, either."

I wanted to ask how come Amelia could afford such a nice place herself, but that was just too rude to get past my lips. "So the witch business supports you?" I asked instead, trying to sound only mildly interested.

She shrugged, but looked pleased I'd asked. Though her mother had left her a lot of money, Amelia was delighted to be self-supporting. I heard it as clearly as if she'd spoken it out loud. "Yeah, I make a living," she said, aiming for a modest tone and just missing. She'd worked hard to become a witch. She was proud of her power.

This was just like reading a book.

"If things get slow, I help out a friend who has a magic shop right off Jackson Square. I read fortunes there," she admitted. "And sometimes I do a magic tour of New Orleans for the tourists. That can be fun, and if I scare 'em enough, I get big tips. So between one thing and another, I do okay."

"You perform serious magic," I said, and she nodded happily. "For who?" I asked. "Since the regular world doesn't admit it's possible."

"The supes pay real well," she said, surprised I had to ask. I didn't really need to, but it was easier to direct her thoughts to the right information if I asked her out loud. "Vamps and Weres, especially. I mean, they don't like witches, but vamps especially want every little advantage they can gain. The rest aren't as organized." With a wave of her hand she dismissed the weaker ones of the supernatural world, the werebats and the shape-shifters and so on. She discounted the power of the other supes, which was a mistake.

"What about fairies?" I asked curiously.

"They have enough of their own magic," she said, shrugging. "They don't need me. I know someone like you might have a hard time accepting that there's a talent that's invisible and natural, one that challenges everything you were taught by your family."

I stifled a snort of disbelief. She sure didn't know anything about me. I didn't know what she and Hadley had talked about, but it hadn't been Hadley's family, for sure. When that idea crossed my mind, a bell rang in the back of my head, one that said that avenue of thought should be explored. But I put it aside to think of later. Right now, I needed to deal with Amelia Broadway.

"So you would say you have a strong supernatural ability?" I said.

I could feel her stifle the rush of pride. "I have some ability," she said modestly. "For example, I laid a stasis spell on this apartment when I couldn't finish cleaning it. And though it's been shut up for months, you don't smell anything, do you?"

That explained the lack of odor wafting from the stained towels. "And you do witchcraft for supernaturals, you read fortunes off Jackson Square, and you lead tour groups sometimes. Not exactly regular office jobs," I said.

"Right." She nodded, happy and proud.

"So you make up your own schedule," I said. I could hear the relief bouncing through Amelia's mind, relief that she didn't have to go into an office any more, though she'd done a stint at the post office for three years until she'd become a full-fledged witch.

"Yes."

"So will you help me clean out Hadley's apartment? I'll be glad to pay you."

"Well, sure I'll help. The sooner all her stuff is out, the sooner I can rent the place. As for your paying me, why don't we wait to see how much time I can give it? Sometimes I get, like, emergency calls." Amelia smiled at me, a smile suitable for a toothpaste ad.

"Hasn't the queen been paying the rent since Hadley passed?"

"Yeah, she has. But it's given me the creeps, thinking of Hadley's stuff up here. And there've been a couple of break-in attempts. The last one was only a couple of days ago." I gave up any pretense of smiling.

"I thought at first," Amelia burbled on, "that it might be like when someone dies and their death notice is in the paper, you get break-ins during the funeral. Course, they don't print obituaries for vampires, I guess because they're already dead or because the other vampires just don't send one to the paper . . . that would be interesting, to see how they handled it. Why don't you try sending in a few lines about Hadley? But you know how vamps gossip, so I guess a few people heard she was definitely dead, dead for the second time. Especially after Waldo vanished from the court. Everyone knows he didn't care for Hadley. And then, too, vamps don't have funerals. So I guess the break-in wasn't related. New Orleans does have a pretty high crime rate."

"Oh, you knew Waldo," I said, to interrupt the flow. Waldo, once the queen's favorite — not in bed, but as a lackey, I thought — had resented being supplanted by my cousin Hadley. When Hadley remained in favor with the queen for an unprecedented length of time, Waldo lured her to St. Louis Cemetery Number One with the ruse of pretending they were going to raise the spirit of Marie Laveau, the notorious voodoo queen of New Orleans. Instead, he'd killed Hadley and blamed it on the Fellowship of the Sun. Mr. Cataliades had nudged me in the right direction until I'd figured out Waldo's guilt, and the queen had given me the opportunity to execute Waldo myself — that was the queen's idea of a big favor. I'd taken a pass on that. But he was finally, definitely dead, now, just like Hadley. I shuddered.

"Well, I know him better than I want to," she said, with the frankness that seemed to be Amelia Broadway's defining characteristic. "I hear you using the past tense, though. Dare I hope that Waldo has gone to his final destination?"

"You can," I said. "Dare, that is."

"Oo-wee," she said happily. "My, my, my."

At least I'd brightened someone's day. I could see in Amelia's thoughts how much she'd disliked the older vampire, and I didn't blame her. He'd been loathsome. Amelia was a single-minded kind of woman, which must make her a formidable witch. But right now she should have been thinking about other possibilities involving me, and she wasn't. There's a downside to being focused on a goal.

"So you want to clear out Hadley's apartment because you think your building won't be targeted any more? By these thieves who've learned that Hadley's dead?"

"Right," she said, taking a final gulp of her coffee. "I kind of like knowing someone else is here, too. Having the apartment empty just gives me the creeps. At least vampires can't leave ghosts behind."

"I didn't know that," I said. And I'd never thought about it, either.

"No vamp ghosts," Amelia said blithely. "Nary a one. Got to be human to leave a ghost behind. Hey, you want me to do a reading on you? I know, I know, it's kind of scary, but I promise, I'm good at it!" She was thinking that it would be fun to give me a touristy-type thrill, since I wouldn't be in New Orleans long; she also believed that the nicer she was to me, the quicker I'd clean out Hadley's place so she could have the use of it back.

"Sure," I said slowly. "You can do a reading, right now, if you want." This might be a good measure of how gifted a witch Amelia really was. She sure didn't bear any resemblance to the witch stereotype. Amelia looked scrubbed and glowing and healthy, like a happy suburban housewife with a Ford Explorer and an Irish setter. But quick as a wink, Amelia extricated a Tarot pack from a pocket of her cargo shorts and leaned over the coffee table to deal them out. She did this in a quick and professional way that didn't make a bit of sense to me.

After poring over the pictures for a minute, her gaze stopped roaming over the cards and fixed on the table. Her face reddened, and she closed her eyes as if she were feeling mortified. Of course, she was.

"Okay," she said at last, her voice calm and flat. "What are you?"

"Telepath."

"I'm always making assumptions! Why don't I learn!"

"No one thinks of me as scary," I said, trying to sound gentle, and she winced.

"Well, I won't make that mistake again," she said. "You did seem more knowledgeable about supes than the ordinary person."

"And learning more every day." Even to myself, my voice sounded grim.

"Now I'll have to tell my advisor that I blew it," my landlady said. She looked as gloomy as it was possible for her to look. Not very.

"You have a . . . mentor?"

"Yeah, an older witch who kind of monitors our progress the first three years of being a professional."

"How do you know when you're a professional?"

"Oh, you have to pass the exam," Amelia explained, getting to her feet and going over to the sink. In a New York minute, she had washed the coffeepot and the filter apparatus, put them neatly in the drainer, and wiped out the sink.

"So we'll start packing up stuff tomorrow?" I said.

"What's wrong with right now?"

"I'd like to go through Hadley's things by myself, first," I said, trying not to sound irritated.

"Oh. Well, sure you would." She tried to look as if she'd thought of that already. "And I guess you have to go over to the queen's tonight, huh?"

"I don't know."

"Oh, I'll bet they're expecting you. Was there a tall, dark, and handsome vamp out there with you last night? He sure looked familiar."

"Bill Compton," I said. "Yes, he's lived in Louisiana for years and he's done some work for the queen."

She looked at me, her clear blue eyes surprised. "Oh, I thought he knew your cousin."

"No," I said. "Thanks for getting me up so I could start work, and thanks for being willing to help me."

She was pleased that she was leaving, because I hadn't been what she'd expected, and she wanted to think about me some and make some phone calls to sisters in the craft in the Bon Temps area. "Holly Cleary," I said. "She's the one I know best."

Amelia gasped and said a shaky good-bye. She left as unexpectedly as she'd arrived.

I felt old all of a sudden. I'd just been showing off, and I'd reduced a confident, happy young witch to an anxious woman in the space of an hour.

But as I got out a pad and pencil — right where they should be, in the drawer closest to the telephone — to figure out my plan of action, I consoled myself with the thought that Amelia had needed the mental slap in the face pretty badly. If it hadn't come from me, it might have come from someone who actually meant her harm.

15

I needed boxes, that was for sure. So I'd also need strapping tape, lots of it, and a Magic Marker, and probably scissors. And finally, I'd need a truck to take whatever I salvaged back to Bon Temps. I could ask Jason to drive down, or I could rent a truck, or I could ask Mr. Cataliades if he knew of a truck I could borrow. If there was a lot of stuff, maybe I would rent a car and a trailer. I'd never done such a thing, but how hard could it be? Since I didn't have a ride right now, there was no way to obtain the supplies. But I might as well start sorting, since the sooner I finished, the sooner I could get back to work and away from the New Orleans vampires. I was glad, in a corner of my mind, that Bill had come, too. As angry as I sometimes felt with him, he was familiar. After all, he'd been the first vampire I'd ever met, and it still seemed almost miraculous to me how it had happened.

He'd come into the bar, and I'd been fascinated with the discovery that I couldn't hear his thoughts. Then later the same evening, I'd rescued him from drainers. I sighed, thinking how good it had been until he'd been recalled by his maker, Lorena, now also definitely dead.

I shook myself. This wasn't the time for a trip down memory lane. This was the time for action and decision. I decided to start with the clothes.

After fifteen minutes, I realized that the clothes were going to be easy. I was going to give most of them away. Not only was my taste radically different from my cousin's, but her hips and breasts had been smaller and her coloring had been different from mine. Hadley had liked dark, dramatic clothes, and I was altogether a lower-key person. I did sort of wonder about one or two of the black wispy blouses and skirts, but when I tried them on, I looked just like one of the fangbangers who hung around Eric's bar. Not the image I was going for. I put only a handful of tank tops and a couple of pairs of shorts and sleep pants in the "keep" pile.

I found a large box of garbage bags and used those to pack the clothes away. As I finished with each bag, I set it out on the gallery to keep the apartment clear of clutter.

It was about noon when I started to work, and the hours passed quickly after I found out how to operate Hadley's CD player. A lot of the music she had was by artists who'd never been high on my list, no big surprise there — but it was interesting listening. She had a horde of CDs: No Doubt, Nine Inch Nails, Eminem, Usher.

I'd started on the drawers in the bedroom when it just began turning dark. I paused for a moment to stand on the gallery in the mild evening, and watch the city wake up for the dark hours ahead. New Orleans was a city of the night now. It had always been a place with a brawling and brazen nightlife, but now it was such a center for the undead that its entire character had changed. A lot of the jazz on Bourbon Street was played these days by hands that had last seen sunlight decades before. I could catch a faint spatter of notes on the air, the music of faraway revels. I sat on a chair on the gallery and listened for a while, and I hoped I'd get to see some of the city while I was here. New Orleans is like no other place in America, both before the vampire influx and after it. I sighed and realized I was hungry. Of course, Hadley didn't have any food in the apartment, and I wasn't about to start drinking blood. I hated to ask Amelia for anything else. Tonight, whoever came to pick me up to go to the queen's might be willing to take me to the grocery store. Maybe I should shower and change?

As I turned to go back into the apartment, I spotted the mildewed towels I'd set out the night before. They smelled much stronger, which surprised me. I would have thought the smell would have diminished by now. Instead, my breath caught in the back of my throat in disgust as I picked up the basket to bring it inside. I intended to wash them. In a corner of the kitchen was one of those washer/dryer sets with the dryer on top. Like a tower of cleanliness.

I tried to shake out the towels, but they'd dried in a stiff crumpled mass. Exasperated, I jerked at the protruding edge of one towel, and with a little resistance, the clots of stuff binding the folds together gave, and the medium blue terrycloth spread out before my eyes.

"Oh, *shit*," I said out loud in the silent apartment. "Oh, *no*."

The fluid that had dried and clumped on the towels was blood.

"Oh, Hadley," I said. "What did you do?"

The smell was as awful as the shock. I sat

down at the small dining table in the kitchen area. Flakes of dried blood had showered onto the floor and clung to my arms. I couldn't read the thoughts of a towel, for God's sake. My condition was of no help to me whatsoever. I needed . . . a witch. Like the one I'd chastened and sent away. Yep, just like that one.

But first I needed to check the whole apartment, see if it held any more surprises.

Oh, yeah. It did.

The body was in the walk-in closet in the hall.

There was no odor at all, though the corpse, a young man, had probably been there for the whole time my cousin had been dead. Maybe this young man had been a demon? But he didn't look anything like Diantha or Gladiola, or Mr. Cataliades, for that matter. If the towels had started to smell, you would think . . . oh well, maybe I'd just gotten lucky. This was something that I would have to find the answer to, and I suspected it lay downstairs.

I knocked on Amelia's door. She answered it immediately, and I saw over her shoulder that her place, though of course laid out exactly like Hadley's, was full of light colors and energy. She liked yellow, and cream, and coral, and green. Her furniture was modern and heavily cushioned, and the wooden bits were polished to the nth degree. As I'd suspected, Amelia's place was spotless.

"Yes?" she said, in a subdued kind of way.

"Okay," I said, as if I were laying down an olive branch. "I've got a problem, and I suspect you do, too."

"Why do you say that?" she asked. Her open face was closed now, as if keeping her expression blank would keep me out of her mind.

"You put a stasis spell on the apartment, right? To keep everything exactly as it was. Before you warded it against intruders?"

"Yes," she said cautiously. "I told you that."

"No one's been in that apartment since the night Hadley died?"

"I can't give you my word on it, because I suppose a very good witch or wizard could have breached my spell," she said. "But to the best of my knowledge, no one's been in there."

"So you don't know that you sealed a body in there?"

I don't know what I expected in the way of reaction, but Amelia was pretty cool about it. "Okay," she said steadily. She may have gulped. "Okay. Who is it?" Her eyelids fluttered up and down a few extra times.

Maybe she wasn't quite so cool.

"I really don't know," I said carefully. "You'll have to come see." As we went up the stairs, I said, "He was killed there, and the mess was cleaned up with towels. They were in the hamper." I told her about the condition of the towels.

"Holly Cleary tells me you saved her son's life," Amelia said.

That took me aback. It made me feel awkward, too. "The police would have found him," I said. "I just accelerated it a little."

"The doctor told Holly if the little boy hadn't gotten to the hospital when he did, the bleeding in his brain might not have been stopped in time," Amelia said.

"That's good then," I said, uncomfortable in the extreme. "How's Cody doing?"

"Well," the witch said. "He's going to be well."

"In the meantime, we got a problem right here," I reminded her.

"Okay, let's see the corpse." Amelia worked hard to keep her voice level.

I kind of liked this witch.

I led her to the closet. I'd left the door open. She stepped inside. She didn't make a sound. She came back out with a slightly green tinge to her glowing tan and leaned against the wall.

"He's a Were," she said, a moment later. The spell she'd put on the apartment had kept everything fresh, as part of the way it worked. The blood had begun to smell a little before the spell had been cast, and when I'd entered the apartment, the spell had been broken. Now the towels reeked of decay. The body didn't have an odor yet, which surprised me a little, but I figured it would any minute. Surely the body would decompose rapidly now that it had been released from Amelia's magic, and she was obviously trying not to point out how well that had worked.

"You know him?"

"Yes, I know him," she said. "The supernatural community, even in New Orleans, isn't that big. It's Jake Purifoy. He did security for the queen's wedding."

I had to sit down. I exited the walk-in closet and slid down the wall until I was sitting propped up, facing Amelia. She sat against the opposite wall. I hardly knew where to start asking questions.

"That would be when she married the King of Arkansas?" I recalled what Felicia had said, and the wedding photo I'd seen in Al Cumberland's album. Had that been the queen, under that elaborate headdress? When Quinn had mentioned making the arrangements for a wedding in New Orleans, was this the wedding he'd meant?

"The queen, according to Hadley, is bi," Amelia told me. "So yes, she married a guy. Now they have an alliance."

"They can't have kids," I said. I know, that was obvious, but I wasn't getting this alliance thing.

"No, but unless someone stakes them, they'll live forever, so passing things on is not a big issue," Amelia said. "It takes months, even years, of negotiations to hammer out the rules for such a wedding. The contract can take just as long. Then they both gotta sign it. That's a big ceremony, takes place right before the wedding. They don't actually have to spend their lives together, you know, but they have to visit a couple of times a year. Conjugal-type visit."

Fascinating as this was, it was beside the point right now. "So this guy in the closet, he was part of the security force." Had he worked for Quinn? Hadn't Quinn said that one of his workers had gone missing in New Orleans?

"Yeah, I wasn't asked to the wedding, of course, but I helped Hadley into her dress. He came to pick her up."

"Jake Purifoy came to pick Hadley up for the wedding."

"Yep. He was all dressed up that night."

"And that was the night of the wedding."

"Yeah, the night before Hadley died."

"Did you see them leave?"

"No, I just . . . No. I heard the car pull up. I looked out my living room window and saw Jake coming in. I knew him already, kind of casually. I had a friend who used to date him. I went back to whatever I was doing, watching TV I think, and I heard the car leave after a while."

"So he may not have left at all."

She stared at me, her eyes wide. "Could be," she said at last, sounding as if her mouth were dry.

"Hadley was by herself when he came to pick her up . . . right?"

"When I came down from her apartment, I left her there alone."

"All I came to do," I said, mainly to my bare feet, "was clean out my cousin's apartment. I didn't much like her anyway. Now I'm stuck with a body. The last time I got rid of a body," I told the witch, "I had a big strong helper, and we wrapped it in a shower curtain."

"You did?" Amelia said faintly. She didn't look too happy to be the recipient of this information.

"Yes." I nodded. "We didn't kill him. We just had to get rid of the body. We thought we'd be blamed for the death, and I'm sure we would have been." I stared at my toenail polish some more. It had been a good job when it started out, a nice bright pink, but now I needed to refresh the paint job or remove it. I stopped trying to think about other things and resumed my gloomy contemplation of the body. He was lying in the closet, stretched out on the floor, pushed under the lowest shelf. He'd been covered with a sheet. Jake Purifoy had been a handsome man, I suspected. He'd had dark brown hair, and a muscular build. Lots of body hair. Though he'd been dressed for a formal wedding, and Amelia had said he looked very nice, now he was naked. A minor question: where were his clothes?

"We could just call the queen," Amelia said. "After all, the body's been here, and Hadley either killed him or hid the body. No way could he have died the night she went out with Waldo to the cemetery."

"Why not?" I had a sudden, awful thought.

"You got a cell phone?" I asked, rising to my feet as I spoke. Amelia nodded. "Call the queen's place. Tell them to send someone over *right now.*"

"What?" Her eyes were confused, even as her fingers were punching in numbers.

Looking into the closet, I could see the fingers of the corpse twitch.

"He's rising," I said quietly.

It only took a second for her to get it. "This is Amelia Broadway on Chloe Street! Send an older vampire over here *right now*," she yelled into the phone. "New vamp rising!" She was on her feet now, and we were running for the door.

We didn't make it.

Jake Purifoy was after us, and he was hungry.

Since Amelia was behind me (I'd had a head start) he dove to grab her ankle. She shrieked as she went down, and I spun around to help her. I didn't think at all, because I would have kept on going out the door if I had. The new vamp's fingers were wrapped around Amelia's bare ankle like a shackle, and he was pulling her toward him across the smooth laminated-wood floor. She was clawing at the floor with her fingers, trying to find something to stop her progress toward his mouth, which was wide open with the fangs extended full length, oh God! I grabbed her wrists and began pulling. I hadn't known Jake Purifoy in life, so I didn't know what he'd been like. And I couldn't find anything human left in his face, anything I could appeal to. "Jake!" I yelled. "Jake Purifoy! Wake up!" Of course, that didn't do a damn bit of good. Jake had changed into something that was not a nightmare but a permanent otherness, and he could not be roused from it: he was it. He was making a kind of *gnarr-gnarr-gnarr* noise, the hungriest sound I'd ever heard, and then he bit down on the calf of Amelia's leg, and she screamed.

It was like a shark had hold of her. If I yanked at her any more, he might take out the bit his teeth had clamped on. He was sucking on the leg wound now, and I kicked him in the head with my heel, cursing my lack of shoes. I put everything I had behind it, and it didn't faze the new vampire in the least. He made a noise of protest, but continued sucking, and the witch kept shrieking with pain and shock. There was a candlestick on the table behind one of the loveseats, a tall glass candlestick with lots of heft to it. I plucked the candle from it, grasped it with both hands, and brought it down as hard as I could on Jake Purifoy's head. Blood began to run from his wound, very sluggishly; that's how vampires bleed. The candlestick came apart with the blow, and I was left with empty hands and a furious vampire. He raised his blood-smeared face to glare at me, and I hope I'm never on the receiving end of another look like that again in my life. His face held the mindless rage of a mad dog.

But he'd let go of Amelia's leg, and she began to scramble away. It was obvious she was hurt, and it was kind of a slow scramble, but she made the effort. Tears were streaming down her face and her breathing was all over the place, harsh in the night's silence. I could hear a siren drawing closer and I hoped it was coming here. It would be too late, though. The vampire launched himself from the floor to knock me down, and I didn't have time to think about anything.

He bit down on my arm, and I thought the teeth would penetrate the bone. If I hadn't thrown up the arm, those teeth would have gripped my neck, and that would have been fatal. The arm might be preferable, but just at this moment the pain was so intense I nearly passed out, and I'd better not do that. Jake Purifoy's body was heavy on top of mine, and his hands were pressing my free arm to the floor, and his legs were on top of mine. Another hunger was wakening in the new vampire, and I felt its evidence pressing against my thigh. He freed a hand to begin yanking at my pants.

Oh, no . . . this was so bad. I would die in the next few minutes, here in New Orleans in my cousin's apartment, far away from my friends and my family.

Blood was all over the new vampire's face and hands.

Amelia crawled awkwardly across the floor toward us, her leg trailing blood behind her. She should have run, since she couldn't save me. No more candlesticks. But Amelia had another weapon, and she reached out with a violently shaking hand to touch the vampire. *"Utinam hic sanguis in ignem commutet!"* she yelled.

The vampire reared back, screaming and clawing at his face, which was suddenly covered by tiny licking blue flames.

And the police came through the door.

They were vampires, too.

For an interesting moment, the police officers thought we had attacked Jake Purifoy. Amelia and I, bleeding and screaming, were shoved up against the wall. But in the meantime, the spell Amelia had cast on the new undead lost its efficacy and he leaped on the nearest uniformed cop, who happened to be a black woman with a proud straight back and a high-bridged nose. The cop whipped out her nightstick and used it with a reckless disregard for the new vamp's

271

teeth. Her partner, a very short man whose skin was the color of butterscotch, fumbled to open a bottle of TrueBlood that was stuck in his belt like another tool. He bit off the tip, and stuck the rubber cap in Jake Purifoy's questing mouth. Suddenly, all was silence as the new vamp sucked down the contents of the bottle. The rest of us stood panting and bleeding.

"He will be quiet now," said the female officer, the cadence of her voice letting me know that she was far more African than American. "I think we have subdued him."

Amelia and I sank onto the floor, after the male cop gave us a nod to let us know we were off the hook. "Sorry we got confused about who was the bad guy," he said in a voice as warm as melted butter. "You ladies okay?" It was a good thing his voice was so reassuring, since his fangs were out. I guess the excitement of the blood and the violence triggered the reaction, but it was kind of disconcerting in a law enforcement officer.

"I think not," I said. "Amelia here is bleeding pretty bad, and I guess I am, too." The bite didn't hurt as badly as it was going to. The vamp's saliva secretes a tiny bit of anesthetic, along with a healing agent. But the healing agent was meant for sealing the pinpricks of fangs, not for actual large tears in human flesh. "We're going to need a doctor." I'd met a vamp in Mississippi who could heal large wounds, but it was a rare talent.

"You both human?" he asked. The female cop was crooning in a foreign language to the new vampire. I didn't know if the former werewolf, Jake Purifoy, could speak the language, but he recognized safety when he saw it. The burns on his face healed as we sat there.

"Yes," I said.

While we waited for the paramedics to come, Amelia and I leaned against each other wordlessly. Was this the second body I'd found in a closet, or the third? I wondered why I even opened closet doors any more.

"We should have known," Amelia said wearily. "When he didn't smell at all, we should have known."

"Actually, I figured that out. Since it was only thirty seconds before he woke up, it didn't do a hell of a lot of good," I said. My voice was just as limp as hers.

Everything got very confusing after that. I kept thinking it would be a good time to faint if I was ever going to, because this was really not a process I wanted to be in on, but I just couldn't pass out. The paramedics were very nice young men who seemed to think we'd been partying with a vamp and it had gotten out of hand. I guessed neither of them would be calling Amelia or me for a date any time soon.

"You don't want to be messing with no vampires, *cherie*," said the man who was working on me. His name tag read DELAGARDIE. "They supposed to be so attractive to women, but you wouldn't believe how many poor girls we've had to patch up. And that was the lucky ones," Delagardie said grimly. "What's your name, young lady?"

"Sookie," I said. "Sookie Stackhouse."

"Pleased to meet you, Miss Sookie. You and your friend seem like nice girls. You need to hang with better people, live people. This city's overrun with the dead, now. It was better when everyone here was breathing, I tell you the truth. Now let's get you to the hospital and get you stitched up. I'd shake your hand if you wasn't all bloody," he said. He gave me a sudden smile, white-toothed and charming. "I'm giving you good advice for free, pretty lady."

I smiled, but it was the last time I was going to be doing that for a while. The pain was beginning to make itself felt. Very quickly, I became preoccupied with coping.

Amelia was a real warrior. Her teeth were gritted as she fought to keep herself together, but she managed all the way to the hospital. The emergency room seemed to be packed. By a combination of bleeding, being escorted by cops, and the friendly Delagardie and his partner putting in a word for us, Amelia and I got put in curtained cubicles right away. We weren't adjacent to each other, but we were in line to see a doctor. I was grateful. I knew that had to be quick, for an urban emergency room.

As I listened to the bustle around me, I tried not to swear at the pain in my arm. In moments when it wasn't throbbing as much, I wondered what had happened to Jake Purifoy. Had the vampire cops taken him to a vampire cell at the jail, or was everything excused since he was a brand new vamp with no guidance? There'd been a law passed about that, but I couldn't remember the terms and strictures. It was hard for me to be too concerned. I knew the young man was a victim of his new state; that the vampire who had made him should have been there to guide him through his first wakening and hunger. The vampire to blame was most likely my cousin Hadley, who had hardly expected to be murdered.

Only Amelia's stasis spell on the apartment had kept Jake from rising months ago. It was a strange situation, probably unprecedented even in vampire annals. And a werewolf who'd become a vampire! I'd never heard tell of such a thing. Could he still change?

I had a while to think about that and quite a few other things, since Amelia was too far away for conversation, even if she'd been up to it. After about twenty minutes, during which time I was disturbed only by a nurse who wrote down some information, I was surprised to see Eric peer around the curtain.

"May I come in?" he asked stiffly. His eyes were wide and he was speaking carefully. I realized that to a vampire, the smell of blood in the emergency room was enchanting and pervasive. I caught a glimpse of his fangs.

"Yes," I said, puzzled by Eric's presence in New Orleans. I wasn't really in an Eric mood, but there was no point in telling the former Viking he couldn't come into the curtained area. This was a public building, and he wasn't bound by my words. Anyway, he could simply stand outside and talk to me through the cloth until he found out whatever he'd come to discover. Eric was nothing if not persistent. "What on earth are you doing here in town, Eric?"

"I drove down to bargain with the queen for your services during the summit. Also, Her Majesty and I have to negotiate how many of my people I can bring with me." He smiled at me. The effect was disconcerting, what with the fangs and all. "We've almost reached an agreement. I can bring three, but I want to bargain up to four."

"Oh, for God's sake, Eric," I snapped. "That's the lamest excuse I've ever heard. Modern invention, known as the telephone?" I moved restlessly on the narrow bed. I couldn't find a comfortable position. Every nerve in my body was jangling with the aftermath of the fear of my encounter with Jake Purifoy, new child of the night. I was hoping that when I finally saw a doctor, he or she would give me an excellent painkiller. "Leave me alone, okay? You don't have a claim on me. Or a responsibility to me."

"But I do." He had the gall to look surprised. "We have a bond. I've had your blood, when you needed strength to free Bill in Jackson. And we've made love often, according to you."

"You *made* me tell you," I protested. And if I sounded a little on the whiny side, well, dammit, I thought it was okay to whine a little. Eric had agreed to save a friend of mine from danger if I'd spill the truth to him. Is that blackmail? Yes, I think so.

But there wasn't any way to untell him. I sighed. "How'd you get here, anyway?"

"The queen monitors what happens to vampires in her city very closely, of course. I thought I'd come provide moral support. And, of course, if you need me to clean you of blood . . ." His eyes flashed as he inspected my arm. "I'd be glad to do it."

I almost smiled, very reluctantly. He never gave up.

"Eric," said Bill's cool voice, and he slipped around the curtain to join Eric at my bedside.

"Why am I not surprised to see you here?" Eric said, in a voice that made it clear he was displeased.

Eric's anger wasn't something Bill could ignore. Eric outranked Bill, and he looked down his substantial nose at the younger vampire. Bill was around one hundred thirty-five years old: Eric was perhaps over a thousand. (I had asked him once, but he honestly didn't seem to know.) Eric had the personality for leadership. Bill was happier on his own. The only thing they had in common was that they'd both made love to me: and just at the moment, they were both pains in my butt.

"I heard over the police band radio at the queen's headquarters that the vampire police had been called in to subdue a fresh vampire, and I recognized the address," Bill said by way of explanation. "Naturally, I found out where Sookie had been brought, and came here as fast as I could."

I closed my eyes.

"Eric, you're tiring her out," Bill said, his voice even colder than usual. "You should leave Sookie alone."

There was a long moment of silence. It was fraught with some big emotion. My eyes opened and went from one face to another. For once, I wished I could read vampire minds.

As much as I could read from his expression, Bill was deeply regretting his words, but why? Eric was looking at Bill with a complex expression compounded of resolve and something less definable; regret, maybe.

"I quite understand why you want to keep Sookie isolated while she's in New Orleans," Eric said. His *r*'s became more pronounced, as they did when he was angry.

Bill looked away.

Despite the pain pulsing in my arm, despite my general exasperation with the both of them, something inside me sat up and took notice. There was an unmistakable significance to Eric's tone. Bill's lack of response was curious . . . and ominous.

"What?" I said, my eyes flicking from one to the other. I tried to prop myself up on my elbows and settled for one when the other arm, the bitten one, gave a big throb of pain. I pressed the button to raise the head of the bed. "What's all the big hinting about, Eric? Bill?"

"Eric should not be agitating you when you've got a lot to handle already," Bill said, finally. Though never known for its expressiveness, Bill's face was what my grandmother would have described as "locked up tighter than a drum."

Eric folded his arms across his chest and looked down at them.

"Bill?" I said.

"Ask him why he came back to Bon Temps, Sookie," Eric said very quietly.

"Well, old Mr. Compton died, and he wanted to reclaim his . . ." I couldn't even describe the expression on Bill's face. My heart began to beat faster. Dread gathered in a knot in my stomach. "Bill?"

Eric turned to face away from me, but not before I saw a shade of pity cross his face. Nothing could have scared me more. I might not be able to read a vampire's mind, but in this case his body language said it all. Eric was turning away because he didn't want to watch the knife sliding in.

"Sookie, you would find out when you saw the queen . . . Maybe I could have kept it from you, because you won't understand . . . but Eric has taken care of that." Bill gave Eric's back a look that could have drilled a hole through Eric's heart. "When your cousin Hadley was becoming the queen's favorite . . ."

And suddenly I saw it all, knew what he was going to say, and I rose up on the hospital bed with a gasp, one hand to my chest because I felt my heart shattering. But Bill's voice went on, even though I shook my head violently.

"Apparently, Hadley talked about you and your gift a lot, to impress the queen and keep her interest. And the queen knew I was originally from Bon Temps. On some nights, I've wondered if she sent someone to kill the last Compton and hurry things along. But maybe he truly died of old age." Bill was looking down at the floor, didn't see my left hand extended to him in a "stop" motion.

"She ordered me to return to my human home, to put myself in your way, to seduce you if I had to . . ."

I couldn't breathe. No matter how my right hand pressed to my chest, I couldn't stop the decimation of my heart, the slide of the knife deeper into my flesh.

"She wanted your gift harnessed for her own use," he said, and he opened his mouth to say more. My eyes were so blurred with tears that I couldn't see properly, couldn't see what expression was on his face and didn't care anyway. But I could not cry while he was anywhere near me. I would not.

"Get out," I said, with a terrible effort. Whatever else happened, I could not bear for him to see the pain he had caused.

He tried to look me straight in the eyes, but mine were too full. Whatever he wanted to convey, it was lost on me. "Please let me finish," he said.

"I never want to see you again, ever in my life," I whispered. "Ever."

He didn't speak. His lips moved, as if he were trying to form a word or phrase, but I shook my head. "Get out," I told him, in a voice so choked with hatred and anguish that it didn't sound like my own. Bill turned and walked past the curtain and out of the emergency room. Eric did not turn around to see my face, thank God. He reached back to pat me on the leg before he left, too.

I wanted to scream. I wanted to kill someone with my bare hands.

I had to be by myself. I could not let anyone see me suffer this much. The pain was tied up with a rage so profound that I had never felt its like. I was sick with anger and hurt. The snap of Jake Purifoy's teeth had been nothing compared to this.

I couldn't stay still. With some difficulty, I eased off the bed. My feet were still bare, of course, and I noticed with an odd detached part of my mind that they were extraordinarily dirty. I staggered out of the triage area, spotted the doors to the waiting room, and aimed myself in that direction. Walking was a problem.

A nurse bustled up to me, a clipboard in her hand. "Miss Stackhouse, a doctor's going to be with you in just a minute. I know you've had to wait, and I'm sorry, but . . ."

I turned to look at her and she flinched, took a step backward. I kept on toward the doors, my steps uncertain but my purpose clear. I wanted out of there. Beyond that, I didn't know. I made it to the doors and pushed and then I was dragging myself through the waiting room thronged with people. I blended in perfectly with the mix of patients and relatives waiting to see a doctor. Some were dirtier and bloodier than

I was, and some were older — and some were way younger. I supported myself with a hand against a wall and kept moving to the doors, to the outside.

I made it.

It was much quieter outside, and it was warm. The wind was blowing, just a little. I was barefoot and penniless, standing under the glaring lights of the walk-in doors. I had no idea where I was in relation to the house, and no idea if that was where I was going, but I wasn't in the hospital any more.

A homeless man stepped in front of me. "You got any change, sister?" he asked. "I'm down on my luck, too."

"Do I *look* like I have *anything?*" I asked him, in a reasonable voice.

He looked as unnerved as the nurse had. He said, "Sorry," and backed away. I took a step after him.

I screamed, *"I HAVE NOTHING!"* And then I said, in a perfectly calm voice, "See, I never had anything to start with."

He gibbered and quavered and I ignored him. I began my walk. The ambulance had turned right coming in, so I turned left. I couldn't remember how long the ride had been. I'd been talking to Delagardie. I had been a different person. I walked and I walked. I walked under palm trees, heard the rich rhythm of music, brushed against the peeling shutters of houses set right up to the sidewalk.

On a street with a few bars, a group of young men came out just as I was passing, and one of them grabbed my arm. I turned on him with a scream, and with a galvanic effort I swung him into a wall. He stood there, dazed and rubbing his head, and his friends pulled him away.

"She crazy," one of them said softly. "Leave her be." They wandered off in the other direction.

After a time, I recovered enough to ask myself why I was doing this. But the answer was vague. When I fell on some broken pavement, scraping my knee badly enough to make it bleed, the new physical pain called me back to myself a little bit more.

"Are you doing this so they'll feel sorry they hurt you?" I asked myself out loud. "Oh my God, poor Sookie! She walked out of the hospital all by herself, driven crazy with grief, and she wandered alone through the dangerous streets of the Big Easy because Bill made her so crazy!"

I didn't want my name to cross Bill's lips ever again. When I was a little more myself — just a little — the depth of my reaction began to surprise me. If we'd still been a couple when I learned what I'd learned this evening, I'd have killed him; I knew that with crystal clarity. But the reason I'd had to get away from the hospital was equally clear; I couldn't have stood dealing with anyone in the world just then. I'd been blindsided with the most painful knowledge: the first man to ever say he loved me had never loved me at all.

His passion had been artificial.

His pursuit of me had been choreographed.

I must have seemed so easy to him, so gullible, so ready for the first man who devoted a little time and effort to winning me. Winning me! The very phrase made me hurt worse. He'd never thought of me as a prize.

Until the structure had been torn down in a single moment, I hadn't realized how much of my life in the past year had been built on the false foundation of Bill's love and regard.

"I saved his life," I said, amazed. "I went to Jackson and risked my life for his, because he loved me." One part of my brain knew that wasn't entirely accurate. I'd done it because I had loved him. And I was amazed, at the same moment, to realize that the pull of his maker, Lorena, had been even stronger than the orders of his queen. But I wasn't in the mood to split emotional hairs. When I thought of Lorena, another realization socked me in the stomach. "I killed someone for him," I said, my words floating in the thick dark night. "Oh, my God. I killed someone for *him*."

I was covered in scrapes, bruises, blood, and dirt when I looked up to see a sign reading CHLOE STREET. That was where Hadley's apartment was, I realized slowly. I turned right, and began to walk again.

The house was dark, up and down. Maybe Amelia was still at the hospital. I had no idea what time it was or how long I had walked.

Hadley's apartment was locked. I went downstairs and picked up one of the flowerpots Amelia had put around her door. I carried it up the stairs and smashed in a glass pane on the door. I reached inside, unlocked the door, and stepped in. No alarm shrieked. I'd been pretty sure the police wouldn't have known the code to activate it when they'd left after doing whatever it was they'd done.

I walked through the apartment, which was still turned upside down by our fight with Jake Purifoy. I had some more cleaning to do in the morning, or whenever . . .

whenever my life resumed. I went into the bathroom and stripped off the clothes I'd been wearing. I held them and looked at them for a minute, at the state they were in. Then I stepped across the hall, unlocked the closest French window, and threw the clothes over the railing of the gallery. I wished all problems were that easily disposed of, but at the same time my real personality was waking up enough to trigger a thread of guilt that I was leaving a mess that someone else would have to clean up. That wasn't the Stackhouse way. That thread wasn't strong enough to make me go back down the stairs to retrieve the filthy garments. Not then.

After I'd wedged a chair under the door I'd broken, and after I'd set the alarm system with the numbers Amelia had taught me, I got into the shower. The water stung my many scrapes and cuts, and the deep bite in my arm began bleeding again. Well, shit. My cousin the vampire hadn't needed any first aid supplies, of course. I finally found some circular cotton pads she'd probably used for removing makeup, and I rummaged through one of the bags of clothes until I found a ludicrously cheerful leopard-patterned scarf. Awkwardly, I bound the pads to the bite and got the scarf tight enough.

At least the vile sheets were the least of my worries. I climbed painfully into my nightgown and lay on the bed, praying for oblivion.

16

I woke up unrefreshed, with that awful feeling that in a moment I would remember bad things.

The feeling was right on the money.

But the bad things had to take a backseat, because I had a surprise to start the day with. Claudine was lying beside me on the bed, propped up on one elbow looking down at me compassionately. And Amelia was at the end of the bed in an easy chair, her bandaged leg propped up on an ottoman. She was reading.

"How come you're here?" I asked Claudine. After seeing Eric and Bill last night, I wondered if everyone I knew followed me around. Maybe Sam would come in the door in a minute.

"I told you, I'm your fairy godmother," Claudine said. Claudine was usually the happiest fairy I knew. Claudine was just as lovely for a woman as her twin Claude was for a man; maybe lovelier, because her more agreeable personality shone through her eyes. Her coloring was the same as his; black hair, white skin. Today she was wearing pale blue capris and a coordinating black-and-blue tunic. She looked ethereally lovely, or at least as ethereal as you can look in capris.

"You can explain that to me right after I go to the bathroom," I said, remembering all the water I'd chugged down when I'd gotten to the sink the night before. All my wanderings had made me thirsty. Claudine swung gracefully from the bed, and I followed her awkwardly.

"Careful," Amelia advised, when I tried to stand up too quickly.

"How's your leg?" I asked her, when the world had righted itself. Claudine kept a grip on my arm, just in case. It felt good to see Claudine, and I was surprisingly glad to see Amelia, even limping.

"Very sore," she said. "But unlike you, I stayed at the hospital and had the wound treated properly." She closed her book and put it on the little table by the chair. She looked a little better than I suspected I did, but she was not the radiant and happy witch she'd been the day before.

"Had a learning experience, didn't we?" I

said, and then my breath caught when I remembered just how much I'd learned.

Claudine helped me into the bathroom, and when I assured her I could manage, she left me alone. I did the necessary things and came out feeling better, almost human. Claudine had gotten some clothes out of my sports bag, and there was a mug on the bedside table with steam rising from it. I carefully sat against the headboard, my legs crossed in front of me, and held the mug to my face so I could breathe in the smell.

"Explain the fairy godmother thing," I said. I didn't want to talk about anything more urgent, not just yet.

"Fairies are your basic supernatural being," Claudine said. "From us come elves and brownies and angels and demons. Water sprites, green men, all the natural spirits . . . all are some form of fairy."

"So you're what?" Amelia asked. It hadn't occurred to Amelia to leave, and that seemed to be okay with Claudine, too.

"I'm trying to become an angel," Claudine said softly. Her huge brown eyes looked luminous. "After years of being . . . well, a good citizen, I guess you'd call it, I got a person to guard. The Sook, here. And she's really kept me busy." Claudine looked proud and happy.

"You're not supposed to prevent pain?" I asked. If so, Claudine was doing a lousy job.

"No, I wish I could." The expression on Claudine's oval face was downcast. "But I can help you recover from disasters, and sometimes I can prevent them."

"Things would be *worse* without you around?"

She nodded vigorously.

"I'll take your word for it," I said. "How come I rated a fairy godmother?"

"I'm not allowed to say," Claudine said, and Amelia rolled her eyes.

"We're not learning a lot, here," she said. "And in view of the problems we had last night, maybe you're not the most competent fairy godmother, huh?"

"Oh, right, Miss I-Sealed-Up-The-Apartment-So-It-Would-Be-All-Fresh," I responded, irrationally indignant at this assault on my godmother's competence.

Amelia scrambled out of her chair, her skin flushed with anger. "Well, I did seal it up! He would have risen like that no matter when he rose! I just delayed it some!"

"It would have helped if we had known he was in there!"

"It would have helped if your ho of a cousin hadn't killed him in the first place!"

We both screeched to a halt in our dialogue. "Are you sure that's what happened?" I asked. "Claudine?"

"I don't know," she said, her voice placid. "I'm not omnipotent or omniscient. I just pop in to intervene when I can. You remember that time you fell asleep at the wheel and I got there in time to save you?"

And she'd nearly given me a heart attack in the process, appearing in the front seat of the car in the blink of an eye. "Yes," I said, trying to sound grateful and humble. "I remember."

"It's really, really hard to get somewhere that fast," she said. "I can only do that in a real emergency. I mean, a life-or-death emergency. Fortunately, I had a bit more time when your house was on fire. . . ."

Claudine was not going to give us any rules, or even explain the nature of the rule maker. I'd just have to muddle through on my belief system, which had helped me out all my life. Come to think of it, if I was completely wrong, I didn't want to know.

"Interesting," said Amelia. "But we have a few more things to talk about."

Maybe she was being so hoity-toity because she didn't have her own fairy godmother.

"What do you want to talk about first?" I asked.

"Why'd you leave the hospital last night?" Her face was tight with resentment. "You should have told me. I hauled myself up these stairs last night to look for you, and there you were. And you'd barricaded the door. So I had to go back down the damn stairs again to get my keys, and let myself in the French windows, and hurry — *on this leg* — to the alarm system to turn it off. And then this doofus was sitting by your bed, and she could have done all of that."

"You couldn't open the windows with magic?" I asked.

"I was too tired," she said with dignity. "I had to recharge my magical batteries, so to speak."

"So to speak," I said, my voice dry. "Well, last night, I found out . . ." and I stopped dead. I simply couldn't speak of it.

"Found out what?" Amelia was exasperated, and I couldn't say as I blamed her.

"Bill, her first lover, was planted in Bon Temps to seduce her and gain her trust," Claudine said. "Last night, he admitted that to her face, and in front of her only other lover, another vampire."

As a synopsis, it was flawless.

"Well . . . that sucks," Amelia said faintly.

"Yeah," I said. "It does."

"Ouch."

"Yeah."

"I can't kill him for you," Claudine said. "I'd have to take too many steps backward."

"That's okay," I told her. "He's not worth your losing any brownie points."

"Oh, I'm not a brownie," Claudine explained kindly. "I thought you understood. I'm a full-blooded fairy."

Amelia was trying not to laugh, and I glared at her. "Just let it go, witch," I said.

"Yes, telepath."

"So what next?" I asked, in general. I would not talk any more about my broken heart and my demolished self-worth.

"We figure out what happened," the witch said.

"How? Call CSI?"

Claudine looked confused, so I guessed fairies didn't watch television.

"No," Amelia said, with elaborate patience. "We do an ectoplasmic reconstruction."

I was sure that my expression matched Claudine's, now.

"Okay, let me explain," Amelia said, grinning all over. "This is what we do."

Amelia, in seventh heaven at this exhibition of her wonderful witch powers, told Claudine and me at length about the procedure. It was time- and energy-consuming, she said, which was why it wasn't done more often. And you had to gather at least four witches, she estimated, to cover the amount of square footage involved in Jake's murder.

"And I'll need real witches," Amelia said. "Quality workers, not some hedgerow Wiccan." Amelia went off on Wiccans for a good long while. She despised Wiccans (unfairly) as tree-hugging wannabes — that came out of Amelia's thoughts clearly enough. I regretted Amelia's prejudice, as I'd met some impressive Wiccans.

Claudine looked down at me, her expression doubtful. "I'm not sure we ought to be here for this," she said.

"You can go, Claudine." I was ready to experiment with anything, just to take my mind off the big hole in my heart. "I'm going to stay to watch. I have to know what happened here. There are too many mysteries in my life, right now."

"But you have to go to the queen's tonight," Claudine said. "You missed last night. Visiting the queen is a dress-up occasion. I have to take you shopping. You don't want to wear any of your cousin's clothes."

"Not that my butt could get into them," I said.

"Not that your butt should want to," she

said, equally harshly. "You can cut that out right now, Sookie Stackhouse."

I looked up at her, letting her see the pain inside me.

"Yeah, I get that," she said, her hand patting me gently on the cheek. "And that sucks big-time. But you have to write it off. He's only one guy."

He'd been the first guy. "My grandmother served him lemonade," I said, and somehow that triggered the tears again.

"Hey," Amelia said. "Fuck him, right?"

I looked at the young witch. She was pretty and tough and off-the-wall nuts, I thought. She was okay. "Yeah," I said. "When can you do the ecto thing?"

She said, "I have to make some phone calls, see who I can get together. Night's always better for magic, of course. When will you go pay your call to the queen?"

I thought for a moment. "Just at full dark," I said. "Maybe about seven."

"Should take about two hours," Amelia said, and Claudine nodded. "Okay, I'll ask them to be here at ten, to have a little wiggle room. You know, it would be great if the queen would pay for this."

"How much do you want to charge?"

"I'd do it for nothing, to have the experience and be able to say I'd done one," Amelia said frankly, "but the others will need some bucks. Say, three hundred apiece, plus materials."

"And you'll need three more witches?"

"I'd like to have three more, though whether I can get the ones I want on this short notice . . . well, I'll do the best I can. Two might do. And the materials ought to be . . ." She did some rapid mental calculations. "Somewhere in the ballpark of sixty dollars."

"What will I need to do? I mean, what's my part?"

"Observe. I'll do the heavy lifting."

"I'll ask the queen." I took a deep breath. "If she won't pay for it, I will."

"Okay, then. We're set." She limped out of the bedroom happily, counting off things on her fingers. I heard her go down the stairs.

Claudine said, "I have to treat your arm. And then we need to go find you something to wear."

"I don't want to spend money on a courtesy call to the vampire queen." Especially since I might have to foot the bill for the witches.

"You don't have to. It's my treat."

"You may be my fairy godmother, but you don't have to spend money on me." I had a sudden revelation. "It's you who paid my hospital bill in Clarice."

Claudine shrugged. "Hey, it's money that came in from the strip club, not from my regular job." Claudine co-owned the strip club in Ruston, with Claude, who did all the day-to-day running of the place. Claudine was a customer service person at a department store. People forgot their complaints once they were confronted with Claudine's smile.

It was true that I didn't mind spending the strip club money as much as I would have hated using up Claudine's personal savings. Not logical, but true.

Claudine had parked her car in the courtyard on the circular drive, and she was sitting in it when I came down the stairs. She'd gotten a first aid kit from the car, and she'd bandaged my arm and helped me into some clothes. My arm was sore but it didn't seem to be infected. I was weak, as if I'd had the flu or some other illness involving high fever and lots of fluids. So I was moving slowly.

I was wearing blue jeans and sandals and a T-shirt, because that was what I had.

"You definitely can't call on the queen in that," she said, gently but decisively. Whether she was very familiar with New Orleans or just had good shopping karma,

Claudine drove directly to a store in the Garden District. It was the kind of shop I'd dismiss as being for more sophisticated women with lots more money than I had, if I'd been shopping by myself. Claudine pulled right into the parking lot, and in forty-five minutes we had a dress. It was chiffon, short-sleeved, and it had lots of colors in it: turquoise, copper, brown, ivory. The strappy sandals that I wore with it were brown.

All I needed was a membership to the country club.

Claudine had appropriated the price tag.

"Just wear your hair loose," Claudine advised. "You don't need fancy hair with that dress."

"Yeah, there is a lot going on in it," I said. "Who's Diane von Furstenburg? Isn't it real expensive? Isn't it a little bare for the season?"

"You might be a little cool wearing it in March," Claudine conceded. "But it'll be good to wear every summer for years. You'll look great. And the queen will know you took the time to wear something special to meet her."

"You can't go with me?" I asked, feeling a little wistful. "No, of course, you can't." Vampires buzz around fairies like hummingbirds around sugar water.

"I might not survive," she said, managing to sound embarrassed that such a possibility would keep her from my side.

"Don't worry about it. After all, the worst thing has already happened, right?" I spread my hands. "They used to threaten me, you know? If I didn't do thus and such, they'd take it out on Bill. Hey, guess what? *I don't care any more.*"

"Think before you speak," Claudine advised. "You can't mouth off to the queen. Even a goblin won't mouth off to the queen."

"I promise," I said. "I really appreciate your coming all this way, Claudine."

Claudine gave me a big hug. It was like an embrace with a soft tree, since Claudine was so tall and slim. "I wish you hadn't needed me to," she said.

17

The queen owned a block of buildings in down town New Orleans, maybe three blocks from the edge of the French Quarter. That tells you what kind of money she was pulling in, right there. We had an early dinner — I realized I was really hungry — and then Claudine dropped me off two blocks away, because the traffic and tourist congestion were intense close to the queen's headquarters. Though the general public didn't know Sophie-Anne Leclerq was a queen, they knew she was a very wealthy vampire who owned a hell of a lot of real estate and spent lots of money in the community. Plus, her bodyguards were colorful and had gotten special permits to carry arms in the city limits. This meant her office building/living quarters were on the tourist list of things to see, especially at night.

Though traffic did surround the building

during the day, at night the square of streets around it was open only to pedestrians. Buses parked a block away, and the tour guides would lead the out-of-towners past the altered building. Walking tours and gaggles of independent tourists included what the guides called "Vampire Headquarters" in their plans.

Security was very evident. This block would be a natural target for Fellowship of the Sun bombers. A few vampire-owned businesses in other cities had been attacked, and the queen was not about to lose her life-after-death in such a way.

The vampire guards were on duty, and they were scary-looking as hell. The queen had her own vampire SWAT team. Though vampires were simply lethal all on their own, the queen had found that humans paid more attention if they found the silhouettes recognizable. Not only were the guards heavily armed, but they wore black bulletproof armor over black uniforms. It was lethal-killer *chic.*

Claudine had prepared me for all this over dinner, and when she let me out, I felt fully briefed. I also felt as if I were going to the Queen of England's garden party in all my new finery. At least I didn't have to wear a hat. But my brown high heels were a risky proposition on the rough paving.

"Behold the headquarters of New Orleans's most famous and visible vampire, Sophie-Anne LeClerq," a tour guide was telling his group. He was dressed colorfully in a sort of colonial outfit: tricorn hat, knee breeches, hose, buckled shoes. My goodness. As I paused to listen, his eyes flickered over to me, took in my outfit, and sharpened with interest.

"If you're calling on Sophie-Anne, you can't go in casual," he told the group, and gestured to me. "This young lady is wearing proper dress for an interview with the vampire . . . one of America's most prominent vampires." He grinned at the group, inviting them to enjoy his reference.

There were fifty other vampires just as prominent. Maybe not as publicly oriented or as colorful as Sophie-Anne Leclerq, but the public didn't know that.

Rather than being surrounded with the appropriate air of exotic deadliness, the queen's "castle" was more of a macabre Disneyland, thanks to the souvenir peddlers, the tour guides, and the curious gawkers. There was even a photographer. As I approached the first ring of guards, a man jumped in front of me and snapped my picture. I was frozen by the flash of light and stared after him — or in what I thought was his direction — while my eyes adjusted. When I was able to see him clearly, I found he was a small, grubby man with a big camera and a determined expression. He bustled off immediately to what I guessed was his accustomed station, a corner on the opposite side of the street. He didn't offer to sell me a picture or tell me where I could purchase one, and he didn't give me any explanation.

I had a bad feeling about this incident. When I talked to one of the guards, my suspicion was confirmed.

"He's a Fellowship spy," said the vampire, nodding in the little man's direction. He'd located my name on a checklist clamped to a clipboard. The guard himself was a sturdy man with brown skin and a nose as curved as a rainbow. He'd been born somewhere in the Middle East, once-upon a time. The name patch attached with Velcro to his helmet said RASUL.

"We're forbidden to kill him," Rasul said, as if he were explaining a slightly embarrassing folk custom. He smiled at me, which was kind of disconcerting, too. The black helmet came down low on his face and the chinstrap was the kind that actually rounded his chin, so I could see only a little bit of his face. At the moment, that bit was mostly sharp, white, teeth. "The Fellowship photographs everyone who goes in and out of this place, and there doesn't seem to be anything we can do about it, since we want to keep the goodwill of the humans."

Rasul correctly assumed I was a vampire ally, since I was on the visitors list, and was treating me with a camaraderie that I found relaxing. "It would be lovely if something happened to his camera," I suggested. "The Fellowship is hunting me already." Though I felt pretty guilty, asking a vampire to arrange an accident to another human being, I was fond enough of my own life to want it saved.

His eyes gleamed as we passed under a streetlight. The light caught them so that for a moment they shone red, like people's eyes sometimes do when the photographer is using a flash.

"Oddly enough, a few things have happened to his cameras already," Rasul said. "In fact, two of them have been smashed beyond repair. What's one more accident? I'm not guaranteeing anything, but we'll do our best, lovely lady."

"Thank you so much," I said. "Anything you can do will be much appreciated. After tonight, I can talk to a witch who could maybe take care of that problem for you. Maybe she could make all the pictures turn out overexposed, or something. You should give her a call."

"That's an excellent idea. Here is Melanie," he said, as we reached the main doors. "I'll pass you on to her, and return to my post. I'll see you when you exit, get the witch's name and address?"

"Sure," I said.

"Did anyone ever tell you that you smell enchantingly like a fairy?" Rasul said.

"Oh, I've been with my fairy godmother," I explained. "She took me shopping."

"And the result was wonderful," he said gallantly.

"You flatterer." I couldn't help but smile back at him. My ego had taken a blow to the solar plexus the night before (but I *wasn't thinking about that*), and a little thing like the guard's admiration was just what I needed, even if it was really Claudine's smell that had triggered it.

Melanie was a delicate woman, even in the SWAT gear. "Yum, yum, you do smell like fairy," she said. She consulted her own clipboard. "You are the Stackhouse woman? The queen expected you last night."

"I got hurt." I held my arm out, showing the bandage. Thanks to a lot of Advil, the pain was down to a dull throb.

"Yes, I heard about it. The new one is having a great night tonight. He received instructions, he has a mentor, and he has a volunteer donor. When he feels more like his new self, he may tell us how he came to be turned."

"Oh?" I heard my voice falter when I realized she was talking about Jake Purifoy. "He might not remember?"

"If it's a surprise attack, sometimes they don't remember for a while," she said, and shrugged. "But it always comes back, sooner or later. In the meantime, he'll have a free lunch." She laughed at my inquiring look. "They register for the privilege, you know. Stupid humans." She shrugged. "There's no fun in that, once you've gotten over the thrill of feeding, in and of itself. The fun was always in the chase." Melanie really wasn't happy with the new vampire policy of feeding only from willing humans or from the synthetic blood. She clearly felt the lack of her former diet.

I tried to look politely interested.

"When the prey makes the first advance, it's just not the same," she grumped. "People these days." She shook her little head in weary exasperation. Since she was so small that her helmet almost wobbled on her head, I could feel myself smiling.

"So, he wakes up and you all herd the volunteer in? Like dropping a live mouse into a snake's tank?" I worked to keep my face serious. I didn't want Melanie to think I was making fun of her personally.

After a suspicious moment, Melanie said, "More or less. He's been lectured. There are other vampires present."

"And the volunteer survives?"

"They sign a release beforehand," Melanie said, carefully.

I shuddered.

Rasul had escorted me from the other side of the street to the main entrance to the queen's domain. It was a three-story office building, perhaps dating from the fifties, and extending a whole city block. In other places, the basement would have been the vampires' retreat, but in New Orleans, with its high water table, that was impossible. All the windows had received a distinctive treatment. The panels that covered them were decorated in a Mardi Gras theme, so the staid brick building was pepped up with pink, purple, and green designs on a white or black background. There were iridescent patches on the shutters, too, like Mardi Gras beads. The effect was disconcerting.

"What does she do when she throws a

party?" I asked. Despite the shutters, the prosaic office rectangle was simply not festive.

"Oh, she owns an old monastery," Melanie said. "You can get a brochure about it before you go. That's where all the state functions are held. Some of the old ones can't go into the former chapel, but other than that . . . it's got a high wall all around, so it's easy to patrol, and it's decorated real nice. The queen has apartments there, but it's too insecure for year-round living."

I couldn't think of anything to say. I doubted I would ever see the queen's state residence. But Melanie seemed bored and inclined to chat. "You were Hadley's cousin, I hear?" she asked.

"Yes."

"Strange, to think of having living relatives." For a moment, she looked far away, and as wistful as a vampire can look. Then she seemed to kind of shake herself mentally. "Hadley wasn't bad for one so young. But she seemed to take her vampire longevity a little too much for granted." Melanie shook her head. "She should never have crossed someone as old and wily as Waldo."

"That's for damn sure," I said.

"Chester," Melanie called. Chester was the next guard in line, and he was standing with a familiar figure clothed in the (what I was coming to think of as) usual SWAT garb.

"Bubba!" I exclaimed, as the vampire said, "Miss Sookie!" Bubba and I hugged, to the vampires' amusement. Vampires don't shake hands, in the ordinary course of things, and hugging is just as outré in their culture.

I was glad to see they hadn't let him have a gun, just the accoutrements of the guards. He was looking fine in the military outfit, and I told him so. "Black looks real good with your hair," I said, and Bubba smiled his famous smile.

"You're mighty nice to say so," he said. "Thank you very much."

Back in the day, everyone in the world had known Bubba's face and smile. When he'd been wheeled into the morgue in Memphis, a vampire attendant had detected the tiniest flicker of life. Since the attendant was a huge fan, he had taken on the responsibility for bringing the singer over, and a legend had been born. Unfortunately, Bubba's body had been so saturated with drugs and physical woes that the conversion hadn't been entirely successful, and the vampire world passed Bubba around like the public relations nightmare he was.

"How long have you been here, Bubba?" I asked.

"Oh, a couple of weeks, but I like it real well," he said. "Lots of stray cats."

"Right," I said, trying not to think about that too graphically. I really like cats. So did Bubba, but not in the same way.

"If a human catches a glimpse of him, they think he's an impersonator," Chester said quietly. Melanie had gone back to her post, and Chester, who'd been a sandy-haired kid from the backwoods with poor dentition when he was taken, was now in charge of me. "That's fine, most often. But every so now and then, they call him by his used-to-be name. Or they ask him to sing."

Bubba very seldom sang these days, though every now and then he could be coaxed into belting out a familiar song or two. That was a memorable occasion. Most often, though, he denied he could sing a note, and he usually got very agitated when he was called by his original name.

He trailed along after us as Chester led me further into the building. We had turned, and gone up a floor, encountering more and more vampires — and a few humans — heading here or there with a purposeful air. It was like any busy office building, any weekday, except the workers were vampires and the sky outside was as dark as the New Orleans sky ever got. As we walked, I noticed that some vampires seemed more at ease than others. I observed that the wary vamps were all wearing the same pins attached to their collars, pins in the shape of the state of Arkansas. These vamps must be part of the entourage of the queen's husband, Peter Threadgill. When one of the Louisiana vampires bumped into an Arkansas vampire, the Arkansan snarled and for a second I thought there would be a fight in the corridor over a slight accident.

Jeesh, I'd be glad to get out of here. The atmosphere was tense.

Chester stopped before a door that didn't look any different from all the other closed doors, except for the two whacking big vampires outside it. The two must have been considered giants in their day, since they stood perhaps six foot three. They looked like brothers, but maybe it was just their size and mien, and the color of their chestnut hair, that sparked the comparison: big as boulders, bearded, with ponytails that trailed down their backs, the two looked like prime meat for the pro wrestling circuit. One had a huge scar across his face, acquired before death, of course. The other had had some skin disease in his original life. They weren't just display items; they were absolutely lethal.

(By the way, some promoter had had the idea for a vampire wrestling circuit a couple of years before, but it went down in flames immediately. At the first match, one vamp had ripped another's arm off, on live TV. Vamps don't get the concept of exhibition fighting.)

These two vampires were hung with knives, and each had an ax in his belt. I guess they figured if someone had penetrated this far, guns weren't going to make a difference. Plus their own bodies were weapons.

"Bert, Bert," Chester said, nodding to each one in turn. "This here's the Stackhouse woman; the queen wants to see her."

He turned and walked away, leaving me with the queen's bodyguards.

Screaming didn't seem like a good idea, so I said, "I can't believe you both have the same name. Surely he made a mistake?"

Two pairs of brown eyes focused on me intently. "I am Sigebert," the scarred one said, with a heavy accent I couldn't identify. He said his name as *See-ya-bairt*. Chester was using a very Americanized version of what must be a very old name. "Dis my brodder, Wybert."

This is my brother, Way-bairt? "Hello," I said, trying not to twitch. "I'm Sookie Stackhouse."

They seemed unimpressed. Just then, one of the pinned vampires squeezed past, casting a look of scarcely veiled contempt at the brothers, and the atmosphere in the corridor became lethal. Sigebert and Wybert watched the vamp, a tall woman in a business suit, until she rounded a corner. Then their attention switched back to me.

"The queen is . . . busy," Wybert said. "When she wants you in her room, the light, it will shine." He indicated a round light set in the wall to the right of the door.

So I was stuck here for an indefinite time — until the light, it shone. "Do your names have a meaning? I'm guessing they're, um, early English?" My voice petered out.

"We were Saxons. Our fadder went from Germany to England, you call now," Wybert said. "My name mean Bright Battle."

"And mine, Bright Victory," Sigebert added.

I remembered a program I'd seen on the History Channel. The Saxons eventually became the Anglo-Saxons and later were overwhelmed by the Normans. "So you were raised to be warriors," I said, trying to look intelligent.

They exchanged glances. "There was nothing else," Sigebert said. The end of his scar wiggled when he talked, and I tried not to stare. "We were sons of war leader."

I could think of a hundred questions to ask them about their lives as humans, but standing in the middle of a hallway in an office building in the night didn't seem the time to do it. "How'd you happen to become vampires?" I asked. "Or is that a tacky question? If it is, just forget I said anything. I don't want to step on any toes."

Sigebert actually glanced down at his feet, so I got the idea that colloquial English wasn't their strong suit. "This woman . . . very beautiful . . . she come to us the night before battle," Wybert said haltingly. "She say . . . we be stronger if she . . . have us."

They looked at me inquiringly, and I nodded to show I understood that Wybert was saying the vampire had implied her interest was in bedding them. Or had they understood she meant to bleed them? I couldn't tell. I thought it was a mighty ambitious vampire who would take on these two humans at the same time.

"She did not say we only fight at night after that," Sigebert said, shrugging to show that there had been a catch they hadn't understood. "We did not ask plenty questions. We too eager!" And he smiled. Okay, nothing so scary as a vampire left with only his fangs. It was possible Sigebert had more teeth in the back of his mouth, ones I couldn't see from my height, but Chester's plentiful-though-crooked teeth had looked super in comparison.

"That must have been a very long time ago," I said, since I couldn't think of anything else to say. "How long have you worked for the queen?"

Sigebert and Wybert looked at each other. "Since that night," Wybert said, astonished I hadn't understood. "We are hers."

My respect for the queen, and maybe my fear of the queen, escalated. Sophie-Anne, if that was her real name, had been brave, strategic, and busy in her career as a vampire leader. She'd brought them over and kept them with her, in a bond that — the one whose name I wasn't going to speak even to myself — had explained to me was stronger than any other emotional tie, for a vampire.

To my relief, the light shone green in the wall.

Sigebert said, "Go now," and pushed open the heavy door. He and Wybert gave me matching nods of farewell as I walked over the threshold and into a room that was like any executive's office anywhere.

Sophie-Anne Leclerq, Queen of Louisiana, and a male vampire were sitting at a round table piled with papers. I'd met the queen once before, when she'd come to my place to tell me about my cousin's death. I hadn't noticed then how young she must have been when she died, maybe no more than fifteen. She was an elegant woman, perhaps four inches shorter than my height of five foot six, and she was groomed down to the last eyelash. Makeup, dress, hair, stockings, jewelry — the whole nine yards.

The vampire at the table with her was her male counterpart. He wore a suit that would have paid my cable bill for a year, and he was barbered and manicured and scented until he almost wasn't a guy any more. In my neck of the woods, I didn't often see men so groomed. I guessed this was the new king. I wondered if he'd died in such a state; actually, I wondered if the funeral home had cleaned him up like that for his funeral, not knowing that his descent below ground was only temporary. If that had been the case, he was younger than his queen. Maybe age wasn't the only requirement, if you were aiming to be royalty.

There were two other people in the room. A short man stood about three feet behind the queen's chair, his legs apart, his hands clasped in front of him. He had close-cut white-blond hair and bright blue eyes. His face lacked maturity; he looked like a large child, but with a man's shoulders. He was wearing a suit, and he was armed with a saber and a gun.

Behind the man at the table stood a woman, a vampire, dressed all in red; slacks, T-shirt, Converses. Her preference was unfortunate, because red was not her color. She was Asian, and I thought she'd come from Vietnam — though it had probably been called something else then. She had very short unpainted nails, and a terrifying sword strapped to her back. Apparently, her hair had been cut off at chin length by a pair of rusty scissors. Her face was the un-enhanced one God had given her.

Since I hadn't had a briefing on the correct protocol, I dipped my head to the queen, said, "Good to see you again, ma'am," and tried to look pleasantly at the king while doing the head-dip thing again. The two standees, who must be aides or bodyguards, received smaller nods. I felt like an idiot, but I didn't want to ignore them. However, they didn't have a problem with ignoring me, once they'd given me an all-over threat assessment.

"You've had some adventures in New

Orleans," the queen said, a safe lead-in. She wasn't smiling, but then I had the impression she was not a smiley kind of gal.

"Yes, ma'am."

"Sookie, this is my husband. Peter Threadgill, King of Arkansas." There was not a trace of affection on her face. She might as well have been telling me the name of her pet cockapoo.

"How-de-do," I said, and repeated my head-bob, adding, "Sir," hastily. Okay, already tired of this.

"Miss Stackhouse," he said, turning his attention back to the papers in front of him. The round table was large and completely cluttered with letters, computer printouts, and an assortment of other papers — bank statements?

While I was relieved not to be an object of interest to the king, I was wondering exactly why I was there. I found out when the queen began to question me about the night before. I told her as explicitly as I could what had happened.

She looked very serious when I talked about Amelia's stasis spell and what it had done to the body.

"You don't think the witch knew the body was there when she cast the spell?" the queen asked. I noticed that though the king's gaze was on the papers in front of him, he hadn't moved a one of them since I'd begun talking. Of course, maybe he was a very slow reader.

"No, ma'am. I know Amelia didn't know he was there."

"From your telepathic ability?"

"Yes, ma'am."

Peter Threadgill looked at me then, and I saw that his eyes were an unusual glacial gray. His face was full of sharp angles: a nose like a blade, thin straight lips, high cheekbones.

The king and the queen were both good-looking, but not in a way that struck any chord in me. I had an impression that the feeling was mutual. Thank God.

"You're the telepath that my dear Sophie wants to bring to the conference," Peter Threadgill said.

Since he was telling me something I already knew, I didn't feel the need to answer. But discretion won over sheer irritation. "Yes, I am."

"Stan has one," the queen said to her husband, as if vampires collected telepaths the way dog fanciers collected springer spaniels.

The only Stan I knew was a head vampire in Dallas, and the only other telepath I'd ever met had lived there. From the queen's few words, I guessed that Barry the Bellman's life had changed a lot since I'd met him. Apparently he worked for Stan Davis now. I didn't know if Stan was the sheriff or even a king, since at the time I hadn't been privy to the fact that vampires had such.

"So you're now trying to match your entourage to Stan's?" Peter Threadgill asked his wife, in a distinctly unfond kind of way. From the many clues thrown my way, I'd gotten the picture that this wasn't a love match. If you asked me to cast a vote, I would say it wasn't even a lust match. I knew the queen had liked my cousin Hadley in a lusty way, and the two brothers on guard had said she'd rocked their world. Peter Threadgill was nowhere near either side of that spectrum. But maybe that only proved the queen was omnisexual, if that was a word. I'd have to look it up when I went home. If I ever got home.

"If Stan can see the advantage in employing such a person, I can certainly consider it — especially since one is easily available."

I was in stock.

The king shrugged. Not that I had formed many expectations, but I would have anticipated that the king of a nice, poor, scenic state like Arkansas would be less sophisticated and folksier, with a sense of humor. Maybe Threadgill was a carpetbagger from New York City. Vampire accents tended to be all over the map — literally — so it was impossible to tell from his speech.

"So what do you think happened in Hadley's apartment?" the queen asked me, and I realized we'd reverted to the original subject.

"I don't know who attacked Jake Purifoy," I said. "But the night Hadley went to the graveyard with Waldo, Jake's drained body landed in her closet. As to how it came there, I couldn't say. That's why Amelia is having this ecto thing tonight."

The queen's expression changed; she actually looked interested. "She's having an ectoplasmic reconstruction? I've heard of those, but never witnessed one."

The king looked more than interested. For a split second, he looked extremely angry.

I forced my attention back to the queen. "Amelia wondered if you would care to, ah, fund it?" I wondered if I should add, "My lady," but I just couldn't bring myself to do it.

"That would be a good investment, since our newest vampire might have gotten us all into a great deal of trouble. If he had gotten loose on the populace . . . I will be glad to pay."

I drew a breath of sheer relief.

"And I think I'll watch, too," the queen added, before I could even exhale.

That sounded like the worst idea in the world. I thought the queen's presence would flatten Amelia until all the magic was squished out. However, there was no way I was going to tell the queen she was not welcome.

Peter Threadgill had looked up sharply when the queen had announced she'd watch. "I don't think you should go," he said, his voice smooth and authoritative. "It will be hard for the twins and Andre to guard you out in the city in a neighborhood like that."

I wondered how the King of Arkansas had any idea what Hadley's neighborhood was like. Actually, it was a quiet, middle-class area, especially compared to the zoo that was vampire central headquarters, with its constant stream of tourists and picketers and fanatics with cameras.

Sophie-Anne was already preparing to go out. That preparation consisted of glancing in a mirror to make sure the flawless façade was still flawless and sliding on her high, high heels, which had been below the edge of the table. She'd been sitting there barefoot. That detail suddenly made Sophie-Anne Leclerq much more real to me. There was a personality under that glossy exterior.

"I suppose you would like Bill to accompany us," the queen said to me.

"No," I snapped. Okay, there was a personality — and it was unpleasant and cruel.

But the queen looked genuinely startled. Her husband was outraged at my rudeness — his head shot up and his odd gray eyes fixed me with a luminous anger — but the queen was simply taken aback by my reaction. "I thought you were a couple," she said, in a perfectly even voice.

I bit back my first answer, trying to remember who I was talking to, and said, almost in a whisper, "No, we are not." I took a deep breath and made a great effort. "I apologize for being so abrupt. Please excuse me."

The queen simply looked at me for a few seconds longer, and I still could not get the slightest indication of her thoughts, emotions, or intentions. It was like looking at an antique silver tray — a shining surface, an elaborate pattern, and hard to the touch. How Hadley could have been adventurous enough to bed this woman was simply beyond my comprehension.

"You are excused," she said finally.

"You're too lenient," her husband said, and his surface, at least, began to thin somewhat. His lips curled in something closely approaching a snarl, and I discovered I didn't want to be the focus of those luminous eyes for another second. I didn't like the way the Asian gal in red was looking at me, either. And every time I looked at her haircut, it gave me the heebie-jeebies. Gosh, even the elderly lady who'd given my gran a permanent three times a year would have done a better job than the Mad Weed Whacker.

"I'll be back in an hour or two, Peter," Sophie-Anne said, very precisely, in a tone that could have sliced a diamond. The short man, his childish face blank, was by her side in a jiffy, extending his arm so she could have his assistance in rising. I guessed he was Andre.

The atmosphere was cuttable. Oh, I so wished I were somewhere else.

"I would feel more at ease if I knew Jade Flower was with you," the king said. He motioned toward the woman in red. Jade Flower, my ass: she looked more like Stone Killer. The Asian woman's face didn't change one iota at the king's offer.

"But that would leave you with no one,"

the queen said.

"Hardly true. The building is full of guards and loyal vampires," Peter Threadgill said.

Okay, even I caught that one. The guards, who belonged to the queen, were separate from the loyal vampires, whom I guessed were the ones Peter had brought with him.

"Then, of course, I would be proud to have a fighter like Jade Flower accompany me."

Yuck. I couldn't tell if the queen was serious, or trying to placate her new husband by accepting his offer, or laughing up her sleeve at his lame strategy to ensure that his spy was at the ectoplasmic reconstruction. The queen used the intercom to call down — or up, for all I knew — to the secure chamber where Jake Purifoy was being educated in the ways of the vampire. "Keep extra guards on Purifoy," she said. "And let me know the minute he remembers something." An obsequious voice assured Sophie-Anne that she'd be the first to know.

I wondered why Jake needed extra guards. I found it hard to get real concerned about his welfare, but obviously the queen was.

So here we went — the queen, Jade Flower, Andre, Sigebert, Wybert, and me. I guess I've been in company just as assorted, but I couldn't tell you when. After a lot of corridor tromping, we entered a guarded garage and piled into a stretch limo. Andre jerked his thumb at one of the guards, indicating that the guard should drive. I hadn't heard the baby-faced vampire utter a word, so far. To my pleasure, the driver was Rasul, who felt like an old friend compared to the others.

Sigebert and Wybert were uncomfortable in the car. They were the most inflexible vampires I'd ever met, and I wondered if their close association with the queen hadn't been their undoing. They hadn't had to change, and changing with the times was the key vampire survival technique before the Great Revelation. It remained so in countries that hadn't accepted the existence of vampire with the tolerance America had shown. The two vampires would have been happy wearing skins and hand-woven cloth and would have looked perfectly at home in handmade leather boots, carrying shields on their arms.

"Your sheriff, Eric, came to speak to me last night," the queen told me.

"I saw him at the hospital," I said, hoping I sounded equally offhanded.

"You understand that the new vampire, the one that was a Were — he had no choice, you understand?"

"I get that a lot with vampires," I said, remembering all the times in the past when Bill had explained things by saying he couldn't help himself. I'd believed him at the time, but I wasn't so sure any more. In fact, I was so profoundly tired and miserable I hardly had the heart to continue trying to wrap up Hadley's apartment and her estate and her affairs. I realized that if I went home to Bon Temps, leaving unfinished business here, I'd just sit and brood when I got there.

I knew this, but at the moment, it was hard to face.

It was time for one of my self-pep talks. I told myself sternly I'd already enjoyed a moment or two of that very evening, and I would enjoy a few more seconds of every day until I built back to my former contented state. I'd always enjoyed life, and I knew I would again. But I was going to have to slog through a lot of bad patches to get there.

I don't think I've ever been a person with a lot of illusions. If you can read minds, you don't have many doubts about how bad even the best people can be.

But I sure hadn't seen this coming.

To my horror, tears began sliding down

my face. I reached into my little purse, pulled out a Kleenex, and patted my cheeks while all the vamps stared at me, Jade Flower with the most identifiable expression I'd seen on her face: contempt.

"Are you in pain?" the queen asked, indicating my arm.

I didn't think she really cared; I was sure that she had schooled herself to give the correct human response for so long that it was a reflex.

"Pain of the heart," I said, and could have bitten my tongue off.

"Oh," she said. "Bill?"

"Yes," I said, and gulped, doing my best to stop the display of emotion.

"I grieved for Hadley," she said unexpectedly.

"It was good she had someone to care." After a minute I said, "I would have been glad to know she was dead earlier than I did," which was as cautiously as I could express it. I hadn't found out my cousin was gone until weeks after the fact.

"There were reasons I had to wait to send Cataliades down," Sophie-Anne said. Her smooth face and clear eyes were as impenetrable as a wall of ice, but I got the definite impression that she wished I hadn't raised the subject. I looked at the queen, trying to

331

pick up on some clue, and she gave a tiny flick of the eye toward Jade Flower, who was sitting on her right. I didn't know how Jade Flower could be sitting in her relaxed position with the long sword strapped to her back. But I definitely had the feeling that behind her expressionless face and flat eyes, Jade Flower was listening to everything that transpired.

To be on the safe side, I decided I wouldn't say anything at all, and the rest of the drive passed in silence.

Rasul didn't want to take the limo into the courtyard, and I recalled that Diantha had parked on the street, too. Rasul came back to open the door for the queen, and Andre got out first, looked around for a long time, then nodded that it was safe for the queen to emerge. Rasul stood at the ready, rifle in his hands, sweeping the area visually for attackers. Andre was just as vigilant.

Jade Flower slithered out of the backseat next and added her eyes to those scanning the area. Protecting the queen with their bodies, they moved into the courtyard. Sigebert got out next, ax in hand, and waited for me. After I'd joined him on the sidewalk, he and Wybert took me through the open gateway with less ceremony than the others had taken the queen.

I'd seen the queen at my own home, unguarded by anyone but Cataliades. I'd seen the queen in her own office, guarded by one person. I guess I didn't realize until that moment how important security was for Sophie-Anne, how precarious her hold on power must be. I wanted to know against whom all these guards were protecting her. Who wanted to kill the Louisiana queen? Maybe all vampire rulers were in this much danger — or maybe it was just Sophie-Anne. Suddenly the vampire conference in the fall seemed like a much scarier proposition than it had before.

The courtyard was well lit, and Amelia was standing on the circular driveway with three friends. For the record, none of them were crones with broomsticks. One of them was a kid who looked just like a Mormon missionary: black pants, white shirt, dark tie, polished black shoes. There was a bicycle leaning up against the tree in the center of the circle. Maybe he *was* a Mormon missionary. He looked so young that I thought he might still be growing. The tall woman standing beside him was in her sixties, but she had a Bowflex body. She was wearing a tight T-shirt, knit slacks, sandals, and a pair of huge hoop earrings. The third witch was about my age, in her mid-to late twenties, and she was Hispanic. She had full cheeks, bright red lips, and rippling black hair, and she was short and had more curves than an S turn. Sigebert admired her especially (I could tell by his leer), but she ignored all the vampires as if she couldn't see them.

Amelia might have been startled by the influx of vampires, but she handled introductions with aplomb. Evidently the queen had already identified herself before I approached. "Your Majesty," Amelia was saying, "These are my co-practitioners." She swept her hand before them as if she were showing off a car to the studio audience. "Bob Jessup, Patsy Sellers, Terencia Rodriguez — Terry, we call her."

The witches glanced at each other before nodding briefly to the queen. It was hard to tell how she took that lack of deference, her face was so glass-smooth — but she nodded back, and the atmosphere remained tolerable.

"We were just preparing for our reconstruction," Amelia said. She sounded absolutely confident, but I noticed that her hands were trembling. Her thoughts were not nearly as confident as her voice, either. Amelia was running over their preparations in her head, frantically itemizing the magic stuff she'd assembled, anxiously reassessing her companions to satisfy herself they were up to the ritual, and so on. Amelia, I belatedly realized, was a perfectionist.

I wondered where Claudine was. Maybe she'd seen the vamps coming and prudently fled to some dark corner. While I was looking around for her, I had a moment when the heartache I was staving off just plain ambushed me. It was like the moments I had after my grandmother died, when I'd be doing something familiar like brushing my teeth, and all of a sudden the blackness would overwhelm me. It took a moment or two to collect myself and swim back to the surface again.

It would be like that for a while, and I'd just have to grit my teeth and bear it.

I made myself take notice of those around me. The witches had assumed their positions. Bob settled himself in a lawn chair in the courtyard, and I watched with a tiny flare of interest as he drew powdered stuff from little snack-size Ziploc bags and got a box of matches out of his chest pocket. Amelia bounded up the stairs to the apartment, Terry stationed herself halfway down the stairs, and the tall older witch, Patsy, was already standing on the gallery looking down at us.

"If you all want to watch, probably up here would be best," Amelia called, and the queen and I went up the stairs. The guards gathered in a clump by the gate so they'd be as far away from the magic as they could be; even Jade Flower seemed respectful of the power that was about to be put to use, even if she did not respect the witches as people.

As a matter of course, Andre followed the queen up the stairs, but I thought there was a less than enthusiastic droop to his shoulders.

It was nice to focus on something new instead of mulling over my miseries, and I listened with interest as Amelia, who looked like she should be out playing beach volleyball, instead gave us instructions on the magic spell she was about to cast.

"We've set the time to two hours before I saw Jake arrive," she said. "So you may see a lot of boring and extraneous stuff. If that gets old, I can try to speed up the events."

Suddenly I had a thought that blinded me by its sheer serendipity. I would ask Amelia to return to Bon Temps with me, and there I would ask her to repeat this procedure in my yard; then I would know what had happened to poor Gladiola. I felt much better once I'd had this idea, and I made myself pay attention to the here and now.

Amelia called out "Begin!" and immediately began reciting words, I suppose in Latin. I heard a faint echo come up from the stairs and the courtyard as the other witches joined in.

We didn't know what to expect, and it was oddly boring to hear the chanting continue after a couple of minutes. I began to wonder what would happen to me if the queen got very bored.

Then my cousin Hadley walked into the living room.

I was so shocked, I almost spoke to her. When I looked for just a second longer, I could tell it wasn't really Hadley. It had the shape of her, and it moved like her, but this simulacrum was only washed with color. Her hair was not a true dark, but a glistening impression of dark. She looked like tinted water, walking. You could see the surface's shimmer. I looked at her eagerly: it had been so long since we'd seen each other. Hadley looked older, of course. She looked harder, too, with a sardonic set to her mouth and a skeptical look to her eyes.

Oblivious to the presence of anyone else in the room, the reconstruction went over to the loveseat, picked up a phantom remote control, and turned on the television. I actually glanced at the screen to see if it would show anything, but of course, it didn't.

I felt a movement beside me and I glanced at the queen. If I had been shocked, she was electrified. I had never really thought the queen could have truly loved Hadley, but I saw now that she had, as much as she was able.

We watched Hadley glance at the television from time to time while she painted her toenails, drank a phantom glass of blood, and made a phone call. We couldn't hear her. We could only see, and that within a limited range. The object she reached for would appear the minute her hand touched it, but not before, so you could be sure of what she had only when she began to use it. When she leaned forward to replace the glass of blood on the table, and her hand was still holding the glass, we'd see the glass, the table with its other objects, and Hadley, all at once, all with that glistening patina. The ghost table was imposed over the real table, which was still in almost exactly the same space as it had been that night, just to make it weirder. When Hadley let go of the glass, both glass and table winked out of existence.

Andre's eyes were wide and staring when I glanced back at him, and it was the most expression I'd seen on his face. If the queen was grieving and I was fascinated and sad, Andre was simply freaked out.

We stood through a few more minutes of this until Hadley evidently heard a knock at the door. (Her head turned toward the door, and she looked surprised.) She rose (the phantom loveseat, perhaps two inches to the right of the real one, became nonexistent) and padded across the floor. She stepped through my sneakers, which were sitting side by side next to the loveseat.

Okay, that was weird. This whole thing was weird, but fascinating.

Presumably the people in the courtyard had watched the caller come up the outside stairs, since I heard a loud curse from one of the Berts — Wybert, I thought. When Hadley opened a phantom door, Patsy, who'd been stationed outside on the gallery, pushed open the real door so we could see. From Amelia's chagrined face, I could tell she hadn't thought that one through ahead of time.

Standing at the door was (phantom) Waldo, a vampire who had been with the queen for years. He had been much punished in the years before his death, and it had left him with permanently wrinkled skin. Since Waldo had been an ultrathin albino before this punishment, he'd looked awful the one and only night I'd known him. As a watery ghost creature, he looked better, actually.

Hadley looked surprised to see him. That expression was strong enough to be easily recognizable. Then she looked disgusted. But she stepped back to let him in.

When she strolled back to the table to pick up her glass, Waldo glanced around him, as if to see if anyone else was there. The temptation to warn Hadley was so strong it was almost irresistible.

After some conversation, which of course we couldn't understand, Hadley shrugged and seemed to agree to some plan. Presumably, this was the idea Waldo had told me about the night he'd confessed to killing my cousin. He'd said it had been Hadley's idea to go to St. Louis Cemetery Number One to raise the ghost of voodooienne Marie Laveau, but from this evidence it seemed Waldo was the one who had suggested the excursion.

"What's that in his hand?" Amelia said, as quietly as she could, and Patsy stepped in from the gallery to check.

"Brochure," she called to Amelia, trying to use equally hushed tones. "About Marie Laveau."

Hadley looked at the watch on her wrist and said something to Waldo. It was something unkind, judging by Hadley's expression and the jerk of her head as she indicated the door. She was saying "No," as clearly as body language could say it.

And yet the next night she had gone with him. What had happened to change her mind?

Hadley walked back to her bedroom and we followed her. Looking back, we watched Waldo leave the apartment, putting the brochure on the table by the door as he departed.

It felt oddly voyeuristic to stand in Hadley's bedroom with Amelia, the queen, and Andre, watching Hadley take off a bathrobe and put on a very fancy dress.

"She wore that to the party the night before the wedding," the queen said quietly. It was a skintight, cut-down-to-here red dress decked with darker red sequins and some gorgeous alligator pumps. Hadley was going to make the queen regret what she was losing, evidently.

We watched Hadley primp in the mirror, do her hair two different ways, and mull her choice of lipsticks for a very long time. The novelty was wearing off the process, and I was willing to fast-forward, but the queen just couldn't get enough of seeing her beloved again. I sure wasn't going to protest, especially since the queen was footing the bill.

Hadley turned back and forth in front of her full-length mirror, appeared satisfied with what she saw, then burst into tears.

"Oh, my dear," the queen said quietly. "I am so sorry."

I knew *exactly* how Hadley felt, and for the first time I felt the kinship with my cousin I'd lost through the years of separation. In this reconstruction, it was the night before the queen's wedding, and Hadley was going to have to go to a party and watch the queen and her fiancé be a couple. And the next night she would have to attend their wedding; or so she thought. She didn't know that she'd be dead by then; finally, definitely dead.

"Someone coming up," called Bob the witch. His voice wafted through the open French windows onto the gallery. In the phantom, ghostly world, the doorbell must have rung, because Hadley stiffened, gave herself a last look in the mirror (right through us, since we were standing in front of it) and visibly braced herself. When Hadley walked down the hall, she had a familiar sway to her hips and her watery face was set in a cold half smile.

She pulled open the door. Since the witch Patsy had left the actual door open after Waldo had "arrived," we could see this happening. Jake Purifoy was dressed in a tux, and he looked very good, as Amelia had said. I glanced at Amelia when he stepped into the apartment, and she was eyeing the phantasm regretfully.

He didn't care for being sent to pick up the queen's honeybun, you could tell, but he was too politic and too courteous to take that out on Hadley. He stood patiently while she got a tiny purse and gave her hair a final combing, and then the two were out the door.

"Coming down out there," Bob called, and we went out the door and across the gallery to look over the railing. The two phantoms were getting into a glistening car and driving out of the courtyard. That was where the area affected by the spell came to an end. As the ghost car passed through the gate area, it winked out of existence right by the group of vampires who were clustered by the opening. Sigebert and Wybert were wide-eyed and solemn, Jade Flower appeared disgruntled, and Rasul looked faintly amused, as if he were thinking of the good stories he'd have to tell in the guards' mess hall.

"Time to fast-forward," Amelia called. She was looking tired now, and I wondered how great a strain coordinating this act of witch-craft was placing on the young witch.

Patsy, Terry, Bob, and Amelia began to say another spell in unison. If there was a weak link in this team effort, it was Terry. The round-faced little witch was sweating profusely and shaking with the effort of keeping her magical end up. I felt a little worried as I saw the strain on her face.

"Take it easy, easy!" Amelia exhorted her team, having read the same signs. Then they all resumed chanting, and Terry seemed to be pacing herself a bit better; she didn't look so desperate.

Amelia said, "Slow . . . down . . . now," and the chanting eased its pace.

The car appeared again in the gate, this time running right through Sigebert, who'd taken a step forward, the better to watch Terry, I suspected. It lurched to an abrupt stop half-in, half-out of the aperture.

Hadley threw herself out of the car. She was weeping, and from the looks of her face, she'd been weeping for some time. Jake Pu-rifoy emerged from his side and stood there, his hands on the top of his door, talking across the roof of the car at Hadley.

For the first time, the queen's personal bodyguard spoke. Andre said, "Hadley, you have to cut this out. People will notice, and the new king will do something about it. He's the jealous kind, you know? He doesn't care about —" Here Andre lost the thread, and shook his head. "He cares about keeping face."

We all stared at him. Was he channeling?

The queen's bodyguard switched his gaze to the ectoplasmic Hadley. Andre said, "But Jake, I can't stand it. I know she has to do this politically, but she's sending me away! I can't take it."

Andre could read lips. Even ectoplasmic lips. He began speaking again.

"Hadley, go up and sleep on it. You can't go to the wedding if you're going to create a scene. You know that would embarrass the queen, and it would ruin the ceremony. My boss will kill me if that happens. This is the biggest event we've ever worked."

He was talking about Quinn, I realized. Jake Purifoy *was* the employee Quinn had told me was missing.

"I can't stand it," Hadley repeated. She was shrieking, I could tell from the way her mouth moved, but luckily Andre saw no need to imitate that. It was eerie enough hearing the words come out of his mouth. "I've done something terrible!" The melodramatic words sounded very strange in Andre's monotone.

Hadley ran up the stairs, and Terry automatically moved out of the way to let her pass. Hadley unlocked the (already open) door and stormed into her apartment. We turned to watch Jake. Jake sighed, straightened up, and stepped away from the car, which vanished. He flipped open a cell phone and punched in a number. He spoke into the phone for less than a minute, with no pause for an answer, so it was safe to assume he'd gotten voice mail.

Andre said, "Boss, I have to tell you I think there's going to be trouble. The girlfriend won't be able to control herself on the day."

Oh my God, tell me Quinn didn't have Hadley killed! I thought, feeling absolutely sick at the thought. But even as the idea formed fully, Jake wandered over to the rear of the car, which appeared again as he brushed against it. He ran his hand lovingly along the line of the trunk, stepping closer and closer to the area outside the gate, and suddenly a hand reached out and grabbed him. The witches' area did not extend beyond the walls, so the rest of the body was absent, and the effect of a hand materializing from nowhere and seizing the unsuspecting Were was as scary as anything in a horror movie.

This was exactly like one of those dreams where you see danger approaching, but you can't speak. No warnings on our part could alter what had already happened. But we were all shocked. The brothers Bert cried out, Jade Flower drew her sword without my even seeing her hand move, and the queen's mouth fell open.

We could see only Jake's feet, thrashing. Then they lay still.

We all stood and looked at each other, even the witches, their concentration wavering until the courtyard began to fill with mist.

"Witches!" Amelia called harshly. "Back to work!" In a moment, everything had cleared up. But Jake's feet were still, and in a moment, their outline grew still more faint; he was fading out of sight like all the other lifeless objects. In a few seconds, though, my cousin appeared on the gallery above, looking down. Her expression was cautious and worried. She'd heard something. We registered the moment when she saw the body, and she came down the stairs with vampiric speed. She leaped through the gate and was lost to sight, but in a moment she was back in, dragging the body by the feet. As long as she was touching it, the body was visible as a table or chair would have been. Then she bent over the corpse, and now we could see that Jake had a huge wound in his neck. The wound was sickening, though I have to say that the vamps watching did not look sickened, but enthralled.

Ectoplasmic Hadley looked around her, hoping for help that didn't come. She looked desperately uncertain. Her fingers never left Jake's neck as she felt for his pulse.

Finally she bent over him and said something to him.

"It's the only way," Andre translated. "You may hate me, but it's the only way." We watched Hadley tear at her wrist with her own fangs and then put her bleeding wrist to Jake's mouth, watched the blood trickle inside, watched him revive enough to grip her arms and pull her down to him. When Hadley made Jake let go of her, she looked exhausted, and he looked as if he were having convulsions.

"The Were does not make a good vampire," Sigebert said in a whisper. "I've never before seen a Were brought over."

It was sure hard for poor Jake Purifoy. I began to forgive him the horror of the evening before, seeing his suffering. My cousin Hadley gathered him up and carried him up the stairs, pausing every now and then to look around her. I followed her up one more time, the queen right behind me. We watched Hadley pull off Jake's ripped clothes, wrap a towel around his neck until the bleeding stopped, and stow him in the closet, carefully covering him and closing the door so the morning sun wouldn't burn the new vampire, who would have to lie in the dark for three days. Hadley crammed the bloody towel into her hamper. Then she stuffed another towel into the open space at the bottom of the door, to make sure Jake was safe.

Then she sat in the hall and thought. Finally she got her cell phone and called a number.

"She asks for Waldo," Andre said. When Hadley's lips began moving again, Andre said, "She makes the appointment for the next night. She says she must talk to the ghost of Marie Laveau, if the ghost will really come. She needs advice, she says." After a little more conversation, Hadley shut her phone and got up. She gathered up the former Were's torn and bloody clothing and sealed it in a bag.

"You should get the towel, too," I advised,

in a whisper, but my cousin left it in the hamper for me to find when I arrived. Hadley got the car keys out of the trouser pockets, and when she went down the stairs, she got into the car and drove away with the garbage bag.

18

"Your Majesty, we have to stop," Amelia said, and the queen gave a flick of her hand that might have been agreement.

Terry was so exhausted she was leaning heavily against the railing of the stairs, and Patsy was looking almost as haggard out on the gallery. The nerdy Bob seemed unchanged, but then he'd wisely seated himself in a chair to start with. At Amelia's wordless signal, they began undoing the spell they'd cast, and gradually the eerie atmosphere lessened. We became an ill-assorted bunch of weird people in a courtyard in New Orleans, rather than helpless witnesses to a magical reenactment.

Amelia went to the corner storage shed and pulled out some folding chairs. Sigebert and Wybert did not understand the mechanism, so Amelia and Bob set the chairs out. After the queen and the witches sat, there was one remaining seat, and I took it after a silent to and fro between me and the four vampires.

"So we know what happened the next night," I said wearily. I was feeling a little silly in my fancy dress and high-heeled sandals. It would be nice to put on my regular clothes.

"Uh, 'scuse me, you might, but the rest of us don't, and we want to know," Bob said. He seemed oblivious to the fact that he ought to be shaking in his sandals in the queen's presence.

There was something kind of likable about the geeky witch. And all four had worked so hard; if they wanted to know the rest of the story, there wasn't any reason they couldn't hear it. The queen raised no objection. Even Jade Flower, who had resheathed her sword, looked faintly interested.

"The next night, Waldo lured Hadley to the cemetery with the story of the Marie Laveau grave and the vampire tradition that the dead can raise the dead — in this case, the voodoo priestess Marie Laveau. Hadley wanted Marie Laveau to answer her questions, which Waldo had told Hadley the ghost could, if the correct ritual was followed. Though Waldo gave me a reason Hadley agreed to do this on the night I met him, now I know he was lying. But I can think of several other reasons she might have agreed to go with Waldo to St. Louis Cemetery," I said. The queen nodded silently. "I think she wanted to find out what Jake would be like when he rose," I said. "I think she wanted to find out what to do with him. She couldn't let him die, you saw that, but she didn't want to admit to anyone that she had created a vampire, especially one that had been a Were."

I had quite an audience. Sigebert and Wybert were squatting on either side of the queen, and they were wrapped up in the story. This must be like going to the movies, for them. All the witches were interested in hearing the backstory on the events they'd just witnessed. Jade Flower had her eyes fixed on me. Only Andre seemed immune, and he was busy doing his bodyguard job, constantly scanning the courtyard and the sky for attack.

"It's possible, too, that Hadley might have believed the ghost could give her advice on how to regain the queen's affections. No offense, ma'am," I added, remembering too late that the queen was sitting three feet away from me in a folding lawn chair with the Wal-Mart price label still hanging on a plastic loop.

The queen waved her hand in a negligent

gesture. She was sunk in thought, so deeply that I wasn't even sure she heard me.

"It wasn't Waldo who drained Jake Purifoy," the queen said, to my amazement. "Waldo could not have imagined that when he succeeded in killing Hadley and reported it to me, blaming it on the Fellowship of the Sun, this clever witch would obey the order to seal the apartment very literally, including a stasis spell. Waldo already had a plan. Whoever killed Jake had a separate plan — perhaps to blame Hadley for Jake's death and his rebirth . . . which would condemn her to jail in a vampire cell. Perhaps the killer thought that Jake would kill Hadley when he rose in three days . . . and possibly, he would have."

Amelia tried to look modest, but it was an uphill battle. It should have been easy, since the only reason she'd cast the spell was to prevent the apartment from smelling like garbage when it finally was reopened. She knew it, and I knew it. But it had been a pretty piece of witchcraft, and I wasn't about to burst her bubble.

Amelia burst it all by herself.

"Or maybe," she said blithely, "someone paid Waldo to get Hadley out of the picture, by one means or another."

I had to shut down my shields immediately, because all the witches began broadcasting such strong panic signals that being around them was unbearable. They knew that what Amelia had said would upset the queen, and when the Queen of Louisiana was agitated, those around her tended to be even more agitated.

The queen shot out of her chair, so we all scrambled to our feet, hastily and clumsily. Amelia had just gotten her legs tucked underneath her, so she was especially awkward, which served her right. Jade Flower took a couple steps away from the rest of the vampires, but maybe she wanted more room in case she had to swing her sword. Andre was the only one who noticed that, besides me. He kept his gaze fixed on the king's bodyguard.

I don't know what would have happened next if Quinn hadn't driven through the gate.

He got out of the big black car, ignored the tense tableau as if it didn't even exist, and strode across the gravel to me. He casually draped an arm over my shoulders and bent to give me a light kiss. I don't know how to compare one kiss to another. Men all kiss differently, don't they? And it says something about their character. Quinn kissed me as if we were carrying on a conversation.

"Babe," he said, when I'd had the last word. "Did I get here at a good time? What happened to your arm?"

The atmosphere relaxed a bit. I introduced him to the people standing in the courtyard. He knew all the vampires, but he hadn't met the witches. He moved away from me to meet and greet. Patsy and Amelia had obviously heard of him and tried hard not to act too impressed at meeting him.

I had to get the rest of the evening's news off my chest. "My arm got bitten, Quinn," I began. Quinn waited, his eyes intent on my face. "I got bitten by a . . . I'm afraid we know what happened to your employee. His name was Jake Purifoy, wasn't it?" I said.

"What?" In the bright lights of the courtyard, I saw that his expression was guarded. He knew something bad was coming; of course, seeing the assembled company, anyone would guess that.

"He was drained and left here in the courtyard. To save his life, Hadley turned him. He's become a vampire."

Quinn didn't comprehend, for a few seconds. I watched as realization dawned as he grasped the enormity of what had happened to Jake Purifoy. Quinn's face became stony. I found myself hoping he never looked at me like that.

"The change was without the Were's consent," the queen said. "Of course, a Were would never agree to become one of us." If she sounded a little snarky, I wasn't too surprised. Weres and vamps regarded each other with scarcely concealed disgust, and only the fact that they were united against the normal world kept that disgust from flaring into open warfare.

"I went by your house," Quinn said to me, unexpectedly. "I wanted to see if you'd gotten back from New Orleans before I drove down here to look for Jake. Who burned a demon in your driveway?"

"Someone killed Gladiola, the queen's messenger, when she came to deliver a message to me," I said. There was a stir among the vampires around me. The queen had known about Gladiola's death, of course; Mr. Cataliades would have been sure to tell her. But no one else had heard about it.

"Lots of people dying in your yard, babe," Quinn said to me, though his tone was absent, and I didn't blame him for that being on his back burner.

"Just two," I said defensively, after a quick mental rundown. "I would hardly call that a lot." Of course, if you threw in the people who'd died in the house . . . I quickly shut off that train of thought.

"You know what?" Amelia said in a high, artificially social voice. "I think we witches will just mosey on down the street to that pizza place on the corner of Chloe and Justine. So if you need us, there we'll be. Right, guys?" Bob, Patsy, and Terry moved faster than I'd thought they were able to the gate opening, and when the vampires didn't get any signal from their queen, they stood aside and let them by. Since Amelia didn't bother retrieving her purse, I hoped she had money in one pocket and her keys in another. Oh well.

I almost wished I were trailing along behind them. Wait a minute! Why couldn't I? I looked longingly at the gate, but Jade Flower stepped into the gap and stared at me, her eyes black holes in her round face. This was a woman who didn't like me one little bit. Andre, Sigebert, and Wybert could definitely take me or leave me, and Rasul might think I wouldn't be a bad companion for an hour on the town — but Jade Flower would enjoy whacking off my head with her sword, and that was a fact. I couldn't read vampire minds (except for a tiny glimpse every now and then, which was a big secret) but I could read body language and I could read the expression in her eyes.

I didn't know the reason for this animosity, and at this point in time I didn't think it mattered a heck of a lot.

The queen had been thinking. She said, "Rasul, we shall go back to the house very shortly." He bowed and walked out to the car.

"Miss Stackhouse," she said, turning her eyes on me. They shone like dark lamps. She took my hand, and we went up the stairs to Hadley's apartment, Andre trailing behind us like something tied to Sophie-Anne's leg with string. I kept having the unwise impulse to yank my hand from the queen's, which of course was cold and dry and strong, though she was careful not to squeeze. Being so close to the ancient vampire made me vibrate like a violin string. I didn't see how Hadley had endured it.

She led me into Hadley's apartment and shut the door behind us. I didn't think even the excellent ears of the vampires below us could hear our conversation now. That had been her goal, because the first thing she said was, "You will not tell anyone what I am about to tell you."

I shook my head, mute with apprehension.

"I began my life in what became northern France, about . . . one thousand, one hundred years ago."

I gulped.

"I didn't know where I was, of course, but I think it was Lotharingia. In the last century I tried to find the place I spent my first twelve years, but I couldn't, even if my life depended on it." She gave a barking laugh at the turn of phrase. "My mother was the wife of the wealthiest man in the town, which meant he had two more pigs than anyone else. My name then was Judith."

I tried hard not to look shocked, to just look interested, but it was a struggle.

"When I was about ten or twelve, I think, a peddler came to us from down the road. We hadn't seen a new face in six months. We were excited." But she didn't smile or look as if she remembered the feeling of that excitement, only the fact of it. Her shoulders rose and fell, once. "He carried an illness that had never come to us before. I think now that it was some form of influenza. Within two weeks of his stay in our town, everyone in it was dead, excepting me and a boy somewhat older."

There was a moment of silence while we thought about that. At least I did, and I suppose the queen was remembering. Andre might have been thinking about the price of bananas in Guatemala.

"Clovis did not like me," the queen said. "I've forgotten why. Our fathers . . . I don't remember. Things might have gone differently if he had cared for me. As it was, he raped me and then he took me to the next town, where he began offering me about. For money, of course, or food. Though the influenza traveled across our region, we never got sick."

I tried to look anywhere but at her.

"Why will you not meet my eyes?" she demanded. Her phrasing and her accent had changed as she spoke, as if she'd just learned English.

"I feel so bad for you," I said.

She made a sound that involved putting her top teeth on her lower lip and making the extra effort to intake some air so she could blow it out. It sounded like *"ffft!"*

"Don't bother," the queen said. "Because what happened next was, we were camped in the woods, and a vampire got him." She looked pleased at the recollection. What a trip down memory lane. "The vampire was very hungry and started on Clovis first, because he was bigger, but when he was through with Clovis, he could take a minute to look at me and think it might be nice to have a companion. His name was Alain. For three years or more I traveled with Alain. Vampires were secret then, of course. Their existence was only in stories told by old women by the fire. And Alain was good at keeping it that way. Alain had been a priest, and he was very fond of surprising priests in their beds." She smiled reminiscently.

I found my sympathy diminishing.

"Alain promised and promised to bring me over, because of course I wanted to be as he was. I wanted the strength." Her eyes flicked over to me.

I nodded heartily. I could understand that.

"But when he needed money, for clothes and food for me, he would do the same thing with me that Clovis had, sell me for money. He knew the men would notice if I was cold, and he knew I would bite them if he brought me over. I grew tired of his failing in his promise."

I nodded to show her I was paying attention. And I was, but in the back of my mind I was wondering where the hell this monologue was heading and why I was the recipient of such a fascinating and depressing story.

"Then one night we came into a village where the head-man knew Alain for what he was. Stupid Alain had forgotten he had passed through before and drained the headman's wife! So the villagers bound him with a silver chain, which was amazing to find in a small village, I can tell you . . . and they threw him into a hut, planning to keep him until the village priest returned from a trip. Then they meant to put him in the sun with some church ceremony. It was a poor village, but on top of him they piled all the bits of silver and all the garlic the people possessed, in an effort to keep him subdued." The queen chuckled.

"They knew I was a human, and they knew he had abused me," she said. "So they didn't tie me up. The headman's family discussed taking me as a slave, since they had lost a woman to the vampire. I knew what that would be like."

The expression on her face was both heartbreaking and absolutely chilling. I held very still.

"That night, I pulled out some weak planks from the rear of the hut and crawled in. I told Alain that when he'd brought me over, I'd free him. We bargained for quite a time, and then he agreed. I dug a hole in the floor, big enough for my body. We planned that Alain would drain me and bury me under the pallet he lay on, smoothing the dirt floor over as best he could. He could move enough for that. On the third night, I would rise. I would break his chain and toss away the garlic, though it would burn my hands. We would flee into the darkness." She laughed out loud. "But the priest returned before three days were up. By the time I clawed my way out of the dirt, Alain was blackened ash in the wind. It was the priest's hut they'd stored Alain in. The old priest was the one who told me what had happened."

I had a feeling I knew the punch line to this story. "Okay," I said quickly, "I guess the priest was your first meal." I smiled brightly.

"Oh, no," said Sophie-Anne, formerly Judith. "I told him I was the angel of death, and that I was passing him over since he had been so virtuous."

Considering the state Jake Purifoy had been in when he'd risen for the first time, I could appreciate what a gut-wrenching effort that must have been for the new vampire.

"What did you do next?" I asked.

"After a few years, I found an orphan like me; roaming in the woods, like me," she said, and turned to look at her bodyguard. "We've been together ever since."

And I finally saw an expression in Andre's unlined face: utter devotion.

"He was being forced, like I had been," she said gently. "And I took care of that."

I felt a cold shiver run down my spine. I couldn't have picked something to say if you had paid me.

"The reason I've bored you with my ancient history," the queen said, shaking herself and sitting up even straighter, "is to tell you why I took Hadley under my wing. She, too, had been molested, by her great-uncle. Did he molest you, too?"

I nodded. I'd had no idea he'd gotten to Hadley. He hadn't progressed to actual penetration, only because my parents had died and I'd gone to live with my grand-mother. My parents hadn't believed me, but I'd convinced my grandmother I was telling the truth by the time he would have felt I was ripe, when I was about nine. Of course, Hadley had been older. We'd had much more in common than I'd ever thought. "I'm sorry, I didn't know," I said. "Thanks for telling me."

"Hadley talked about you often," the queen said.

Yeah, thanks, Hadley. Thanks for setting me up for the worst . . . no, wait, that was unfair. Finding out about Bill's massive deception was *not* the worst thing that had ever happened to me. But it wasn't too far down on my personal list, either.

"That's what I've found out," I said, my voice as cold and crisp as a celery stick.

"You are upset that I sent Bill to investigate you, to find out if you could be of use to me," the queen said.

I took a deep breath, forced my teeth to unclench. "No, I'm not upset with you. You can't help being the way you are. And you didn't even know me." Another deep breath. "I'm *upset* with Bill, who *did* know me and went ahead with your whole program in a very thorough and calculated way." I had to drive away the pain. "Besides, why would you care?" My tone was bordering on insolent, which was not wise when you're dealing with a powerful vampire. She'd touched me in a very sore spot.

"Because you were dear to Hadley," Sophie-Anne said unexpectedly.

"You wouldn't have known it from the way she treated me, after she became a teenager," I said, having apparently decided that reckless honesty was the course to follow.

"She was sorry for that," the queen said, "once she became a vampire, especially, and found out what it was like to be a minority. Even here in New Orleans, there is prejudice. We talked about her life often, when we were alone."

I didn't know which made me more uncomfortable, the idea of the queen and my cousin Hadley having sex, or having pillow talk about me afterward.

I don't care if consenting adults have sex, no matter what that sex consists of, as long as both parties agree beforehand. But I don't necessarily need to hear any details, either. Any prurient interest I might have had has been flooded over the years with images from the minds of the people in the bar.

This was turning out to be a long conversation. I wanted the queen to get to the point.

"The point is," the queen said, "I am grateful that you — through the witches — gave me a better idea of how Hadley died. And also you have let me know there is a wider plot against me than just Waldo's jealous heart."

I had?

"So I am in your debt. Tell me what I can do for you now."

"Ah. Send over a lot of boxes so I can pack up Hadley's stuff and get back to Bon Temps? Get someone to take the stuff I don't want to a charity drop-off?"

The queen looked down, and I swear she

was smothering a smile. "Yes, I think I can do that," she said. "I'll send some human over tomorrow to do those things."

"If someone could pack the stuff I want into a van and drive it up to Bon Temps, that would be real good," I said. "Maybe I could ride back in that van?"

"Also not a problem," she said.

Now for the big favor. "Do I actually have to go with you to this conference thing?" I asked, which I knew was kind of pushing it.

"Yes," she said.

Okay, stonewall there.

She added, "But I'll pay you handsomely."

I brightened. Some of the money I'd gotten for my previous vampire services was still in my savings account, and I'd gotten a big financial break when Tara "sold" me her car for a dollar, but I was so used to living close to the financial bone that a cushion was always welcome. I was always scared I'd break my leg, or my car would throw a rod, or my house would burn down . . . wait, that had already happened . . . well, that some disaster would happen, like a high wind would blow off the stupid tin roof my grandmother had insisted on, or something.

"Did you want something of Hadley's?" I asked her, my train of thought having veered away from money. "You know, a remem-brance?"

Something flashed in her eyes, something that surprised me.

"You took the words right out of my mouth," said the queen, with an adorable hint of a French accent.

Uh-oh. It couldn't be good that she'd switched on the charm.

"I did ask Hadley to hide something for me," she said. My bullshit meter was beeping like an alarm clock. "And if you come across it in your packing, I'd like to have it back."

"What does it look like?"

"It's a jewel," she said. "My husband gave it to me as an engagement gift. I happened to leave it here before I got married."

"You're welcome to look in Hadley's jewelry box," I said immediately. "If it belongs to you, of course you have to have it back."

"That's very kind of you," she said, her face back to its regular glassy smoothness. "It's a diamond, a large diamond, and it's fixed on a platinum bracelet."

I didn't remember anything like that in Hadley's stuff, but I hadn't looked care-fully. I'd planned to pack Hadley's jewelry box intact so I could pick through it at my leisure in Bon Temps.

"Please, look now," I suggested. "I know that it would be like a faux pas to lose a present from your husband."

"Oh," she said gently, "you have no idea." Sophie-Anne closed her eyes for just a second, as if she were too anxious for words. "Andre," she said, and with that word he took off for the bedroom — didn't need any directions, I noticed — and while he was gone, the queen looked oddly incomplete. I wondered why he hadn't accompanied her to Bon Temps, and on an impulse, I asked her.

She looked at me, her crystalline eyes wide and blank. "I was not supposed to be gone," she said. "I knew if Andre showed himself in New Orleans, everyone would assume I was here, too." I wondered if the reverse would be true. If the queen was here, would everyone assume Andre was, also? And that sparked a thought in me, a thought that had gone before I could quite grasp hold of it.

Andre came back at that moment, the tiniest shake of his head telling the queen he hadn't found what she wanted to reclaim. For a moment, Sophie-Anne looked quite unhappy. "Hadley did this in a minute of anger," the queen said, and I thought she was talking to herself. "But she may bring me down from beyond the veil." Then her face relaxed into its usual emotionless state.

"I'll keep an eye open for the bracelet," I said. I suspected that the value of the jewelry did not lie in its appraisal. "Would that bracelet have been left here the last night before the wedding?" I asked cautiously.

I suspected my cousin Hadley had stolen the bracelet from the queen out of sheer pique that the queen was getting married. That seemed like a Hadley thing to do. If I'd known about Hadley's concealment of the bracelet, I would have asked the witches to roll the clock back on the ectoplasmic reconstruction. We could have watched Hadley hide the thing.

The queen gave one short nod. "I must have it back," the queen said. "You understand, it's not the value of the diamond that concerns me? You understand, a wedding between vampire rulers is not a love match, where much can be forgiven? To lose a gift from your spouse, that's a very grave offense. And our spring ball is scheduled for two nights from now. The king expects to see me wearing his gifts. If I'm not . . ." Her voice trailed away, and even Andre looked almost worried.

"I'm getting your point," I said. I'd noticed

the tension already rolling through the halls at Sophie's headquarters. There'd be hell to pay, and Sophie-Anne would be the one to pay it. "If it's here, you'll get it back. Okay?" I spread my hands, asking her if she believed me.

"All right," she said. "Andre, I can't spend any more time here. Jade Flower will report the fact that I came up here with Sookie. Sookie, we must pretend to have had sex."

"Sorry, anyone who knows me knows I don't do women. I don't know who you expect Jade Flower's reporting to . . ." (Of course I did, and that would be the king, but it didn't seem tactful to say "I know your business," just then.) "But if they've done any homework, that's just a fact about me."

"Perhaps you had sex with Andre, then," she said calmly. "And you let me watch."

I thought of several questions, the first one being, "Is that the usual procedure with you?" followed by, "It's not okay to misplace a bracelet, but okay to bump pelvises with someone else?" But I clamped my mouth shut. If someone were holding a gun to my head, I'd actually have to vote for having sex with the queen rather than with Andre, no matter what my gender preference, because Andre creeped me out big-time.

But if we were just pretending . . .

In a businesslike way, Andre removed his tie, folded it, put it in his pocket, and undid a few shirt buttons. He beckoned to me with a crook of his fingers. I approached him warily. He took me in his arms and held me close, pressed against him, and bent his head to my neck. For a second I thought he was going _____ re of absolu_____ aled. That's _____

"Put _____ said, after a _____ pstick will tr_____

I did as he told me. He was cold as ice. This _____ was like . . . well, this was weird. I thought of the picture-taking session with Claude; I'd spent a lot of time lately *pretending* to have sex.

"I love the smell of fairy. Do you think she knows she has fairy blood?" he asked Sophie-Anne, while I was in the process of transferring my lipstick.

My head snapped back then. I stared right into his eyes, and he stared right back at me. He was still holding me, and I understood that he was ensuring I would smell like him and he would smell like me, as if we'd actually done the deed. He definitely wasn't up for the real thing, which was a relief.

"I what?" I hadn't heard him correctly, I was sure. "I have what?"

"He has a nose for it," the queen said. "My Andre." She looked faintly proud.

"I was hanging around with my friend Claudine earlier in the day," I said. "She's a fairy. That's where the smell is coming from." I really must need to shower.

"You permit?" Andre asked, and without waiting for an answer, he jabbed my wounded arm with a fingernail, right above the bandage.

"Yow!" I said in protest.

He let a little blood trickle onto his finger, and he put it in his mouth. He rolled it around, as if it were a sip of wine, and at last he said, "No, this smell of fairy is not from association. It's in your blood." Andre looked at me in a way that was meant to tell me that his words made it a done deal. "You have a little streak of fairy. Maybe your grandmother or your grandfather was half-fey?"

"I don't know anything about it," I said, knowing I sounded stupid, but not knowing what else to say. "If any of my grandparents were other than a hundred percent human, they didn't pass that information along."

"No, they wouldn't," the queen said, matter-of-factly. "Most humans of fairy descent hide the fact, because they don't really believe it. They prefer to think their parents are mad." She shrugged. Inexplicable! "But that blood would explain why you have supernatural suitors and not human admirers."

"I don't have human admirers because I don't want 'em," I said, definitely piqued. "I can read their minds, and that just knocks them out of the running. If they're not put off from the get-go by my reputation for weirdness," I added, back into my too-much-honesty groove.

"It's a sad comment on humans that none of them are tolerable to one who can read their minds," the queen said.

I guess that was the final word on the value of mind-reading ability. I decided it would be better to stop the conversation. I had a lot to think about.

We went down the stairs, Andre leading, the queen next, and me trailing behind. Andre had insisted I take off my shoes and my earrings so it could be inferred that I had undressed and then just slipped back into the dress.

The other vampires were waiting obediently in the courtyard, and they sprang to attention when we began making our way down. Jade Flower's face didn't change at all when she read all the clues as to what we'd been up to in the past half hour, but at least she didn't look skeptical. The Berts looked knowing but uninterested, as if the scenario of Sophie-Anne watching her bodyguard engaging in sex (with a virtual stranger) were very much a matter of routine.

As he stood in the gateway waiting for further driving instructions, Rasul's face expressed a mild ruefulness, as if he wished he had been included in the action. Quinn, on the other hand, was pressing his mouth in such a grim line that you couldn't have fed him a straight pin. There was a fence to mend.

But as we'd walked out of Hadley's apartment, the queen had told me specifically not to share her story with anyone else, emphasis on the *anyone.* I would just have to think of a way to let Quinn know, without letting him *know.*

With no discussion or social chitchat, the vampires piled into their car. My brain was so crowded with ideas and conjectures and everything in between that I felt punch-drunk. I wanted to call my brother, Jason, and tell him he wasn't so irresistible after all, it was the fairy blood in him, just to see what he'd say. No, wait, Andre had implied that humans weren't affected by the nearness of fairies like vampires were. That is, humans didn't want to consume fairies, but did find them sexually attractive. (I thought of the crowd that always surrounded Claudine at Merlotte's.) And Andre had said that other supernaturals were attracted by fairy blood too, just not in the eat-'em-up way that vamps were. Wouldn't Eric be relieved? He would be so glad to know he didn't really love me! It was the fairy blood all along!

I watched the royal limo drive away. While I was fighting a wave compounded of about six different emotions, Quinn was fighting only one.

He was right in front of me, his face angry. "How'd she talk you into it, Sookie?" he asked. "If you'd yelled, I'd have been right up there. Or maybe you wanted to do that? I would have sworn you weren't the type."

"I haven't gone to bed with anyone this evening," I said. I looked him straight in the eyes. After all, this wasn't revealing anything the queen had told me, this was just . . . correcting an error. "It's fine if others think that," I said carefully. "Just not you."

He looked down at me for a long moment, his eyes searching mine as if he were reading some writing on the back of my eyeballs.

"Would you *like* to go to bed with someone this evening?" he asked. He kissed me. He kissed me for a long, long time, as we stood glued together in the courtyard. The witches did not return; the vampires stayed gone. Only the occasional car going by in the street or a siren heard in the distance reminded me we were in the middle of a city. This was as different from being held by Andre as I could imagine. Quinn was warm, and I could feel his muscles move beneath his skin. I could hear him breathe, and I could feel his heartbeat. I could sense the churn of his thoughts, which were mostly now centered on the bed he knew must be somewhere upstairs in Hadley's apartment. He loved the smell of me, the touch of me, the way my lips felt . . . and a large part of Quinn was attesting to that fact. That large part was pressed between us right at this very moment.

I'd gone to bed with two other males, and both times it hadn't worked out well. I hadn't known enough about them. I'd acted on impulse. You should learn from your mistakes. For a second, I wasn't feeling especially smart.

Luckily for my decision-making ability, Quinn's phone chose that moment to ring.

God bless that phone. I'd been within an ace of chucking my good resolutions right out the window, because I'd been scared and lonely throughout the evening, and Quinn felt relatively familiar and he wanted me so much.

Quinn, however, was not following the same thought processes — far from it — and he cursed when the phone rang a second time.

"Excuse me," he said, fury in his voice, and answered the damn phone.

"All right," he said, after listening for a moment to the voice on the other end. "All right, I'll be there."

He snapped the tiny phone shut. "Jake is asking for me," he said.

I was so at sea with a strange combination of lust and relief that it took me a moment to connect the dots. Jake Purifoy, Quinn's employee, was experiencing his second night as a vampire. Having been fed some volunteer, he was enough himself to want to talk to Quinn. He'd been in suspended animation in a closet for weeks, and there was a lot he would need to catch up on.

"Then you have to go," I said, proud that my voice was practically rock steady. "Maybe he'll remember who attacked him. Tomorrow, I have to tell you about what I saw here tonight."

"Would you have said yes?" he asked. "If we'd been undisturbed for another minute?"

I considered for a minute. "If I had, I would've been sorry I did," I said. "Not because I don't want you. I do. But I had my eyes opened in the past couple of days. I know that I'm pretty easy to fool." I tried to sound matter-of-fact, not pitiful, when I said that. No one likes a whiny woman, least of all me. "I'm not interested in starting that up with someone who's just horny at the moment. I never set out to be a one-night-stand kind of woman. I want to be sure, if I have sex with you, that it's because you want to be around for a while and because you like me for who I am, not what I am."

Maybe a million women had made approximately the same speech. I meant it as sincerely as any one of those million.

And Quinn gave a perfect answer. "Who would want just one night with you?" he said, and then he left.

19

I slept the sleep of the dead. Well, probably not, but as close as a human would ever come. As if in a dream, I heard the witches come carousing back into the courtyard. They were still congratulating one another with alcohol-lubricated vigor. I'd found some real, honest cotton sheets among the linens (Why are they still called linens? Have you seen a linen sheet in your life?) and I'd tossed the black silky ones into the washer, so it was very easy to slip back into sleep.

When I got up, it was after ten in the morning. There was a knocking at the door, and I stumbled down the hall to unlock it after I'd pulled on a pair of Hadley's spandex exercise pants and a hot pink tank top. I saw boxes through the peephole, and I opened the door feeling really happy.

"Miss Stackhouse?" said the young black man who was holding the flattened boxes. When I nodded, he said, "I got orders to bring you as many boxes as you want. Will thirty do to start with?"

"Oh, yes," I said. "Oh, that'll be great."

"I also got instructions," he said precisely, "to bring you anything related to moving that you might need. I have here strapping tape, masking tape, some Magic Markers, scissors, and stick-on labels."

The queen had given me a personal shopper.

"Did you want colored dots? Some people like to put living room things in boxes with an orange dot, bedroom things in boxes with a green dot, and so on."

I had never moved, unless you counted taking a couple of bags of clothes and towels over to Sam's furnished duplex after the kitchen burned, so I didn't know the best way to go about it. I had an intoxicating vision of rows of neat boxes with colored dots on each side, so there couldn't be any mistake from any angle. Then I snapped back to reality. I wouldn't be taking that much back to Bon Temps. It was hard to form an estimate, since this was unknown territory, but I knew I didn't want much of the furniture.

"I don't think I'll need the dots, thanks anyway," I said. "I'll start working on these boxes, and then I can call you if I need any more, okay?"

"I'll assemble them for you," he said. He had very short hair and the curliest eyelashes I'd ever seen on a person. Cows had eyelashes that pretty, sometimes. He was wearing a golf-type shirt and neatly belted khakis, along with high-end sneakers.

"I'm sorry, I didn't catch your name," I said, as he whipped a roll of strapping tape from a large lumpy plastic shopping bag. He set to work.

"Oh, 'scuse me," he said, and it was the first time he'd sounded natural. "My name is Everett O'Dell Smith."

"Pleasure to meet you," I said, and he paused in his work so we could shake hands. "How did you come to be here?"

"Oh, I'm in Tulane Business School, and one of my professors got a call from Mr. Cataliades, who is, like, *the* most famous lawyer in the vampire area. My professor specializes in vampire law. Mr. Cataliades needed a day person; I mean, he can come out in the day, but he needed someone to be his gofer." He'd gotten three boxes done, already.

"And in return?"

"In return, I get to sit in court with him on his next five cases, and I get to earn some money I need real bad."

"Will you have time this afternoon to take me to my cousin's bank?"

"Sure will."

"You're not missing a class now, are you?"

"Oh, no, I got two hours before my second class."

He'd already been to a class and accumulated all this stuff before I'd even gotten up. Well, he hadn't been up half the night watching his dead cousin walk around.

"You can take these garbage bags of clothes to the nearest Goodwill or Salvation Army store." That would clear the gallery and make me feel productive all at the same time. I'd gone over the garments quite carefully to make sure Hadley hadn't hidden anything in them, and I wondered what the Salvation Army would make of them. Hadley had been into Tight and Skimpy; that was the nicest way to put it.

"Yes, ma'am," he said, whipping out a notebook and scribbling in it. Then he waited attentively. "Anything else?" he prompted me.

"Yes, there's no food in the house. When you come back this afternoon, can you bring me something to eat?" I could drink tap water, but I couldn't create food out of nothing.

Just then a call from the courtyard made

me look over the railing. Quinn was down there with a bag of something greasy. My mouth began watering.

"Looks like the food angle is covered," I told Everett, waving Quinn up.

"What can I do to help?" Quinn asked. "It struck me your cousin might not have coffee and food, so I brought some beignets and some coffee so strong it'll make you grow hair on your chest."

I'd heard that quite a few times, but it still made me smile. "Oh, that's my goal," I said. "Bring it on. There's actually coffee here, but I didn't have a chance to make it because Everett here is such a take-charge kind of guy."

Everett smiled up from his tenth box. "You know that's not true, but it's good to hear you say it," he said. I introduced the two men, and after Quinn handed me my bag, he began to help Everett assemble boxes. I sat at the glass-topped dining table and ate every crumb of the beignets that were in the bag and drank every drop of the coffee. I got powdered sugar all over me, and I didn't care a bit. Quinn turned to look at me and tried to hide his smile. "You're wearing your food, babe," he said.

I looked down at the tank top. "No hair on my chest, though," I said, and he said,

"Can I check?"

I laughed and went to the back to brush my teeth and hair, both essential tasks. I checked out Hadley's clothes that I'd wriggled into. The black spandex workout pants came to midthigh. Hadley probably had never worn them, because they would have been too big, to her taste. On me, they were very snug, but not the snug Hadley liked, where you could count the . . . oh, never mind. The hot pink tank top left my pale pink bra straps showing, to say nothing of a couple of inches of my middle, but thanks to Peck's Tan-a-Lot (located inside Peck's Bunch-o-Flicks, a video rental place in Bon Temps), that middle was nice and brown. Hadley would have put a piece of jewelry in her belly button. I looked at myself in the mirror, trying to picture myself with a gold stud or something. Nah. I slipped on some sandals decorated with crystal beads and felt quite glamorous for about thirty seconds.

I began talking to Quinn about what I planned to do that day, and rather than yell, I stepped from the bedroom into the hall with my brush and my elastic band. I bent over at the waist, brushed my hair while I was inverted, and gathered it into a ponytail on top of my head. I was sure it was centered, because the movements were just automatic after all these years. My ponytail came down past my shoulder blades now. I looped the band, ran the ponytail through, and I straightened, ponytail flying back over my shoulders to bounce in the middle. Quinn and Everett had stopped their task to stare. When I looked back at them, the two men hastily bent back to their tasks.

Okay, I didn't get that I'd done anything interesting, but apparently I had. I shrugged and vanished into the master bathroom to slap on some makeup. After another glance in the mirror, it occurred to me that maybe anything I did in that outfit was fairly interesting, if you were a fully functional guy.

When I came out, Everett had gone and Quinn gave me a slip of paper with Everett's cell number on it. "He says to call him when you need some more boxes," Quinn said. "He took all the bagged clothes. Looks like you don't need me at all."

"No comparison," I said, smiling. "Everett didn't bring me grease and caffeine this morning, and you did."

"So what's the plan, and how can I help?"

"Okay, the plan is . . ." I didn't exactly have one more specific than "go through this stuff and sort it out," and Quinn couldn't do that for me.

"How's this?" I asked. "You get everything out of the kitchen cabinets, and set it out where I can see it all, and I'll make a 'keep or toss' decision. You can pack what I want to keep, and put what I want to toss out on the gallery. I hope the rain stays away." The sunny morning was clouding over, fast. "While we work, I'll fill you in on what happened here last night."

Despite the threat of bad weather, we worked all morning, called in a pizza for lunch, and resumed work in the afternoon. The stuff I didn't want went into garbage bags, and Quinn furthered his muscular development by carrying all the garbage bags down to the courtyard and putting them in the little shed that had held the lawn chairs, still set up on the grass. I tried to admire his muscles only when he wasn't looking, and I think I was successful. Quinn was very interested to hear about the ectoplasmic reconstruction, and we talked about what it might all mean without reaching any conclusions. Jake didn't have any enemies among the vampires that Quinn knew of, and Quinn thought that Jake must have been killed for the embarrassment it would cause Hadley, rather than for any sin of Jake's own.

I saw neither hide nor hair of Amelia, and I wondered if she'd gone home with the Mormonish Bob. Or maybe he'd stayed with her, and they were having a fabulous time in Amelia's apartment. Maybe he was a real ball of fire under that white shirt and those black pants. I looked around the courtyard. Yes, Bob's bicycle was still propped against the brick wall. Since the sky was getting darker by the minute, I put the bike in the little shed, too.

Being with Quinn all day was stoking my fire a bit hotter every moment. He was down to a tank top and jeans, and I found myself wondering what he'd look like without those. And I didn't think I was the only one conjecturing about what people would look like naked. I could catch a flash from Quinn's mind every now and then as he was toting a bag down the stairs or packing pots and pans into a box, and those flashes weren't about opening his mail or doing his laundry.

I had enough practical presence of mind left to switch on a lamp when I heard the first peal of thunder in the distance. The Big Easy was about to be drenched.

Then it was back to flirting with Quinn wordlessly — making sure he had a good view when I stretched up to get a glass down from the cabinets or bent down to wrap that glass in newspaper. Maybe a quarter of me was embarrassed, but the rest of me was having fun. Fun had not been a big factor in my life recently — well, ever — and I was enjoying my little toddle on the wild side.

Downstairs, I felt Amelia's brain click on, after a fashion. I was familiar with the feel of this, from working in a bar: Amelia had a hangover. I smiled to myself as the witch thought of Bob, who was still asleep beside her. Aside from a basic, "How could I?" Amelia's most coherent thought was that she needed coffee. She needed it bad. She couldn't even turn on a light in the apartment, which was darkening steadily with the approach of the storm. A light would hurt her eyes too much.

I turned with a smile on my lips, ready to tell Quinn we might be hearing from Amelia soon, only to find he was right behind me, and his face was intent with a look I could not mistake. He was ready for something entirely different.

"Tell me you don't want me to kiss you, and I'll back off," he said, and then he was kissing me.

I didn't say a word.

When the height difference became an issue, Quinn just picked me up and put me on the edge of the kitchen counter. A clap of thunder sounded outside as I parted my knees to let him get as close to me as he could. I wrapped my legs around him. He pulled the elastic band out of my hair, not a totally pain-free process, and ran his fingers through the tangles. He crushed my hair in his hand and inhaled deeply, as if he were extracting the perfume from a flower.

"This is okay?" he asked raggedly, as his fingers found the bottom back edge of my tank top and sneaked up under it. He examined my bra tactilely and figured out how to open it in record time.

"Okay?" I said, in a daze. I wasn't sure whether I meant, "Okay? Hell, yes, hurry up!" or "Which part of this is okay, you want to know?" but Quinn naturally took it as a green light. His hands pushed the bra aside and he ran his thumbs across my nipples, which were already hard. I thought I was going to explode, and only the sure anticipation of better things to come kept me from losing it right then and there. I wriggled even further to the edge of the counter, so the big bulge in the front of Quinn's jeans was pressed against the notch in my pants. Just amazing, how they fit. He pressed against me, released, pressed again, the ridge formed by the stretch of the jeans over his penis hitting just the right spot, so easy to reach through the thin and stretchy spandex. Once more, and I cried out, holding on to him through the blind moment of orgasm when I could swear I'd been catapulted into another universe. My breathing was more like sobbing, and I wrapped myself around him like he was my hero. In that moment, he certainly was.

His breathing was still ragged, and he moved against me again, seeking his own release, since I had so loudly had mine. I sucked on his neck while my hand went down between us, and stroked him through his jeans, and suddenly he gave a cry as ragged as mine had been, and his arms tightened around me convulsively. "Oh, God," he said, "oh, God." His eyes closed tight with his release, he kissed my neck, my cheek, my lips, over and over. When his breathing — and mine — was a little more even, he said, "Babe, I haven't come like that since I was seventeen, in the backseat of my dad's car with Ellie Hopper."

"So, that's a good thing," I mumbled.

"You bet," he said.

We stayed clinched for a moment, and I became aware that the rain was beating against the windows and the doors, and the thunder was booming away. My brain was thinking of shutting down for a little nap, and I was lazily aware of Quinn's brain going equally drowsy as he rehooked my bra at my back. Downstairs, Amelia was making coffee in her dark kitchen and Bob the witch was waking up to the wonderful smell and wondering where his pants were. And in the courtyard, swarming silently up the stairs, enemies were approaching.

"Quinn!" I exclaimed, just in the moment his sharp hearing picked up the shuffle of the footsteps. Quinn went into fighting mode. Since I hadn't been home to check the calendar symbols, I'd forgotten we were close to the full moon. There were claws on Quinn's hands now, claws at least three inches long, instead of fingers. His eyes slanted and became altogether gold, with dilated black pupils. The change in the bones of his face had made him alien. I'd made a form of love with this man in the past ten minutes, and now I would hardly have known him if I'd passed him on the street.

But there wasn't time to think about anything but our best defense. I was the weak link, and I had better depend on surprise. I slid off the counter, hurried past him to the door, and lifted the lamp from its pedestal. When the first Were burst through the door, I bashed him upside the head, and he staggered, and the one coming in right after him tripped over his flailing predecessor, and Quinn was more than ready for the third one.

Unfortunately, there were six more.

20

It took just two of them to subdue me, and I was kicking and screaming, biting and hitting, with every bit of energy I had. It took four for Quinn, but those four succeeded only because they used a stun gun. Otherwise, I'm sure he could have taken six or eight of them out of action, instead of the three he took care of before they got him.

I knew I would be overcome, and I knew I could save myself some bruises and maybe a broken bone if I just assented to be taken. But I have my pride. More practically, I wanted to be sure that Amelia heard what was happening above her. She'd do something. I wasn't sure what she'd do, but she'd act.

I was hustled down the stairs, my feet hardly touching them, by two husky men I'd never seen before. These same two men had bound my wrists together with duct tape. I'd done my best to arrange for a little slack, but I was afraid they'd done a fair job of it.

"Mmm, smells like sex," the shorter one said as he pinched my butt. I ignored his tacky leer and took some satisfaction in eyeing the bruise I'd given him on his cheekbone with my fist. (Which, by the way, was aching and smarting over the knuckles. You can't hit someone without paying for it yourself.)

They had to carry Quinn, and they weren't gentle about it. He got banged around against the stairs, and once they dropped him. He was a big guy. Now he was a bleeding big guy, since one of the blows had cut the skin above his left eye. He'd had the duct tape treatment, too, and I wondered how the fur would react to the tape.

We were being held side by side in the courtyard, briefly, and Quinn looked over at me as if he desperately wanted to speak to me. The blood was running down his cheek from the wound over his eyes, and he looked groggy from the stun gun. His hands were changing back to regular hands. I lunged toward him, but the Weres kept us apart.

Two vans drove into the circular drive, two vans that said BIG EASY ELECTRIC on the side. They were white and long and windowless in the back, and the logo on the side had been covered up with mud, which looked highly suspicious. A driver jumped out of the cab of each van, and the first driver threw open the doors to the rear of the first vehicle.

While our captors were hustling Quinn and me over to that van, the rest of the raiding party was being brought down the stairs. The men Quinn had managed to hurt were damaged far worse than Quinn, I'm glad to say. Claws can do an amazing amount of damage, especially wielded with the force a tiger can exert. The guy I'd hit with the lamp was unconscious, and the one who'd reached Quinn first was possibly dead. He was certainly covered with blood and there were things exposed to the light that should have been neatly packed in his belly.

I was smiling with satisfaction when the men holding me shoved me into the back of the van, which I discovered was awash with trash and absolutely filthy. This was a high-class operation. There was a wide-mesh screen between the two front seats and the open rear, and the shelves in the rear had been emptied, I supposed for our occupancy.

I was crammed into the narrow aisle between the shelves, and Quinn was jammed in after me. They had to work hard because he was still so stunned. My two escorts were slamming the rear van doors on the two of us as the hors de combat Weres were loaded into the other van. I was guessing the vans had been parked out on the street briefly so we wouldn't hear the vehicles pulling into the driveway. When they were ready to load us up, our captors had pulled into the courtyard. Even the people of a brawling city like New Orleans would notice some battered bodies being loaded into vans . . . in the pouring rain.

I hoped the Weres wouldn't think of grabbing Amelia and Bob, and I prayed that Amelia would think cleverly and hide herself, rather than do some impulsive and brave witch thing. I know it's a contradiction, right? Praying for one thing (asking God a favor) while at the same time hoping your enemies would be killed. All I can say is, I have a feeling Christians have been doing that from the get-go — at least bad ones, like me.

"Go, go, go," bellowed the shorter man, who'd hopped into the front seat. The driver obliged with a completely unnecessary squealing of tires, and we lurched out of the courtyard as if the president had just been shot and we had to get him to Walter Reed.

Quinn came to completely as we turned

off Chloe Street to head for our final destination, wherever it might be. His hands were bound behind him, which is painful, and he hadn't quit bleeding from the head. I'd expected him to remain groggy and shocked. But when his eyes focused on my face, he said, "Babe, they beat you bad." I must not look too good.

"Yeah, well, you seem to be in the same boat," I said. I knew the driver and his companion could hear us, and I didn't give a damn.

With a grim attempt at a smile, he said, "Some defender I turned out to be."

In the Weres' estimation, I wasn't very dangerous, so my hands had been bound in front. I squirmed until I was able to put pressure on the cut on Quinn's forehead. That had to have hurt even more, but he didn't say a word in protest. The motion of the van, the effects of the beating, and the constant shifting and smell of the trash all around us combined to make the next ten minutes very unpleasant. If I'd been very clever, I could have told which way we were going — but I wasn't feeling very clever. I marveled that in a city with as many famed restaurants as New Orleans had, this van was awash with Burger King wrappers and Taco Bell cups. If I got a chance to rummage through the debris, I might find something useful.

"When we're together, we get attacked by Weres," Quinn said.

"It's my fault," I said. "I'm so sorry I dragged you into this."

"Oh, yeah," he said. "I'm known for hanging with a desperate crowd."

We were lying face to face, and Quinn sort of nudged me with his leg. He was trying to tell me something, and I wasn't getting it.

The two men in the front seat were talking to each other about a cute girl crossing the street at a traffic light. Just listening to the conversation was almost enough to make you swear off men, but at least they weren't listening to us.

"Remember when we talked about my mental condition?" I said carefully. "Remember what I told you about that?"

It took him a minute because he was hurting, but he got the hint. His face squinched up as if he were about to chop some boards in half, or something else requiring all his concentration, and then his thought shoved into my head. *Phone in my pocket,* he told me. The problem was, the phone was in his right pocket, and he was lying on that side. There was hardly room for him to turn over.

This called for a lot of maneuvering, and

I didn't want our captors to see it. But I managed, finally, to work my fingers into Quinn's pocket, and made a mental note to advise him that, under this set of circumstances, his jeans were too tight. (Under other circumstances, no problem with the way they fit.) But extricating that phone, with the van rocking, while our Were assailants checked on us every minute or so, that was difficult.

Queen's headquarters on speed dial, he told me when he felt the phone leave his pocket. But that was lost on me. I didn't know how to access speed dial. It took me a few moments to make Quinn understand that, and I'm still not sure how I did it, but finally he *thought* the phone number at me, and I awkwardly punched it in and pressed SEND. Maybe we hadn't thought that through all the way, because when a tiny voice said, "Hello?" the Weres heard it.

"You didn't search him?" the driver asked the passenger incredulously.

"Hell no, I was trying to get him in the back and get myself out of the rain," the man who had pinched me snarled right back. "Pull over, dammit!"

Has someone had your blood? Quinn asked me silently, though this time he could have spoken, and after a precious second, my brain kicked in. "Eric," I said, because the Weres were out their doors and running to open the rear doors of the van.

"Quinn and Sookie have been taken by some Weres," Quinn said into the phone I was holding to his mouth. "Eric the Northman can track her."

I hoped Eric was still in New Orleans, and I further hoped whoever answered the phone at the queen's headquarters was on the ball. But then the two Weres were yanking open the van doors and dragging us out, and one of them socked me while the other hit Quinn in the gut. They yanked the phone from my swollen fingers and tossed it into the thick undergrowth at the side of the road. The driver had pulled over by an empty lot, but up and down the road were widely spaced houses on stilts in a sea of grasses. The sky was too overcast for me to get a fix on our direction, but I was sure now we'd driven south into the marshes. I did manage to read our driver's watch, and was surprised to find out it was already past three in the afternoon.

"You dumb shit, Clete! Who was he calling?" yelled a voice from the second van, which had pulled over to the side of the road when we did. Our two captors looked at each other with identical expressions of consternation, and I would have been laughing if I hadn't been hurting so badly. It was as if they'd practiced looking stupid.

This time Quinn was searched very thoroughly, and I was, too, though I had no pockets or anywhere else to conceal anything, unless they wanted to do a body cavity check. I thought Clete — Mr. Pinch-Ass — was going to, just for a second, as his fingers jabbed the spandex into me. Quinn thought so, too. I made an awful noise, a choked gasp of fear, but the sound that came from Quinn's throat was beyond a snarl. It was a deep, throaty, coughing noise, and it was absolutely menacing.

"Leave the girl alone, Clete, and let's get back on the road," the tall driver said, and his voice had that "I'm done with you" edge to it. "I don't know who this guy is, but I don't think he changes into a nutria."

I wondered if Quinn would threaten them with his identity — most Weres seemed to know him, or know of him — but since he didn't volunteer his name, I didn't speak.

Clete shoved me back into the van with a lot of muttering along the lines of "Who died and made you God? You ain't the boss of me," and so on. The taller man clearly *was* the boss of Clete, which was a good thing. I wanted someone with brains and a shred of decency between me and Clete's probing fingers.

They had a very hard time getting Quinn into the van again. He didn't want to go, and finally two men from the other van came over, very reluctantly, to help Clete and the driver. They bound Quinn's legs with one of those plastic things, the kind where you run the pointed tip through a hole and then twist it. We'd used something similar to close the bag when we'd baked a turkey last Thanksgiving. The tie they used on Quinn was black and plastic and it actually locked with what looked like a handcuff key.

They didn't bind my legs.

I appreciated Quinn's getting angry at their treatment of me, angry enough to struggle to be free, but the end result was that my legs were free and his weren't — because I still didn't present a threat to them, at least in their minds.

They were probably right. I couldn't think of anything to do to prevent them from taking us wherever we were going. I didn't have a weapon, and though I worried at the duct tape binding my hands, my teeth didn't seem to be strong enough to make a weak spot. I rested for a minute, shutting my eyes wearily. The last blow had opened a cut on my cheek. A big tongue rasped over my bleeding face. Then again.

"Don't cry," said a strange, guttural voice, and I opened my eyes to check that it was, indeed, coming from Quinn.

Quinn had so much power that he could stop the change once it had begun. I suspected he could trigger it, too, though I'd noticed that fighting could bring it on in any shape-shifter. He'd had the claws during the fight in Hadley's apartment, and they'd almost tipped the balance in our favor. Since he'd gotten so enraged at Clete during the episode by the side of the road, Quinn's nose had flattened and broadened. I had a close-up view of the teeth in his mouth, teeth that had altered into tiny daggers.

"Why didn't you change fully?" I asked, in a tiny whisper.

Because there wouldn't be enough room for you in this space, babe. After I change, I'm seven feet long and I weigh about four hundred fifty pounds.

That will make any girl gulp. I could only be grateful he'd thought that far ahead. I looked at him some more.

Not grossed out?

Clete and the driver were exchanging recriminations about the phone incident.

"Why, grandpa, what big teeth you have," I whispered. The upper and lower canines were so long and sharp they were really scary. (I called them *canines;* to cats, that might be an insult.)

Sharp . . . they were sharp. I worked my hands up close to his mouth, and begged him with my eyes to understand. As much as I could tell from his altered face, Quinn was worried. Just as our situation aroused his defensive instincts, the idea I was trying to sell to him excited other instincts. *I will make your hands bleed,* he warned me, with a great effort. He was partially animal now, and the animal thought processes didn't necessarily travel the same paths as the human.

I bit my own bottom lip to keep from gasping as Quinn's teeth bit into the duct tape. He had to exert a lot of pressure to get the three-inch canines to pierce the duct tape, and that meant that those shorter, sharp incisors bit into my skin, too, no matter how much care he took. Tears began rolling down my face in an unending stream, and I felt him falter. I shook my bound hands to urge him on, and reluctantly he bent back to his task.

"Hey, George, he's biting her," Clete said

from the passenger's seat. "I can see his jaw moving."

But we were so close together and the light was so poor that he couldn't see that Quinn was biting the binding on my hands. That was good. I was trying hard to find good things to cling to, because this was looking like a bleak, bleak world just at this moment, lying in the van traveling through the rain on an unknown road somewhere in southern Louisiana.

I was angry and bleeding and sore and lying on my already injured left arm. What I wanted, what would be ideal, would be to find myself clean and bandaged in a nice bed with white sheets. Okay, clean and bandaged and in a clean nightgown. And then Quinn would be in the bed, completely in his human form, and he would be clean and bandaged, too. And he'd have had some rest, and he'd be wearing nothing at all. But the pain of my cut and bleeding arms was becoming too demanding to ignore any longer, and I couldn't concentrate enough to cling to my lovely daydream. Just when I was on the verge of whimpering — or maybe just out-and-out screaming — I felt my wrists separate.

For a few seconds I just lay there and panted, trying to control my reaction to the pain. Unfortunately Quinn couldn't gnaw on the binding on his own hands, since they'd been bound behind him. He finally succeeded in turning over so I could see his wrists.

George said, "What are they doing?"

Clete glanced back at us, but I had my hands together. Since the day was dark, he couldn't see very clearly. "They're not doing anything. He quit biting her," Clete said, sounding disappointed.

Quinn succeeded in getting a claw hooked into the silvery duct tape. His claws were not sharp-edged along their curve like a scimitar; their power lay in the piercing point backed by a tiger's huge strength. But Quinn couldn't get the purchase to exercise that strength. So this was going to take time, and I suspected the tape was going to make a ripping noise when he succeeded in slicing it open.

We didn't have much time left. Any minute even an idiot like Clete would notice that all was not well.

I began the difficult maneuvering to get my hands down to Quinn's feet without giving away the fact that they weren't bound any longer. Clete glanced back when he glimpsed my movement, and I slumped against the empty shelves, my hands clasped together in my lap. I tried to look hopeless, which was awfully easy. Clete got more interested in lighting a cigarette after a second or two, giving me a chance to look at the plastic strap binding Quinn's ankles together. Though it had reminded me of the bag tie we used last Thanksgiving, this plastic was black and thick and extra tough, and I didn't have a knife to cut it or a key to unlock it. I did think Clete had made a mistake putting the restraint on, however, and I hurried to try to take advantage of it. Quinn's shoes were still on, of course, and I unlaced them and pulled them off. Then I held one foot pointed down. That foot began to slide up inside the circle of the tie. As I'd suspected, the shoes had held his feet apart and allowed for some slack.

Though my wrists and hands were bleeding onto Quinn's socks (which I left on so the plastic wouldn't scrape him) I was managing pretty well. He was being stoic about my drastic adjustments to his foot. Finally I heard his bones protest at being twisted into a strange position, but his foot slid up out of the restraint. Oh, thank God.

It had taken me longer to think about than to do. It had felt like hours.

I pulled the restraint down and shoved it into the debris, looked up at Quinn, and nodded. His claw, hooked in the duct tape, ripped at it. A hole appeared. The sound hadn't been loud at all, and I eased myself back full length beside Quinn to camouflage the activity.

I stuck my thumbs in the hole in the duct tape and yanked, achieving very little. There's a reason duct tape is so popular. It's a reliable substance.

We had to get out of that van before it reached its destination, and we had to get away before the other van could pull up behind ours. I scrabbled around through the chalupa wrappers and the cardboard french fry cartons on the floor of the van and finally, in a little gap between the floor and the side, I found an overlooked Phillips screwdriver. It was long and thin.

I looked at it and took a deep breath. I knew what I had to do. Quinn's hands were bound and he couldn't do it. Tears rolled down my face. I was being a crybaby, but I just couldn't help it. I looked at Quinn for a moment, and his features were steely. He knew as well as I did what needed to be done.

Just then the van slowed and took a turn from a parish road, reasonably well paved, onto what felt like a graveled track running into the woods. A driveway, I was sure. We were close to our destination. This was the best chance, maybe the last chance, we would have.

"Stretch your wrists," I murmured, and I plunged the Phillips head into the hole in the duct tape. It became larger. I plunged again. The two men, sensing my frantic movement, were turning as I stabbed at the duct tape a final time. While Quinn strained to part the perforated bindings, I pulled myself to my knees, gripping the latticed partition with my left hand, and I said, "Clete!"

He turned and leaned between the seats, closer to the partition, to see better. I took a deep breath and with my right hand I drove the screwdriver between the crosshatched metal. It went right into his cheek. He screamed and bled and George could hardly pull over fast enough. With a roar, Quinn separated his wrists. Then Quinn moved like lightning, and the minute the van slammed into Park, he and I were out the back doors and running through the woods. Thank God they were right by the road.

Beaded thong sandals are not good for running in the woods, I just want to say here, and Quinn was only in his socks. But we covered some ground, and by the time the startled driver of the second van could pull over and the passengers could leap out in pursuit, we were out of sight of the road. We kept running, because they were Weres, and they would track us. I'd pulled the screwdriver out of Clete's cheek and had it in my hand, and I remember thinking that it was dangerous to run with a pointed object in my hand. I thought about Clete's thick finger probing between my legs, and I didn't feel so bad about what I'd done. In the next few seconds, while I was jumping over a downed tree snagged in some thorny vines, the screwdriver slipped from my hand and I had no time to search for it.

After running for some time, we came to the swamp. Swamps and bayous abound in Louisiana, of course. The bayous and swamps are rich in wildlife, and they can be beautiful to look at and maybe tour in a canoe or something. But to plunge into on foot, in pouring rain, they suck.

Maybe from a tracking point of view this swamp was a good thing, because once we were in the water we wouldn't be leaving any scent. But from my personal point of view, the swamp was awful, because it was dirty and had snakes and alligators and God knows what else.

I had to brace myself to wade in after Quinn, and the water was dark and cool since it was still spring. In the summer, it would feel like wading through warm soup. On a day so overcast, once we were under the overhanging trees, we would be almost invisible to our pursuers, which was good; but the same conditions also meant that any lurking wildlife would be seen approximately when we stepped on it, or when it bit us. Not so good.

Quinn was smiling broadly, and I remembered that some tigers have lots of swamps in their natural habitat. At least one of us was happy.

The water got deeper and deeper, and soon we were swimming. There again, Quinn swam with a large grace that was kind of daunting to me. I was trying with all my might just to be quiet and stealthy. For a second, I was so cold and so frightened I began to think that . . . no, it wouldn't be better to still be in the van . . . but it was a near thing, just for a second.

I was so tired. My muscles were shaking with the aftermath of the adrenalin surge of our escape, and then I'd dashed through the woods, and before that there'd been the fight in the apartment, and before that . . . oh my God, I'd had sex with Quinn. Sort of. Yes, definitely sex. More or less.

We hadn't spoken since we'd gotten out

of the van, and suddenly I remembered I'd seen his arm bleeding when we'd burst out of the van. I'd stabbed him with the Phillips head, at least once, while I was freeing him.

And here I was, whining. "Quinn," I said. "Let me help you."

"Help me?" he asked. I couldn't read his tone, and since he was forging through the dark water ahead of me, I couldn't read his face. But his mind, ah, that was full of snarled confusion and anger that he couldn't find a place to stuff. "Did I help you? Did I free you? Did I protect you from the fucking Weres? No, I let that son of a bitch stick his finger up you, and I watched, I couldn't do anything."

Oh. Male pride. "You got my hands free," I pointed out. "And you can help me now."

"How?" he turned to me, and he was deeply upset. I realized that he was a guy who took his protecting very seriously. It was one of God's mysterious imbalances, that men are stronger than women. My grandmother told me it was his way of balancing the scales, since women are tougher and more resilient. I'm not sure that's true, but I knew that Quinn, perhaps because he was a big, formidable guy and, perhaps because he was a weretiger who could turn into this fabulously beautiful and lethal beast, was in a funk because he hadn't killed all our attackers and saved me from being sullied by their touch.

I myself would have preferred that scenario a lot, especially considering our present predicament. But events hadn't fallen out that way. "Quinn," I said, and my voice was just as weary as the rest of me, "they have to have been heading somewhere around here. Somewhere in this swamp."

"That's why we turned off," he said in agreement. I saw a snake twined around a tree branch overhanging the water right behind him, and my face must have looked as shocked as I felt, because Quinn whipped around faster than I could think and had that snake in his hand and snapped it once, twice, and then the snake was dead and floating away in the sluggish water. He seemed to feel a lot better after that. "We don't know where we're going, but we're sure it's away from them. Right?" he asked.

"There aren't any other brains up and running in my range," I said, after a moment's checking. "But I've never defined how big my range is. That's all I can tell you. Let's try to get out of the water for a minute while we think, okay?" I was shivering all over.

Quinn slogged through the water and

gathered me up. "Link your arms around my neck," he said.

Sure, if he wanted to do the man thing, that was fine. I put my arms around his neck and he began moving through the water.

"Would this be better if you turned into a tiger?" I asked.

"I might need that later, and I've already partially changed twice today. I better save my strength."

"What kind are you?"

"Bengal," he said, and just then the pattering of the rain on the water stopped.

We heard voices calling then, and we came to a stop in the water, both of our faces turned to the source of the sound. As we were standing there stock-still, I heard something large slide into the water to our right. I swung my eyes in that direction, terrified of what I'd see — but the water was almost still, as if something had just passed. I knew there were tours of the bayous south of New Orleans, and I knew locals made a good living out of taking people out on the dark water and letting them see the alligators. The good thing was, these natives made money, and out-of-staters got to see something they'd never have seen otherwise. The bad thing was, sometimes the locals threw treats to attract the gators. I figured the gators associated humans with food.

I laid my head on Quinn's shoulder and I closed my eyes. But the voices didn't get any closer, and we didn't hear the baying of wolves, and nothing bit my leg to drag me down. "That's what gators do, you know," I told Quinn. "They pull you under and drown you, and stick you somewhere so they can snack on you."

"Babe, the wolves aren't going to eat us today, and neither will the gators." He laughed, a low rumble deep in his chest. I was so glad to hear that sound. After a moment, we began moving through the water again. The trees and the bits of land became close together, the channels narrow, and finally we came up on a piece of land large enough to hold a cabin.

Quinn was half supporting me when we staggered out of the water.

As shelter, the cabin was poor stuff. Maybe the structure had once been a glorified hunting camp, three walls and a roof, no more than that. Now it was a wreck, halfway fallen. The wood had rotted and the metal roof had bent and buckled, rusting through in spots. I went over to the heap of man-tailored material and searched very carefully, but there didn't seem to be anything we could use as a weapon.

Quinn was occupied by ripping the remnants of the duct tape off his wrists, not even wincing when some skin went with it. I worked on my own more gently. Then I just gave out.

I slumped dismally to the ground, my back against a scrubby oak tree. Its bark immediately began making deep impressions in my back. I thought of all the germs in the water, germs that were doubtless speeding through my system the moment they'd gained entry through the cuts on my wrists. The unhealed bite, still covered by a now-filthy bandage, had doubtless received its share of nasty particles. My face was swelling up from the beating I'd taken. I remembered looking in the mirror the day before and seeing that the marks left by the bitten Weres in Shreveport had finally almost faded away. Fat lot of good that had done me.

"Amelia should have done something by now," I said, trying to feel optimistic. "She probably called vampire HQ. Even if our own phone call didn't reach anyone who'd do something about it, maybe someone's looking for us now."

"They'd have to send out human employees. It's still technically daylight, even though the sky's so dark."

"Well, at least the rain's over with," I said. At that moment, it began to rain again.

I thought about throwing a fit, but frankly, it didn't seem worth using up the energy. And there was nothing to do about it. The sky was going to rain, no matter how many fits I threw. "I'm sorry you got caught up in this," I said, thinking that I had a lot for which to apologize.

"Sookie, I don't know if *you* should be telling me *you're* sorry." Quinn emphasized the pronouns. "Everything has happened when we were together."

That was true, and I tried to believe all this wasn't my fault. But I was convinced that somehow, it really was.

Out of the blue, Quinn said, "What's your relationship with Alcide Herveaux? We saw him in the bar last week with some other girl. But the cop, the one in Shreveport, said you'd been engaged to him."

"That was bullshit," I said, sitting slumped in the mud. Here I was, deep inside a southern Louisiana swamp, the rain pelting down on me . . .

Hey, wait a minute. I stared at Quinn's mouth moving, realized he was saying something, but waited for the trailing end of a thought to snag on something. If there'd been a lightbulb above my head, it

419

would have been flashing. "Jesus Christ, Shepherd of Judea," I said reverently. "That's who's doing this."

Quinn squatted in front of me. "You've picked who's been doing what? How many enemies do you have?"

"At least I know who sent the bitten Weres, and who had us kidnapped," I said, refusing to be sidetracked. Crouched together in the downpour like a couple of cave people, Quinn listened while I talked.

Then we discussed probabilities.

Then we made a plan.

21

Once he knew what he was doing, Quinn was relentless. Since we couldn't be any more miserable than we already were, he decided we might as well be moving. While I did little more than follow him and stay out of his way, he began to scour the area for smells. Finally he got tired of crouching, and he said, "I'm going to change." He stripped quickly and efficiently, rolling the clothes into a compact (but sopping) bundle and handing them to me to carry. Every conjecture I'd had about Quinn's body was absolutely on target, I was pleased to note. He'd begun taking off his clothes without a single hesitation, but once he noticed I was looking, he held still and let me look. Even in the dark, dripping rain, he was worth it. Quinn's body was a work of art, though a scarred work of art. He was one large block of muscle, from his calves to his neck.

"Do you like what you see?" he asked.

"Oh, *boy*," I said. "You look better than a Happy Meal to a three-year-old."

Quinn gave me a broad, pleased smile. He bent to crouch on the ground. I knew what was coming. The air around Quinn began to shimmer and tremble, and then within that envelope Quinn began to change. Muscles rippled and flowed and reformed, bones reshaped, fur rolled out of somewhere inside him — though I knew that couldn't be, that was the illusion. The sound was dreadful. It was a kind of gloppy, sticky sound, but with hard notes in it, as if someone were stirring a pot of stiff glue that was full of sticks and rocks.

At the end of it, the tiger stood across from me.

If Quinn had been a gorgeous naked man, he was an equally beautiful tiger. His fur was a deep orange slashed with black stripes, and there were touches of white on his belly and face. His eyes slanted, and they were golden. He was maybe seven feet long and at least three feet tall at the shoulder. I was amazed at how big he was. His paws were fully developed and as big as some dinner plates. His rounded ears were just plain cute. He walked over to me silently, with a grace unusual in such a massive form. He rubbed his huge head against me, almost knocking me down, and he purred. He sounded like a happy Geiger counter.

His dense fur was oily to the touch, so I figured he was pretty well waterproofed. He gave a barking cough, and the swamp went silent. You wouldn't think Louisiana wildlife would recognize the sound of a tiger, right? But it did, and it shut its mouth and hid.

We don't have the same special space requirements with animals that we do with people. I knelt beside the tiger that had been Quinn, in some magical way was still Quinn, and I put my arms around his neck, and I hugged him. It was a little disturbing that he smelled so much like an actual tiger, and I forced my mind around the fact that he was a tiger, that Quinn was inside him. And we set out through the swamp.

It was a little startling to see the tiger mark his new territory — this is not something you expect to see your boyfriend do — but I decided it would just be ridiculous to mind the display. Besides, I had enough to think about, keeping up with the tiger. He was searching for scents, and we covered a lot of ground. I was growing more and more exhausted. My sense of wonder faded, and I was simply wet and chilly, hungry and grumpy. If someone had been thinking right under my feet, I'm not sure my mind would have picked the thoughts up.

Then the tiger froze, nose testing the air. His head moved, ears twitching, to search in a particular direction. He turned to look at me. Though tigers can't smile, I got the definite wave of triumph from the huge cat. The tiger turned his head back to the east, rotated his massive head to look at me, and turned his head to the east again. *Follow me,* clear as a bell.

"Okay," I said, and put my hand on his shoulder.

Off we went. The trip through the swamp lasted an eternity, though later I estimated that "eternity," in this case, was probably about thirty minutes. Gradually the ground grew firmer, the water scarcer. Now we were in forest, not swamp.

I'd figured we'd gotten close to our abductors' destination when the van had turned off onto the side road. I'd been right. When we came to the edge of the clearing surrounding the little house, we were to the west side of the north-facing house. We could see both front and back yards. The van that had held us captive was parked in the back. In the tiny clearing at the front was a car, some kind of GMC sedan.

The little house itself was like a million other houses in rural America. It was a box of a place: wooden, painted tan, with green shutters on the windows and green uprights to support the roof over the tiny front porch. The two men from the van, Clete and George, were huddled on the concrete square because of that bit of shelter, however inadequate it was.

The matching structure at the rear of the house was a little deck outside the back door, scarcely large enough to hold a gas grill and a mop. It was open to the elements. By the way, the elements were really going to town.

I stowed Quinn's clothes and shoes at the foot of a mimosa tree. The tiger's lips pulled back when he scented Clete. The long teeth were as frightening as a shark's.

The afternoon of rain had lowered the temperature. George and Clete were shivering in the damp cool of the evening. They were both smoking. The two Weres, in human form and smoking, would not have a better sense of smell than regular people. They showed no sign of being aware of Quinn at all. I figured they would react pretty dramatically if they caught the scent of tiger in southern Louisiana.

I worked my way through the trees around the clearing until I was very close to the van. I eased my way around it and crept up to the passenger side. The van was unlocked, and I could see the stun gun. That was my goal. I took a deep breath and opened the door, hoping the light that came on wasn't interesting to anyone who could see out the back window. I grabbed the stun gun from the jumble of stuff between the front seats. I shut the door as quietly as a van door can be shut. Luckily, the rain seemed to muffle the noise. I gave a shaky sigh of relief when nothing happened. Then I duckwalked back into the edge of the woods and knelt by Quinn.

He licked my cheek. I appreciated the affection in the gesture, if not the tiger breath, and I scratched his head. (Somehow, kissing his fur had no appeal.) That done, I pointed to the left west window, which should belong to a living room. Quinn didn't nod or give me a high five, both of which would have been untigerlike gestures, but I guess I had expected him to give me some kind of green light. He just looked at me.

Picking up my feet carefully, I stepped out into the little open space between the forest and the house, and very carefully I made my way to the lit window.

I didn't want to pop into view like a jack-in-the-box, so I hugged the side of the house and inched sideways until I could peer in at the very corner of the glass. The older Pelts, Barbara and Gordon, were sitting on an "early American" loveseat dating from the sixties, and their body language clearly proclaimed their unhappiness. Their daughter Sandra paced back and forth in front of them, though there wasn't much room for such an exhibition. It was a very small family room, a room that would be comfortable only if you had a family of one. The older Pelts looked as if they were going to a Lands' End photo shoot, while Sandra was more adventurously clad in skintight stretch khakis and a bright striped short-sleeved sweater. Sandra was dressed for trolling for cute guys at the mall, rather than torturing a couple of people. But torturing was what she'd been planning to do. There was a straight-backed chair crammed into the room, too, and it had straps and handcuffs already attached.

On a familiar note, there was a roll of duct tape sitting ready beside it.

I'd been pretty calm until I saw the duct tape.

I didn't know if tigers could count, but I held up three fingers in case Quinn was watching. Moving slowly and carefully, I squatted down and moved south until I was below the second window. I was feeling

427

pretty proud of my sneaking ability, which should have alerted me to potential disaster. Pride goeth before a fall.

Though the window was dark, when I eased up into position, I was looking through the glass right into the eyes of a small swarthy man with a mustache and goatee. He was sitting at a table right by the window, and he'd been holding a cup of coffee in his hand. In his shock, he let it drop to the table and the hot backsplash hit his hands and chest and chin.

He shrieked, though I wasn't sure he was using actual words. I heard a commotion at the front door and in the front room.

Well . . . eff.

I was around the corner of the house and up the steps to the little deck faster than you could say Jack Robinson. I yanked open the screen door and pushed in the wooden door, and I leaped into the kitchen with the stun gun on. The small guy was still patting at his face with a towel while I zapped him, and he went down like a sack of bricks. Wow!

But the stun gun had to recharge, I discovered, when Sandra Pelt, who'd had the advantage of already being on her feet, charged into the kitchen, teeth bared. The stun gun didn't do a damn thing to her, and she was on me like an — well, like an enraged wolf.

However, she was still in the form of a girl, and I was desperate and desperately angry.

I've seen at least two dozen bar fights, ranging from halfhearted punches to rolling-on-the-ground biting, and I know how to fight. Right now I was willing to do whatever it took. Sandra was mean, but she was lighter and less experienced, and after some wrestling and punching and hair pulling that went by in a flash, I was on top of her and had her pinned to the floor. She snarled and snapped but she couldn't reach my neck, and I was prepared to head-butt her if I had to.

A voice in the background bellowed, "Let me in!" and I assumed it was Quinn behind some door. "Come on now!" I yelled in answer. "I need help!"

She was squirming underneath me, and I dared not let go to shift my grip. "Listen, Sandra," I panted, "hold still, dammit!"

"Fuck you," she said bitterly, and her efforts redoubled.

"This is actually kind of exciting," a familiar voice said, and I glanced up to see Eric looking down at us with wide blue eyes. He looked immaculate: neat as a pin in blue jeans that had a crease and a starched blue-

and-white striped dress shirt. His blond hair was shining clean and (here was the most enviable part) dry. I hated his guts. I felt nasty to the nth degree.

"I could use some help here," I snapped, and he said, "Of course, Sookie, though I'm enjoying the wiggling around. Let go of the girl and stand up."

"Only if you're ready for action," I said, my breathing ragged with the effort of holding Sandra down.

"I'm always ready for action," Eric said, with a glowing smile. "Sandra, look at me."

She was too smart for that. Sandra squeezed her eyes shut and fought even harder. In a second, she freed one of her arms and swung it back to get momentum for her punch. But Eric dropped to his knees and caught the hand before it could fly at my head.

"That's enough," he said in an entirely different tone, and her eyes flew open in surprise. Though he still couldn't catch her with his eyes, I figured he had charge of her now. I rolled off the Were to lie on my back in what remained of the floor in the tiny kitchen. Mr. Small and Dark (and Burned and Stunned), who I figured owned this house, was crumpled by the table.

Eric, who was having almost as much

trouble with Sandra as I'd had, took up a lot more of the available space. Exasperated with the Were, he adopted a simple solution. He squeezed the fist he'd caught, and she screamed. And shut up — and quit struggling.

"That's just not fair," I said, fighting a wave of weariness and pain.

"All's fair," he said quietly.

I didn't like the sound of that. "What are you talking about?" I asked. He shook his head. I tried again. "Where's Quinn?"

"The tiger has taken care of your two abductors," Eric said, with an unpleasant smile. "Would you like to go see?"

"Not particularly," I said, and closed my eyes again. "I guess they're dead?"

"I'm sure they wish they were," Eric said. "What did you do to the little man on the floor?"

"You wouldn't believe me if I told you," I said.

"Try me."

"I scared him so bad he spilled hot coffee on himself. Then I hit him with a stun gun that I got out of the van."

"Oh." There was a kind of breathy sound, and I opened my eyes to see that Eric was laughing silently.

"The Pelts?" I asked.

"Rasul has them covered," Eric said. "You have another fan, it seems."

"Oh, it's because of the fairy blood," I said irritably. "You know, it's not fair. Human guys don't like me. I know about two hundred of 'em who wouldn't want to date me if I came with a Chevy truck. But because supes are attracted to the fairy smell, I get accused of being a guy magnet. How wrong is that?"

"You have fairy blood," Eric said, as if his own lightbulb had just lit up. "That explains a lot."

That hurt my feelings. "Oh no, you couldn't just like me," I said, tired and hurting beyond coherence. "Oh no, gosh, there has to be a *reason.* And it's not gonna be my sparkling personality, oh no! It's gonna be my blood, because it's *special.* Not me, *I'm* not special . . ."

And I would have gone on and on, if Quinn hadn't said, "I don't give a damn about fairies, myself." Any available room left in the kitchen vanished.

I scrambled to my feet. "You okay?" I asked in a wobbly voice.

"Yes," he said, in his deepest rumble. He was altogether human again, and altogether naked. I would've hugged him, but I felt a little embarrassed about embracing him in

432

the altogether, in front of Eric.

"I left your clothes out there in the woods," I said. "I'll go get 'em."

"I can."

"No, I know where they are, and I couldn't get any wetter." Besides, I'm not sophisticated enough to be comfortable in a room with a naked guy, an unconscious guy, a real horrible girl, and another guy who's been my lover.

"Fuck you, bitch," the charming Sandra called after me, and shrieked again, as Eric made it clear he didn't care for name calling.

"Right back at you," I muttered, and trudged out into the rain.

Oh, yes, it was still raining.

I was still brooding over the fairy-blood thing as I scooped up the bundle of Quinn's sodden clothes. It would be easy to slide into a depressed trough if I thought the only reason anybody ever liked me was because I had fairy blood. Of course, there was always the odd vampire who had been ordered to seduce me . . . I was sure the fairy blood had just been a bonus, in that case . . . no, no, no, *wasn't going there.*

If I looked at it in a reasonable way, the blood was just as much a part of me as my eye color or the thickness of my hair. It hadn't done a thing for my half-fairy grand-mother, assuming the gene had come to me through her and not one of my other grand-parents. She'd married a human man who hadn't treated her any differently than he would have if her blood had been plain old grade A human. And she'd been killed by a human who hadn't known anything about her blood other than the color of it. Follow-ing the same assumption, fairy blood hadn't made a bit of difference to my father. He'd never in his life encountered a vampire who might be interested in him because of it — or if he had, he'd kept it mighty close. That didn't seem likely. And the fairy blood hadn't saved my father from the flash flood that had washed my parents' truck off the bridge and into the swollen stream. If the blood had come to me through my mother, well, she'd died in the truck, too. And Linda, my mother's sister, had died of cancer in her midforties, no matter what kind of heritage she had.

I didn't believe this wonderful fairy blood had done all that much for me, either. Maybe a few vampires had been a little more interested in me and friendly to me than they would have been otherwise, but I couldn't say that had been much of an advantage.

In fact, many people would say the vampire attention had been a big negative factor in my life. I might be one of those people. Especially since I was standing out here in the pouring rain holding someone else's wet clothes and wondering what the hell to do with them.

Having come full circle, I slogged back to the house. I could hear a lot of moaning coming from the front yard: Clete and George, presumably. I should have gone to check, but I couldn't muster up the energy.

Back in the kitchen, the small dark man was stirring a little, his eyes opening and shutting and his mouth twitching. His hands were tied behind him. Sandra was bound with duct tape, which cheered me up quite a bit. It seemed a neat piece of poetic justice. She even had a neat rectangle squarely over her mouth, which I presumed was Eric's work. Quinn had found a towel to secure around his waist, so he looked very . . . preppy.

"Thanks, babe," he said. He took his clothes and began squeezing them out over the sink. I dripped on the floor. "I wonder if there's a dryer?" he asked, and I opened another door to find a little pantry/utility room with shelves on one wall and on the other a water heater and a tiny washer and dryer.

"Pass 'em in here," I called, and Quinn came in with his clothes. "Yours need to go in there, too, babe," he said, and I noticed he sounded as tired as I felt. Changing into and out of tiger form without the full moon, in such a short space of time, must have been very difficult. "Maybe you can find me a towel?" I asked, pulling off the wet pants with great effort. Without a single joke or leer, he went to see what he could find. He returned with some clothes, I assumed from the small man's bedroom: a T-shirt, shorts, socks. "This is the best I could do," he said.

"It's better than I hoped for," I said. After I'd used the towel and I had pulled on the clean, dry clothes, I almost wept with gratitude. I gave Quinn a hug and then went to find out what we were going to do with our hostages.

The Pelts were sitting on the floor, securely handcuffed, in the living room, watched by Rasul. Barbara and Gordon had looked so mild when they'd come to Merlotte's to meet with me in Sam's office. They looked mild no longer. Rage and malice sat oddly on their suburban faces.

Eric brought Sandra in, too, and dumped her by her parents. Eric stood in one doorway, Quinn in another (which a glance told me led into Small and Dark's bedroom). Rasul, gun in hand, relaxed his vigilance a little now that he had such formidable backup. "Where's the little guy?" he asked. "Sookie, I'm glad to see you looking so well, even though your ensemble falls below your usual standards."

The shorts were baggy cargo shorts, the shirt was big, and the white socks were the capper. "You really know how to make a girl feel beautiful, Rasul," I said, scraping together maybe half a smile to offer him. I sat down in the straight-backed chair and I asked Barbara Pelt, "What were you going to do with me?"

"Work on you until you told us the truth, and Sandra was satisfied," she said. "Our family couldn't be at peace until we knew the truth. And the truth lies in you, I just know it."

I was troubled. Well, beyond troubled. Because I didn't know what to say to her just yet, I looked from Eric to Rasul. "Just the two of you?" I asked.

"Any time two vampires can't handle a handful of Weres is the day I become human again," Rasul said, with an expression so snooty I was tempted to laugh. But he'd been exactly right (though of course he'd had a tiger who helped). Quinn was propped in the doorway looking picturesque, though just at the moment his great expanse of smooth skin didn't interest me at all.

"Eric," I said, "what should I do?"

I don't think I'd ever asked Eric for advice before. He was surprised. But the secret wasn't only mine.

After a moment, he nodded.

"I'll tell you what happened to Debbie," I said to the Pelts. I didn't ask Rasul and Quinn to leave the room. I was getting rid of this right now, both the lingering guilt and the hold Eric had on me.

I'd thought about that evening so often that my words came automatically. I didn't cry, because all my tears had been shed months ago, in private.

Once I'd finished the story, the Pelts sat and stared at me, and I stared back.

"That sounds like our Debbie," said Barbara Pelt. "This has the ring of truth."

"She did have a gun," said Gordon Pelt. "I gave it to her for Christmas two years ago." The two Weres looked at each other.

"She was . . . proactive," Barbara said, after a moment. She turned to Sandra. "Remember when we had to go to court, when she was in high school, because she put superglue in that cheerleader's hair-

438

brush? The one that was dating her ex-boyfriend? That does sound like Debbie, huh?"

Sandra nodded, but the duct tape wouldn't permit her speech. Sandra had tears rolling down her cheeks.

"You still don't remember where you put her?" Gordon asked Eric.

"I would tell you if I did," Eric said. *Not that I care,* his tone implied.

"You guys hired the two kids who attacked us in Shreveport," Quinn said.

"Sandra did," Gordon admitted. "We didn't know about it until Sandra had already bitten them. She'd promised them . . ." He shook his head. "She'd sent them to Shreveport on her errand, but they would have returned home to collect their reward. Our Jackson pack would have killed them. Mississippi doesn't permit bitten Weres. They kill them on sight. The boys would have named Sandra as their maker. The pack would have abjured her. Barbara's dabbled with witchcraft, but nothing of the level that would have sealed the boys' mouths. We hired an out-of-state Were to track them when we found out. He couldn't stop them, couldn't prevent their arrest, so he had to be arrested and go into the jail system with them, to take care of the problem." He looked up at us, shook his head sternly. "He bribed Cal Myers to put him in the cell with them. Of course, we punished Sandra for that."

"Oh, did you take away her cell phone for a week?" If I sounded sarcastic, I thought I had a right to be. Even cooperative, the Pelts were pretty horrible. "We were both hurt," I said, nodding toward Quinn, "and those two kids are dead now. Because of Sandra."

"She's our daughter," Barbara said. "And she believed she was avenging her murdered sister."

"And then you hired all the Weres that were in the second van, and the two Weres lying out in the front yard. Are they going to die, Quinn?"

"If the Pelts don't take them to a Were doctor, they may. And they sure can't go to any human hospital."

Quinn's claws would have left distinctive marks.

"Will you do that?" I asked skeptically. "Take Clete and George to a Were doctor?"

The Pelts looked at each other and shrugged. "We figured you were going to kill us," Gordon said. "Are you going to let us walk away? With what assurances?"

I'd never met anyone quite like the Pelts

before, and it was easier and easier to see where Debbie had gotten her charming personality, adopted or not.

"With assurances that I never hear of this again," I said. "Neither I nor Eric."

Quinn and Rasul had been listening silently.

"Sookie is a friend of the Shreveport pack," Quinn said. "They are very upset she was attacked, in their own city, and now we know you're responsible for that attack."

"We heard she was no favorite of the new packleader." Barbara's voice held a trace of contempt. She was reverting to her own personality, since she no longer feared her own death. I liked them better when they were scared.

"He may not be packleader for long," Quinn said, his voice a quiet threat. "Even if he stays in office, he can't rescind the pack's protection, since it was guaranteed by the previous packleader. The honor of the pack would be destroyed."

"We'll make reparations to the Shreveport pack," Gordon said wearily.

"Did you send Tanya to Bon Temps?" I asked.

Barbara looked proud of herself. "Yes, I did that. You know our Debbie was adopted? She was a werefox."

I nodded. Eric looked quizzical; I didn't think he'd met Tanya.

"Tanya is a member of Debbie's birth family, and she wanted to do something to help. She thought if she went to Bon Temps and began working with you, you might let something spill. She said you were too suspicious to warm up to her offer of friendship. I think she might stay in Bon Temps. I understand finding the bar owner so attractive was an unexpected bonus."

It was kind of gratifying to discover Tanya was as untrustworthy as I'd suspected. I wondered if I had the right to tell Sam this whole story, by way of warning. I'd have to think about that later.

"And the man who owns this house?" I could hear him groaning and moaning from the kitchen.

"He's a former high school buddy of Debbie's," Gordon said. "We asked him if we could borrow his house for the afternoon. And we paid him. He won't talk after we leave."

"What about Gladiola?" I asked. I remembered the two burning body sections on my driveway. I remembered Mr. Cataliades's face, and Diantha's grief.

They all three stared at me blankly. "Gladiola? The flower?" Barbara said, looking genuinely puzzled. "It's not even the right season for glads, now."

That was a dead end.

"Do you agree we're square on this?" I asked baldly. "I've hurt you, you've hurt me. Even?"

Sandra shook her head from side to side, but her parents ignored her. Thank God for duct tape. Gordon and Barbara nodded at each other.

Gordon said, "You killed Debbie, but we do believe that you killed her in self-defense. And our living daughter took extreme and unlawful methods to attack you. . . . It goes against my grain to say this, but I think we have to agree to leave you alone, after this day."

Sandra made a lot of weird noises.

"With these stipulations." Gordon's face suddenly looked hard as a rock. The yuppie man took a backseat to the Were. "You won't come after Sandra. And you stay out of Mississippi."

"Done," I said instantly. "Can you control Sandra enough to make her keep to this agreement?" It was a rude but valid question. Sandra had enough balls for an army, and I doubted very much if the Pelts had ever really had control over either of their daughters.

"Sandra," Gordon said to his daughter. Her eyes blazed at him from her forcibly mute face. "Sandra, this is law. We are giving our word to this woman, and our word is binding on you. If you defy me, I'll challenge you at the next full moon. I'll take you down in front of the pack."

Both mother and daughter looked shocked, Sandra more so than her mother. Sandra's eyes narrowed, and after a long moment, she nodded.

I hoped Gordon lived a long time and enjoyed good health while he lived. If he grew ill, or if he died, Sandra wouldn't feel bound by this agreement, I felt pretty darn sure. But as I walked out of the little house in the swamp, I thought I had a reasonable chance of not seeing the Pelts again in my life, and that was absolutely okay with me.

22

Amelia was rummaging through her walk-in closet. It was just after dark the next day. Suddenly the hangers quit sliding across the rack at the very back of the closet.

"I think I have one," she called, sounding surprised. I waited for her to emerge, sitting on the edge of her bed. I'd had at least ten hours' sleep, I'd had a careful shower, I'd had some first aid, and I felt a hundred times better. Amelia was glowing with pride and happiness. Not only had Bob the Mormony witch been wonderful in bed, they'd been up in time to watch Quinn's and my abduction, and to have the brilliant idea of calling the vampire queen's mansion instead of the regular police. I hadn't told her yet that Quinn and I had made our own call, because I didn't know which one had been more effective, and I enjoyed seeing Amelia so happy.

I hadn't wanted to go to the queen's shindig at all until after my trip to the bank with Mr. Cataliades. After I'd returned to Hadley's apartment, I'd resumed packing my cousin's stuff and heard a strange noise when I'd put the coffee into a box. Now if I wanted to avert disaster, I had to go to the queen's spring party, the supernatural event of the year. I'd tried getting in touch with Andre at the queen's headquarters, but a voice had told me he was not to be disturbed. I wondered who was answering the phones at Vampire Central that day. Could it be one of Peter Threadgill's vamps?

"Yes, I do!" Amelia exclaimed. "Ah, it's kind of daring. I was the bridesmaid at an extreme wedding." She emerged from the closet with her hair disheveled, her eyes lit with triumph. She rotated the hanger so I could get the full effect. She'd had to pin the dress to the hanger because there was so little to hang.

"Yikes," I said, uneasily. Made mostly of lime-green chiffon, it was cut in a deep V almost down to the waist. A single narrow strap ran around the neck.

"It was a movie star wedding," Amelia said, looking as if she had a lot of memories of the service. Since the dress was also backless, I was wondering how those Hollywood women kept their boobs covered. Double-sided tape? Some kind of glue? As I hadn't seen Claudine since she vanished from the courtyard before the ectoplasmic reconstruction, I had to assume she'd gone back to her job and her life in Monroe. I could have used her special services just about now. There had to be a fairy spell that would make your dress stay still.

"At least you don't need a special bra to wear under it," Amelia said helpfully. That was true; it wasn't possible to wear a bra at all. "And I've got the shoes, if you can wear a seven."

"That's a big help," I said, trying to sound pleased and grateful. "I don't suppose you can do hair?"

"Nah," Amelia said. She waved a hand at her own short 'do. "I wash it, brush it, and that's that. But I can call Bob." Her eyes glowed happily. "He's a hairdresser."

I tried not to look too astonished. *At a funeral home?* I thought, but I was smart enough to keep that to myself. Bob just looked no way like any hairdresser I'd ever seen.

After a couple of hours, I was more or less into the dress, and fully made up.

Bob had done a good job with my hair, though he'd reminded me several times to keep very still, in a way that had made me a little nervous.

And Quinn had shown up on time in his car. When Eric and Rasul had dropped me off at about two in the morning, Quinn had just gotten in his car and driven away to wherever he was staying, though he'd put a light kiss on my forehead before I started up the stairs. Amelia had come out of her apartment, all happy I was safely back, and I'd had to return a call from Mr. Cataliades, who wondered if I was quite all right, and who wanted me to go to the bank with him to finalize Hadley's financial affairs. Since I'd missed my chance to go with Everett, I'd been grateful.

But when I'd returned to Hadley's apartment after the bank trip, I'd found a message on Hadley's answering machine telling me that the queen expected to see me at the party at the old monastery tonight. "I don't want you to leave the city without seeing me again," the queen's human secretary had quoted her as saying, before informing me that the dress code was formal. After my discovery, when I realized I'd have to attend the party, I'd gone down the stairs to Amelia's in a panic.

The dress caused another kind of panic. I was better-endowed than Amelia, though a bit shorter, and I had to stand really straight.

"The suspense is killing me," said Quinn, eyeing my chest. He looked wonderful in a tux. My wrist bandages stuck out against my tan like strange bracelets; in fact, one of them was acutely uncomfortable, and I was anxious to take it off. But the wrist would have to stay covered a while, though the bite on my left arm could remain uncovered. Maybe the suspense about my boobs would distract partygoers from the fact that my face was swollen and discolored on one side.

Quinn, of course, looked as though nothing had ever happened to him. Not only did he have the quick-healing flesh of most shape-shifters, but a man's tux covers up a lot of injuries.

"Don't you make me feel any more self-conscious than I already do," I said. "For about a dime, I'd go crawl back into bed and sleep for a week."

"I'm up for that, though I'd reduce the sleep time," Quinn said sincerely. "But for our peace of mind, I think we better do this first. By the way, my suspense was about the trip to the bank, not your dress. I figure, with your dress, it's a win-win situation. If you stay in it, good. If you don't, even better."

I looked away, trying to control an involuntary smile. "The trip to the bank." That seemed like a safe topic. "Well, her bank account didn't have a lot in it, which I figured would be the case. Hadley didn't have much sense about money. Hadley didn't have much sense, period. But the safe-deposit box . . ."

The safe-deposit box had held Hadley's birth certificate, a marriage license, and a divorce decree dated more than three years ago — both naming the same man, I was glad to see — and a laminated copy of my aunt's obituary. Hadley had known when her mother had died, and she'd cared enough to keep the clipping. There were pictures from our shared childhood, too: my mother and her sister; my mother and Jason, me, and Hadley; my grandmother and her husband. There was a pretty necklace with sapphires and diamonds (which Mr. Cataliades had said the queen had given to Hadley), and a pair of matching earrings. There were a couple more things that I wanted to think about.

But the queen's bracelet was not there. That was why Mr. Cataliades had wanted to accompany me, I think; he half expected the bracelet would be there, and he seemed quite anxious when I held the lockbox out to him so he could see its contents for himself.

"I finished packing the kitchen stuff this afternoon after Cataliades took me back to Hadley's apartment," I said to Quinn, and watched his reaction. I would never again take the disinterestedness of my companions for granted. I found myself fairly convinced Quinn had not been helping me pack the day before in order to search for something, after I saw that his reaction was perfectly calm.

"That's good," he said. "Sorry I didn't make it over to help you today. I was closing out Jake's dealings with Special Events. I had to call my partners, let them know. I had to call Jake's girlfriend. He wasn't steady enough to be around her, if she even wants to see him again. She's not a vamp lover, to put it mildly."

At the moment, I wasn't either. I couldn't fathom the true reason the queen wanted me at the party, but I had found another reason to see her. Quinn smiled at me, and I smiled back at him, hoping that some good would come out of this evening. I had to admit to myself that I was a bit curious about seeing the queen's party barn, so to speak — and I was also kind of glad to dress up and be pretty after all the swamp slogging.

As we drove, I almost opened a conversation with Quinn at least three times — but on every occasion, when it got to the point, I kept my mouth shut.

"We're getting close," he told me when we'd reached one of the oldest neighborhoods in New Orleans, the Garden District. The houses, set in beautiful grounds, would cost many times what even the Bellefleur mansion would fetch. In the middle of these marvelous homes, we came to a high wall that extended for a whole block. This was the renovated monastery that the queen used for entertaining.

There might be other gates at the back of the property, but tonight all the traffic was moving through the main front entrance. It was heavily protected with the most efficient guards of all: vampires. I wondered if Sophie-Anne Leclerq was paranoid, or wise, or simply did not feel loved (or safe) in her adopted city. I was sure the queen also had the regular security provisions — cameras, infrared motion detectors, razor wire, maybe even guard dogs. There was security out the ying-yang here, where the elite vampires occasionally partied with the elite humans. Tonight the party was supes only, the first large party the newlyweds had given since they'd become a couple.

Three of the queen's vampires were at the

gate, along with three of the Arkansas vampires. Peter Threadgill's vampires all wore a uniform, though I suspected the king called it livery. The Arkansas bloodsuckers, male and female, were wearing white suits with blue shirts and red vests. I didn't know if the king was ultrapatriotic or if the colors had been chosen because they were in the Arkansas state flag as well as the U.S. flag. Whichever, the suits were beyond tacky and into some fashion hall of shame, all on their own. And Threadgill had been dressed so conservatively! Was this some tradition I'd never heard of? Gosh, even I knew better than that, tastewise, and I bought most of my clothes at Wal-Mart.

Quinn had the queen's card to show to the guards at the gate, but still they called up to the main house. Quinn looked uneasy, and I hoped he was as concerned as I was about the extreme security and the fact that Threadgill's vampires had worked so hard to distinguish themselves from the queen's adherents. I was thinking hard about the queen's need to offer the king's vamps a reason she would go upstairs with me at Hadley's. I thought of the anxiety she displayed when she asked about the bracelet. I thought of the presence of both camps of vampires at the main gate. Neither

monarch trusted the spouse to provide protection.

It seemed like a long time before we were
given leave to pass through. Quinn was as
quiet as I while we waited.

The grounds seemed to be beautifully
landscaped and kept, and they were certainly well lit.

"Quinn, this is just wrong," I said. "What's
going on here? Do you think they'd let us
leave?" Unfortunately, it seemed as though
all my suspicions were true.

Quinn didn't look any happier than I was.
"They won't let us out," he said. "We have
to go on now." I clutched my little evening
bag closer to me, wishing there was something more lethal in it than a few small
items like a compact and a lipstick, and a
tampon. Quinn drove us carefully up the
winding drive to the front of the monastery.

"What did you do today, besides work on
your outfit?" Quinn asked.

"I made a lot of phone calls," I said. "And
one of them paid off."

"Calls? Where to?"

"Gas stations, all along the route from
New Orleans to Bon Temps."

He turned to stare at me, but I pointed
just in time for Quinn to apply the brakes.

A lion strolled across the drive.

"Okay, what's that? Animal? Or shifter?" I was edgier by the minute.

"Animal," Quinn said.

Scratch the idea of dogs roaming the enclosure. I hoped the wall was high enough to keep the lion in.

We parked in front of the former monastery, which was a very large two-story building. It hadn't been built for beauty, but for utility, so it was a largely featureless structure. There was one small door in the middle of the façade, and small windows placed regularly. Again, fairly easy to defend.

Outside the small door stood six more vampires, three in fancy but unmatching clothes — surely Louisiana bloodsuckers — and three more from Arkansas, in their glaringly garish outfits.

"That's just butt-ugly," I said.

"But easy to see, even in the dark," Quinn said, looking as if he were thinking deep, significant thoughts.

"Duh," I said. "Isn't that the point? So they'll instantly . . . oh." I mulled it over. "Yeah," I said. "No one would wear anything close to that, on purpose or by accident. Under any circumstances. Unless it was really important to be instantly identifiable."

Quinn said, "It's possible that Peter

Threadgill is not devoted to Sophie-Anne."

I gave a squawk of laughter just as two Louisiana vampires opened our car doors in a move so coordinated it must have been rehearsed. Melanie, the guard vampire I'd met at the queen's downtown headquarters, took my hand to help me from the car, and she smiled at me. She looked a lot better out of the overwhelming SWAT gear. She was wearing a pretty yellow dress with low heels. Now that she wasn't wearing a helmet, I could see her hair was short, intensely curly, and light brown.

She took a deep, dramatic breath as I passed, and then made an ecstatic face. "Oh, the odor of the fairy!" she exclaimed. "It makes my heart sing!"

I swatted at her playfully. To say I was surprised would be an understatement. Vampires, as a whole, are not noted for their sense of humor.

"Cute dress," Rasul said. "Kind of on the daring side, huh?"

Chester said, "Can't be too daring for me. You look really tasty."

I thought it couldn't be a coincidence that the three vampires I'd met at the queen's headquarters were the three vampires on door duty tonight. I couldn't figure out what that could mean, though. The three Arkansas vampires were silent, regarding the to-and-fro between us with cold eyes. They were not in the same relaxed and smiling mood as their fellows.

Something definitely off-kilter here. But with the acute vampire hearing all around, there wasn't anything to say about it.

Quinn took my arm. We walked into a long hall that seemed to run nearly the length of the building. A Threadgill vampire was standing at the door of a room that seemed to serve as a reception area.

"Would you like to check your bag?" she asked, obviously put out at being relegated to a hat-check girl.

"No, thanks," I said, and thought she was going to pull it out from under my arm.

"May I search it?" she asked. "We screen for weapons."

I stared at her, always a risky thing to do to a vampire. "Of course not. I have no weapons."

"Sookie," Quinn said, trying not to sound alarmed. "You have to let her look in your purse. It's procedure."

I glared at him. "You could have told me," I said sharply.

The door guard, who was a svelte young vamp with a figure that challenged the cut of the white pants, seized my purse with an air of triumph. She turned it out over a tray, and its few contents clattered to the metal surface: a compact, a lipstick, a tiny tube of glue, a handkerchief, a ten-dollar bill, and a tampon in a rigid plastic applicator, completely covered in plastic wrap.

Quinn was not unsophisticated enough to turn red, but he did glance discreetly away. The vampire, who had died long before women carried such items in their purses, asked me its purpose and nodded when I explained. She repacked my little evening bag and handed it to me, indicating with a hand gesture that we should proceed down the hall. She'd turned to the people who'd come in behind us, a Were couple in their sixties, before we'd even exited the room.

"What are you up to?" Quinn asked, in the quietest possible voice, as we moved along the corridor.

"Do we have to pass through any more security?" I asked, in a voice just as hushed.

"I don't know. I don't see any up ahead."

"I have to do something," I said. "Excuse me, while I find the nearest ladies' room." I tried to tell him, with my eyes, and with the pressure of my hand on his arm, that in a few minutes everything would be all right, and I sincerely hoped that was the truth. Quinn was clearly not happy with me, but he waited outside the ladies' room (God knows what that had been when the building was a monastery) while I ducked into one of the stalls and made a few adjustments. When I came out, I'd tossed the tampon container into the little bin in the stall, and one of my wrists had been rebandaged. My purse was a little heavier.

The door at the end of the corridor led into the very large room that had been the monks' refectory. Though the room was still walled with stone and large pillars supported the roof, three on the left and three on the right, the rest of the decor was considerably different now. The middle of the room was cleared for dancing, and the floor was wooden. There was a dais for musicians close to the refreshments table, and another dais at the opposite end of the room for the royalty.

Around the sides of the room were chairs in conversational groupings. The whole room was decorated in white and blue, the colors of Louisiana. One of the walls had murals depicting scenes from around the state: a swamp scene, which made me shudder; a Bourbon Street montage; a field being plowed and lumber being cut; and a fisherman hoisting up a net in the Gulf Coast. These were all scenes featuring humans, I thought, and wondered what the thinking was behind that. Then I turned to look at the wall surrounding the doorway I'd just entered, and I saw the vampire side of Louisiana life: a group of happy vampires with fiddles under their chins, playing away; a vampire police officer patrolling the French Quarter; a vampire guide leading tourists through one of the Cities of the Dead. No vamps snacking on humans, no vamps drinking anything, I noticed. This was a statement in public relations. I wondered if it really fooled anyone. All you had to do was sit down at a supper table with vampires, and you'd be reminded how different they were, all right.

Well, this wasn't what I'd come to do. I looked around for the queen, and I finally saw her standing by her husband. She was wearing a long-sleeved orange silk dress, and she looked fabulous. Long sleeves maybe seemed a little strange in the warm evening, but vampires didn't notice such things. Peter Threadgill was wearing a tux, and he looked equally impressive. Jade Flower was standing behind him, sword strapped to her back even though she was wearing a red sequined dress (in which, by the way, she looked awful). Andre, also fully armed, was at his station behind the queen.

Sigebert and Wybert couldn't be far off. I spotted them on either side of a door that I assumed led to the queen's private apartments. The two vampires looked acutely uncomfortable in their tuxes; it was like watching bears who'd been made to wear shoes.

Bill was in the room. I caught a glimpse of him in the far corner, in the opposite direction from the queen, and I shivered with loathing.

"You have too many secrets," Quinn complained, following the direction of my gaze.

"I'll be glad to tell you a few of 'em, real soon," I promised, and we joined the tail end of the reception line. "When we reach the royals, you go ahead of me. While I'm talking to the queen, you distract the king, okay? Then I will tell you everything."

We reached Mr. Cataliades first. I guess he was sort of the queen's secretary of state. Or maybe attorney general would be more appropriate?

"Good to see you again, Mr. Cataliades," I said, in my most correct social tone. "I've got a surprise for you," I added.

"You may have to save it," he said with a kind of stiff cordiality. "The queen is about to have the first dance with her new king.

And we're all so looking forward to seeing the present the king gave her."

I glanced around but I didn't see Diantha. "How's your niece?" I asked.

"My surviving niece," he said grimly, "is at home with her mother."

"That's too bad," I said. "She should be here this evening."

He stared at me. Then he looked interested.

"Indeed," he said.

"I heard that someone from here stopped to get gas a week ago Wednesday, on her way to Bon Temps," I said. "Someone with a long sword. Here, let me tuck this in your pocket. I don't need it any more." When I stepped away from him and faced the queen, I had one hand over my injured wrist. The bandage had vanished.

I held out my right hand, and the queen was forced to take it in her own. I had counted on obliging the queen to follow the human custom of shaking hands, and I was mighty relieved when she did. Quinn had passed from the queen to the king, and he said, "Your Majesty, I'm sure you remember me. I was the event coordinator at your wedding. Did the flowers turn out like you wanted?"

Somewhat startled, Peter Threadgill

turned his large eyes on Quinn, and Jade Flower kept her eyes on what her king did.

Trying very hard to keep my movements swift but not jerky, I pressed my left hand and what was in it onto the queen's wrist. She didn't flinch, but I think she thought about it. She glanced down at her wrist to see what I'd put on it, and her eyes closed in relief.

"Yes, my dear, our visit was lovely," she said, at random. "Andre enjoyed it very much, as did I." She glanced back over her shoulder, and Andre picked up his cue, and inclined his head to me, in tribute to my supposed talents in the sack. I was so glad to get the ordeal over with that I smiled at him radiantly, and he looked a shade amused. The queen raised her arm slightly to beckon him closer, and her sleeve rode up. Suddenly Andre was smiling as broadly as I was.

Jade Flower was distracted by Andre's movement forward, and her eyes followed his. They widened, and she was very much not smiling. In fact, she was enraged. Mr. Cataliades was looking at the sword on Jade Flower's back with a completely blank face.

Then Quinn was dismissed by the king and it was my turn to pay homage to Peter Threadgill, King of Arkansas.

"I hear that you had an adventure in the swamps yesterday," he said, his voice cool and indifferent.

"Yes, sir. But it all worked out okay, I think," I said.

"Good of you to come," he said. "Now that you have wrapped up your cousin's estate, I am sure you will be returning to your home?"

"Oh, yes, quick as can be," I said. It was the absolute truth. I would go home providing I could just survive this evening, though at the moment the chances weren't looking too good. I had counted, as well as I was able in a throng like this. There were at least twenty vampires in the room wearing the bright Arkansas outfit, and perhaps the same number of the queen's homies.

I moved away, and the Were couple that had entered after Quinn and me took my place. I thought he was the lieutenant governor of Louisiana, and I hoped he had good life insurance.

"What?" Quinn demanded.

I led him over to a place against the wall, and gently maneuvered him until his back was against it. I had to face away from any lip-readers in the room.

"Did you know the queen's bracelet was missing?" I asked.

He shook his head. "One of the diamond bracelets the king gave her as a wedding present?" he asked, his head ducked to baffle any watchers.

"Yes, missing," I said. "Since Hadley died."

"If the king knew the bracelet was missing, and if he could force the queen to acknowledge that she'd given it to a lover, then he would have grounds for divorce."

"What would he get then?"

"What *wouldn't* he get! It was a vampire hierarchal marriage, and you don't get any more binding than that. I think the wedding contract was thirty pages."

I understood much better now.

A beautifully dressed vampire woman wearing a gray-green gown strewn with gleaming silver flowers raised her arm to get the attention of the crowd. Gradually the assembled people fell silent.

"Sophie-Anne and Peter welcome you to their first joint entertainment," the vamp said, and her voice was so musical and mellow that you wanted to listen to her for hours. They should get her to do the Oscars. Or the Miss America pageant. "Sophie-Anne and Peter invite all of you to have a wonderful evening of dancing, eating, and drinking. To open the dancing, our host and hostess will waltz."

Despite his glitzy surface, I thought Peter might be more comfortable doing a square dance, but with a wife like Sophie-Anne, it was waltz or nothing. He advanced on his wife, his arms at the ready to receive her, and in his carrying vampire voice he said, "Darling, show them the bracelets."

Sophie-Anne swept the crowd with a smile and raised her own arms to make the sleeves slide back, and a matching bracelet on each wrist shone at the guests, the two huge diamonds winking and blinking in the chandelier lights.

For a moment Peter Threadgill was absolutely still, as if someone had zapped him with a freeze gun. He altered his stance as he moved forward, after that, and took one of her hands in both of his. He stared down at one bracelet, then released her hand to take the other. That bracelet, too, passed his silent test.

"Wonderful," he said, and if it was through his fangs you'd only think they'd extended because he was horny for his beautiful wife. "You're wearing both of them."

"Of course," Sophie-Anne said. "My darling." Her smile was just as sincere as his.

And away they danced, though something

about the way he swung her let me know the king was letting his temper get the better of him. He'd had a big plan, and now I'd spoiled it . . . but thankfully, he didn't know my part. He just knew that somehow Sophie-Anne had managed to retrieve her bracelet and save her face, and he had nothing to justify whatever he'd plotted to do. He would have to back down. After this, he'd probably think of another way to subvert his queen, but at least I'd be out of the fray.

Quinn and I retreated to the refreshments table, located to the south side of the large room, beside one of the thick pillars. Servers were there with carving knives to shave off ham or roast beef. There were yeasty rolls to pile the meat on. It smelled wonderful, but I was too nervous to think of eating. Quinn got me a cup of ginger ale from the bar. I stared at the dancing couple and waited for the ceiling to fall in.

"Don't they look lovely together?" a well-dressed gray-haired woman said. I realized she was the one who'd come in after me.

"Yes, they do," I agreed.

"I'm Genevieve Thrash," she said. "This is my husband, David."

"Pleased to meet you," I said. "I'm Sookie Stackhouse, and this is my friend, John

467

Quinn." Quinn looked surprised. I wondered if that was actually his first name.

The two men, tiger and Were, shook hands while Genevieve and I watched the couple dance a bit longer.

"Your dress is so pretty," Genevieve said, giving every indication she was speaking sincerely. "It takes a young body to show off a gown like that."

"I appreciate your saying so," I said. "I'm showing a bit more of that body than I'm comfortable with, so you've made me feel better."

"I know your date appreciates it," she said. "And so does that young man over there." She nodded her head subtly, and I glanced in the direction she was indicating. Bill. He looked very good in his tuxedo, but even being in the same room made something within me twist with pain.

"I believe your husband is the lieutenant governor?" I said.

"You're absolutely correct."

"And how do you like being Mrs. Lieutenant?" I asked.

She told some amusing stories about people she'd met while she followed David's political career. "And what does your young man do?" she asked, with that eager interest that must have helped her husband up that ladder.

"He's an events coodinator," I said, after a moment's hesitation.

"How interesting," Genevieve said. "And yourself, you have a job?"

"Oh, yes ma'am," I said. "I'm a barmaid."

That was a bit startling to the politician's wife, but she grinned at me. "You're the first I've ever met," she said cheerfully.

"You're the first Mrs. Lieutenant Governor I've ever met," I said. Damn, now that I'd met her and liked her, I felt responsible for her. Quinn and David were just chatting away, and I think fishing was their topic.

"Mrs. Thrash," I said, "I know you're a Were and that means you're tough as tough can be, but I'm going to give you a piece of advice."

She looked at me quizzically.

"This advice is pure gold," I said.

Her eyebrows flew up. "Okay," she said, slowly. "I'm listening."

"Something very bad is going to happen here in the next hour or so. It's going to be so bad that it might get a lot of people killed. Now you can stay and have a good time until it happens, and then you'll wonder why you didn't listen to me, or you can leave now after acting like you've been

469

taken ill, and you can save yourself a lot of unhappiness."

Her gaze was intent. I could hear her wondering whether to take me seriously. I didn't seem like a weirdo or a crazy person. I seemed like a normal, attractive, young woman with a heck of a handsome date.

"Are you threatening me?" she asked.

"No, ma'am. I'm trying to save your ass."

"We'll get one dance in first," Genevieve Thrash said, making up her mind. "David, honey, let's take a spin around the dance floor and then make our excuses. I've got the worst headache you ever felt." David obligingly broke off his conversation with Quinn to take his wife to the clear space and begin waltzing along with the royal vampire couple, who looked relieved to have company.

I was beginning to relax my posture again, but a glance from Quinn reminded me to stand very straight. "I *love* the dress," he said. "Shall we dance?"

"You can waltz?" I hoped my jaw hadn't dropped too far.

"Yep," he said. He didn't ask if I could, though as a matter of fact I'd been watching the queen's steps intently. I can dance — can't sing, but I love a dance floor. I'd never waltzed, but I figured I could do it.

It was wonderful to have Quinn's arm around me, to be moving so gracefully around the floor. For a moment, I just forgot everything and enjoyed looking up at him, feeling the way a girl feels when she's dancing with a guy she expects she'll make love with, sooner or later. Quinn's fingers touching my bare back just made me tingle.

"Sooner or later," he said, "we're gonna be in a room with a bed, no phones, and a door that will lock."

I smiled up at him and spied the Thrashes easing out of the door. I hoped their car had been brought around. And that was the last normal thought I had for some time.

A head flew past Quinn's shoulder. It was moving too fast for me to pin down whose head it was, but it looked familiar. A spray of blood created a ruddy cloud in the head's wake.

I made a sound. It wasn't a scream or a gasp; more like "Eeeeep."

Quinn stopped dead, though the music didn't for a long moment. He looked in all directions, trying to analyze what was happening and how we could survive it. I'd thought one dance would be okay, but we should have gone with the Were couple. Quinn began pulling me over to the side of the ballroom, and he said, "Backs against the wall." We'd know from which direction the danger was coming: good thinking. But someone cannoned into us and Quinn's hold on my hand was broken.

There was a lot of screaming and a lot of movement. The screaming was all from the Weres and other supes who'd been invited to the party, and the movement was mostly from the vampires, who were looking for their allies amid the chaos. This was where the horrible outfits worn by the king's followers came into their own. It was instantly easy to see who belonged to the king. Of course, that made them an easy target, too, if you didn't happen to like the king and his minions.

A thin black vampire with dreadlocks had whipped a sword with a curved blade out of nowhere, apparently. The blade was bloody, and I thought Dreadlocks was the head-lopper. He was wearing the awful suit, so he was someone I wanted to dodge. If I had any allies here, it wasn't anyone working for Peter Threadgill. I'd gotten behind one of the pillars holding up the ceiling of the west end of the refectory, and I was trying to figure out the safest way from the room when my foot bumped something that shifted. I looked down to see the head. It belonged to Wybert. I wondered for a fraction of a second if it would move or speak, but decapitation is pretty final, no matter what species you are.

"Oh," I moaned, and decided I'd better get a good hold on myself, or I was gonna look just like Wybert, at least in one important respect.

Fighting had broken out throughout the room. I hadn't seen the precipitating incident, but on some pretext the black vampire had attacked Wybert and cut off his head. Since Wybert was one of the queen's bodyguards and Dreadlocks was one of Peter's attendants, the beheading was a pretty decisive act.

The queen and Andre were standing back to back in the middle of the floor. Andre was holding a gun in one hand and a long knife in the other, and the queen had acquired a carving knife from the buffet. There was a circle of white coats surrounding them, and when one fell, another would take its place. This was like Custer's last stand, with the queen standing in for Custer. Sigebert was equally besieged on the bandstand, and the orchestra, part Were or shifter and part vampire, had separated into its various components. Some were joining in the combat, while others were trying to flee. Those who were doing their best to get the hell out of there were clogging the door leading to the long corridor. The effect was a logjam.

The king was under attack from my three friends Rasul, Chester, and Melanie. I was sure I'd find Jade Flower at his back, but she was having her own problems, I was glad to see. Mr. Cataliades was doing his best to — well, it looked like he was just trying to touch her. She was parrying his attempts with her whacking big sword, the sword that had sliced Gladiola in two, but neither of them looked like they were giving up any time soon.

Just then I was knocked flat to the floor, losing my breath for a minute. I struck out, only to have my hand trapped. I was smushed under a big body. "I've got you," Eric said.

"What the hell are you doing?"

"Protecting you," he said. He was smiling with the joy of battle, and his blue eyes were glittering like sapphires. Eric loved a brawl.

"I don't see anybody coming after me," I said. "It seems to me like the queen needs you more than I do. But I appreciate it."

Carried away on a wave of excitement, Eric kissed me long and hard and then scooped up Wybert's head. "Bowling for vampires," he said happily, and flung the disgusting object at the black vampire with an accuracy and force that knocked the sword out of the vampire's hand. Eric was on it with a great leap, and the sword swung on its owner with deadly force. With a war cry that had not been heard in a thousand years, Eric attacked the circle around the queen and Andre with a savagery and abandon that was almost beautiful in its way.

A shifter trying to find another way out of the room knocked against me with enough force to dislodge me from behind my comparatively secure position. Suddenly, there were too many people between me and the pillar, and the way back was blocked. Damn! I could see the door Wybert and his brother had been guarding. The door was across the room, but it was the only empty passage. Any way out of this room was a good way. I began sidling around the walls to reach it, so I wouldn't have to cross the dangerous open spaces.

One of the whitecoats leaped in front of me.

"We're supposed to find you!" he bellowed. He was a young vampire; there were clues, even at such a moment. This vamp had known the amenities of modern life. He had all the signs — superstraight teeth that had known braces, a husky build from modern nutrition, and he was big-boned and tall.

"Look!" I said, and pulled one side of my bodice away. He did, God bless him, and I kicked him in the balls so hard I thought they'd come out through his mouth. That's gonna get a man on the floor, no matter what their nature is. This vampire was no exception. I hurried around him and reached the east wall, the one with the door.

I had maybe a yard to go when someone grabbed my foot, and down I went. I slipped in a pool of blood and landed on my knees in it. It was vamp blood, I could tell by the color.

"Bitch," said Jade Flower. "Whore." I didn't think I'd ever heard her talk before. I could have done without it now. She began dragging me, hand over hand, toward her extended fangs. She wasn't getting up to kill me, because one of her legs was missing. I almost threw up but became more concerned with getting away than with ralphing. My hands scrabbled at the smooth wood floor, and my knees tried to get purchase so I could pull away from the vampire. I didn't know if Jade Flower would die of this terrible wound or not. Vampires could survive so many things that would kill a human, which of course was a big part of the attraction . . . *Snap to, Sookie!* I told myself fiercely.

The shock must be getting to me.

I threw out my hand and managed to get a grip on the door frame. I pulled and pulled, but I couldn't break free from Jade Flower's hold, and her fingers were digging into the flesh of my ankle. Soon she would snap the bones, and then I wouldn't be able to walk.

With my free foot I kicked the little Asian woman in the face. I did it again and again. Her nose was bleeding, and her lips were, too, but she would not let go. I don't think she even felt it.

Then Bill jumped on her back, landing with enough force to break her spine, and her hold on my ankle relaxed. I scrambled away while he raised a carving knife very like the one the queen had had. He sank it into Jade Flower's neck, over and over, and then her head was off and he was looking at me.

He didn't speak, just gave me that long, dark look. Then he was up and gone, and I had to get the hell out of there.

The queen's apartments were dark. That wasn't good. Beyond where the light penetrated from the ballroom, who knew what could be lurking?

There just had to be an outside door through here. The queen wouldn't leave herself bottled up. She'd have a way to get outside. And if I was remembering the orientation of the building, I needed to walk straight ahead to reach the correct wall.

I gathered myself and decided I'd just stride right on through. No more of this skulking around the wall. The hell with it.

And to my surprise, it worked, up to a point. I went through one room — a sitting room, I figured — before I ended up in what must have been the queen's bedroom. A whisper of movement in the room retriggered my fear switch, and I fumbled along the wall for the light. When I flipped it, I found I was in the room with Peter Threadgill. He was facing Andre. A bed was between them, and on the bed was the queen, who had been badly wounded. Andre didn't have his sword, but then neither did Peter Threadgill. Andre did have a gun, and when I turned on the light, he shot the king right in the face. Twice.

There was a door beyond the body of Peter Threadgill. It had to lead to the grounds. I began to sidle around the room, my back pressed against the wall. No one paid a bit of attention to me.

"Andre, if you kill him," the queen said quite calmly, "I'll have to pay a huge fine." She had a hand pressed to her side, and her beautiful orange dress was dark and wet with her blood.

"But wouldn't it be worth it, lady?"

There was a thoughtful silence on the queen's part, while I unlocked about six locks.

"On the whole, yes," Sophie-Anne said. "After all, money isn't everything."

"Oh, *good*," Andre said happily, and raised the gun. He had a stake in the other hand, I saw. I didn't stick around to see how Andre did the deed.

I set off across the lawn in my green evening shoes. Amazingly, the evening shoes were still intact. In fact, they were in better shape than my ankle, which Jade Flower had hurt pretty badly. I was limping by the time I'd taken ten steps. "Watch out for the lion," called the queen, and I looked behind me to see that Andre was carrying her out of the building. I wondered whose side the lion was on.

Then the big cat appeared right in front of me. One minute my escape route was clear, and the next it was filled by a lion. The outside security lights were off, and in the moonlight the beast looked so beautiful and so deadly that fear pulled the air right out of my lungs.

The lion made a low, guttural sound.

"Go away," I said. I had absolutely nothing to fight a lion with, and I was at the end of my rope. "Go away!" I yelled. "Get out of here!"

And it slunk into the bushes.

I don't think that is typical lion behavior. Maybe it smelled the tiger coming, because a second or two later, Quinn appeared, moving like a huge silent dream across the grass. Quinn rubbed his big head against me, and we went over to the wall together. Andre laid down his queen and leaped up on top with grace and ease. For his queen, he pulled apart the razor wire with hands just barely cushioned with his torn coat. Then down he came and carefully lifted Sophie-Anne. He gathered himself and cleared the wall in a bound.

"Well, I can't do that," I said, and even to my own ears, I sounded grumpy. "Can I stand on your back? I'll take my heels off." Quinn snugged up to the wall, and I ran my arm through the sandal straps. I didn't want to hurt the tiger by putting a lot of weight on his back, but I also wanted to get out of there more than I've wanted anything, just about. So, trying to think light thoughts, I balanced on the tiger's back and managed to pull myself, finally, to the top of the wall. I looked down, and it seemed like a very long way to the sidewalk.

After all I'd faced this evening, it seemed stupid to balk at falling a few feet. But I sat on the wall, telling myself I was an idiot, for several long moments. Then I managed to flip over onto my stomach, let myself down as far as I could reach, and said out loud, "One, two, three!" Then I fell.

For a couple of minutes I just lay there, stunned at how the evening had turned out.

Here I was, lying on a sidewalk in historical New Orleans, with my boobs hanging out of my dress, my hair coming down, my sandals on my arm, and a large tiger licking my face. Quinn had bounded over with relative ease.

"Do you think it would be better to walk back as a tiger, or as a large naked man?" I asked the tiger. "Because either way, you might attract some attention. I think you stand a better chance of getting shot if you're a tiger, myself."

"That will not be necessary," said a voice, and Andre loomed above me. "I am here with the queen in her car, and we will take you where you need to go."

"That's mighty nice of you," I said, as

Quinn began to change back.

"Her Majesty feels that she owes you," Andre said.

"I don't see it that way," I said. Why was I being so frank, now? Couldn't I just keep my mouth shut? "After all, if I hadn't found the bracelet and given it back, the king would have . . ."

"Started the war tonight anyway," Andre said, helping me to my feet. He reached out and quite impersonally pushed my right breast under the scanty lime-green fabric. "He would have accused the queen of breaking her side of the contract, which held that all gifts must be held in honor as tokens of the marriage. He would have brought suit against the queen, and she would have lost almost everything and been dishonored. He was ready to go either way, but when the queen was wearing the second bracelet, he had to go with violence. Ra Shawn set it off by beheading Wybert for bumping against him." Ra Shawn had been Dreadlock's name, I assumed.

I wasn't sure I got all that, but I was equally sure Quinn could explain it to me at a time when I had more brain cells to spare for the information.

"He was so disappointed when he saw she had the bracelet! And it was the right one!"

Andre said merrily. He was turning into a babbling brook, that Andre. He helped me into the car. "Where was it?" asked the queen, who was stretched across one of the seats. Her bleeding had stopped, and only the way she was holding her lips indicated what pain she was in.

"It was in the can of coffee that looked sealed," I said. "Hadley was real good with arts and crafts, and she'd opened the can real carefully, popped the bracelet inside, and resealed it with a glue gun." There was a lot more to explain, about Mr. Cataliades and Gladiola and Jade Flower, but I was too tired to volunteer information.

"How'd you get it past the search?" the queen asked. "I'm sure the searchers were checking for it."

"I had the bracelet part on under my bandage," I said. "The diamond stood out too far, though, so I had to prize it out. I put it in a tampon holder. The vampire who did the searching didn't think of pulling out the tampon, and she didn't really know how it was supposed to look, since she hadn't had a period in centuries."

"But it was put together," the queen said.

"Oh, I went into the ladies room after I'd had my purse searched. I had a little tube of superglue in my purse, too."

The queen didn't seem to know what to say. "Thank you," she told me, after a long pause. Quinn had climbed into the back with us, quite bare, and I leaned against him. Andre got into the driver's seat, and we glided off.

He dropped us off in the courtyard. Amelia was sitting on the pavement in her lawn chair, a glass of wine in her hand.

When we emerged, she set the glass down very carefully on the ground and then looked us over from head to toe.

"Okay, don't know how to react," she said, finally. The big car glided out of the courtyard as Andre took the queen to some safe hideaway. I didn't ask, because I didn't want to know.

"I'll tell you tomorrow," I said. "The moving truck will be here tomorrow afternoon, and the queen promised me people to load it and drive it. I have to get back to Bon Temps."

The prospect of going home seemed so sweet I could taste it on my tongue.

"So you got lots to do at home?" Amelia asked, as Quinn and I began going up the stairs. I guessed Quinn could sleep in the same bed. We were both too tired to plunge into anything; tonight was not the night to begin a relationship, if I hadn't already begun one. Maybe I had.

"Well, I have a lot of weddings to go to," I said. "I have to get back to work, too."

"Got an empty guest bedroom?"

I stopped about halfway up the stairs. "I might. Would you be needing one?"

It was hard to tell in the poor light, but Amelia might be looking embarrassed. "I tried something new with Bob," she said. "And it didn't exactly work out right."

"Where is he?" I asked. "In the hospital?"

"No, right there," she said. She was pointing at a garden gnome.

"Tell me you're joking," I said.

"I'm joking," she said. "This is Bob." She picked up a big black cat with a white chest that had been curled up in an empty planter. I hadn't even noticed him. "Isn't he cute?"

"Sure, bring him along," I said. "I've always been fond of cats."

"Babe," said Quinn, "I'm glad to hear you say that. I was too tired to completely change."

For the first time, I really looked at Quinn. Now he had a tail.

"You're definitely sleeping on the floor," I said.

"Ah, babe."

"I mean it. Tomorrow you'll be able to be all human, right?"

"Sure. I've changed too many times lately. I just need some rest."

Amelia was looking at the tail with wide eyes. "See you tomorrow, Sookie," she said. "We'll have us a little road trip. And then I'll get to stay with you for a while!"

"We'll have such fun," I said wearily, trudging up the rest of the stairs and feeling profoundly glad I'd stuck my door key in my underwear. Quinn was too tired to watch me retrieve it. I let the remnants of the dress fall back into place while I un-locked the door. "Such fun."

Later, after I'd showered and while Quinn was in the bathroom himself, I heard a tentative knock on the door. I was decent enough in my sleep pants and tank top. Though I wanted to ignore it more than anything, I opened the door.

Bill was looking pretty good for someone who'd fought in a war. The tuxedo would never be functional again, but he wasn't bleeding, and whatever cuts he might have sustained had already healed over.

"I have to talk to you," he said, and his voice was so quiet and limp that I took a step out of the apartment. I sat down on the gallery floor, and he sat with me.

"You have to let me say this, just once," he said. "I loved you. I love you."

I raised a hand to protest, and he said, "No, let me finish. She sent me there, true. But when I met you — after I came to know you — I really . . . loved you."

How long after he'd taken me to bed had this supposed love come about? How could I possibly believe him, since he'd lied so convincingly from the very moment I'd met him — playing disinterested because he could read my fascination with the first vampire I'd ever met?

"I risked my life for you," I said, the words coming out in a halting sequence. "I gave Eric power over me forever, for your sake, when I took his blood. I killed someone for you. This is not something I take for granted, even if you do . . . even if that's everyday existence for you. It's not, for me. I don't know if I can ever not hate you."

I got up, slowly and painfully, and to my relief he didn't make the mistake of trying to help me. "You probably saved my life tonight," I said, looking down at him. "And I thank you for that. But don't come into Merlotte's any more, don't hang around in my woods, and don't do anything else for me. I don't want to see you again."

"I love you," he said stubbornly, as if that fact were so amazing and such an undeniable truth that I should believe him. Well, I had, and look at where it had gotten me.

"Those words are not a magical formula," I said. "They're not going to open my heart to you."

Bill was over a hundred and thirty years old, but at that moment I felt I could match him. I dragged myself inside, shut the door behind me and locked it, and made myself go down the hall to the bedroom.

Quinn was drying himself off, and he turned around to show me his muscular derriere. "Fur-free," he said. "Can I share the bed?"

"Yes," I said, and crawled in. He got in the other side, and he was asleep in thirty seconds. After a minute or two, I slid over in the bed and put my head on his chest.

I listened to his heartbeat.

23

"What was the deal with Jade Flower?" Amelia asked the next day. Everett was driving the U-Haul, and Amelia and I were following in her little car. Quinn had left the next morning by the time I'd gotten up, leaving me a note telling me he was going to call me after he'd hired someone to take Jake Purifoy's place and after his next job, which was in Huntsville, Alabama — a Rite of Ascension, he said, though I had no idea what that was. He ended the note with a very personal comment about the lime-green dress, which I won't repeat here.

Amelia had her bags packed by the time I'd dressed, and Everett was directing two husky men in loading up the boxes I wanted to take back to Bon Temps. When he returned, he would take the furniture I didn't want to Goodwill. I'd offered it to him, but he'd looked at the fake antiques and politely said they weren't his style. I'd tossed my own stuff in Amelia's trunk, and off we'd driven. Bob the cat was in his own cage on the backseat. It was lined with towels and also held a food and water bowl, which was kind of messy. Bob's litter box was on the floorboard.

"My mentor found out what I'd done," Amelia said gloomily. "She's very, very unhappy with me."

I wasn't surprised, but it didn't seem tactful to say so, when Amelia had been such a help to me.

"He is missing his life now," I pointed out, as mildly as I could manage.

"Well, true, but he's having a hell of an experience," Amelia said, in the voice of someone determined to look on the bright side. "I'll make it up to him. Somehow."

I wasn't sure this was something you could "make up" to someone. "I'll bet you can get him back to himself soon," I said, trying to sound confident. "There are some really nice witches in Shreveport who might help." If Amelia could conquer her prejudice against Wiccans.

"Great," the witch said, looking more cheerful. "In the meantime, what the hell happened last night? Tell me in detail."

I figured it was all over the supernatural community today, so I might as well spill the beans. I told Amelia the whole story.

"So how did Cataliades know Jade Flower had killed Gladiola?" Amelia asked.

"Um, I told him," I said, my voice small.

"How'd you know?"

"When the Pelts told me they hadn't hired anyone to watch the house, I figured the murderer was someone sent by Peter Threadgill to delay my getting the message from Cataliades. Peter Threadgill knew all along that the queen had lost the bracelet to Hadley. Maybe he had spies among the queen's own people, or maybe one of her dumber followers, like Wybert, let it slip. It wouldn't be hard to watch the movements of the two goblin girls the queen used as messengers. When one of them came to deliver the queen's message to me, Jade Flower followed her and killed her. The wound was pretty drastic, and after I saw Jade Flower's sword and watched her whip it out so fast I couldn't see it move, I figured she was a likely candidate for the designated killer. Plus, the queen had said if Andre was in New Orleans, everyone had to assume she was, too . . . so the reverse had to be true, right? If the king was in New Orleans, everyone would assume Jade Flower was, too. But she was outside my house, in the woods." I shuddered all over at the memory.

"I found out for sure after calling a lot of gas stations. I talked to a guy who definitely remembered Jade Flower."

"So why did Hadley steal the bracelet?"

"Jealousy, I guess, and the desire to put the queen in a bad spot. I don't think Hadley understood the implications of what she'd done, and by the time she did, it was too late. The king had laid his plans. Jade Flower watched Hadley for a while, snatched the opportunity to take Jake Purifoy and kill him. They hoped it would be blamed on Hadley. Anything that would discredit Hadley would discredit the queen. They had no way of knowing she would turn him."

"What will happen to Jake now?" Amelia looked troubled. "I liked him. He was a nice guy."

"He still may be. He's just a vampire nice guy."

"I'm not sure there's such a thing," my companion said quietly.

"Some days, I'm not sure either." We rode for a while in silence.

"Well, tell me about Bon Temps," Amelia said, to get us out of our conversational doldrums.

I began to tell her about the town, and the bar where I worked, and the wedding shower I'd been invited to attend, and all the upcoming weddings.

"Sounds pretty good," Amelia said. "Hey, I know I kind of asked myself along. Do you mind, I mean, really?"

"No," I said, with a speed that surprised even me. "No, it'll be nice to have company . . . for a while," I added cautiously. "What will you do about your house in New Orleans while you're gone?"

"Everett said he wouldn't mind living in the upper apartment, because his mom was getting kind of hard to take. Since he's got such a good job with Cataliades, he can afford it. He'll watch my plants and stuff until I get back. He can always e-mail me." Amelia had a laptop in her trunk, so for the first time there'd be a computer in the Stackhouse home. There was a pause, and then she said, her voice tentative, "How are you feeling now? I mean, with the ex and all?"

I considered. "I have a big hole in my heart," I said. "But it'll close over."

"I don't want to sound all Dr. Phil," she said. "But don't let the scab seal the pain in, okay?"

"That's good advice," I said. "I hope I can manage it."

I'd been gone a few days, and they'd been eventful ones. As we drew closer to Bon

Temps, I wondered if Tanya had succeeded in getting Sam to ask her out. I wondered if I'd have to tell Sam about Tanya's role as spy. Eric didn't have to be confused about me any more, since our big secret was out. He didn't have a hold on me. Would the Pelts stick to their word? Maybe Bill would go on a long trip. Maybe a stake would accidentally fall on his chest while he was gone.

I hadn't heard from Jason while I was in New Orleans. I wondered if he was still planning on getting married. I hoped Crystal had recovered. I wondered if Dr. Ludwig accepted insurance payments. And the Bellefleur double wedding should be an interesting event, even if I was working while I was there.

I took a deep breath. My life was not so bad, I told myself, and I began to believe that was true. I had a new boyfriend, maybe; I had a new friend, surely; and I had events to look forward to. This was all good, and I should be grateful.

So what if I was obliged to attend a vampire conference as part of the queen's entourage? We'd stay in a fancy hotel, dress up a lot, attend long boring meetings, if everything other people had told me about conferences was true.

Gosh, how bad could that be?
Better not to think about it.